Ghost Star
By Kal Spriggs

Books by Kal Spriggs

The Shadow Space Chronicles

The Fallen Race
The Shattered Empire
The Prodigal Emperor
The Sacred Stars
The Temple of Light
Ghost Star
The Star Engine*

The Renegades

Renegades: Origins
Renegades: Out of the Cold
Renegades Out of Time

The Eoriel Saga

Echo of the High Kings
Wrath of the Usurper
Fate of the Tyrant (Forthcoming)

The Star Portal Universe

Children of Valor
Valor's Child
Valor's Calling
Valor's Duty
Valor's Cost
Valor's Stand*

The Rising Wolf

Fenris Unchained
Odin's Eye
Jormungandr's Venom*

Prologue

June 3, 2410
Sanctuary Station, Faraday System
United Colonies

Lieutenant Elvis Medica really hoped that the Marines guarding the hatch to the *Widowmaker* didn't notice the stunwand he'd tucked in the back of his trousers. As he and Lieutenant Commander Forrest Perkins walked towards the hatch, he felt a nervous sweat break out on his forehead.

If Lieutenant Commander Perkins felt nervous, he certainly didn't show it, his face split in a wide, goofy grin as he continued to tell his story, "So," he said, "there we were, skunk drunk off moonshine, and they dragged us in front of the Baron..."

"Right," Elvis said, not even really listening as he nervously ran a hand over the biometric scanner next to the hatch. Forrest didn't, and as they started towards the hatch, Elvis let himself feel a spurt of hope.

"Gentlemen," one of the Marines stepped in front of them, "Sorry, but you *both* need to scan in." Her voice was polite and professional, but Elvis's stomach sank all the same. Stealing a ship was ever so much harder when people did their jobs.

Elvis gave a nervous smile, "I'm authorized to access the vessel," he gestured at the scanner, "surely I can authorize the Lieutenant Commander?"

"I'm afraid not, sir," the Marine said. "We've been instructed that only authorized personnel can access this ship."

"Sure," Forrest gave the Marine a smile, "I'll just do that right now."

Shit, Elvis thought to himself as Forrest turned back towards the scanner. That was the signal. Elvis drew the stun wand from behind his back, even as Forrest turned back, as if to say something. Elvis hit the nearest Marine just under the chin and the stunwand discharged twenty thousand volts to incapacitate the Marine even as it administered a tranquilizer dose.

Elvis looked back and saw that Forrest had the second Marine down as well. Forrest spoke into his comm for a moment and then he nodded at Elvis, "Corporal Wandry and Corporal

Wicklund are on their way."

Elvis could only nod nervously. Forrest had brought in about a dozen of their crew from the escape. The two Marines had volunteered immediately, both of them eager to get some revenge on Marius Giovanni. Yet both of them were hotheads and Elvis just hoped they didn't blow this whole operation.

He tried hard not to think about what the operation involved as he and his nominal superior dragged the two unconscious Marines down the corridor and stashed them in a storage locker. Thankfully, this was the research portion of the station and was mostly empty at these hours. Most of Sanctuary Station was empty, really. The station lay on the outer edges of the Faraday system and it still hadn't expanded to its full capacity, other than the shipyards. Most of the berths for warships were empty, the United Colonies Fleet scattered across dozens of star systems.

In another five years, Elvis knew that the fleet buildup would reach its stride, tens of thousands, possibly *hundreds* of thousands of spacers and Marines would move through these corridors. But for now, it was mostly empty... which was good since Elvis and Lieutenant Commander Forrest Perkins had just committed multiple felonies when they assaulted these two Marines.

By the time they got back to the airlock, Petty Officer Chap Godbey and Staff Sergeant Dawn Witzke stood outside the hatch. Staff Sergeant Witzke gave them both respectful nods, her face cheerful. "Skipper, Lieutenant."

"Any trouble?" Elvis asked.

"Negative, sir. Your code authorized access, we started moving people aboard in small groups, as the Skipper instructed."

"Good," Lieutenant Commander Perkins said. "Once the last of our group get aboard, secure the hatch."

On impulse, Elvis passed his comm unit over to Petty Officer Godbey. The station employed smart jamming in the research section to prevent unauthorized transmissions. Since he'd been assigned to the station, his comm unit should be able to reach the vessel's bridge and let Forrest know if there were any issues.

Elvis followed his superior aboard, "We sure about this Skipper?"

"I think we're a little bit beyond the point of no return at this point," Forrest grinned at him. They worked their way up to the bridge of the *Widowmaker* and Forrest's smile grew broad as he stroked the arm of the command chair. "You know," he said after a long moment, "I didn't think they'd ever let me command again after what happened to the *Bowie*."

"Uh," Elvis rolled his eyes, "technically they haven't." Forrest had been exonerated of wrongdoing in the initial board of inquiry, but that was hardly a statement of approval. There'd been rumors, too, of politicians wanting to drag him and other officers close to Emperor Lucius Giovanni through the mud. If those rumors were true, Lieutenant Commander Forrest Perkins might well never command again.

"True enough. Get down to engineering," Forrest said after a moment. "Fire up the reactor and let me know when we're good to go."

"Sure thing, Skipper," Elvis said. Despite his doubts about this whole thing, he trusted Forrest's judgment. He had no idea whether Forrest was right about Princess Alannis Giovanni being alive or if this was the best way to go about rescuing her... but he had faith in Forrest's experience and capabilities to determine the right course of action.

Elvis brought the antimatter reactor up with only a few minutes work. In fact, it was easier than he had expected, it wasn't even in full standby mode, merely at idle. As the matter and antimatter matrix began feeding power to the ship's systems, he messaged Lieutenant Commander Perkins, "We're ready, Skipper."

"Roger," he replied. "I've disconnected us from the station. We're getting calls from the station, but I've bluffed them so far, saying we're doing some systems tests, but that won't last long. I'm bringing up the drives."

Elvis began to feed power to the ship's drives, watching everything carefully. The automated systems controlled everything well, but it still required his direct attention, a glitch in the process would either ramp up the reactor's power too quickly or could result in the grav-drives over drawing and locking out. The one would shut down the reactor and leave the ship without power and the other would knock out the drives long enough for them to reset. Either way, it wold mean they wouldn't escape the system. Not before some kind of response team could take over the ship.

Under normal operation, Elvis would have engine techs who

could monitor the process... but to say that Lieutenant Commander Perkins had assembled a skeleton crew would be something of an overstatement. Including Corporal Wandry and Corporal Wicklund, they had ten people to operate the destroyer. Despite the vessel's extensive automation, the ship was still designed for a crew of thirty or more. *That's not even counting the bunk-space for fifty marines,* he thought. The ship had been built in the Centauri Confederation as one of their hunter-killers, designed to insert teams of commandos on raids against rebel factions within the Centauri Confederation. Elvis wasn't terribly impressed with the armament, but it's stealth capabilities were damned impressive.

"Okay," Forrest called out over the intercom," we're clear of the station." Elvis let out a tense breath. That meant they were past the point of no return. Everyone aboard the ship was now guilty of piracy and mutiny. "I've just sent a formal message to Sanctuary Station's commanding officer, informing him that I've instructed my crew that we're on secret orders from Emperor Giovanni and that I bear all responsibility for our actions from this moment forward."

Elvis swallowed as he realized what that meant. While it might not save their careers, it could be enough to avoid criminal charges for the rest of the crew.

Of course, even if they somehow accomplished the impossible, then Forrest would *still* be hung out to dry. He'd not only stolen the vessel, but he'd shouldered all the responsibility for it. Elvis's lips pressed into a flat line. He stormed out of the engine room, headed for the bridge. He'd be damned if he let Forrest take all the blame for this.

He ran into a couple of men in civilian ship suits in the corridor.

"What is going on?" Rory demanded, running hand through his thinning hair. "We were in the middle of a delicate calibration process..." He blinked at Elvis, "Wait, what are *you* doing here?"

"This is most unusual," Feliks gave a stork-like head bob, "you should know better than to run some kind of systems function while we conduct our work."

"What the hell are you two doing here?" Elvis demanded. The two civilian engineers were supposed to be at work on several of the Balor vessel retrofits. That was why Elvis had let Forrest know that it was clear to steal the ship. *No one* was supposed to be aboard the ship. "Is there anyone else aboard?"

"Of *course* there isn't anyone else aboard!" Rory sputtered. "That's why we're *doing* these calibrations tonight! You have no idea how annoying it is to have 'help' on hand getting in the way and messing things up!"

"Very counterproductive," Feliks nodded. "Especially when one of them manages to injure themselves because they don't follow safety procedures." His dour expression and morose voice added extra weight to his statement, as if he saw such injuries on a regular basis.

With how these two are, it's a wonder they haven't killed anyone, Elvis thought.

"All the blood and screaming," Rory nodded. "Very distracting. And I *hate* blood."

"Look, we need to get you off the ship, now!" Elvis snapped. The last thing he wanted to add to his criminal record just now was kidnapping.

"That's ridiculous!" Rory shouted. "I'm in the middle of a very delicate--"

"Jump is calculated," Forrest said over the intercom, "jumping in ten seconds."

"No!" Elvis shouted. Then he remembered that he'd passed his comm unit to Petty Officer Godbey. He turned and ran for the engineering console. The two engineers were bad enough to work with. He was not going to be stuck with them for weeks in shadow space, especially not after kidnapping them...

His hand slammed down on the intercom system, "Skipper, this is Lieutenant Medica, you can't jump to shadow space we--"

The ship dropped into shadow space before he could finish.

***

"I can't believe you stole a ship!" Rory shook his head, looking between Lieutenant Medica and Forrest Perkins. "There should be a law against that, right?"

"Several," Feliks nodded, "especially for interrupting our work."

"Explain to me again, why exactly you're aboard?" Forrest asked rubbing his face tiredly.

"I *already* told your jack-booted accomplices!" Rory

protested. "We're calibrating some sensitive equipment..."

"*What* equipment?!" Forrest demanded.

"Uh," Rory looked at Feliks, "I don't think we're authorized to tell you." Yet the expression of the short, overweight man was one of worry. He looked as if he were afraid that they might find something out.

"Your schedule didn't show you here," Forrest mused aloud. "You were aboard the ship at two in the morning, standard time. You had no assistants, nothing was scheduled..." His eyes went narrow, "You were doing something you weren't supposed to be doing, weren't you?"

"How does he know that?" Rory waved at Feliks, "He's not supposed to be smart enough to know that!"

"I don't have to tell you anything," Feliks muttered.

"Right!" Rory nodded and raised a fist, "We don't have to tell you anything! You're the criminals, here! We won't be bullied!"

"Setting aside some issues with that," Forrest said. "If you assume that we *are* criminals.... what is to stop us from venting you out an airlock if you don't tell us what we want to know?"

"You *wouldn't*," Rory's eyes went big. He looked over at Lieutenant Medica for support, but the engineering officer folded his arms and scowled. From what Forrest had heard, the Lieutenant had plenty of pent up irritation with the two men.

"Corporal Wicklund," Forrest pressed a button on the arm of the command chair, "Please ready your ship's suit and come up to the bridge. There's a little detail I have for you to take care of."

"Okay, okay!" Rory sputtered. "It's not really *that* big of a secret. It's just that, well, Feliks and I got a message from one of our friends, working for General Shaden."

"She's not really a friend," Feliks commented. "Rory thinks she's cute."

"She *is* cute," Rory snapped. "And she was bragging about how they've made adjustments to their ship's drives that lets psychics screen the vessel's signatures, sort of a psionic screen that makes it harder for the Balor to target them..."

"And?" Forrest asked.

"Well, it got Feliks and I to wondering if this ship's active stealth system might do something similar, if those mystery aliens we've encountered might have telepathic abilities, which was why they weren't able to see this ship at all."

"Yes," Feliks nodded, and blinked, his eyes big behind his thick glasses. "After you fired on the enemy ship, it should have been able to track your weapons fire back and engage you, but it didn't."

"I know that," Forrest said, "I assumed their active sensors just weren't good enough to pick us up, even at that range."

"No, see that doesn't make any sense, not after what we've seen of their other capabilities!" Rory protested. "Look, their weapons fire is extremely accurate, their systems, despite being made with human components, are at least a generation ahead of anything we can make. We've gone under the assumption that their radar systems, based off the emissions we've seen, are just very sophisticated, which aids their accuracy. But what if that's not the case at all? What if their radar emissions are just a spoof, so that we *don't* realize they're psionic?"

Forrest frowned, "Why would they do that?"

Feliks and Rory looked at one another, "Seriously, he's this dense? No wonder he got captured..." Forrest felt a spike of rage as they made light of the ambush that had killed his last command and over a hundred of his crew.

"Explain," Forrest snapped, "now."

"*Fine*," Rory rolled his eyes. "Look, we've assumed until now that any kind of ansible interception must be done through some technological means. But that's impossible."

"Highly improbable," Feliks interrupted.

"Yes, well, it would be like intercepting a single photon in a star system and determining its energy state *without* preventing it from reaching its destination, only far, far harder," Rory said. "These are transmissions beamed *through* shadow space. To intercept them, either you'd need machinery that senses things through shadow space and can detect, intercept, and re-transmit communications faster than real-time or..."

"Or you would need someone capable of sensing things in shadow space without altering the state of whatever they're sensing," Feliks finished. "Which would imply a psychic ability, as yet never-before-seen. Which these aliens might be capable of... and if they can do that, then they could also possess other psionic abilities, such as senses powerful enough to use to target enemy ships."

Forrest sat back in his command chair. "That's... that's an interesting assumption."

"Yes. It would suggest that the active emissions we've picked up from their vessels are a further byproduct of their low-shielded reactors rather than being active sensors. So we were studying the ship's stealth systems and comparing it to the stealth systems aboard one of the modified combat shuttles the Dreyfus Mutineers possessed, to see if we could detect the modification and what frequencies it might operate upon."

That explains the combat shuttle docked in our internal launch bay. There hadn't been any such craft aboard when Forrest had stolen the vessel from Marius Giovanni. "Well?" Forrest asked.

Rory looked at Feliks. Neither spoke for a long moment, "Well, our results are as yet inconclusive, however, we estimate a thirty percent--"

"Ten percent at most," Feliks muttered.

"Really, that low?" Rory asked. He pursed his lips, "Well, a *twenty* percent possibility that the modifications performed on this vessel by the people *you* hijacked it from the *first* time, were designed to screen it from psionic senses... and that they were done by the people who captured you... the people who planned to use the ship against these unknown aliens before you stole it."

"What's the other eighty percent chance?" Lieutenant Medica asked.

"Oh, uh," Rory looked at Feliks, who shrugged, "That's the likelihood that they didn't understand the systems well enough and that their modifications didn't work as intended. Either way, it has the same result. We think this ship would be completely invisible to any psychic senses. It would be like it didn't exist!"

"It isn't perfect," Feliks interjected. "There will be ways that a psychic could locate it if they knew it was present, but it is still an unprecedented achievement."

"Okay," Forrest mused, "so they modified this ship and now those mystery aliens can't see it and it is still very hard to detect to almost everyone else..." He looked at Lieutenant Medica. This didn't really change much, if anything. "Can we dump them at Formosa Station?"

The engineering officer scowled at the two scientists. "I'm not sure they'd survive."

Rory's back went straight, "I'll have you know that I can take care of myself--"

"Formosa Station," Forrest interrupted, "is an independent station sometimes frequented by pirates and slavers. I'm assuming you have no hard currency on you?"

As Rory and Feliks shook their heads, Forrest sighed, "We have some, but probably not enough to buy you passage back to the United Colonies. Certainly not enough to pay for passage on a trustworthy vessel. An untrustworthy captain might sell you into slavery... or just steal everything you own and dump you out an airlock."

"Uh, maybe we should stay aboard the ship," Rory looked over at Feliks.

"That seems to be the better option," Feliks nodded.

"We don't have enough people aboard to babysit you," Lieutenant Medica growled. Forrest winced at the reminder. They had ten people to operate the destroyer. Normally that would have made the task impossible. However, the *Widowmaker* was heavily automated, so the skeleton crew could manage, if only barely. At least, until serious maintenance issues came due, anyway. Lieutenant Medica went on after a moment, "We can't afford to have you getting in the way at the last minute and getting us all killed."

"We can be helpful!" Rory protested. "We've been studying the ship's systems, we know far more about the stealth systems and how they interact with the rest of the vessel's systems than you could have learned in your time aboard."

Forrest pursed his lips, "Fine, it isn't as if we have many options. You stay aboard... but if you get in the way, or if Lieutenant Medica says you're a nuisance or risk, we'll drop you at the first port." In reality, he knew the two men were too valuable to risk them, but he didn't have many options. Hopefully they'd stay out of the way and be somewhat useful. Forrest almost wanted to turn around and drop them off in United Colonies territory, but there was too much risk that word would have gone out about the theft of the ship.

"Of course," Rory nodded, "We'll be very helpful, not a worry at all... uh, by the way, why are we going to this pirate station?"

"There's a rumor that some of Marius Giovanni's people

might resupply at the station," Forrest said. "And we're trying to track them down."

"Wait," Rory looked at Feliks, "isn't that the guy..."

"Yes," Feliks nodded, "he's related to the new Nova Roman Emperor, correct?"

"He's Emperor Lucius Giovanni's father... or a clone of his father, anyway," Forrest shrugged. "More importantly to our business, he's the father of Alannis Giovanni, and for that reason I'm hoping that she's still alive."

"I'm confused," Rory said. "We saw the footage, the shuttle she was aboard was destroyed at Kapteyn's Star. I don't see *how* it would be possible for her to have survived."

"There's a chance," Lieutenant Medica said, "that she's still alive. The Skipper thinks it wasn't really her aboard the shuttle."

"Why on Earth..." Rory shook his head, "What logical reason would you have to think that? I mean, Reese Leone wanted to take control of the Enforcer Platform. We have transmissions from him as he tried to dock with the station. We searched the planet below. All his people said he was aboard the shuttle along with Princess Giovanni. What evidence do you have to prove otherwise?"

"Little things," Forrest snapped. It felt good to speak about it to someone who wasn't inclined to believe him. The intelligence branch people he'd briefed had looked at him like he was crazy. The nine members of his former crew who he'd talked into helping him were already loyal to him, they trusted his judgment. Rory and Feliks were about as impartial as he could expect anyone to be. "She didn't address me by my first name, she and Reese didn't bring up my relationship with her, just... little things."

"Wait, you were in a relationship with the *princess*?" Rory demanded. He shook his head, "Great... this is about a girl. He stole a unique, irreplaceable, and *priceless,* warship because of a girl."

"Women," Feliks nodded somberly. "Women ruin everything."

***

June 5, 2410
Saariskella Colony, Ottokar System
Colonial Republic

Colonel Price propped his feet up and enjoyed the warm fire as he sipped at his whisky. He stared at the old-fashioned paper book in his lap without really seeing it. Officially, Commander Bowder had requested leave after the Battle of Kapteyn's Star. Unofficially, he'd mentioned he was thinking about retiring, too sick of death and war to take it much longer.

He'd slipped any potential observers and left a trail that would indicate that Commander Bowder might have taken his own life... should he fail to return.

Colonel Price had shaken off the false identity, donned a different one, and boarded a transport here. Saariskella was a cold, damp world, renowned for its skiing and for its secluded hunting lodges. The colonists eked out a living by catering to tourists and hunters. Since most people wore heavy coats with goggles and hoods, it was also a good world for doing business anonymously.

He looked up at a knock on the door. His hand settled to the Sako TR-7 in his lap, underneath his book, "Come in." It wasn't the only bit of protection he had. There was an entire security team, men he'd trained himself, along the perimeter, ready to take down any potential attackers.

The door opened and a man stomped inside, shaking snow off and throwing back his hood. "Colonel Price," Admiral Collae said, his stony face harsh in the light from the fire. "I see you're interested in my offer after all?"

"Well, I'm willing to listen to what you have to say," Colonel Price replied. "After all, things happened mostly as you predicted back at Kapteyn's Star. Though I *will* admit the bit with Princess Giovanni being killed was something of a surprise."

Admiral Collae gave a narrow smile, "Yes. Some things are best as surprises. I have an associate coming soon who'll put your mind at ease about some of our other plans, but in the meantime, I wanted to know if your facility, the antimatter production one... is it secure?"

"Very secure," Colonel Price said. "It's located in deep space, only the people there and myself know the coordinates." He gave a wolfish grin, "The crews of supply ships I charter tend to be unhappy when they realize how I keep it that way."

Admiral Collae nodded, "Excellent. My organization is in need of a secure base of operations with a massive power output. I think your organization could help us out."

"I'll assume you *aren't* talking about the CRAN?" Colonel Price asked. Admiral Collae probably hadn't lured him all the way out here just to murder him and try to take his resources... but that didn't mean Colonel Price was going to drop his guard.

"No," Admiral Collae snorted, "I'm not."

There was a knock at the door, but Colonel Price didn't jump. His security team had already alerted him to the second guest. "Come on in," he said.

The second guest came in and then put back his hood and pulled off his goggles, "Cold out there," he said with an easy, boyish smile. The horribly disfiguring scars marred that smile, somewhat, but Colonel Price wasn't bothered by scars. "Couldn't we meet somewhere nice, like a beach?"

Colonel Price recognized Reese Leone. He felt a real spurt of surprise as he saw him, though. "You're supposed to be dead."

"So are you, Colonel Price," Reese smiled broadly. "And like you, I've found death to be remarkably... liberating." He gestured at a chair, "May I sit?"

Colonel Price nodded slowly. He contemplated Reese's presence, combined with Admiral Collae's presence. *Admiral Collae's people didn't just seize his transports,* Colonel Price mused, *he evacuated Reese, all of us none the wiser.* That meant that the attempt to board the Enforcer Platform had been another ruse. He felt oddly relieved that the end goal hadn't been the alien station.

"So," Reese said, taking a seat in the chair and then leaning forward, elbows on his knees, his blue eyes flickering with odd reflections of the fire. "Colonel Price, tell me about this station of yours. I need to know *exactly* how much power you can produce."

***

June 10th, 2410
124R36 System
Unclaimed Space

Aromata Atagi grinned as the four destroyers emerged from shadow space dead in the middle of his ambush. *Engage,* he sent and as one, the five frigates of his squadron opened fire.

Each of the frigates were substantially smaller than the three destroyers they faced, but at close range and with the element of surprise, that didn't matter much. Thirty mass driver rounds smashed into the lead pair of destroyers, an overwhelming barrage against foes who had no idea that they were even under attack.

The frigates had angling shots above and below the belly-bands of the destroyers' defense screens. Armor shattered and engine pods detonated under the salvo of tungsten-tipped depleted uranium rounds. Yet both ships went to battle stations, radar lashing out, weapons systems coming online and flailing blindly in an attempt to suppress the incoming fire.

Second salvo, Aromata commanded. These enemy ships were immaterial, but they needed to be removed so that he could hit his true target. His lieutenants replied, even as they volleyed another thirty mass drivers into the two lead ships.

One of the two destroyers broke in half, its midships shattered, all systems offline. The other was a powerless hulk, venting its hydrogen fuel and atmosphere from massive rents in its hull.

But in the time it took those two destroyers to die, they bought the next pair of ships time to get their systems online, time to search for the killers of their brethren... and Aromata's smile faded a bit as he sensed that the fight had shifted.

Flank them, he commanded, and his five frigates surged forward, *single firing pass.* He didn't need to give them more detail than that. His commanders knew how to move in coordination, they'd conducted raids similar to this one dozens, even hundreds, of times together. They had the initiative to move and maneuver, they knew their orders... and they knew why this one mission was different and why it was very important that they follow his direction perfectly... even if it meant that some of them might not survive.

Aromata's frigate went high, while the other four split into pairs that swung low, firing their mass drivers from knife range, all four focusing fire on the third destroyer. Aromata, however, had a different target.

He took over weapons, reaching out with his psychic senses as he did so, feeling for the exact position of the Defiance-class destroyer... and it's very important passenger. *There you are,* he thought, even as he aimed his frigate's mass drivers, taking the time to line up the shot perfectly.

The frigate's single turret fired, three mass driver rounds lanced out, too close to dodge, and smashed through the side armor of the fourth destroyer. The ship shuddered, but power stayed online and both its engine pods remained intact. That ship was Reese's flag ship, and Aromata Atagi's shot had just destroyed the vessel's shadow space drive.

Reese Leone's destroyer continued to spit mass driver rounds in reply and Aromata's frigate shuddered under multiple impacts, glancing blows, but still enough that alarms wailed through the bridge. He saw that the third destroyer was crippled, the vessel yawing over, still returning fire, but spinning like a dying beast.

Mission accomplished, Aromata sent, *withdraw.*

All five of his frigates had sustained damage, two of them severely, but they retained their shadow space drives. They'd already plotted their escape routes and they jumped to shadow, leaving the wounded and crippled destroyers behind.

It would look like they'd been driven off, like a pirate ambush that had expected merchant ships rather than a military force. *That is what Reese and his master need to believe,* Aromata told himself. The five frigates he'd used had been taken from pirates, their systems cobbled together, wholly unworthy of the name of warships.

Every bit of evidence would suggest that Reese Leone had run into a pirate ambush by sheer bad luck. The damage to his surviving vessels would require him to make a stop at Formosa Station to either repair or transfer to another ship. Someone would recognize him, someone would talk.

And from there, it would merely be a matter of making certain that the other game pieces were set in motion. Five pirate frigates had just set in motion the downfall of all of Reese's efforts. Aromata's smile grew broad as he considered that. His master would be very pleased and Aromata knew that would translate to better rewards... and a better chance at overall victory. After all, while some Shadow Lords favored overwhelming force, Aromata's master appreciated a more subtle hand.

Shadow Lord Invictus manipulated from behind the scenes, his focus always upon greater victory.

***

June 12, 2410
Formosa Station, 124R36 System
Unclaimed Space

Ricky One-Eye scratched at his bald head. The rash that had made all his hair fall out hadn't gone away, despite the various drugs he'd stolen from the pharmacy. Nor had he been able to regain much of the weight he'd lost while living on garbage and rats in Yaitsik Station's waste system. At least he didn't match any of the wanted posters that had popped up for his capture across civilized space.

"Look," he said in as ingratiating a tone as he could manage, "all I'm trying to do is get back home to see my ailing mother." He gave a friendly smile, even as he scanned the bar for any potential bounty hunters or law enforcement.

"You look disease ridden," the freighter's owner growled. The captain had the only ship going out towards the periphery and he'd been pretty hard to talk around into letting Ricky aboard. Then again, since Ricky planned to murder the man and seize his ship if given the chance, that was probably wise of him.

Ricky's smile wavered, "Well, you look..."

He trailed off as he recognized the man over the freighter captain's shoulder, just walking out of the bar. "I understand, entirely, thanks for your time," Ricky said absently as he rose from the table. He had to have been mistaken, there was no *way* that he'd seen right. He rubbed at his one good eye and then blinked disbelievingly at the retreating figure.

Ricky stepped out into the station's corridors, he found his target and followed the man. There was no mistaking the blonde hair or the set of his shoulders. As Reese Leone paused in outside a docking port and looked over his shoulder, Ricky had to rub his one good eye in disbelief. Yet there was no mistaking him. The man sported an impressive set of scars across his face and head, but the shape of his jaw, the blue eyes, and the rest of him was unmistakable. But... by all reports, Reese Leone was dead. *Everyone* was talking about that, and Ricky had consoled himself in the fact that the same navy boys that had ruined him had killed Reese not long afterward.

That son of a bitch, Ricky thought to himself. His hand fell to where his pistol should have rested, but then the pirate remembered that he'd had to leave his stolen weapons behind when he boarded the last transport. Ricky knew a guy on the station who *could* have got him a weapon, but that would have risked the criminal turning him in. After all, last time he'd been here at Formosa Station, Ricky *had* shorted the fence.

Ricky didn't want to risk fighting Reese hand to hand. Besides, there was no profit in revenge.

But there *might* be profit in reporting the man's survival. Ricky gave a wicked grin as he thought about that. If this *was* Reese and if his many enemies still wanted him dead, then finding out more about his presence here at Formosa Station could be very, very valuable.

Ricky ducked his head and moved past the man, but he stopped a short distance away and pretended to consult a station map. Soon enough, another man joined Reese at the docking collar. "You've made the arrangements?" Reese asked.

"Yes, sir," the subordinate replied, "we've uploaded the coordinates to the rendezvous and we've completed our repairs. The Lord Admiral says that our replacement escort will meet us and provide us with the final coordinates to Golgotha." Ricky nearly choked at those words. *Golgotha,* he thought to himself, *that's impossible, the place is just a myth...*

He'd become so distracted that he missed whatever Reese said in reply. Reese's underling went on, "Yes, sir, we'll get them aboard immediately. The rest of the cargo has been loaded, would you like for me to lead you to your suite?"

"No, thank you," Reese said. "I know the way. Please see to our other guests." The man turned and scanned the crowd and Ricky felt sweat bead his brow as Reese's blue eyes settled on him.

Ricky pawed at the map, as if he were tracing a route. He kept his gaze locked forward, even as he watched the renegade military officer out of the corner of his eyes. After a moment, Reese turned back and walked past the guards and onto the ship.

Ricky swallowed nervously. The news of Reese's survival would be invaluable... but he didn't have any proof. No one would believe him, especially not with a bogus destination like Golgotha. The place was a myth, a rumored system filled with alien ruins and a star that was too dim to see with the unaided eye. It was legendary, a place of fabulous treasures... and a place where so many treasure hunters had reputedly died that Amalgamated Worlds had erased the location from the star charts.

There had to be some way to turn this information to his use, Ricky decided. Even if most people wouldn't believe his story, there was bound to be someone desperate enough to do so. Ricky would find that person and he'd milk the information for everything it was worth.

***

Chapter I

June 15, 2410
Formosa Station, 123R36 System
Unclaimed Space

Lieutenant Commander Forrest Perkins scowled at the one-eyed pirate seated across from him. "Reese Leone," Forrest demanded, "you swear it was this man?"

"I've been trying to kill him for the past year and a half," Ricky One-Eye sneered. "Of *course* I recognized him."

Forrest didn't trust the pirate as far as he could throw him. Ricky was known to be a slaver and pirate. He and his people had tried to kill United Colonies personnel before.

"And you're certain you heard where he's going?" Forrest snapped.

"That's what I said, isn't it?" Ricky One-Eye leered. "And I'll tell you... when I see payment for that information. I'm sure your government could repay me very, very well. Enough to live the rest of my life on women and drugs, right? Maybe even a full pardon?"

Forrest kept his expression level. In truth, he had a bit of petty cash, every bit of money that he'd had in his accounts, withdrawn for hard currency just before he stole the *Widowmaker*... and most of that had gone towards needed supplies. It wouldn't be anywhere near enough to pay what Ricky seemed to think this information was worth. *He doesn't need to know that,* Forrest thought.

"I doubt it," Forrest sat back his eyes ranging the bar to see if the pirate had any kind of backup. "All we have is your word. Without some kind of confirmation..."

Ricky leaned forward, his voice raising, "I'm telling you, you'll *want* this information. This is the kind of thing that can make or break a nation. This is the kind of chance that comes along once in a lifetime--"

Ricky was so intent on his pitch that he didn't see Lieutenant Medica walk up behind him and hit him in the back with a stun wand. As the pirate jerked and twitched from the electrical current, Forrest didn't miss the fact that the engineer held the stun wand on a bit longer than necessary. Then again, Forrest didn't blame him.

No one in the bar so much as looked over as Ricky One-Eye twitched and fell to the floor. The pirate's face was drawn back in a grimace of pain, right up until the tranquilizers from the stun wand took effect.

As Forrest stood up, the bartender looked over, "You can't leave that here."

"We'll take care of it," Forrest replied. He grabbed the slaver's feet and Lieutenant Medica grabbed the slaver by the arms. The two of them carried the man out of the bar.

"You sure he knows something?" Lieutenant Medica asked.

Forrest shrugged, "He seems to think so. Enough that he was trying to weasel out a pardon, anyway."

"Well, if not, we can always space him and be rid of him," Lieutenant Medica grunted. Forrest looked up in surprise at Lieutenant Medica's harsh tone. The Lieutenant shrugged, "My parents were killed by a pirate like this one."

"Shit," Forrest said, "sorry, I didn't know."

"It's not something I talk about much," Elvis Medica replied. Neither of them seemed to attract any attention walking through the station with a limp body. Forrest felt an odd sense of detachment as they walked down the corridors to the ship.

As they came up the ramp, they moved over to the side and Lieutenant Medica dropped the pirate's arms, the man's head hitting the metal deck with a thud. Forrest gave the man a look, but Lieutenant Medica just shrugged, "Oops."

***

Ricky One-Eye rubbed at the back of his aching head and glowered at the navy officer. His lumpy head had a few more lumps back there than he remembered. "I'm not telling you a damned thing." He hadn't expected them to be sneaky about things and kidnap him right out of the bar. That was his job, not what military folks would do.

"Let me explain this to you, using small words," the navy officer snapped back. "You tell us, or we space you out the airlock and then we go find someone else who *will* talk."

Ricky smirked, "Right, like that's an option. Besides, you're the good guys, right?" Navy types *might* vent pirates out airlocks, but they only did it after a proper trial. Besides, it wasn't as if they were going to torture him.

"You seem to be operating under a misconception," the naval officer said. "We *were* naval officers... but we stole this ship. We're not going after Reese because we want to capture him. We're going after him to kill him."

Ricky stared at the naval officer, for a moment the words didn't make any sense. He looked over at the other navy boy, the one this one had called Skipper. The tall, skinny man gave him a cold smile, his dark eyes intense. Ricky felt sweat bead on his forehead.

He looked back at the first one, "You're mutineers?"

"Yeah, you could say that," he said. "But we really don't like pirates. Think of us more as vigilantes. We've got a nasty ship, we're hunting our prey... and you're the man who knows where he is. So do you think we're going to draw the line on anything?"

Ricky's throat constricted a bit. "You... you wouldn't."

"I've already discussed this with the Captain," the officer said. "I'm not a big fan of pirates. I like slavers even worse. If you don't tell me what I need to know, then I'll put you in the airlock and I'll turn the pressure down *real* slow. You know what slow depressurization does to someone? Your blood vessels in your soft tissue will burst, in your eyes, in your lungs.... Then we'll pump air back in and we'll ask you again. If you don't tell us, I'll drop the pressure again. Pretty soon your tissue in your throat will give out. We don't have a ship's doctor, by the way, so once you lose your voice, we'll just vent you."

Ricky swallowed and looked back and forth between the two men.

The Captain raised his hands, "Don't look at me, you're the one who insisted you're not going to tell us anything."

Ricky raised his hands, "Okay, I'll talk, I'll talk, just... give me *something*. I've got nothing left, *nothing*. Promise me you'll drop me off at a halfway decent planet and I'll tell you what you want to know."

"We'll drop you somewhere," the Captain said after a moment's thought. "Give you some money, enough to survive."

Ricky licked his lips. "Okay... Reese said he was going to Golgotha."

"Well, shit," the Captain said after a moment.

**

"Golgotha?" Elvis asked a few minutes later as he and Forrest stood in the ship's conference room.

"It's a myth, I think. Or at least, I *thought.*" Forrest said after a long moment. "It's a system that Amalgamated Worlds discovered. It was chock-full of alien ruins and treasure hunters flooded the place. Supposedly it was so dangerous that they wiped every record of it from existence." He looked over at Rory and Feliks. "Do you two know anything?"

"No, of course not," Rory ran a hand through his thinning brown hair. "Nothing that connects to anything else we know. Well, we know it was real, but we don't know anything about the race that lived there, if they were one we encountered before or if they only were in the system, or really much about them at all."

"What about the system?" Forrest demanded.

"Rumors," Feliks shrugged, "nothing concrete. It's supposed to have a counter-rotation, it moves against the rotation of the rest of the galaxy. It made plotting a jump there difficult, as it is in constant differential motion. There were theories that it might therefore have extra-galactic origins."

Forrest rubbed his chin and looked at Elvis, "Do you think Ricky was telling the truth?"

"Probably," the Lieutenant replied after a long moment. "Want me to put him in an airlock?"

Forrest winced. He hoped that Elvis was joking. Not that the pirate didn't really deserve it, but more in the sense that Forrest didn't want to do any more extrajudicial killing than necessary. Forrest's career was over and he'd probably face serious jail-time, but as long as he kept his crew's actions by-the-book, then they might be able to plead ignorance and be reinstated after all this was over. "No, we'll go with this, for now. He closed his eyes in thought. "Amalgamated Worlds would not have completely erased info on the system, they'll have left information somewhere..."

"Skipper," Lieutenant Medica began, "you think they'd have that info with the files they brought with the Dreyfus Fleet?"

"Yeah, maybe," Forrest said. "But that's not really an option, is it?" By now, there was no going back to the Faraday System. They *might* believe Ricky One-Eye, but odds were that they'd simply throw the man in prison to rot... along with Forrest and his crew. Even if they were prepared to believe the ridiculous story, there was no way they'd let Forrest be any part of the effort to find Reese.

Forrest wasn't prepared to be on the sideline, especially not on just the *chance* that someone else would go find and rescue Alannis. The Emperor might want to do just that, if he could be convinced that his sister was alive. Anyone short of him, though, Forrest wasn't about to trust, not with this.

He looked at Lieutenant Medica, "There are archives, right? One in the Centauri Confederation at Elysia?"

"You mean the old military archives?" Lieutenant Medica asked. He frowned in thought, "I suppose. You think they'd have a record of the system?"

"Yeah," Forrest nodded, "maybe. Isn't there one on Mars, too?"

Lieutenant Medica pulled out his datapad and began browsing through data. "Let's see, there's one at Hugo Base, it used to be an Amalgamated Worlds military base... and yeah, they sell data." He blanched, "I don't know if their price is still the same, but boss, we can't afford *this*."

He passed his datapad over to Forrest, who winced at the stated price. "A million a minute?!"

"Yeah, they have a 'special rate' for multiple users, but that's one point five million a minute for two users, so that doesn't really help us," Lieutenant Medica said.

"Could we get inside, hack their systems maybe?" Forrest asked.

"Are you kidding?" Lieutenant Medica shook his head. "They'll have military grade software and judging by the rates they charge, they probably have the security to back them up."

"That may not be *entirely* true," Rory spoke up.

"Excuse me?" Forrest asked.

"Well," Rory glanced at Feliks, "what do you think?"

"There is a high probability," Feliks brought up his datapad and began tapping at it. "You could be right. But I don't really see how it would help."

Rory nodded and brought out his own datapad, "If we're right, then we should be able to pull up the spec, they'll have included it..."

"Excuse me," Forrest said.

"Ah, they did, excellent," Rory went on, ignoring Forrest. He moved over to the conference room display and linked it to his datapad. "So, if we're right, and the systems are of that generation..."

The two scientists bent over the display, bickering. Forrest walked around and looked at the display. It looked like technical readouts, but he couldn't make sense of them. "Excuse me," Forrest repeated himself.

"...the third module is definitely of that tier, but I don't see how that would change the underlying problem," Feliks went on.

"That's because your focus is *far* too narrow," Rory waved his hands. "You've got to look at the overall pattern, the flaws that they built into the greater system. When you do that..." He did something on his datapad and the display shifted color, with systems flashing in orange and red. "See, it all comes down when you trigger the cascade."

"Ah, yes, but you can't do that without initiating it from *inside* the system," Feliks protested.

Rory threw his hands in the air, "Well, of *course*--"

"Excuse me!" Forrest snapped.

The two scientists looked over at him, as if they'd forgotten about his presence. "Sorry, what?"

Forrest restrained a sigh, "What are you two talking about?"

"Oh, well, they've utilized old hardware, the legacy system that Amalgamated Worlds built. They can't have changed the hardware out because the existing security protocols that Amalgamated Worlds Fleet built into their secure military hardware. If they tried to copy it out without the appropriate security and command codes, they'd trigger a system purge."

"What does any of that matter?" Forrest demanded.

"They have made essential software upgrades, but their hardware is old, probably repaired bit by bit, using salvaged equipment or custom-built sections to match as closely as possible to the original," Feliks said. "But over time, there will have been more and more systems cobbled together, a general shift away from the original configuration. They'll have tweaked the main system and patched the software as much as they could, but they're still out of alignment with the original configuration, which introduces an overall risk."

"Why couldn't they copy everything over onto a new system?" Lieutenant Medica asked. "If all they needed were the appropriate command codes, they could have acquired those by this time." Amalgamated Worlds command codes could be bought fairly commonly, both at black market hubs and in standard network trading. Most of them didn't have much value, but there were always treasure hunters who collected codes just in case they came across an abandoned facility or ship.

"Only by the time they had the codes, they'll have modified the systems, so if they try to use those codes, they could trigger the security system purge anyway," Rory grinned. "So they won't want to risk their cash cow."

Forrest mulled that over, "Okay, so how does that help us?"

"This is trivial, da?" Feliks said. "They are out of alignment with their original configuration. Any half-way decent engineer could trigger a system reset, which would then identify every bit of their cobbled together pieces and parts and start a security alert. If someone triggered those security systems, there would be enough time to copy over a limited amount of data before the entire system purges itself. There would be a brief window of complete access, as the system consumes itself."

"That doesn't sound like good security," Forrest said.

"It's *terrible* security," Rory nodded as he ran a hand through his thinning hair. "But it's not designed into their system, it is a consequence of their systematic upgrades that they can't avoid. Of course, it's all theoretical."

"Yes," Feliks nodded, "there's no way we could trigger the system collapse."

"What, why not?" Forrest demanded.

Rory snorted, "You'd need to have hardware access to one of their terminals. It would take Feliks or me, since no one else would have the required expertise. And in the process, we'd be destroying exabytes of stored information: scientific data, ship designs, weapon plans, historical military records... it would be destroying priceless information..."

"That probably is already stored elsewhere, either in the Dreyfus Fleet or at Centauri, right?"

"I suppose..." Rory looked over at Feliks, who shrugged.

"Well, yes. But still, you'd need to get either myself or Feliks--"

"Probably both of us," Feliks said.

"Yes, probably both of us, inside a high security facility where they no doubt have shoot on sight orders for intruders. And I'm sorry, but there's no way that..." Rory trailed off and stared at Forrest in horror. "Wait, you can't be seriously considering..."

"Why not?" Forrest smiled.

"It's like destroying the Library of Alexandria to pull out a single scroll!" Rory protested.

"Or destroying a priceless painting to recover the artist's signature," Feliks nodded.

"And you're putting our lives at risk!" They both protested.

Forrest shrugged, "But think of just how much credibility it will give you. You'll have done the impossible, think of all the bragging rights."

Rory's mouth opened and closed. For a long moment, he seemed incapable of speaking. Finally he just looked at Lieutenant Medica, "Did he just say that I should *brag* about burning down the Library of Alexandria?"

"Yeah," Lieutenant Medica nodded, "I think he did. But remember, you have another option."

"We do?" Feliks asked hopefully.

"We could drop you off here at Formosa Station where you'll probably be robbed and murdered."

"Oh," Rory licked his lips. "Well, when you put it that way..."

***

June 15, 2410
Sanctuary Station, Faraday System
United Colonies

"Attention on deck!" Someone called and Senior Captain Daniel Beeson rose to his feet along with the rest of the briefing room.

Rear Admiral Boris Kaminsky walked through the hatch and moved to the head of the conference table, his face stern and unreadable. "As you were," he growled. Daniel and the other officers settled to their seats. The big, florid-faced Rear Admiral swept his gaze around table, his dark eyes lingering on each of the seated officers.

Daniel really wasn't certain what to expect at this briefing. Until a few days ago, he'd still been under an official inquiry about the events at Kapteyn's Star. The dual military-civilian inquiry had dragged on for months. Daniel had come to feel more and more that after the death of Princess Alannis Giovanni, they'd never let him command again.

All that had changed only a few days earlier with the news that Lieutenant Commander Forrest Perkins had stolen a vessel. The inquiry had been put on hold. Daniel had been ordered to report to his ship... and then a few hours earlier, he'd been summoned to attend this staff meeting.

"Twelve days ago, Lieutenant Commander Forrest Perkins stole a unique warship from here at Sanctuary Station. Intelligence suspects that either Lieutenant Commander Perkins suffered a mental break after the loss of his destroyer, the *Bowie* and most of his crew... or that he was mentally programmed by Marius Giovanni during his captivity and is operating under compulsion."

Daniel winced at the words. The theft of the ship was bad enough, but neither of those accusations sounded at all like the strong-willed, quick-witted officer he had served with.

"Seven days ago, I asked for and was given orders to hunt him and his stolen vessel down," Rear Admiral Kaminsky said. "I have assembled all of you to accomplish this mission." He activated the display and a dozen vessels appeared. "We have three Nagyr-class battlecruisers, two Constellation-class cruisers, two Jouster-class light cruisers, three Kriss-class destroyers, and two Archer-class destroyers. Together, we will assemble as Task Force Hunter. The reason for the make-up of our forces is that the Centauri Confederation has just ejected our diplomats." A mutter of unease went around the conference table and more than a few officers looked in Daniel's direction. Removal of diplomats was a predecessor to a declaration of war and there was no doubt that it was in response to the events at Kapteyn's Star. "In addition to that, Emperor Giovanni has ordered an aggressive approach against Marius Giovanni's support structure. The Fleet is spread rather thin... which means that Task Force Hunter is all the vessels available to resolve this problem."

"Sir," Commander Shaw spoke up, "I don't see why the one destroyer warrants an entire task force. I've just been pulled away from the Anvil system, where we had finally got the pirate situation under control. I've already received word from one of my contacts that almost a dozen civilian freighters have disappeared just in the past week since my departure. What can one rogue destroyer be against that?"

Rear Admiral Kaminsky cocked his head and stared at the officer. He didn't speak for a long moment, long enough that the captain shifted uncomfortably in his chair. When he finally did speak, his gruff voice was calm and surprisingly soft. "The stealth technology on the hunter-killer class vessel is very advanced. Our best scientists, our *very* best scientists, were still trying to figure it out when it was stolen. That single vessel could infiltrate any star system, could volley its missiles or engage with its primary weapon, and then escape in the following confusion. Imagine if Lieutenant Commander Perkins has had a break with reality, if he somehow becomes convinced that destroying a city or even all life on a planet is necessary? The ship's stealth systems are capable enough to allow that and its armament is powerful enough."

Rear Admiral Kaminsky swept his gaze around the table, "Task Force Hunter's orders are to find him and stop him before he does anything of the sort. Ships will depart in three hours and there's a host of reports that we'll need performed before then. You are dismissed, ladies and gentlemen."

Daniel rose with the others, but then the Rear Admiral pointed at him, "Senior Captain Beeson, a word, if you would."

And here it is, Daniel thought.

***

"So," Rear Admiral Boris Kaminsky studied the Senior Captain for a long moment. "You've served with Lieutenant Commander Perkins for some time?"

"Yes, sir," Captain Beeson replied. He considered it for a moment, "Off and on, for seven years."

"He was the Emperor's Flag Lieutenant while you were his Chief of Staff," Boris said. "He also served aboard the Constellation, first as the assistant tactical officer, then as the tactical officer, and finally as your XO. Were you close?"

To his credit, Beeson didn't flinch at the interrogatory tone. "We were. I consider him an outstanding officer and a friend."

Boris asked, "But he didn't contact you prior to his theft of the *Widowmaker*?"

"No, sir," Beeson straightened, "he did not."

Undoubtedly because you were already in enough difficulty, Boris thought. The Senior Captain had been under an ongoing inquiry. It had started out fairly straightforward, but it had quickly become mired in politics. Senator Harris Penwaithe and his allies had seen it as an opportunity to damage one of the Emperor's favored officers and, by extension, to tarnish the Emperor's reputation. They'd seen it as a way to change policies they didn't like... but in the process they might end up destroying several officers' careers.

Senior Captain Beeson had not called upon the Emperor for assistance in the grueling review board of his actions at Kapteyn's Star. Nor had he asked for Emperor Lucius Giovanni's help in the senate inquiry. Since he'd once served as the Emperor's Flag Captain, in theory he could have asked for that help. He hadn't, and it said more to the positive about the commander of the *Constellation*

"Have you heard the specifics of his theft of the vessel?" Boris asked. When the officer shook his head in reply, Boris went on, "He has, in several interviews with Fleet Intelligence, stated that he doesn't believe that Princess Alannis Giovanni died at Kapteyn's Star. He thinks that Reese Leone faked his --and by extension, her-- death. He was recommended to see a psychologist. Have you heard anything about that?"

Senior Captain Beeson winced. "No, sir, I hadn't. I'm not certain how Reese could have pulled that off. Having some kind of recording is one thing, but the shuttle wasn't a drone, it had a crew. We found some of Reese's people who saw him board it with his prisoners, and while we couldn't search the entire Temple, not in the time we had, we found no sign of Reese or his core crew." He straightened his shoulders, though, "Still, I don't think he would have come to such a conclusion without good reason."

"Are you aware that Lieutenant Commander Perkins was in a relationship with Princess Giovanni?" Boris asked.

Senior Captain Beeson looked away. As far as Boris knew,

this information hadn't come out in the inquiry. The relationship had, technically, been within regulations. They hadn't been directly in each other's chain of command. Still, it was the kind of salacious bit of gossip that would end up all over the news media if it came out. "Yes, sir, I was aware."

"The going hypothesis among the intelligence officers tasked for the investigation is that Lieutenant Commander Perkins became deranged after the losses of his ship and crew and then obsessive over Princess Giovanni during his captivity. They've even got a psychologist who thinks that he's snapped, that he suffered a break with reality. They cite the letter that he sent to the Emperor, in which he informs him of his intent to steal the vessel and that he deceived his crew, claiming they're operating under secret orders. They claim it as further evidence of his obsession as some kind of attention-seeking measure."

Beeson grimaced that that, "What do you think, sir?"

Boris took a seat and put his feet up on the conference table. "You worked with Forrest on and off for seven years? I was prisoner with him in the Chxor penal system for over a decade. He and I and a handful of others survived aboard Melcer Station and other hellholes for *ten years* where life is normally measured in hours... and by the time I met him, he'd already spent five years in Chxor custody." He pulled out an archaic cigar and --ignoring fleet regulations-- lit it and puffed at it.

Captain Beeson wrinkled his nose at the smell, but he waited patiently. It said something about him that he tolerated the filthy habit. Boris hated it himself, but he'd taken up smoking when he served in the Centauri Confederation Fleet and while he'd kicked the habit once, he'd picked it up again dealing with certain former Amalgamated Worlds officers during the lead-up to the Dreyfus Coup.

"I think Forrest could be wrong. I think he could be confused or deceived... but do I think he's crazy? Not a chance. If fifteen years of living under Chxor occupation didn't break him, then a few months in Marius Giovanni's prison wouldn't do the trick, either." He cocked his head and looked at Daniel Beeson. "I specifically requested you because of any other potential officers, I expect you to have a bond with Forrest Perkins. That might come in handy if we're going to talk him down from doing anything... hasty."

The officer nodded and he cleared his throat, "Admiral, has Emperor Giovanni weighed in on this at all?"

Boris had already expected the question. "No, he hasn't made any official statement. I expect he's monitoring the situation, but he's too busy with the current situation with the Centauri Confederation to become personally involved." It wasn't the full truth, but Boris wasn't about to discuss his secret orders with anyone, not unless the time came to act upon them.

"Now," Boris said, "I know you've been out of the loop with the inquiries and that you'll need to shake down new crew and get your ship in fighting state, so I won't take up any more of your time. You're dismissed, Senior Captain, and welcome to the squadron."

As Beeson saluted and stepped out of the room, Boris hoped that he had read the other officer correctly. If not, it would make bringing Forrest back alive a difficult proposition.

***

Chapter II

July 12, 2410
Sol System
Neutral Space

"Ladies and Gentlemen," Lieutenant Commander Forrest Perkins said softly, "welcome to the Sol System."

They had emerged at the edge of the system, far out from Earth, Mars, and most of the inhabited portions of the system. The energy bleed-off from their emergence from shadow space shouldn't show at that range on any of the various sensors in the system.

"You sure about this plan, Skipper?" Lieutenant Medica asked.

"More or less," Forrest gave the engineer a grin. "We get in, we get what we need, we get out. What can go wrong, right?"

"At least we don't have to feel guilty about taking down their network and main source of income," Lieutenant Medica growled.

Forrest nodded at that. Hugo Base had been one of the handful of Amalgamated Worlds military facilities to survive the Shadow Lords' attack on the system. The Martian base had become a point of refuge for senior Amalgamated Worlds officers... many of whom hadn't been content to live out the rest of their lives on the edge of survival. Run by a tight-knit cabal, Hugo Base had become a center of an extortion ring.

One of their first crimes had been to seize humanitarian aid sent to Earth after the initial sacking, which had possibly killed tens or even hundreds of thousands in the chaos after the fall of Amalgamated Worlds. As a secondary source of income, they sold information from their data networks for money that then purchased more weapons and mercenaries, which they used to extort regions of Mars and other key colonies in the system. Hugo Base didn't have the manpower to actually control the Sol system, but they used what they had to dominate commerce in the system and to make certain that they had the lion's share of wealth. It was an open secret that a handful of individuals controlled Hugo Base and from there, much of the star system. They ran protection rackets on surviving colonies and there was a great deal of suspicion that they'd actually destroyed several surviving cities on Earth, in order to eliminate any self-sufficient competition.

The base had also become something of a status symbol for wealthy elite and those who fawned upon the staff of Hugo Base. All kinds of the "right" people had been granted citizenship, often in ceremonies that showed off their wealth as the remnants of Amalgamated Worlds bestowed their benedictions.

"Are Rory and Feliks ready for this?" Forrest asked.

"They were hard at work on their datapads last I saw," Lieutenant Medica said. "Hopefully that's a good thing. They still seem aghast at the idea of destroying all the other information in their systems."

"You aren't?" Forrest asked. He would have thought that Elvis Medica, as an engineer, would feel the same way.

"Not particularly," Lieutenant Medica shrugged. "Most of what the base will have in their systems is going to be reports and administrative data from almost a century ago. Yeah, I'm sure that has some historical relevance... but in the grand scheme... who cares? We're doing this to save lives."

Forrest had a bit more reservations about it than that, but then again, this was all far more personal to him. The prospect of Alannis being prisoner to Marius Giovanni and Reese Leone disturbed him on multiple levels. Reese was dangerously obsessive and that was bad enough. But Marius... if it even *was* the real Marius Giovanni and not another clone... he had admitted to brainwashing thousands of innocent men and women. He routinely stripped people of their free will and forced them into his service... and what would a man like that do to Alannis?

Forrest felt sweat break out on his forehead and his stomach roiled. *Even if I do rescue her, will it have been too late?* He hoped that Marius's or Reese's links to Alannis Giovanni would prevent them from using such tactics on her, but he couldn't count on it. Time was of the essence. Every hour that she was in their grasp was another hour that Alannis was in danger.

"Lots of sensor contacts," Lieutenant Medica muttered, looking over Forrest's shoulder at the sensor display. At least three clusters of numerous ships sat in orbit over Mars. Forrest picked out dozens of individual warships in separate orbits, spaced out to give those ships room to fight if it came to that. *What the hell is going on?*

"Official broadcast is that there's some kind of peace conference between Tau Ceti and Centauri, sir," Petty Officer Godbey spoke up.

He tapped at his display and the main display showed a broadcast. A pretty Asiatic woman spoke, her voice cheerful and her attitude perky, "...historic meeting continues between President Spiridon's representative Annabelle Spiridon and Chancellor Andreas Tautmann, after the revelation that dozens of senior military personnel from the Centauri Confederation may have been compromised. Tanis has offered to mediate and Chairman-Admiral Amelie Ortega is present as their representative along with a small number of their vessels present to enforce the neutrality of the location. The ongoing discussions range from unification of military investigations to possibly healing the long-standing divide within the Confederation. Sources close to President Spiridon have claimed that he has no intention of instituting a police state and that any fears of dictatorship in the Confederation are purely speculation and have no resemblance to the truth."

"Yeah," Forrest muttered, "if you'll believe that, then I've got some prime frontier colony land I'd like to sell you in New Eden." President Spiridon ruled his part of the Centauri Confederation with an iron fist. This meeting with the Tau Ceti Seperatists might patch things over, but once Spiridon got his hands on a system, he wasn't going to let go. Even if Forrest hadn't seen enough of the President of the Centauri Confederation, he'd heard an earful about the dictator from his old friend Boris.

Forrest dismissed the broadcast and brought up the updated sensor track. There *were* a lot of ships in orbit around Mars, which was bad enough. There were also a lot more sensor platforms than he had expected. "Isn't Sol supposed to be neutral territory?"

"Yeah, that's what I thought," Lieutenant Medica shook his head. "Sir, that's a lot more than a few legacy systems. It looks like they have the system on lockdown."

"Why, though?" Forrest asked. "I mean, the system's been a backwater since the Shadow Lords sacked it almost a century ago." He shook his head, "I thought they destroyed a lot of this stuff in the process, and some of the energy signatures on these sensor platforms... these are military grade, and that's not the kind of expense you go to for a strategically unimportant system."

"Maybe it's related to this meeting?" Lieutenant Medica asked.

"Still, it would take months to set this up." Forrest shook his head. He didn't understand it and he certainly didn't like it. This kind of sensor buildup was what someone would do for a system capital or a major military base. It was what someone would do if they had to expect or plan for a surprise attack. It was not what you would think to find around the mostly abandoned home system of humanity.

"Can we slip through?" Lieutenant Medica asked in a quiet voice.

Forrest shot him a raised eyebrow, and the engineering officer shrugged, "Skipper, I'm an engineer, not a pilot. I know our ship's specs, that doesn't mean I know how it will perform in conjunction with maneuvers."

"Well," Forrest quirked a crooked smile, "Assuming that your specs are right, then yeah, we should slip through, no problem. Most of these platforms are on power-saving mode, which means the outer perimeter is on timed active scans and constant passive scanning. They're on a random interval, but we can still play the law of averages as we move through. The *inner* system perimeter is fully active, but that's where the *Widowmaker'*s active stealth system is going to be put to its full use."

Unfortunately, she had been built in the Centauri Confederation, so if anyone would know what to be watching for, it would be the Centauri or their perennial opponents, the Tau Ceti. *We take it slow,* Forrest told himself, *we avoid their clusters of ships, and we don't do anything to draw attention to ourselves.*

The *Widowmaker* was harder to spot than a hole in space. The active stealth system actually bent light and radio waves around it. The result was a bit of distortion, almost impossible to spot without knowing what to look for. "We could fly right through one of their relay beams and they shouldn't pick us up. The only thing the field doesn't mask entirely is our mass, and there's enough ships flying around that they shouldn't notice us." Gravitational sensors were passive sensors anyway, they didn't send out any kind of signal to track. The gravitational field of the destroyer would be relatively small.

The ship's own emissions were transformed into heat, and in

conjunction with the vessel's heat sinks and cooling units, the heat would be stored and emitted in a safe direction. That wouldn't be a problem in the outer system, but once they reached the inner system, they'd be on the clock. As they built up heat, the ship's cooling systems would lose efficiency, gradually failing until either they were forced to shut everything down and vent heat or they were able to vent it in a safe direction.

If the system were on a real war-footing, then they'd have personnel on their gravitational sensors scanning for any kind of intrusion. Forrest's best hope in that case was to come in close to some stellar object or even a ship and use its known presence to mask the *Widowmaker*'s.

Fortunately, since this was a peace talk of some kind, no one should be planning any kind of military operations in the system. Forrest just hoped all that goodwill meant that both sides would be a little more relaxed and paying a little less attention to one another.

***

"I want our passive scans at one hundred percent effectiveness," Kapitan zur Weltraum Langsdorff snapped. "If the Centauri so much as fart, I want to know what they had for breakfast, am I understood?" From someone else, that would have elicted a laugh. His crew, though, knew him well enough to realize that he was deadly serious.

"Jawohl, Herr Kapitan," his sensors officer replied.

Langsdorff didn't bother to hide his scowl as he surveyed the various displays of the "referendum." This assignment was, on the surface, a plum job, providing escort and security for Chancellor Tautmann. Both Centauri and Tau Ceti media had played this as a meeting of the minds, as the beginning of an end to hostilities within the Confederation. It could be a historic event, a cessation of over eighty years of civil war between the two strongest members of the Confederation. The way some of the politicians talked it up, children a century from this day would brag about how their grandparent was a sailor aboard one of the ships at Sol system when they signed the peace agreements.

Langsdorff understood the reality of the situation better than most of his crew. Tau Ceti and Centauri had both been hurt, very badly, by the massive loss of trust of their officer corps. Dozens of senior officers had been implicated, several had been confirmed, as brainwashed plants by Marius Giovanni. Worse, many of them had been in place for months or even *years*. The damage they could have done was unimaginable. It would take a decade to sift through personnel transfers, promotions, and even logistical and supply agreements. The compromises in security and planning alone left Langsdorff terrified. The strategic implications were horrifying.

That level of compromises meant that heads were going to roll. Already over a dozen senior officers who *hadn't* been implicated had been forced to resign. Entire elements of military and civilian security had been relieved and replaced within Tau Ceti space... and rumors suggested that President Spiridon of the Centauri had begun a ruthless purge of his officer corps.

In theory, Langsdorff's involvement with the United Colonies personnel who had uncovered the infiltration would have helped his career. He had shown that he wasn't part of the infiltration and he wasn't implicated in any way, shape, or form.

The political reality, however, was far more bleak. The embarrassment over the arrest of the terrorist Tomas Kanreich in the neighboring Alpha Canis Majoris system had not only revealed corruption within that star system, but it had revealed close and direct ties to corrupt politicians within the Tau Ceti system, complete with data on illegal payments from the Slivko crime family to several high ranking members of the National Council. Many of them had been forced to resign and at least two were facing criminal charges... but their political allies on all ends of the spectrum weren't about to forget that a certain Kapitan zur Weltraum Langsdorff had accompanied ships of a foreign power to raid a notional ally's system because Tau Ceti and Confederation military ships and officers had been compromised.

The senior military officers, too, weren't about to forgive or forget his involvement in destroying the careers of dozens of officers who'd been implicated in Marius Giovanni's brainwashing scheme. Certainly they understood that it was a security threat... probably better than Langsdorff understood. But because they hadn't uncovered the odd behavior and strange decisions made by their former friends and associates, it reflected badly upon them.

Thus, when they tried to find someone to send for this escort mission, they had chosen Langsdorff. No one, military officer or politician, really thought that anything would come of this referendum. At best, they expected a stalemate, at worst... well, it wasn't beyond President Spiridon to instigate some kind of military or diplomatic incident that would then provoke a violent upsurge in the ongoing civil war.

There were dozens of ways they could do that, from provoking the Tau Ceti Defense Forces vessels to fire upon them to staging some kind of surprise attack, even to blowing up one of their own ships and claiming it was done by TCDF. Even Tanis's vessels weren't beyond suspicion, they *were* mercenaries, after all... their loyalty could be bought.

And when something happened, the voters back home would want someone to pin it all upon. Kapitan zur Weltraum Langsdorff understood that. Which didn't mean that he was going to let his political enemies make it easy. He was going to do his duty and if anything seemed out of place, he was going to make certain that his people didn't pay the price for it.

***

Minder tuned out the bickering of his human "advisers" and sent a mental message to his daughter. *How do the discussions progress?* The opportunity to further stir the pot had been too good to pass up and he had insured that his daughter would be the representative to attend.

As expected, so far, she replied. *The fact that we have infiltrated both major sides of the conflict means that we need not resort to telepathic meddling. Tensions are already high enough and both major parties grievances are well entrenched so discussions are going nowhere, while each of the smaller factions is afraid of being sold out and so they're cutting back-room deals and agreements that they can't possibly keep.*

Minder felt pleasure at that. In reality, the vast majority of his job was simply to fan the existing paranoia and fear within the major powers of human space. The Centauri Confederation continued to devour itself and the disorganized mess of the Colonial Republic could be further destabilized with a few targeted assassinations whenever one of their generals or admirals grew too powerful. Of course, he didn't count on that. That was why he'd put into place several contingencies for a variety of outcomes. Those ranged from agents in positions aboard both Tau Ceti and Centauri vessels to open fire... as well as assassins among the diplomatic staff who, while entirely human, were mentally controlled so that they could be triggered to kill a variety of dignitaries.

The targets included his own daughter, though she didn't know it. In some ways, that would have been the most effective method to secure a guaranteed war. But it brought with it the cost of replacing her. Minder hadn't entirely dismissed it, but he hesitated to go to the effort, particularly since she'd begun to prove extremely effective.

His agents had also taken over the senior personnel of Hugo Base. He'd used the paranoid and ambitious former Amalgamated Worlds officers as a lever on multiple occasions, going as far as to have them play factions of the Centauri Confederation against each other for prized access to their data storage. Even better, the secrets buried there went far beyond mere data. Minder felt a spurt of pleasure as he considered just how dangerous the Martian base was... and how valuable the secrets there could be. With the diplomatic staff meeting at Hugo Base as neutral territory, Minder controlled every aspect of the meeting, on dozens of levels. It wasn't a question of how it could go wrong... merely when he wanted it to end in violence and bloodshed.

Any further progress on identifying Marius Giovanni's infiltrators? He asked.

None beyond the ones we had initially identified, her frustration-laden response matched his own irritation.

Let me know if anything changes, Minder sent to his daughter. The majority of the mental tampering that Marius Giovanni's brainwashing had done was brute force, clearly driven by standard methods of drugs and mental conditioning. Those types of infiltrators were easy for Minder's kind to identify and neutralize. Minder had even left a few of them in place, positioned where he could monitor the information they could access and any actions they could take.

However, there were several that seemed to be far more carefully modified. Whether that was through more advanced techniques or even psionics, Minder's people hadn't been able to learn. Most such agents didn't even seem aware of the changes to their loyalties... or there weren't any changes. Five of the released officers from the base at 767A36 had proven compromised. Two had shown no other symptoms of such programming beyond impossible assertions about *other* senior officers being compromised. The other three had killed themselves, either upon being revealed or after accomplishing whatever task they'd been assigned.

The problem was: Minder's people had already discovered at least a dozen other officers and civilian officials who had *also* been adjusted. Five of them in the process of accomplishing their missions. At least one of them had been successful, and the action had erased over fourteen hours of sensor logs for the entire Centauri system. Another had five minutes of uninterrupted access to the military archives, and Minder's best human programmers still weren't sure what exactly the man had done before a security officer had noticed the breach and put a bullet through the back of his head.

Minder didn't know the intent, but this wave of sleeper agents was a threat that he had to address... and he didn't know what Marius Giovanni's end game could be.

I hate that, Minder thought to himself. For decades he had operated in the shadows, manipulating the players of the human race, secure in the fact that no humans knew of his agenda or existence. Now he knew that *Marius* had done the same thing... and Marius's goals seemed to directly oppose Minder's. Worse than that, he seemed perfectly capable of making absolutely ruthless decisions to accomplish his goals.

At least I foiled his main effort at Kapteyn's Star, Minder reminded himself. Sidewinder had delivered one major setback to Marius Giovanni's forces in the killing of his main agent, Reese Leone. Minder didn't want to think about how close the human's plans had come to success. Humanity's very flaws that allowed Minder to manipulate them also sowed the seeds of making them difficult to manage.

Minder returned his attention to his human advisers as they stared at him expectantly. He'd managed to follow the majority of their discussion with an idle part of his mind and he had already come to the decision even before this meeting. "I think we'll focus our efforts on increasing our military spending. I want to see complete reports on vessel procurement and ground force buildup."

He formed a pleasant, pleased smile as he went on, his mind

shifting to the human facade that he had managed as the ruler of a star nation for decades. It was an act that he had played for so long that he did it without effort. It was a challenge that he had come to savor.

He would be disappointed if the decision ever came down from his superiors to exterminate humanity once and for all.

***

"You have got to be kidding me," Forrest grumbled as he looked over the intercepted transmission. "The peace talk is happening at Hugo Base?!"

"Yes, sir," Petty Officer Godbey nodded, his expression tight and his voice clipped. "Apparently the ships are just a show, the real meeting is happening planet-side." He licked his lips, "I suppose it makes sense, skipper. Lots more room planet-side for discussions and meetings than aboard any ship."

"Well... crap," Forrest rubbed his temples. "This is insane. This is *beyond* insane."

"Are we going to abort?" Lieutenant Medica asked.

"No!" Forrest blurted. As Elvis Medica raised an eyebrow at him, Forrest realized just how desperate his reply had sounded. Not for the first time, he wondered if this *was* crazy. If Alannis Giovanni really was dead... then Forrest had destroyed his own career and quite probably those of the men and women who'd followed him. He'd stolen an advanced, stealthy warship... and he planned to infiltrate a peace summit to steal information on a location given to him by a pirate.

"We use this peace talk as cover. We slip in, get what we need, and we get out."

"Skipper..." Lieutenant Medica looked around the bridge, as if to make certain that no one else was here besides Petty Officer Godbey, who looked as if he *didn't* want to be here. "Boss, there's over fifty capital ships in orbit around Mars. Light and heavy cruisers, mostly, but also battlecruisers. The orbits are so heavy with sensors you could practically walk on them. Hugo Base is going to be locked down tighter than ever... and it isn't just Hugo Base security. There's also going to be Tanis Defense Force personnel, Tau Ceti military personnel, and Centauri Confederation personnel." Elvis clenched his jaw, "Hell, skipper. This is what amounts to a terrorist attack on a diplomatic summit. We're talking about grounds for a declaration of war!"

Forrest closed his eyes. He thought about Alannis. He pictured her smile, her laugh. He thought about what she might be going through as a prisoner. What that bastard Reese might be doing to her, right now. He thought about her strapped, helpless, in some machine as it rewrote her mind.

He thought about what might happen to the United Colonies if he was wrong. Or even if he *wasn't* wrong, but if this all went back on them anyway. A rogue United Colonies officer had been the one leading the attack on Kapteyn's Star. Marius Giovanni, the man behind the attack, was the father of Emperor Lucius Giovanni of the United Colonies. If Forrest or any of his personnel were identified or if Centauri Confederation realized that United Colonies personnel were involved in any way...

Forrest's head dropped. "Okay," he said. "Let's talk with Rory and Feliks, maybe they'll have some way to do this remotely." A cyber attack on the network might not be seen as an act of war. Even better if they'd figured some way to get the information without taking down the entire network.

Elvis Medica didn't seem entirely satisfied by that, but he gave Forrest a nod.

"Rory, Feliks, to the bridge," Forrest sent over the intercom.

A few minutes later, Rory and Feliks arrived. In contrast to their long-standing scowls and frowns, the two wore broad grins. They also had bloodshot eyes. Rory's thinning brown hair stood on end and Felix's hair was disheveled. "A very good morning to you, Lieutenant Commander!" Rory said.

"Yes, good morning!" Feliks bobbed his head.

Forrest glanced at the chrono. "It's almost six in the evening, ship time."

"Oh, well," Rory glanced at his datapad. "I thought we'd just pulled an all-nighter. At least we have a few days to recover before we get to Mars, right?"

"We're almost in orbit," Forrest bit out. "How long have you two been awake?"

"That is a good question," Feliks blinked owlishly.

"That doesn't matter," Rory waved a dismissive hand. "What matters is what we've figured out!"

"It is fantastic news," Feliks nodded. "All of our effort is worth it!"

Forrest's eyebrows went up, "You figured out how to remotely access the data we need?"

"What?" Rory snorted with laughter, "No, that's *impossible.*"

"Yes, and a waste of time, too," Feliks nodded. "No, we figured out something far more important. We learned--"

"I thought that we agreed that *I* could tell them since *I* was the one with the idea," Rory interrupted.

"Yes, but your idea wouldn't have worked without my algorithm!" Feliks protested.

"Your simple little algorithm are meaningless compared to the data compression work that I came up with!" Rory shouted.

"Gentlemen," Forrest tried to interrupt.

"Simple!" Feliks waved his long, thin arms at Rory, "It is a seven variable decryption algorithm. It shouldn't have a solution, but I managed to create one! Your data compression software is a patched together bit of software that you modified based upon watching a toilet flush!"

Rory's face had gone red, "Well, at least--"

"Shut up!" Forrest snapped. As the two scientists stared at him, he clinched his jaw. "We have a fleet of over two hundred vessels in orbit over our destination. Hugo Base is under a secure lock down and is the center for some kind of diplomatic summit. Now, one of you explain why I'm supposed to be impressed?"

"Oh," Rory said after a moment. "Well, we figured out how to download the entire contents of their network. But since it's impossible for us to get inside, I guess that doesn't matter."

"The entire contents?" Forrest's eyebrows went up. "That's several petabytes, right?"

"We are actually dealing with exabytes," Feliks corrected. "Which is why the process was so hard to solve. We will have less than thirty seconds from when we neutralize security to when the system wipes itself. During that time we will need to decrypt and download all of that information."

"That's where his algorithm and *my* data compression comes in," Rory stood as tall as his short, pudgy frame would allow. "We can save *everything!* We could steal the digital equivalent to five billion Libraries of Alexandria!"

"Even better," Feliks said, "we would have access to all of it!"

"Well, does this process work remotely?" Forrest asked.

"Of course not!" Rory waved his hands, "that would be impossible. No this will require a direct, hard-line connection. We'll need to access a terminal inside the base."

"That's the problem," Forrest repeated, "because there's no way we're slipping into that base without creating a major diplomatic incident." His face went grim as he contemplated the situation. There was only one choice left to him. "We're going to scrap the mission."

***

Minder's daughter, or Fixer as she had started to think of herself, tuned out the drone of the speaking official and she felt a flutter of unease as she tasted the emotions of the normal humans around her.

They were a weak, easily manipulated lot. Many of them were so complacent from decades at being among the ranks of the elite that they didn't really understand challenge or struggle. The elite of the most wealthy star systems in human space, they reaped the benefits of their forebears who had arranged things to keep their families in positions of power and prosperity.

Like I was... once, she thought absently. Not that she regretted her transformation. She was stronger, sharper, and far more capable after her father had transformed her.

Normally the most pampered and content of humanity were the most easily influenced and until the past few days, that had proven true... until her rival had countered that.

That was where the flutter of unease came from. The tall, beautiful woman, the scion of another powerful family... and unlike many here, she had worked for her position. She'd also proven remarkably astute at influencing those around her... and despite Fixer's earlier messages to Minder, there had begun to be a disturbing amount of progress at the meeting.

Fixer didn't like that on many levels. She knew the stakes as well as her father. She knew just how dangerous humanity could be, not in what they themselves could do, but what they could enable as a possibility.

She also knew that Minder would go to any extreme to prevent even the remote possibility of such an event. Despite her father's ability to keep secrets, she knew of many of his contingencies here at this meeting as well as throughout human space. He would kill billions of them without hesitation. Fixer suspected that he would sacrifice any and all of his subordinates... even her or Sidewinder.

Which I understand, she thought, even as she stared at her hated rival. Fixer wouldn't hesitate to do the same, after all. Her species was a collective, but her kind, those who hid amongst humanity, they were --by necessity-- individuals. In doing so, they were at once a part of the greater whole... but the intelligent and aware of their kind needed the ability to act as individuals. That enabled them to have singular goals and emotions... such as a survival instinct or ambition.

Fixer didn't necessary *dream* of supplanting Minder... but if the opportunity came, she wouldn't pass it up. Loyalty went only so far, and as she saw it, the successes that Marius Giovanni and his agents had found were a result of Minder's focus on the core human systems and his failure to monitor the overall situation. He'd lost sight of the larger picture. Which was why she'd begun to look deeper into his plans and actions... just as a precaution, of course.

Yet for all that, Fixer knew that her situation at this conference was precarious. Should Minder decide to trigger one of his contingencies, there was every possibility that he would go for an extreme solution. And Fixer didn't doubt that her death in such a fashion would enhance her father's efforts. He might regret her loss, but he wouldn't hesitate to sacrifice her. After all, she, like all of her kind, was replaceable.

She opened herself to the emotions around her and what she felt gave her a trill of nervousness. The fear, the anger, the paranoia... the emotions that she had manipulated so well... those were subdued. They had been replaced by confidence and satisfaction. Her rival had caused that, Fixer knew. The powerful, assured woman spoke so eloquently, so confidently, that the others couldn't help but listen to her. Now, as her rival stood, prepared to speak, Fixer saw the group of senior officers and politicians lean forward in their seats, ready to hear her words.

Fixer had to stop her.

She made the decision in a split second and, without any outward sign, she sent out a tendril of thought to one of the military officers that she had prepared for just this eventuality. It had taken her a few hours, every day, for the past week for her to plant the compulsion in his mind, but he had picked up the composite pistol from where her people had positioned it for him. He wore it now, and as she reached into his mind, she activated the secondary compulsion.

Flottilen-Admiral Krause of Tau Ceti stood, walked in front of Fixer's rival, drew the concealed pistol, and fired two rounds into her chest from point blank range.

As Fixer's rival fell back, in the heartbeats before the room exploded into shouting, confusion, and chaos, Fixer allowed herself a small, satisfied smile.

***

Chapter III

July 13, 2410
Mars Orbit, Sol System
Neutral Territory

Kapitan zur Weltraum Langsdorff of the Tau Ceti Defense Forces cut off the panicked transmission from the surface, "All ships, battle stations," he snapped orders to his squadron. He didn't know what had happened at Hugo Base, but it sounded as if gunfire had interrupted the main summit. "Order the *Michel* to launch shuttles to the surface and extract all of our personnel."

"Kapitan Langsdorff," his executive officer spoke up, "should we wait for confirmation from Chancellor Tautmann?" The woman was a political appointee, Langsdorff knew. She'd been assigned as his watch-dog.

Langsdorff leveled a basilisk glare upon his XO. "I am responsible for the safeguarding of all personnel. We have reports of gunfire, we will pull them out before this escalates."

She licked her lips, "But this might provoke..."

"There are reports of shots fired," Kapitan zur Weltraum Langsdorff snapped. "That is sufficient to tell us that the situation has gone beyond diplomatic and into the military." He looked past his XO to see that shuttles had already launched per his orders. "Do you duty, XO, and allow me to do mine."

He turned back to his displays, "What are the Centauri vessels doing?"

His sensors officer looked up, her face pale, "They've powered up their weapons batteries and they've gone to active sensors."

Langsdorff's lips went in a flat line as he considered that. "Bring our weapons systems online and break orbit. Initiate withdrawal plan..." he glanced at his display and selected a predesignated course, "Operation Danzig." That withdrawal would put space between his vessels and the others in orbit while still allowing his combat shuttles to evacuate the civilian personnel from Hugo Base.

The Tanis Defense Force vessels in orbit had begun to form up into a defensive formation and had also launched their shuttles.

No one from any of the three task forces had sent any communications to one another, Langsdorff realized. The dozens of single vessels that had carried the smaller faction's representatives had either broken orbit or remained in place, their ships crews reacting in a variety of fashions.

The Tau Ceti officer considered transmitting to the other ships, but he dismissed that after a moment's thought. Anything he sent to them wouldn't be taken at face value. The summit had collapsed in violence and someone out there was behind it. The last thing he wanted was for his ships and personnel to become the focus of that firepower. The uncertainty right now was his ally. The Centauri would either open fire and implicate themselves or they would hold their fire, hoping that Langsdorff's people would be the first to shoot.

"Break orbit," he snapped, "Use Plan Belhaven." That course would get them out of low orbit and put some distance between themselves and the Centauri vessels, but it would keep them close enough to support their shuttles. "I want tight control on all weapons batteries," Langsdorff snapped into his command net. "Fire *only* if you are hit by targeting sensors and only with command authorization." He let out a tense breath, "that said, do *not* allow the enemy to engage us first. If you have eminent threat, engage with all weapons." His ships already had firing parameters based upon their passive sensors. The enemy might have those as well, but odds were, they'd want to go to active targeting before they fired. That would give his people some warning... time enough for them to preemptively engage the enemy. At this range, the firefight would be devastating and Langsdorff would rather get his shots off first.

At the end of the day, Langsdorff would face the board of inquiry and the destruction of his career over allowing the men and women under his command to die needlessly.

He just hoped it wouldn't come to that.

***

Lieutenant Commander Forrest Perkins let out a tense breath. "Alright, there's nothing we can do now." He nodded at Rory and Feliks, "I appreciate your hard work. I'm sure you put a lot of effort into it. But since we can't continue this mission without endangering the United Colonies--"

"Uh, Skipper?" Petty Officer Godbey started to speak.

"One moment," Forrest said, raising a hand. He looked at the two scientists. "Unfortunately, I'm going to have to call this entire operation off. I'll make the official announcement to the crew after this--"

"Sir, you really need to see this," Petty Officer Godbey interrupted.

Forrest looked over at the sensor display and it took him a long moment to make sense of what he saw. The orderly rows of ships had exploded into chaos. All three forces had broken orbit and launched shuttles to the surface. Both the Tau Ceti and Centauri fleet elements had powered up their weapons systems.

No one had fired a shot... not yet, but it looked like it was about to become a serious fight. Forrest looked up at Lieutenant Medica. "Get the shuttle prepped, and launch it *now*."

***

Fixer kept the smile off her face as her security team moved her to her private shuttle. She *could* have evacuated a number of her nation's people with her, but she was content to allow them to find their own ways off of Hugo Base.

The alarm klaxons heightened the tension, especially as the Hugo Base security personnel forced their way through crowds. It was probably time for her to contact her father. *Minder,* she sent, *things have fallen apart. One of Tau Ceti's officers drew a pistol and opened fire.* It was best not to give too much information, especially when it was difficult, if not impossible, for her to lie in direct mental communication with him.

Conceal the truth, yes, but actual deceit would be entirely different.

What? Minder sent back. *One of ours?*

Fixer mentally interpreted that as one of "their" kind or one of Minder's agents. *No,* she sent back.

Well, perhaps it was one of Giovanni's damned sleeper agents, Minder replied, irritation clear in his mental projection. *Either way, this works to our favor. Are you where you can safely evacuate?*

She didn't miss the weight he put on that question and she wondered if he hoped she would say that she couldn't get clear... and if he'd use one of his contingencies to ensure that. *I'm nearly to my shuttle,* Fixer sent back.

There was a few seconds pause and Fixer's escort had her aboard her shuttle within that time. She ordered them to shut the door and lift off.

Very well, Minder's thoughts carried his confidence, *you are present, take charge of my agents, there. Escalate it to violence, draw in as many factions as you can. Now that it has devolved, I want maximum chaos.*

Of course, father, Fixer sent back and she didn't hide her sense of pleasure at the opportunity.

She broke off her connection to him and sent a mental tendril to her father's agent here at Hugo Base. The former human and most of his senior ranks had been transformed into her kind. They'd secretly run Hugo Base for decades, ensuring that the Sol system colonies remained fractured and distrustful of one another. *My shuttle is lifting off,* she sent, *are the other nations sending shuttles for their representatives?*

His response came a moment later, *Yes. The three task forces have broken orbit. What do you want me to do?*

Fixer couldn't help a pleased smile as she contemplated what would happen next. *Clearly this was a betrayal of the neutrality of the summit. Order your human subordinates to engage all landing shuttles as a security measure. Seize any human dignitaries that you can... execute any who resist.*

***

"Kaptain Langsdorff!" His sensor officer looked up, "Our landing shuttles have begun taking fire!"

"From the Centauri?!" Langsdorff demanded. He didn't see how the Centauri would dare to open fire on the shuttles as they landed, not with their own shuttles intermixed.

"No, sir, from the *base.*"

Langsdorff swore as he brought up the display. It was too late to order his shuttles out. Many had gone on evasive patterns, but others tried to drive through the gunfire. The position of his ships meant that they couldn't safely fire on the weapons platforms of the base, not without endangering their shuttles and certainly not without endangering Centauri or Tanis shuttles sent to evacuate their own personnel.

"Has Hugo Base sent any transmissions?" Langsdorff demanded. This couldn't be some ploy of the Centauri. They were losing shuttles of their own.

"Yes, sir," his communications officer reported.

He brought it up, and the bearded commander of the base appeared on the screen. "Due to multiple assassination attempts, my personnel have initiated a lockdown of Hugo Base," Johann Kalsi said. "We will not allow any invasion forces to land. Any attempt to land will be met with deadly force and all dignitaries on the planet will be detained until we can ascertain who is behind this senseless violence."

Langsdorff's face went hard at that. The man spoke of peace while engaging dozens of unarmed shuttles. He cut off the transmission. "How long to arm our reserve shuttles and get them on-site?"

"Fifteen minutes, sir," his XO said.

Langsdorff bit back a snarl. His XO had been the one to remind him that the terms of this meeting had required them to disarm their shuttles. He leveled a baleful glare on her, but she was studiously working at her station and didn't meet his gaze. *How many good people are dying down there while I can't do anything to save them?*

***

"Are we sure this is a good idea?" Rory asked as the stealth shuttle screamed through the Martian upper atmosphere.

"It does seem particularly risky," Feliks nodded. "Hostilities could break out at any moment, we do not have a transponder, and our stealth field on this shuttle has not been successfully tested under these kinds of conditions."

"Shut up," Elvis snapped at the two scientists. As the ranking officer after Forrest, he knew why he was here. That didn't mean he was eager to be present.

"This is insane!" Ricky One-Eye snapped. "I didn't sign up for a combat mission! Why am I even here!?"

Elvis leveled a glare at the pirate. "You're here because we're short handed. I watch the scientists, Wandry and Wicklund watch my back, and *you* watch our exit." He gave the man an unpleasant smile as the shuttle rocked, "and if you get any ideas about abandoning us, Corporal Wandry and Petty Officer Cartwright both have instructions to shoot you on sight if you come back to the shuttle without us."

Ricky One Eye looked over at the Marine, her face hidden behind her visor. Granted, Corporal Lin Wicklund was a big woman, nearly two meters tall. She came from a heavy gravity world, Elvis knew. She also didn't like pirates.

Evidently the threat was sufficient and Ricky shut up.

Which was good, because Elvis didn't need any further distractions. He reviewed the map overlay on his helmet display again. Hopefully the base defenses would be overwhelmed by the chaos of shuttle landings and evacuations.

"Lieutenant!" Petty Officer Godbey barked from the cockpit, "I need you up here!"

Elvis unstrapped and then staggered forward. The ride had just become far rougher and he pulled himself into the cockpit and braced in the hatch. He saw why, immediately.

Explosions and ionized trails of energy weapons fire scarred the sky. Elvis blanched as he saw the weight of fire coming up from the planet's surface. "Holy crap," he shook his head, "Hugo Base opened fire?!"

"Yes, sir," Petty Officer Godbey said grimly. "They've splashed over fifteen shuttles at this point. Four of them taking off."

"*Shit*," Elvis gasped. If the defenders suspected someone was dropping a regiment of troops to secure the base, that would be one thing, but these people were trying to evacuate. "Do we have a firing solution on their weapon emplacements?" When they'd planned the initial entry, Elvis had picked out what he suspected was three sensor towers and five weapon emplacements. He didn't think they'd get all of the weapon emplacements, but without the sensor towers, those should be blind.

Petty Officer Godbey whipped his head around, eyes wide, "Sir, that would give away our presence *and* it's opening fire on a neutral nation!"

Elvis nodded, "Yes, but people are dying."

"Sir, I have their weapons emplacement locations loaded in the targeting computers. They are, however, conducting multi-spectrum jamming and deploying chaff and thermal flares. I'll be sending our birds in without guidance. If there's something in the way, I may splash them."

Elvis watched another shuttle vanish in a fireball. "Do it."

***

Wachtmiester Horst ducked down as weapon fire scythed across the platform and two more of his security detail went down. He had Chancellor Tautmann wedged behind him in the doorway of the landing pad, but most of his security detail was down at this point. He looked up as one of their shuttles banked over the enemy position, the pilot directing the flare of his engines down on the weapons team.

"Alder this is LC77 we are landing on your position, prepare to load VIPs," the shuttle pilot barked over the net.

"Affirmative!" Wachtmiester Horst called in reply. Alder was his callsign as the protective detail for the Chancellor.

The shuttle began to land, just as an automated turret rotated in its direction. "LC77, break off, break off now!" Horst shouted.

The pilot didn't have time to respond. The turret opened up, railgun rounds punched through it's armored hull from point blank range and the shuttle exploded, pieces of debris raining down behind the shockwave that blasted Horst's people down from the platform.

Down the corridor, he heard more gunfire and screams as Hugo Base personnel continued to fight his people. He felt his stomach go cold as he realized that he wasn't going to be able to get the Chancellor out. "All LC elements, this is Alder, break off, there's no way to get through their defenses."

***

Elvis watched as Petty Officer Godbey activated the weapons systems and launched.

The Molnir-class shuttle carried eight Interceptor missiles. All eight of them detached and streaked out. The Interceptor missiles were designed for missile and fighter interception at hundreds of thousands of kilometers. In the planet's atmosphere, their warheads didn't even activate, they went in as purely kinetic weapons and the missile spread impacted square on the targets that Elvis had identified.

Each of those missiles traveled at two hundred and fifty

kilometers per second upon impact. The eight detonations happened so closely together that they might as well have been one explosion. The shockwaves rolled through the thin martian atmosphere and Elvis couldn't help a whistle of appreciation. *I hope we didn't nail any civilians with those,* he thought absently to himself.

Jamming and weapon fire cut off within seconds. "Bring us in," Elvis snapped.

***

Fixer's pleasure vanished as explosions blossomed across Hugo Base. "What was that?" she demanded. None of the ships in orbit should have dared to open fire and she had not expected any of the human shuttles to be armed.

Her human military adviser rushed over. "I'm not sure, Madame. Our other shuttles were under fire, but someone or something took out several of Hugo Base's defenses."

Fixer sent back a mental message to the suborned commander of the base, but he was either dead or too busy to respond. If it was the former, then someone needed to take charge of things and make certain that none of her father's agents were exposed... if it was the latter, then her presence might be enough to tip things back the right way.

"Bring us back down there," Fixer snapped. "Get us on the ground, now!"

***

Wachtmiester Horst grinned as the weapon platform overlooking the landing pad detonated. Debris and shrapnel exploded outward, but Horst would take that any day over aimed fire. He covered Chancellor Tautmann with his body even as he activated his comm. "Good job!" Horst shouted, "Nice LC's, you splashed the turret, we're currently clear! Get us out of here, now!"

A few moments later, he saw dozens of shuttles begin to land. Horst didn't wait for the turbines to even wind down on the nearest one, he grabbed Chancellor Tautmann by the collar and dragged the VIP through the light Martian gravity in three bounds. As the ramp dropped, Horst shoved the crew chief out of the way. "We have the Chancellor aboard, get us off the ground!"

There were other Tau Ceti diplomats, officers, and politicians who needed transport, but those weren't his problem. "Roger," the pilot responded over the net, "We are now LC Alder. LC Alder is outbound with cargo."

The engines warbled up, even as the ramp came up. Horst looked over at the crew chief, "Damned fine shooting, by the way. You nailed that turret perfectly."

"That wasn't us," the crew chief scowled. "We haven't got any ammo, our standing orders had us disarmed."

Horst stared at the other man, "Then who the hell just saved us?"

***

"Go, go go!" Elvis Medica shouted as he pushed Rory and Feliks ahead of him.

Ahead of them he saw Corporal Wiklund take a knee behind a bit of wreckage and open fire while Staff Sergeant Dawn Witzke rushed to the shelter of the hatchway. In the thin air and light gravity, the biggest problem was staying low.

Rory put a bit too much behind a step and went bounding into the air. As tracers cut through the air above him, Elvis reached up a hand, caught the engineer by his ankle, and yanked him back downwards.

"Damn it, stay low!" Elvis shouted.

"They're *shooting* at us!" Rory shouted.

"Well, yeah," Elvis snapped, even as he shoved the two of them into the hatch that Staff Sergeant Witzke had cleared. "We sort of blew up half their base."

"What?!" Rory said.

"Don't worry about it," Elvis replied. He flipped the emergency override on the side of the hatch, and when that didn't work, he bit back a curse and started ripping out wires. It was clear that the base had gone to some kind of emergency lock down. What that meant as far as who had started this mess, Elvis didn't know. What he did know was that they didn't have time to waste. There were shuttles landing all around the facility and hundreds of dignitaries and their escorts fleeing the base in all directions. Sooner or later, though, someone would notice their group going *inside* and that would be a problem.

He overrode the remote lock down and the hatch ground open. "Okay," he looked at Rory and Feliks, "stay close to me and keep your heads down." They didn't have any kind of body armor for either of the two scientists. It wasn't something that Elvis would have thought to bring, even if he'd realized the two men would be aboard the *Widowmaker* when they took it. He really hoped that neither of the two men got killed. As annoying as they could be, they were sort of irreplaceable.

Elvis nodded at Staff Sergeant Witzke who led the way down the corridor, followed by Corporal Wandry. The two moved in bounds, one covering a section of corridor while the other moved up. Elvis turned to look at Ricky One-Eye. The pirate crouched near the airlock, his face pale, gasping in the thin air. Mars had been inhabited for centuries and while it wasn't exactly prime real estate, it at least had a mostly breathable atmosphere.

Which was good for Ricky, since they didn't have a ship suit for him.

Elvis was honest enough with himself to admit that he didn't mind watching the slaver gasp for air. "Guard this hatch. It's our way out. If you see anyone approach, you notify us immediately."

"What if they see me?" Ricky whiined.

"Radio me," Elvis snapped back, pointing at the handheld comm unit in the pirate's hand.

"What if they're armed?!" Ricky whined as Elvis turned away.

"Then try not to piss yourself before you die!" Elvis shouted over his shoulder. He pushed the two scientists ahead of him. They had landed at one of the base's utility pads and this section of corridor, under normal conditions, should have only been used for maintenance crews.

Right now, it was mostly empty. Elvis figured that most of the security would be focused on the outer parts of the base, where everyone was trying to escape. That would only last for so long, though. He glanced up as they passed a security door and noticed the array of sensors. The group had to be setting off alarms... the question was if anyone had time to notice.

Staff Sergeant Witzke came to the end of the corridor and waved a hand. "Hatch is secured, sir," she reported, even as Corporal Wandry came up to secure the cross corridor just behind her. "Do we go in fast or slow?"

Down the corridors, Elvis could hear gunfire dropping off. The distant sounds of explosions had ceased. *We're running out of time,* Elvis thought to himself.

"Blow it," he snapped.

He could hear the grin in Staff Sergeant Witzke's voice as he replied, "Yes, sir!" The Marine pulled a charge out of her combat gear, attached it to the door, and then stepped back. "Fire in the hole!"

The thin air didn't transfer the shock as powerfully and the directional plasma charge focused the vast majority of the energy inwards. The armored hatch disintegrated, the ceramic composite armor shattering and scything into the room beyond. Staff Sergeant Witzke gave an excited shout as she charged inside.

At the same time, the alarms and klaxons seemed to climb in pitch. A moment later, Elvis heard, "Warning, security breach of data core, security breach of the data core..."

"Move!" Elvis shouted as he pushed the two scientists ahead of him into the room. His gaze skipped over the red ruin of what had been a person near the hatch. Staff Sergeant Witzke had swept around the corner and into the control room where a half-dozen technicians raised their hands, their faces pale and terrified.

"Down on the floor, now!" Staff Sergeant Witzke shouted and all of them hurried to comply. That included Rory and Feliks who both ducked down as the Marine turned back to face them.

"Not you two," Elvis scowled, hoisting them back to their feet and pushing them towards the control room's consoles. "Do your thing."

"Right, right," Rory said, absently patting at his helmet. He looked at Feliks, "You brought the case, right?"

"We've got movement in the side corridor," Corporal Wandry reported.

Feliks looked around, "I thought that *you* brought the case..."

Out in the corridor Corporal Wandry opened fire. Elvis heard return fire, the sharp sound gunfire muffled in the thin atmosphere.

Elvis reached over and unstrapped the case from Rory's back and put it in his hands. "There, ready?"

"Right!" Rory moved over and plugged into the main

terminal. One of the technicians started to his feet, "You can't!"

Staff Sergeant Witzke clubbed the man back down with the butt of her rifle. "Anyone else feel like interrupting?"

No one else stood up. The gunfire in the corridor redoubled and Elvis gave the Marine a nod, "Go help Wandry," he ordered. Elvis drew his pistol and checked it. He wasn't a particularly good shot, but the technicians in the room all seemed fairly cowed. Hopefully he wouldn't have to use it.

"Okay," Rory spoke, "wow, they didn't even have these terminals locked down. That's pretty sloppy. Oh, hey, look, they left the original data link installed, that's really sloppy!"

Elvis looked at Rory, "The *Widowmaker* was designed and built by the Centauri, who make use of a lot of Amaglamated Worlds designs and technology. Couldn't we have modified the *Widowmaker*'s transmitter and used legacy Amalgamated Worlds military codes to access the information, then?"

"Well, yes," Rory looked up from his terminal, "but you'd have to have legacy Amalgamated Worlds security codes to get this system to deliver the data. And it would require authorization *here*, so someone still would have to be in the control room."

Elvis shook his head, "Not if you used command override codes and tricked the authorization with a command loop. The security net would default to authorized from a command override and it would give us what we needed."

"I hadn't thought of that," Rory admitted. "I suppose that would have worked..."

"That is quite a good idea," Feliks said from where he plugged in cables to the terminal. "If we had thought of that, none of this would be necessary."

Out in the corridor, the sound of gunfire redoubled. *None of this was necessary,* Elvis thought to himself, even as he turned away from the two engineers. "Staff Sergeant, status?"

"Holding, just a few local security, no one with heavy firepower so far, sir," Staff Sergeant Witzke reported. "Any chance you can lock down some of these side corridors, sir?"

"Uh," Elvis turned back to one of the terminals and brought up the base layout. The systems really were pretty similar to those aboard the *Widowmaker.* He activated a lockdown of the adjacent corridors and the sound of gunfire died off. "That should do it."

"Roger, sir," Staff Sergeant Witzke replied. "That won't hold them for long, but I'm going to move Corporal Wandry to the midpoint to cover our retreat. How much longer, sir?"

Elvis looked over at where Rory and Feliks worked. "Not much, I hope."

* * *

"Captain, the Tanis Defense Force shuttles have opened fire on the base," Kaptain zur Weltraum Langdorff's sensor officer reported.

The Tau Ceti officer looked up in surprise. He knew that as the peacekeepers for this summit, the Tanis vessels and shuttles had been allowed to remain armed. Intellectually, he knew that the Tanis Defense Force had been selected for the task of enforcing the peace at this meeting. But he had expected them to withdraw at the first sign of hostilities. However sharp a blow to their image the outbreak of violence might be, they were a single-system star nation and Langsdorff had not expected them to become involved in the fight.

Unless they were bought off, he thought to himself.

"Who are they attacking?" Kaptain zur Weltraum Langsdorff demanded.

"The surviving base weapons as well as any defenders still firing on shuttles," the sensor officer reported. "It looks as if they're suppressing the base and preparing to land troops."

Langsdorff looked at his displays. His own shuttles and personnel were nearly armed and ready to go back down to Mars. He could call that strike off and let Tanis's people do it... but only if he trusted them to do so impartially. If they'd been bought off...

He winced as he considered the consequences if the Centauri had purchased Tanis's loyalty. The single-system nation lay behind Tau Ceti, astride the main trade routes out to the Colonial Republic. If Tanis had abandoned their neutrality, then they could create a stranglehold on Tau Ceti, which would devastate the economy and Tau Ceti's ability to resist Centauri influence.

He pursed his lips, "Open a channel to their flagship."

A moment later, Chairman-Admiral Ortega appeared on his screen. The coldly beautiful woman met his gaze with her exotic lavender-colored eyes. "Kapitan zur Weltraum Langsdorff," she said, "I take it you have questions about our intentions?"

He favored her rather straightforward attitude. "I do. We still have a large number of dignitaries and personnel on the planet." He didn't mention that the Chancellor had made it aboard one of the Tau Ceti shuttles, thanks in large part to whoever had initially opened fire on the base.

"Our intention is to seize the base and to return captive personnel to their appropriate vessels," Chairman-Admiral Ortega replied. "The personnel of Hugo Base have violated the terms of the peace summit and therefore they will be detained and questioned. I ask that your people stay out of the area until my people can resolve the situation." She gave a humorless smile, "My second-in-command is now informing the Centauri contingent the same thing."

Kapitan zur Weltraum Langsdorff stared at the woman for a long moment. If she were telling the truth, she would be doing much to defuse the situation... but only if she were telling the truth. And if her personnel were going down to take hostages, then with her ships in position and her people in charge of the base, Langsdorff would be unable to counter her.

Yet if he launched his combat shuttles, he would be violating the peace. Not only would the Centauri have grounds to open fire, but so would the Chairman-Admiral. "Very well," Kapitan zur Weltraum Langsdorff said with a matching humorless smile, "I will await the results of your efforts, Chairman Admiral."

***

Ricky One-Eye ducked down as an explosion went off nearby and dust settled down from the ceiling. He gasped, his lungs fighting for air in the thin atmosphere. Ricky looked down the corridor at where the others had gone. The lights flickered under another explosion and then went out.

The navy lieutenant had threatened him, but Ricky wasn't scared of him, not really. He was already a dead man if any of his enemies got hold of him. Ricky had vented enough people to know that it was painful... but Ricky was a survivor.

There's plenty *of shuttles out there,* he thought to himself. He glanced out the door just as another shuttle came in to land, this one only a hundred meters or less from the hatch.

I can do it, he thought to himself. A hundred meters of open ground. If he stayed low, he could make it to the pad. There were enough scrambling soldiers and civilians that he could blend in, maybe even get the clothes off a dead civilian, pretend to be wounded...

Without another thought, Ricky slipped away from the door and scrambled across the broken ground. In the light gravity he had to fight to keep from bounding into the air. Combined with the thin air, he felt lightheaded and he had to stop as his stomach protested. Ricky threw up, feeling the sharp, acid burn of vomit in his nostrils, even as bullets snapped overhead and the sound of gunfire picked up nearby.

He tried to get himself under control, but his stomach continued to heave as he vomited his last meal across the red Martian soil and his own clothing.

At last, after what seemed like an eternity, he managed to crawl, wiping vomit off his face and his vision blurred by tears. He moved slower, careful not to over exert himself as he moved towards where he thought the shuttle had landed.

His hand found flesh and he rubbed at his eyes. The corpse lay splayed out next to several others, blood staining their clothing. Ricky didn't hesitate, pulling the stained jacket off the nearest of the dead men and then doing the same with the pants. They wouldn't have fit him a few months earlier, but he'd lost a lot of weight. He crawled away from the bodies and spied a shuttle, the hatch open and a pair of armed guards just coming out. He couldn't make out the flag on the shuttle's tail, but it didn't matter.

A dozen civilians rushed towards the shuttle and Ricky bounded over and joined the group. Most of the gunfire had ceased, but Ricky forced his way to the center of the group, careful to give himself both cover against any further weapons fire and concealment within the group.

As they came up to the shuttle ramp, he noticed the uniformed guards were pushing the milling group to the side. He worried that they were checking identities, but they only seemed to be checking for injuries or weapons.

He had to hide a smile, even as he panted for air. Once the shuttle took off, he could jump one of the guards, get his weapon, and then take over the shuttle. These civilians had to be worth something, and Ricky would bargain with their lives to get free of the system. If that didn't work, he could always head to Earth and at least sell the shuttle for something.

As one of the guards waved him towards the hatch, Ricky didn't bother to hide his feeling of relief. His hands shook a bit as he reached for the ladder railing.

I don't even need to tell anyone about Reese or Marius Giovanni, he thought to himself.

"Stop him," a woman's cold voice spoke.

Strong arms caught Ricky and lifted him up. He found himself face to face with a beautiful woman. Her expression was hard, though, and her green eyes flashed in rage. "Secure this man," she snapped. "Alive. Post two guards. He speaks to no one."

Ricky felt a spurt of terror as he stared at her, there was something inhuman about the way she stared at him. It was the same look he used when he appraised slaves, deciding whether they were worth the cost of transport or if he should space them.

A shuttle went overhead and fired off some kind of weapon. Nearby, something exploded. Ricky wet himself a bit.

"Get him aboard," the woman snapped, "don't let *anything* happen to him."

***

"And..." Rory looked up, "we're in."

"I thought you said this would be quick," Elvis snapped. He knew just how complicated the process was, but still, Rory and Feliks had spent as much time bickering as they had actually working.

"Now that we are connected, yes, it should all be over soon," Feliks spoke without looking up. "I will trigger the initial reset and..."

The lights on a box that Rory had hooked into the terminal began to flash. Elvis didn't like the looks of that. They were angry, orange and red strobes. "What is that?"

"Oh, that?" Rory looked over. "Oh, hmm, it shouldn't be doing that."

"I told you we should have looked at the possibility of a fail-safe," Feliks replied.

"It's not a problem, I'll just override... oh, that's not working," Rory pulled out his datapad. "Let me try something else..."

"What are you talking about?" Elvis demanded. He had to

remind himself that shooting either of the two scientists, no matter how much they annoyed him, would be counterproductive.

"Amalgamated Worlds sometimes installed fail-safes to protect their most important facilities from capture," Feliks said.

"What, like some kind of lock down?" Elvis asked. Lots of military facilities did things like that, as soon as they experienced a data breach, all doors and access routes went to security lock down. That would be bad, but he figured that worse came to worse, he could transmit the data to the *Widowmaker* somehow.

"In this case," Feliks didn't look up from where he worked, "it is fifty megaton antimatter bomb." His harsh Centauri accent had become distinctly more pronounced.

"Wait... *what*?" Elvis demanded.

"It's fine, I can handle it," Rory said.

Elvis's head snapped around at the sound of distant explosions and dust began to slowly fall from the ceiling. "Petty Officer Cartwright?"

"Inbound shuttles, sir," the pilot reported. "I'm seeing weapons fire at defensive emplacements. It looks like someone is blowing the *hell* out of this base."

"Tell me about it," Elvis muttered, looking at the angry, flashing lights on the box.

All of the displays in the control room went blank, and then angry letters flashed across the screens: *Code Noah Ward*

"What is that?" Elvis demanded as alarms began to wail.

"It is final warning to base staff, a scorched earth trigger that will destroy this entire facility," Feliks said, his voice still calm. He looked over at Rory, "The download is nearly complete."

"Oh, this is really, really, bad," Rory said. "We tanked the entire system, we have all the data... but the self-destruct is an entirely *separate* system. It could take *hours* just to establish protocols to communicate with it, and this whole thing is going to go up in minutes!"

"There's over ten thousand people in this base!" Elvis snapped. It would be one thing if they were all security personnel, but they weren't. There were civilians, and military families, this was a small city... and Elvis might well have just sentenced all of them to death. Them and whoever was here from the peace summit who hadn't managed to evacuate.

Rory ran a hand through his thinning hair, "Look... I can stop it, but the rest of you need to get out of here."

Elvis pursed his lips, "No, you're essential to the war effort. I'm expendable... and I'm the one in charge of this mission. Tell me what I need to do."

"Rory," Feliks shook his head, "you are the one who wrote the encryption code..."

"Just go!" Rory snapped. "I don't have time to explain all this and--"

Elvis swung his arm and struck Rory across the temple with the butt of his pistol. As the scientist collapsed, he turned his attention to Feliks. "Get him and the data out of here. I'll take care of this." He felt a heavy weight settle on his shoulders as he picked up Rory's datapad. The tall, stork-like Feliks dragged his companion out of the room and Elvis looked around to see the technicians in the room staring at him with wide eyes. "I would suggest," Elvis said in a cold voice, "that all of you get out of here."

***

At this point, Kapitan zur Weltraum Langsdorff expected nothing but further bad news. Reality met his expectations soon enough.

"Kapitan zur Weltraum Langsdorff!" his sensor officer reported. "We have detected a power spike from the base's antimatter reactors. They will overload in minutes!"

Langsdorff sighed. "Of course. Do we know if they were damaged or deliberately sabotaged?"

"Indications are that this is a controlled detonation," the sensors officer reported, licking his lips. "Kapitan zur Weltraum Langsdorff, if they detonate at full yield, the resulting explosion will devastate the planet."

Langsdorff brought up the estimates on his personal display. He blanched a bit at the projected yield. "Is there anything we can do?"

His tactical officer shook her head, "Sir, any kind of weapons fire from orbit will only damage the control system, which might trigger a detonation early. All of these structures are too deeply buried to guarantee hits that would put the reactor in shutdown versus overload status."

"Message Chairman-Admiral Ortega," Kapitan zur Weltraum Langsdorff said in a dead voice. "Tell her what we have observed."

His communication officer reported a moment later, "Apparently the Chairman-Admiral returned to the surface with her shuttle. Her second-in-command has informed me that they do not have time to reach a safe distance, but that they are moving on the control room section now to secure it."

That *might* work, he supposed. But if the base staff were determined to take themselves out, then he didn't see how it could help. A reactor overload was hard to achieve, but if someone had the dedication to kill themselves and the time to set it up, then it was extremely hard to stop.

He didn't see *why* anyone at the base would resort to something so destructive. They would kill not only themselves, but their families and the high yield detonation would spread radioactive debris across the planet. Four hundred years of terraforming work would be undone and Mars's surface would be unlivable for centuries.

God in heaven, he thought to himself, *please prevent this from coming to pass.*

***

Staff Sergeant Witzke grabbed a scientist with each arm and ran down the corridor, covering three hundred meters in less than a minute. The light gravity aided her movement, but stopping was going to be a bitch.

These two probably won't know how to properly land, so I'll have to take the brunt of it, she thought, even as she bounded out the hatch and into the Martian atmosphere. Ahead, she saw the shuttle, but dozens of troops were swarming the area. Instinctively, she shouted, "Primary wounded, make a hole!"

Since her weapon was slung, these people either didn't see her as a threat or they just didn't care about her. They moved out of her way and continued to rush towards the hatch from which she'd come. Ahead of her, Corporal Wandry had already reached their shuttle and he and Corporal Wicklund clearly understood her plan as she took progressively larger and larger bounds, going a dozen meters or more into the air with each bound.

She had to do this just right...

"Petty Officer Cartwright," Staff Sergeant Witzke snapped as she started his final descent, "Prep for takeoff!"

She spun around in the thin air, the two scientists thrashing and fighting with her. "Hold still!" she barked, even as she held both of them up against her chest and tucked her chin. This was really going to hurt...

She blacked out as she struck the two other Marines braced to catch them as they hurtled through the shuttle's open hatch and into the drop bay.

***

Elvis saw sweat run down his nose and dribble onto the faceplate of his helmet, but he was too focused on the task at hand. He'd seen right away what Rory had tried: a complicated set of programs designed to override the base's self-destruct protocols-- this *Code Noah Ward.* Just why the designers of Hugo Base thought destroying everything was a viable solution to losing control was something that Elvis didn't want to think about.

Elvis had thrown all of Rory's work out. He approached the entire thing from the perspective of an engineer. The reactor couldn't overload if he put it into shutdown status first.

He worked frantically. First he cut all of the physical connections under the terminal, then he pulled out Rory's datapad and went to work, isolating as much of the software as he could. There were hardware links that he couldn't sever. The reactor was buried a half-mile below the control room. But he *could* convince the reactor software not to receive signals from those connections.

Once he did that, he could put the reactor into shutdown mode and then the entire base would shut down. It would kill life-support and all other systems. There'd be ten thousand people trapped in the dark until someone could bring power safely back online, but it wouldn't blow up the planet, so there was that at least.

He looked up at a shout as a team of armed men swarmed the room. Only one of them kept a weapon on him as the others fanned out. As that one centered his sights on Elvis's face, Elvis spoke in a calm, smooth tone, "Look, you're probably here for the same reason I am. I've got to shut everything down or we're all dead."

"Don't move!" one of the armed men snapped.

Elvis glanced down at his datapad. They were almost out of

time.

"I've got to put the reactor into shutdown mode. If I don't do that in the next thirty seconds, this whole place is going to go up."

A tall, black-haired, woman in a suit, of all things, with a face mask for the thin atmosphere came into the room, followed by still more armed men. Elvis now had over a dozen weapons aimed at his head. He met the woman's lavender eyes and he hoped she would see his sincerity

His datapad pinged at him and speakers in the room started to blare, "Code Noah Ward, Code Noah Ward."

"I've got to stop this, *now!*" Elvis said. The face of the woman looked conflicted, but the armed men all went tense.

There were fourteen thousand lives on the line. Elvis didn't hesitate. He activated the datapad. He heard a gunshot and then the world went black.

***

"Shuttle is aboard, Skipper," Petty Officer Godbey reported.

Lieutenant Forrest Perkins nodded, though the motion came slowly, as if from an old man. He tried not to think of how many lives he'd endangered. He tried not to think of how Staff Sergeant Witzke was unconscious and severely injured and how Corporal Wandry and Wicklund both had bruised, possibly cracked ribs. He tried not to think of Lieutenant Elvis Medica, left behind at Hugo Base. The engineering officer might well have given his life to fix the mistake that Forrest had caused. Elvis must have stopped the self destruct, but there'd been no messages from him and Forrest worried that in the chaotic situation on the ground, the engineer might not have survived the effort.

"Take us out of here," Forrest said, "withdrawal course delta bravo."

The *Widowmaker* drew away from the planet. As the red planet withdrew, Forrest tried not to think. He told himself that if there was even a chance that Alannis was still alive, that this sacrifice was worth it. Yet his earlier confidence and assurance were bitter. His hope that this would be easy had died with Elvis Medica in the red sands of Mars.

***

Chapter IV

Minder made certain that he was alone and that his mind was totally focused before he decided to answer his daughter's message.

Please tell me that this is some kind of bad joke, he sent after a moment. Humor wasn't something that his species really understood, but his kind, those who had infiltrated humanity in particular, sometimes developed peculiarities.

No, father, her response was cold and heavy with bitterness, *I wish it was. The prisoner I obtained at Hugo Base seems entirely certain that Reese Leone was at Formosa Station and that his destination was Golgotha.*

This was impossible. It was *worse* than impossible... it was a disaster.

If Minder's superiors learned of this... Minder could not help but shudder as he considered his fate. All his power, all his influence, and though he hated to admit it, the very many human luxuries that he had come to enjoy... all that would be taken away.

His species would destroy him. Not as punishment; they didn't think in those terms. No, they would consider it a precaution. He had proven unfit for the task so he would be removed. The decades of hard work on his part would have little meaning to them. They didn't think as individuals, just as parts of a greater whole... and when one part failed to function, it would be removed and replaced.

Father, she sent to him, *what do we do?*

He couldn't report this, not until he confirmed it. *The prisoner could be mistaken, the information could be inaccurate,* he sent back. All the same, he knew that this wasn't a mistake. Marius Givoanni and Reese Leone somehow knew the truth. There could be no other purpose for the humans to be at Golgotha.

It should be impossible, he told himself. He had spent eighty years steering the human race away from that knowledge. He had killed tens of millions of humans to prevent the rise of powerful psychics with political power. He had encouraged the paranoia and isolation of the human Shadow Lords. Minder had destroyed or hidden every bit of information on Golgotha that he could get his hands on. *Somehow,* he thought, *somehow I have failed... and somehow Marius Giovanni knows the truth of what I've tried to hide.*

They needed to know more. The humans hunting Marius Giovanni, they would be a good place to start. *What did you learn of their ship, the* Widowmaker*?*

Not as much as I would like, his daughter replied. Fixer's voice held much frustration, not that he could blame her. *It is the same vessel stolen by Reese, the vessel that apparently the prisoners used to escape from Marius Giovanni's base. The ship's stealth systems have been modified. I could not sense it, not with my mind at all and reviewing our ship's sensors has not yet located it's course or destination.*

The ship's capabilities terrified him almost as much as the news of Reese's survival. Technology that could hide vessels from psychic senses would be devastating against his species. *It may be the same vessel that Sidewinder reported at Kapteyn's Star,* he sent. *You said that the ship is renegade, that they have no support network?*

Yes, she sent back.

Minder contemplated things for a moment. There were few ports near the Sol system where such a ship might find refuge and resupply. In all likelihood, with the chaos at Hugo Base, they'd want to regroup and resupply, before they went after Marius Giovanni.

Idarian Station, he sent back, *they probably won't stay there long...* Minder knew that if his daughter did the jump calculations, that she could get her forces there in time to catch the vessel... but she'd give away too much of her nature to those ship's officers and crews in the process. *Send their commander, this Perkins, a message,* he sent, *convince him to come to us, offer him weapons, support, anything he wants... make him believe us.*

When he arrives? Fixer asked.

Take the ship, kill their junior personnel and rip every scrap of information from their commander's mind. I need to know everything that he knows, Minder sent. He couldn't risk a chance that any of this information would get out. Golgotha had become a place of legend to the rest of humanity. It needed to be forgotten... and Minder couldn't risk anyone venturing there. *Then kill him.*

***

August 11, 2410
Idarian Station, 804E81 System
Unclaimed Space

"We have good seal at the airlock, Skipper," Petty Officer Godbey reported.

"Right," Forrest said. "Wandry, open up the airlock, bring their doctor to see our wounded." They'd already coordinated with the station, telling them they had injured men aboard. The jump from the Sol System to the edges of the Centauri System, and then the short jump to the 804E81 system had taken twenty-seven days. Wandry and Wicklund were at least mobile, with cracked ribs, but Forrest still wanted them checked out.

"Skipper, we have two messages waiting for us in the station's ansible logs."

Forrest's eyes went wide, "What?" He pulled up the two messages, both listed contact numbers with no other information and he swallowed nervously as he contemplated that. His first hope had been that somehow, Elvis Medica had survived and escaped, that he had guessed where Forrest was headed and got a message to him.

Yet if that were the case, he would have left an actual message.

These two messages were the type that someone would send as a blind. If he called either number, he risked whoever he contacted having confirmation of his location. From there, they could contact the station's managers and seize the ship. Idarian Station was a neutral port of call, but that didn't mean the authorities couldn't be convinced to hold a ship.

No one *should* know that he'd be coming here, yet they could have sent messages to likely ports throughout the region.

Still, if they knew his ship, then they *might* have captured Lieutenant Medica alive. Forrest owed it to the man to at least find out if he was still alive.

He looked up the ansible rates for both numbers. Whoever had left each of the messages had also apparently covered his ship for a return call. *Nice of them,* he thought absently, *though that's a bit more evidence for a trap.*

He looked up from his display. "Petty Officer Godbey,

monitor the station. If there's any sign that they're locking our ship or that any personnel are moving to our airlock, pull us away. If neccesary, utilize emergency protocols for detachment." The emergency protocols that warships mounted would use compressed gasses to blast free of the station.

"Yes, sir," the noncommissioned officer nodded. If the prospect of potentially damaging, possibly severely, a neutral station with an emergency detachment bothered him, he didn't show it.

Forrest wasn't certain which number to dial first. He chose one at random, queued up a neutral background for himself, and dialed the number.

His display went to a holding screen. He counted off the seconds, wondering if he were dooming his ship and crew. Finally, however, the screen transitioned. A strawberry-blonde-haired woman stared at him, her green eyes cheerful and friendly. She wore smart, professional civilian clothing that looked like something from the core colonies, utilitarian and streamlined. "Lieutenant Commander Perkins, I'm glad you chose to communicate with me."

"You have the advantage of me," Forrest said. "Who are you?"

"I'm sorry, I realize you may not be entirely up on Centauri Confederation VIP's," she managed to refer to herself as a VIP with a tone of slight sarcasm, as if it embarrassed her a bit. "I'm Annabelle Spiridon, daughter to President Spiridon of the Confederation."

Forrest choked a bit, "I see."

"You probably don't," she said and her face and voice went solemn, "you see, I was at Hugo Base, I barely survived an assassination attempt, and if your shuttle *hadn't* intervened, then I'd be dead. And while you violated a number of diplomatic protocols by firing on Hugo Base, if you hadn't done that, then thousands of innocent lives might have been lost."

"We were there on our own business," Forrest flushed.

"Yes, so I've learned," her expression went hard, "my people captured one of your crew. We didn't know who he was and he was badly injured, so they ran him through a rapid field interrogation while they attempted to save his life." She gave a slight frown, "I'm afraid he didn't survive the process."

Shit, Forrest thought. She could only mean Elvis Medica.

"I understand that you are in pursuit of Reese Leone and Marius Giovanni. These men are both criminals. We had assumed Mister Leone, at least, was dead. Your United Colonies claimed they had accomplished his death, so we assumed that they knew what they were talking about... mistakenly, it would seem.

"They have every reason to believe so," Forrest said, his voice defensive. The casual disregard for the United Colonies Fleet and Baron Giovanni rubbed him the wrong way.

"Of course, I'm sorry," Annabelle Spiridon gave him an apologetic smile. "I meant no offense. In fact, knowing your mission, I actually want to help you."

"Help?" Forrest asked, his eyebrows going up in surprise.

"You, no doubt, are low on supplies, you can't have many crew aboard, all volunteers. Your destination, as I understand it, is Golgotha." She said that off-handedly, yet Forrest realized that she was fishing for information. *She doesn't know for certain.* He didn't miss how she paused, as if waiting for confirmation. When he didn't respond, she went on, "The Centauri Confederation has a vested interest in stopping Marius Giovanni. We believe it was his agents who disrupted our peace summit, that they suborned the officers of Hugo Base and that they bought off Chairman-Admiral Ortega of the Tanis Defense Forces. Reese Leone is responsible for the loss of our entire garrison force at Kapteyn's Star. We have every reason to want to stop them, and as you already intend to venture to Golgotha and confirm his location..."

She raised her hands as she trailed off, as if to suggest that this deal offered them both an ideal solution.

The thought of supplies, weapons, even manpower tempted Forrest more than he would like to admit. He needed replacement munitions for the shuttle, he'd need a team for the rescue, and his personal funds were basically gone. *I'll need to buy foodstuffs, equipment, ship parts...*

"What do you plan to do about Reese and Marius?" Forrest asked.

Her friendly expression went hard, "Both of them are responsible for the deaths of thousands of Confederation personnel. They might well be responsible for the deaths of *millions* with how they have sabotaged the peace summit. Honestly, if not for that, we would have ships and troops to spare to send to Golgotha. As it is, providing you with supplies will be all we can manage without confirmation of some kind."

"I see," Forrest said after he considered it. On face value, it made sense. Still, with how precarious his situation was, he hesitated to trust her. "Where would I meet your people?"

"I'm headed for the Delta Pavonis system, where our military forces will regroup. We're waiting to see what the response from the Tau Ceti will be, but they've already put their forces to full military alert." She gave a grim smile, "Despite all protests on our part, they seem to think *we* are behind all this."

Forrest gave a noncommittal grunt. While he would imagine that President Spiridon *did* want peace, he figured the kind of peace that he wanted was one that he ruled over. In fact, if his daughter had been a bit less friendly and more pragmatic from the beginning, he might have trusted her more.

"In any case," she went on, "if you meet me at Delta Pavonis, I can provide you with a group of volunteers as well as munitions and other supplies. I have no doubt that your ship is in need of resupply."

"I'll have to think about it," Forrest said.

"Lieutenant Commander," Annabelle Spiridon replied, "this is a rare opportunity. You are without allies, with limited resources, and you're going against a very dangerous man. I'm asking you, please, accept my help. If you go in there by yourself and *fail*, then you'll give away the fact that we know Marius Giovanni's base of operations. As we learned from the Kapteyn's Star debacle, he will have a backup base and escape plan."

Forrest met her green eyes. "I said I would think about it, Miss Spiridon. Now, if you'll excuse me, I have to see to my ship."

He cut the call and looked over at Petty Officer Godbey. "Any sign of hostile intent from the station?"

"Negative, sir," he said after a moment, "all quiet."

"Right, let's see who this other contact is..."

This time he waited quite a bit longer on a holding screen. It was more than enough time for someone to reach their terminal and ready themselves. Forrest glanced over at Petty Officer Godbey, but the noncommisioned officer just shook his head. No sign of any kind of trap... yet.

The screen finally went live and Forrest found himself face to face with a woman in military dress. "Lieutenant Commander Perkins," she spoke in a cold, level voice. "I am Chairman-Admiral Ortega of the Tanis Defense Force." Her raven-black hair was drawn back in a severe style and her harsh-planed face wore a disapproving expression.

"Ma'am," Forrest said, "to what do I owe the pleasure?"

"To the fact that your vessel infiltrated a secure peace summit and violated the terms of that summit, which I was charged to enforce," she snapped. "Furthermore, your shuttle fired upon Hugo Base, which potentially endangered hundreds of innocent bystanders... which was just the prelude to several of your personnel triggering the facility's self-destruct protocols."

"Ah," Forrest said nervously, "those are some pretty big accusations to level."

"I wouldn't bother to deny it," she snapped. "I have both physical and material evidence of the presence of your people. I also have a prisoner. He hasn't given me much information, as yet, but his very presence at the base is enough to put you and your vessel here, despite sensor logs to the contrary."

Prisoner... he thought. His shuttle had returned with all his personnel except for Lieutenant Medica. For a minute, his mind went blank. Then he remembered Ricky One-Eye. The pirate would probably hold out, trying to make some kind of deal, but he'd give information about Forrest far more readily than the information about Reese's survival.

"Okay," Forrest said, trying to buy some time, "assuming that my ship was there... then what? Whoever fired those missiles at the base prevented dozens of shuttles from being shot down. Hugo Base opened fire first."

"You attacked the base in the middle of a criminal enterprise to steal their data!" Chairman-Admiral Ortega snapped. "It doesn't matter if your shuttle improved the situation, I'm not inclined to believe that your shuttle didn't open fire to protect themselves or out of some panic that they'd been detected." Her lavender eyes were clouded and angry. "I already have read the report of your theft of the *Widowmaker*, which was originally stolen from the Brockman Shipyards at Tanis. That vessel was allowed to be retained by the United Colonies as salvage, since they captured it from Marius Giovanni's forces. However, you, as a private citizen do not qualify under that exemption. I could have you arrested for piracy, you and your crew could face lengthy, possibly life-time, prison sentences."

Now she's going to appeal to my better nature, Forrest thought to himself.

"Do yourself a favor, turn yourself in. I understand that some of the data you acquired is some kind of continued personal investigation of Marius Giovanni," the Chairman-Admiral adopted a more moderate tone. "If you turn that information over to me, along with your ship and crew, I will see to it that your crew faces minimal charges, possibly even asylum at Tanis. You might face a token sentence, five years at the most, for cooperation."

Forrest's face went hard. "Chairman-Admiral, assuming I was dedicated enough to hijack a ship from my nation, to throw away my military career, and to open fire on a peace summit... what makes you think I'd be willing to surrender?"

"You can't do this on your own," she replied. Her cold expression cracked just a bit and Forrest saw actual concern. "If you're really after Marius Giovanni, you have to know that he has an entire fleet. Your Emperor's forces are spread thin and even if they weren't, you've stolen a ship from them so they won't exactly be inclined to trust you. The Centauri and Tau Ceti don't even know of your presence or mission and even if they did, you can't trust either of them. The Centauri would betray you and take your ship and your secrets, while the Tau Ceti would spend weeks or months bickering about what to do on a committee."

Her voice had gone low and intense, "Your nation's allies, the Shogunate, are in an ongoing war with the Colonial Republic and wouldn't risk irritating the United Colonies, so they'd imprison you and your crew. It would take them months to ship you back to your home system, months that Marius Giovanni would be allowed to do his work."

"In the meantime," she said, "I have a task force that could strike within days, my ships are at the Alpha Canis Majoris system. All I need, Lieutenant Commander, is a destination. Meet me here, and I promise you that my entire force will go after him."

"Why would you go after him?" Forrest asked.

"Reese Leone stole a vessel from Tanis, he violated our neutrality and that has gone unpunished for too long," her response came quickly, too quickly. "Marius Giovanni is a criminal who needs to face justice."

Forrest's eyes narrowed. "I thought justice was something for sale in Tanis, just like everything else."

Chairman-Admiral Ortega's lavender eyes flashed with anger. "Do not mistake my generosity for weakness, Lieutenant Commander." Her lips drew back in a sneer, "You may hide behind your affected New Texas accent, but I've done my homework on you. You were Alannis Giovanni's lover, possibly her suitor. You were born into the lowest classes of Saragossa, where you managed to claw your way into their Academy and commissioned as a merchant officer." She cocked her head, her voice becoming analytical. "You graduated at the middle of your class, the school records pegged you as ambitious but hard-working. After the fall of Saragossa, you were interned by the Chxor. You spent fifteen years surviving in their penal system. Fifteen years in a prison labor system where most people's lives are measured in hours."

She leaned forward, her face intent, "A man like you, Forrest Perkins, is a survivor. Driven. You don't go through something like that, you don't survive something like that, without being some kind of monster, do you?"

Forrest met her gaze without flinching. "I'm not a monster. I'm just too stupid to give up."

"Interesting," she sat back, "and then when you encountered Princess Giovanni, you courted her... completely irrespective of her political connections? You served as her brother's flag lieutenant as a bare ensign. Tell me, did you stumble into such an arrangement on accident? You received a citation for your efforts during the Dreyfus Mutiny. Tell me, were you Emperor Giovanni's assassin, or did you just arrange for executions to be carried out?"

Forrest's lips went into a flat line. "I'm no murderer. I did my duty, nothing less. I'm no ass-kisser, either. And my interest in Alannis has nothing to do with who she's related to." He realized that he'd slipped up by referring to her in the present tense, but the Tanis officer didn't seem to have noticed.

She gave a humorless smile, "I'm sure. Well, in a completely altruistic appeal, think of this: if you and your crew provide us with the information that leads to the capture of Marius Giovanni, I will wave all charges, grant your crew asylum on Tanis. You can live out the rest of your lives in relative luxury, paid for by Tanis System

Control. You will have stopped a criminal and in the process, gain access to luxuries and comfortable lives."

Had Forrest only cared about bringing Marius, or even Reese, to justice, then he would have found her offer very tempting indeed. Not for himself, but for his crew. He'd already gotten Elvis killed. Staff Sergeant Witzke's wounds were serious. Worse, he and the rest of his crew could still face charges of mutiny and piracy.

But if Alannis was alive, then Forrest was still her best chance at survival. Forrest wasn't doing this for himself or for revenge, he was doing it for Alannis. She deserved better than to be abandoned... and Forrest had let her down when he'd bought Reese's faking of her death. He wasn't going to let her down again.

"No," Forrest said, "I don't think I'll take you up on that offer."

"Lieutenant Commander," Chairman-Admiral Ortega's lavender eyes went narrow, "I suggest you rethink your decision. You have no resources, no allies--"

Forrest cut the call off. "Well, that wasn't going anywhere, anyway." He looked at Petty Officer Godbey, "Any word on the doc?"

"He just finished looking at Staff Sergeant Witzke," he replied. "Says that she needs about a month of bed-rest, but after that she should be good to go. Head trauma wasn't as bad as we thought and the meds we were giving her was what kept her unconscious. He gave us some different stuff."

Forrest let out a tense breath, that was good news, anyway.

He considered the risk of staying at Idarian Station against the chance that the Chairman-Admiral would either buy off the station manager and security or try to get someone here in time to capture the *Widowmaker*.

"Thank the doctor for his time," Forrest said. "Do we have some supplies onboard?"

"Initial supplies, yes," Petty Officer Godbey nodded. "Just foodstuffs and water. Rory hasn't had a chance to order any parts or anything like that, sir."

We don't have the money for that anyway, Forrest reminded himself. "Signal station control that we intend to undock. We're headed out."

"You can't be serious," Rory's high pitched voice came on the intercom a moment later, "we've got a dozen systems that need some kind of maintenance. We're dangerously low on parts, I don't know if we can make it another week without some of these repairs!"

"And we're down our engineering officer, I know," Forrest replied. "I'll deal with it." This mission was his and he would finish it. He didn't need anyone's help and he didn't want anyone to know where they were headed... just in case.

Yet as they undocked, he reconsidered his decision. Did he *really* want to do this all on his own? It would be one thing if he had nothing to go on... but he had a location. Rory and Feliks had managed to extract the projected coordinates for the Golgotha system in the data they'd stolen.

With the recorded interrogation from Ricky One-eye, that might be enough.

Annabelle Spiridon seemed inclined to believe him already. She knew where to go... she was willing to resupply Forrest's ship, to give him a crew. He could leverage that, mount a rescue...

Or he could send a whole fleet to Alpha Canis Majoris. Chairman-Admiral Ortega seemed willing to take *all* of her ships in pursuit of Marius Giovanni.

Forrest gnawed at his lip. He didn't want to rely on either of them. He'd taken *some* precautions before all this, but that didn't meant that those would work out. Was it just his own hubris? Worse, was he doing just what Reese had? Alannis had told him about her ex-husband, how he'd refused help, refused to trust anyone... and how that had led to his own break with reality.

Was this a mistake? He didn't know if he could trust either of the two women who'd offered help... but he did know that he needed supplies and resources to stand a chance. Their initial scan of the data indicated that Golgotha was twenty days travel from the 804E81 system. If he went to Delta Pavonis, it would add fifteen days to that travel time, while Alpha Canis Majoris would add another twenty-one days to that.

Alannis needed his help. And even if she *was* dead, Marius Giovanni needed to be stopped. Haring off without any kind of help wouldn't accomplish either of those results.

Forrest let out a harsh sigh. He coded up a message to send by ansible. It took every bit of his resolve to type three words, to enter in the ansible code, and to send the simple text message.

See you soon.

Forrest brought up the navigational computer and started plotting the course. He just hoped he had made the right decision.

***

Fixer rejoiced as she read the message. She'd worried that she had overplayed her hand, yet it seemed the human officer had fallen for her ploy. Yet the human officer's message had followed shortly after. *See you soon.* She had listened to her rival's attempt to get the *Widowmaker* to come to her. It had made her nervous, first to realize that the woman had survived her assassination attempt and then that she might be able to convince Lieutenant Commander Perkins to accept her offer. Still, Fixer could barely repress a snort of amusement at how the woman had unwittingly driven Lieutenant Forrest Perkins towards Fixer's trap.

And trap it would be. She had boarding teams preparing, made up of trusted subordinates who would keep their mouths shut. They were the product of intensive training and though they were human, they served her interests far more than they did humanity's... or even her father's.

She didn't bother to suppress her pleasure at that thought. The *Widowmaker* possessed unique technology, with the ability to infiltrate even a heavily scanned system and to elude her own kind's ability to sense it's presence. With the right crew aboard, the ship would be perfect for removing the one obstacle to her ambitions.

Face it, she thought, *father has become to enamored of his plots, this is a game to him and he's lost focus. Clearly he's been too gentle on humanity.* Her father's plans to fracture humanity and play them off against each other hadn't worked. No, the time had come to seize power, to rule humanity and to prevent them from ever becoming a threat.

She would be far better suited to that task.

But first, she needed to set things into motion. *Father,* she sent, *the human ship will meet my forces soon. I will have them in my control in a matter of days.*

His response came back quickly, a sure sign that he anticipated such a communication... which suggested that he had her under observation. *Excellent,* he sent, *have you prepared a team to secure the ship and crew?*

I have, she replied, aware that he probably knew that much. *But I'd like your permission to embark a crew to scout Golgotha.*

He didn't respond for a long moment and she had to focus on keeping her emotions separate from her mental link with him. *Sidewinder's forces can attack Golgotha, but the human's modifications to the* Widowmaker *will make it possible to scout the system and determine the disposition of Giovanni's forces. That way we can prevent his escape.*

That much was true. The last thing they wanted was for Marius Giovanni or Reese Leone to escape, especially if they knew even a fraction of the full significance of Golgotha.

Of course, the destroyer would allow her to strike her father, too, as soon as Sidewinder completed his attack. With how well protected he was, it wouldn't be a surgical attack. She'd order the crew to utilize antimatter warheads. Civilian casualties would be catastrophic, but much of their planet's colonies were underground. It would only make the strike all the more emotional for the rest of humanity, without destroying the industry and labor of the planet.

It would be easy to then dispose of the crew and plant evidence to implicate political and military enemies as the source of the attack. She could then ride popular support as the survivor of such a tragedy. Combined with her father's remaining network, she would be able to conquer most of human space.

Very well, his response dragged her back to the present. *Prepare a crew. But I'll want you to personally oversee the scouting operation.*

Fixer couldn't help a spurt of pleasure. That would work out even better than she could have planned. *Of course, father, thank you for this opportunity.*

Her father ended the mental link without response. She enjoyed the bit of triumph, even as she adjusted her clothing and went to the door of her suite. She opened it, then looked at her civilian and military aides. Most of them had been converted to her kind, but a handful were fully human, entirely unaware of her true nature.

It was a role she had played for four years. As a human, she had been a cheerful, friendly personality with an utterly ruthless core. Now that she'd been converted, she maintained that appearance, backed up with psionic abilities that made her far more dangerous than any human realized. Fixer was her inner persona, but in this forum, she adopted her outer nature.

"Prep our team for the arrival of the *Widowmaker*," Annabelle Spiridon said, her voice cheerful. "I want their crew taken down quickly and from there, I want a volunteer crew assembled. I will take overall command of the vessel."

***

August 13, 2410
Alpha Canis Majoris
Tau Ceti Seperatist Aligned, Centauri Confederation

Task Force Hunter arrived at the Alpha Canis Majoris system and Senior Captain Daniel Beeson listened with half an ear as Admiral Kaminsky communicated with the Tanis Defense Force fleet. Admiral Kaminsky had quietly given Daniel access to the communications, with a note to listen but not to speak up on the net.

"Thank you, again, Chairman-Admiral, for the information and invitation," Admiral Kaminsky said.

"Unfortunately," Chairman-Admiral Ortega replied after a slight delay, "I think your coming here will prove fruitless. Intelligence sources among the Centauri have informed me that they offered material support to the *Widowmaker* and that they expect the vessel to head to Delta Pavonis."

Daniel couldn't help but wince. To say that the United Colonies' relationship with the Centauri Confederation had deteriorated would be an understatement. President Spiridon had claimed the Volaterra and Lavinium star systems, which had once been part of the Nova Roma Empire. Centauri ships and troops had defended the systems against the Chxor... but they'd also seized all government and military installations.

Emissaries from both systems had called for help from Emperor Giovanni. As yet, the United Colonies wasn't prepared to go to war over it, but Daniel knew that it was only a matter of time. People were dying. Worse, citizens were being dragged off into the night, taken away by Spiridon's Centauri Security Bureau and other paramilitary organizations. *And the CSB has gained a level of infamy throughout human space for their utter ruthlessness.* He really didn't want to think about what the organization was reputed to do to the people they made disappear.

"I see, Chairman Admiral," Admiral Kaminsky replied. "That is unfortunate. Thank you, at least, for notifying me of your intention to have him come here." Daniel could hear an edge of irritation in the Admiral's voice, one that the man didn't bother to hide very well.

Not that I can blame him, Daniel thought. The Chairman-Admiral could have notified them on their way, saving them the time and expense of moving their task force out here. They'd been gathering information from the Cumae system. There *was* a direct route from there to Alpha Canis Majoris, but it had been a long trip.

Besides, Daniel thought, *we're technically violating Centauri Confederation space, even meeting here at the edge of the system.* The Chairman-Admiral's message had suggested that she'd worked something out with the locals, but that didn't mean that such an arrangement couldn't be rescinded. Right now, the very last thing the United Colonies needed was for the Centauri to have a legitimate grievance about a territory violation.

"I'm sorry I didn't notify you earlier. We only received the news within the past few hours. Since you are here anyway, perhaps we could discuss future coordination? Possibly even aboard my flagship?" The Chairman-Admiral's words were innocuous enough, but there was no need to discuss coordination in person, not unless she wanted to completely avoid any possibility of someone learning what they discussed.

Such a proposal might be a simple security measure, or it could be a prelude to espionage or passing of critical information. For that matter, it could be a quiet offer of alliance against the Centauri Confederation, should war break out. Tanis had maintained their neutrality since before the fall of Amalgamated Worlds... but war was coming, whether they liked it or not.

"Since we are here anyway, Chairman-Admiral, it seems prudent to discuss future coordination in person," Admiral Kaminsky answered. "I'll bring Senior Captain Beeson along, as my second in command."

"That might be prudent," Chairman-Admiral Ortega replied. There was just a hair's-breadth of hesitation in her voice, as if she wanted to add something, but she didn't want to risk it. "I'll see you soon."

She cut the connection and Daniel straightened in his command chair. He nodded at his XO, "I'll be taking a shuttle to meet aboard the Tanis Defense Force's flagship. Have them prep the shuttle."

He just wondered what this was all about... and how dangerous it would prove to himself and his crew.

* * *

"Thanks for meeting me in person, we have come to suspect that all long range communications may be compromised," Chairman Admiral Ortega said, her expression hard. She gave Captain Beeson a slight nod, more of an acknowledgment than any real form of greeting, before moving back to her desk. "We have learned that your Lieutenant Commander Perkins may have evidence that Reese Leone still lives. We also believe that Marius Giovanni has set up base in an unknown system, however, we haven't been able to pin him down. I think that your Lieutenant Commander Perkins has acquired that location, though I'm not certain how."

Admiral Boris Kaminsky sighed, "We haven't yet ascertained his base of operations, either. I know it is a priority for the Emperor, but his focus has had to be the Centauri Confederation after some of their more recent provocations."

"Ma'am," Captain Beeson spoke up, "perhaps if you could let me communicate with Lieutenant Commander Perkins, I could get him to come here, instead?"

She gave him a calculating look, "Forgive me, Senior Captain, but wasn't he formerly under your command? I would think that you would have been one of the first ones he would have come to... if he trusted you." Her cold tone suggested that she was far more upset about the circumstances than she'd earlier suggested.

Daniel's face went hard. "Chairman-Admiral, I was under a great deal of attention during the formal inquires into the events at Kapteyn's Star. I think that Lieutenant Commander Perkins may have feared that he would have made my situation more precarious. If anyone might convince him to surrender, it would be me."

She nodded, "Fair enough. Unfortunately, he and his ship departed Idarian Station. The *Widowmaker* doesn't have an on-board ansible system, it's too small for the standard Centauri design... unless you've refitted it with the Nova Roma ansible system?"

"No," Admiral Kaminsky replied, "We have not."

"How did you manage to find out so much?" Daniel asked.

The Chairman-Admiral didn't reply for a long moment. When she did, her voice was leached of emotion. "During the peace summit, one of the Tau Ceti senior officers attacked me."

Daniel glanced at Admiral Kaminsky, who didn't show any change of expression.

"Flottilen-Admiral Krause fired three shots into my chest from close range, without any warning. If I hadn't been wearing my body armor, I'd be dead," the Chairman-Admiral continued. "This threw the entire peace conference into chaos. Most of the dignitaries fled, my personnel evacuated me to a shuttle, while my people tried to keep things calm both on the station and in orbit."

"It wasn't until we launched from the base that the second part of the attack took place. Someone, most probably the base command staff, set the automated defenses to open fire on all air traffic. Over two hundred personnel died, many of them senior officers or high-ranking political figures from the Centauri Confederation and Tau Ceti. Not long after that, Hugo Base personnel opened fire on my peacekeeping staff and neutral personnel at the base. Over five hundred men and women died."

Daniel blanched at that. This was the kind of violent event that triggered wars... and apparently Tanis had been in charge of security.

"I immediately ordered a launch of our ready shuttles, prepped to storm the base, to overwhelm the defenses and secure the entire facility. Our goal was to seize Hugo Base's network and examine their entire record system. Just before that, however, someone opened fire with a shuttle concealed by a stealth system."

Daniel glanced at Admiral Kaminsky, but the Admiral didn't change expression. *The Widowmaker shouldn't have had a shuttle aboard and Forrest shouldn't have been able to bring the destroyer into Martian atmosphere without someone noticing...*

"That shuttle destroyed multiple weapons emplacements and neutralized Hugo Base's targeting sensors. One of those missiles *also* blasted the base's command bunker, which was the central node for the automated defenses. The shuttle then landed at a maintenance pad and disembarked six personnel. Those six personnel targeted the base's computer network center where they hacked the system and downloaded the entire contents of the base's systems... and also triggered a self-destruct protocol, Code Noah Ward. It would have overloaded the base's antimatter reactors and killed everyone at the base. My engineers have estimated the yield at over three hundred megatons."

Daniel swallowed as he considered that. Three hundred megatons, detonated at or just below ground level, would probably have spread radioactive material for thousands of kilometers. Whoever had made such a fail-safe must have wanted to leave nothing but a radioactive crater of Hugo Base.

"To be fair to your Lieutenant Commander Perkins, I don't think he intended to do that, and one of his people remained behind to stop it... which is why I offered him the chance to come and surrender to me," Chairman-Admiral Ortega said. "In fact, all evidence points to General Johann Kalsi, the base's senior officer, as the origin of the attacks as well as the originator of the Noah Ward fail-safe protocol. Though we suspect that an inner cabal of at least five of the base's senior personnel were behind the overall violence at the conference. After my people seized the base, my investigators tied much of it back to Hugo Base personnel, following orders from their commanding officers, all the way to the top."

Her lips pressed in a firm line, "That doesn't change the fact that Lieutenant Commander Perkins entered restricted airspace and fired upon a peace conference or that personnel under his command triggered the Noah Ward protocol, which if they hadn't managed to bypass, it would have killed tens of thousands of men, women, and children."

Admiral Kaminsky nodded, "I do not present any excuse for their actions, Chairman Admiral. However, I might note that you said one of their personnel remained behind to bypass the self destruct?"

"Yes," she nodded, "you did. Which is how I know that it *was* Lieutenant Commander Perkins and the *Widowmaker*." She tapped a control on her desk and the display brought up an image and records. The image was of Lieutenant Elvis Medica, his military photo and records next to it. "Lieutenant Medica was the one to remain behind at the base, attempting to disarm the destruct protocol. He managed to accomplish it, too, though one of my over-zealous security personnel nearly shot him."

"Nearly?" Admiral Kaminsky asked.

She ignored his question. "I had him run through basic interrogation methods, but he has proven resistant beyond offering up that they were after Marius Giovanni... and that Reese Leone may be alive. We've pieced together that he was part of the crew of the *Widowmaker* and is one of the suspected hijackers. From their position at Mars and your own official notice about the vessel, we projected where Lieutenant Commander Perkins would head. Because he has been uncooperative, I'm tempted to offer him up to the Centauri as a scapegoat. As you might imagine, both they and the Tau Ceti want someone to pin all this upon. Since General Johann Kalsi and his staff all perished in the shuttle's attack when that missile took out the command node, I've got no one to give to them... no one but young Lieutenant Medica."

"But he had *nothing* to do with the attack!" Daniel protested.

Admiral Kaminsky gave him a hard look, but Chairman-Admiral Ortega gave a slight smile, "Senior Captain Beeson, you have a great deal to learn about politics in the Centauri Confederation if you think that innocence has anything to do with justice or punishment." Her expression went cold again, "Right now, *Tanis* is on the hook for this. I'm too senior to take the fall, my father and the Tanis System Command board would have to defend me or else they'd look weak. General Kalsi would have been a perfect scapegoat... but he's dead... far too conveniently dead."

"You don't think that young Lieutenant Medica is a little junior to go down for this?" Admiral Kaminsky shook his head, "You'll provoke a war between the United Colonies and the Centauri Confederation.

"Better the United Colonies than Tanis," Chairman Admiral Ortega snapped.

"If you turn him over to us," Daniel said, "I could get information from him. He was one of my officers--"

"If you would see him turned over to you... then I need *something*. Tau Ceti and the Centauri are both aware of Marius Giovanni's infiltrations, if I could provide them with a location, with *something*, and then suggest that it was his assassin who attacked me, then I could deflect the coming storm," Chairman-Admiral Ortega jabbed a finger at her desk. "Otherwise, gentlemen, I will turn him over to the Centauri in a heartbeat. Believe me, when I say that they will drug him and torture him so that he will confess to *any* crimes that they want to attribute to him... and your nation with him."

Daniel scowled at her, "That's pretty damned heartless of you."

Her lavender-eyed gaze went to him, her expression hard, "We're talking interstellar war. If our situations were reversed, wouldn't you make the same decision?"

Daniel didn't flinch. "Give me five minutes with him, I will get you something."

Admiral Kaminsky quirked a slight smile, "Well, Chairman-Admiral, the ball is in your court."

She looked between the two of them and for a moment, Daniel wondered if she were going to reject the offer just to be contrary, but then she gave a nod and activated a toggle on her desk. "Executive-Captain Harlan, please have a security team escort Senior Captain Beeson to our security section to interview our prisoner," she looked up and met Daniel's gaze as she went on, "I want full audio and visual recordings of their discussion."

***

"Sir!" Lieutenant Elvis Medica stood up as Daniel entered the cell. For a moment he looked worried, "Sir, have you been captured..."

He trailed off, though, as he saw that Daniel was in his dress uniform. "Is there some kind of trial then?"

"Trial?" Daniel asked. "No... not yet." Daniel cocked his head, "Lieutenant, do you even know who you've been captured by?"

"I figured it was the Centauri, sir, with how they've treated me," Lieutenant Medica replied. "I haven't seen any uniforms, no one has identified themselves..."

"It's Tanis," Daniel interrupted, "but they plan to turn you over the the Centauri... I'm here to try to talk you into giving us something to give them." Daniel hesitated to say more, but then he decided to lay the cards out on the table. "They're recording this entire conversation."

"I figured as much, sir," Lieutenant Medica replied. "You have to understand, sir, we didn't intend to blow the hell out of the base. I ordered the missile strike, those bastards were slaughtering the shuttles trying to take off... I couldn't let it go on!"

Daniel felt his throat constrict, even knowing he was probably damning himself, Lieutenant Medica didn't hesitate to accept responsibility. "What were you even doing there?" Daniel asked moving over to take a seat next to the engineering officer. "You downloaded Hugo Base's entire network, what were you after?"

Lieutenant Medica looked down. "Sir, I'm not sure that I should say."

Daniel caught the distinction. The Lieutenant had not said that he didn't want to tell Daniel, he didn't know if it was safe to say it where Tanis Defense Force personnel could overhear.

"We already know it relates to Marius Giovanni," Daniel chose his own words with care. He hoped that the Chairman-Admiral chose the personnel with access to the cell block with care. But Daniel didn't know for certain and he didn't really trust the woman. "Is it his base of operations?"

Lieutenant Medica's lips went in a flat line. It was more than that, but he didn't want Tanis knowing. Daniel rubbed his forehead in frustration. "Look, I know that Lieutenant Commander Perkins stopped at Formosa Station before he headed to the Sol System. We know that he found some information there that led him to Mars." Daniel considered his next words carefully, "Either he found some confirmation there that reinforced his conclusion and sent him to Hugo Base on Mars... or he found direct information about Marius Giovanni." Chairman-Admiral Ortega didn't know that Forrest had hijacked the *Widowmaker* to rescue the (assumed) deceased Princess Alannis Giovanni. Elvis Medica might be trying to keep that information quiet. *She's third in line of succession after the Emperor and his daughter, so she's something of a prize.*

Lieutenant Medica nodded, slightly. *A bit of both, then,* Daniel realized. From what he knew of Forrest Perkins, that meant that he didn't trust the lead they had to be strong enough to allocate resources, or possibly just enough resources soon enough to matter. "Did you learn the location of Marius Giovanni's base of operations?"

Lieutenant Medica gave a single, firm, nod.

"Can you give that to us without jeopardizing the lives of United Colonies personnel?" Daniel asked. If he didn't want to disclose it, then he might be worried that someone else could get there first... or that an attack on Marius Giovanni's base might kill her.

Lieutenant Medica hesitated. "Sir, I'm not sure."

Daniel sat back, "If I can obtain a voucher for the safety of *all* our personnel, would you disclose the information we need?"

Lieutenant Medica met his gaze, "Yes, sir."

I hope that will be enough, Daniel thought. Because this was a race. Forrest would reach the Centauri in a matter of hours and once they had the *Widowmaker* and the knowledge of Marius Giovanni's location, they'd send forces of their own.

***

Minder absently wondered if Fixer's scheming and backstabbing came as a consequence of their unique tasks they'd been assigned or if it was an element of her former human nature blending through due to the hasty process he'd used in improving her.

Probably a little bit of both, he decided as he put the final plans together for taking care of that particular issue. Ambition was not a natural motivator for his species. They worked as a collective, so individual achievement was immaterial. In reality, they didn't even care about their overall dominance of the galaxy. The segment assigned to this region had one task: to prevent the return of their enemy.

It was a stronger sector than most, in part because this was the place that their enemies had been strongest. This had been where they had fought their last battle... this had been where they had nearly won. And now, humanity might bring his race's great enemy back.

Minder had unified his race's infiltrators. Before his efforts, they had worked as single cells, undermining humanity and other threats to prevent them from becoming coordinated enough to present a cohesive threat. They had worked under his direction for decades, ever since he had helped to orchestrate the destruction of Amalgamated Worlds.

Minder had parented a human family in that time, had played the role of a father and leader for not just a world, but for an entire stellar nation. No one had questioned President Spiridon's motives as inhuman. They'd seen him as another corrupt oligarch who sought to consolidate power. No one had ever even suspected that he wasn't really human at all... that he had been incubated inside a human host and supplanted the creature's higher order intelligence.

Even his political opponents had furthered his plans as they opposed his efforts, for they'd led to further fracturing and dissolution of human society and effort. When terrorists and revolutionaries fought his police state tactics, he'd utilized pawns within their ranks to destroy government facilities that held data he wanted to conceal. When military opponents had sought new methods, he'd directed their weapon and defensive programs away from areas that could have proven to be dangerous to his cause.

Even the tiny handful of precognitives had been easy to manipulate or detract. When they'd presented their prophesies of the Giovanni, his agents had encouraged Marius Giovanni's downfall and instigated the Shadow Lords into opposing him. Furthermore, he thought he had subverted the entire course when he had taken the exiled Marius Giovanni under his wing.

Only it wasn't the right Giovanni, he reminded himself, *it was just a copy.* The information had come as a shock to him when Lucius Giovanni had broken it. Minder had never suspected the one he'd had was a copy. Worse, the Shadow Lords had their copies of Marius Giovanni, too, it seemed... and the real one was either dead or lost.

Meanwhile, *Lucius* Giovanni had established a powerful, thriving nation. Minder's superiors had not been amused... not that they even remotely understood the concept of humor. Minder had hoped to utilize the Chxor to crush the threat, yet the powerful Chxor Empire had crumbled. *What else could you expect from the product of a failed Ben-Yam-Gar experiment.* He should never have relied upon them, just as his predecessors should never have counted on the Wrethe Incursions being successful.

And that brought him back to his current dilemma.

Fixer thought that he had failed. She thought that she could replace him and do a better job than he could. Was it his pride, his individualism, that rejected her ambition... or was it cold logic? Minder *had* failed. Marius Giovanni had gone around him and even now, he might be activating the ancient devices hidden at Golgotha.

Was Fixer capable of replacing him? Should Minder allow

her to do that? He didn't know her exact plan, though he could guess well enough. She wouldn't endanger the galaxy by allowing Marius Giovanni to succeed. She would scout Golgotha and wait for Sidewinder to complete his task. Then she'd utilize a direct method, probably a large scale terrorist strike, to kill Minder.

His daughter would then wave the bloody shirt and use that to unify forces to her. With the feared President Spiridon dead, many humans would be more willing to deal with his personable daughter. She might then convert them, either slowly or rapidly into more of their splinter species.

In a generation, she could potentially rule all of humanity... but that wasn't the goal of their species. Humanity might not be governable. Their kind did not need them unified, they needed them exterminated or reduced to quarreling groups. Humans had a tendency to rebel against even their own.

No, he thought to himself, *Fixer's plan will not work in the long term. Even if she succeeds, then she'll become a threat to our own kind.* That terrified him, for while he had instigated war among the humans, he had never even imagined doing so among his species. Doing so would invite defeat by their enemies.

Fixer would not succeed, could not be allowed to succeed. Minder would have to see to it.

But first, he had to deal with Marius Giovanni. The human ship would arrive soon, his daughter would have it, and she would scout Golgotha for Sidewinder's forces.

It is all coming together, only a few hours now...
***

"Golgotha?" Chairman-Admiral Ortega demanded. "You can't be serious."

Lieutenant Elvis Medica looked between her, Admiral Kaminsky, and Captain Beeson, "Ma'am, sirs, I am entirely serious. The pirate--"

"A wanted fugitive who's known for pulling scams, human trafficking, murder, rape, and a host of other crimes," the Chairman-Admiral's lavender eyes flashed with anger.

"--he seemed entirely certain," Elvis continued. "Amalgamated Worlds had the star-charts scrubbed of Golgotha's location, so we went to Hugo Base to obtain the coordinates."

"You invaded a *peace conference* in order to steal the location of a system judged too dangerous to visit by Amalgamated Worlds, who were known for accepting extreme risks. You did all this on the word of someone who cannot be trusted," Chairman-Admiral Ortega demanded. The cold anger in her voice showed what she thought of their judgement.

"We followed the evidence," Elvis replied. "No one else seemed interested in finding out the truth. What choice did we have?" He regretted the words right after he said them, particularly with the look of hurt on Captain Beeson's face.

It's not his fault, Elvis thought, *but the situation being what it was...*

"Does the United Colonies know the location of Golgotha?" Chairman-Admiral Ortega demanded.

"We *may* have it on file," Admiral Kaminsky said. "There's a great deal of data in the fleet archives that we haven't fully investigated. The location of the system would not have been a priority. The problem would be finding out the information in a timely fashion. We believe that ansible transmissions are no longer secure."

"You'd have to send a dispatch ship," Chairman-Admiral Ortega nodded. "We don't know who may be listening. That could take months or more."

"We have single use cyphers," Admiral Kaminsky admitted. "It would be possible to send a message in that fashion, but the more often we send such messages, the more likely it is that our enemies will realize it and will adapt."

Elvis felt far out of his depth. He listened to them speak and he just felt a sense of relief. This was out of his hands now, someone else, someone with far more experience, would deal with it.

"What about Lieutenant Medica?" Captain Beeson asked.

Chairman-Admiral Ortega looked at Elvis. He swallowed nervously as she stared at him. "While he has provided us with information, it has not appreciably changed the situation."

"He volunteered information that could be crucial," Captain Beeson objected.

"The Centauri Confederation will want a target as a whole to attack over this. Tanis is powerful, but as a single system, we do not have the resources to hold off their combined forces." Chairman-

Admiral Ortega grimaced, "Initial indications are that the Tau Ceti Separatists have put aside their distrust for the Centauri in order to resolve the situation. Their emissaries are en route to meet with President Spiridon and establish a unified reaction to the attacks. If I do not provide them with an appropriate target, they will turn on Tanis."

"You're going to give me to them?" Elvis's jaw dropped in shock. He had expected to go home and face trial after giving the information to them. Possibly to face some kind of trial and punishment in the Tanis system. But to be handed over to the Centauri...

"I may have no choice. Especially if your Lieutenant Commander Perkins goes to them," she replied. "They will use you and the rest of the *Widowmaker*'s crew as an excuse to launch an attack on the United Colonies... but they will leave Tanis alone."

Elvis stared at her, realizing that, far from being over, his troubles had just begun.

***

Chapter V

August 26, 2410
Aboard the *Widowmaker*
Shadow Space

"So the Golgotha system *does* move counter-rotation to the rest of the galaxy," Rory went on excitedly. "And the data we've got on the system, I can't *believe* that Amalgamated Worlds quarantined the system and purged all records of it's location! The place is a veritable treasure trove..."

"All I need is a location and navigational plotting for any planets or stellar debris," Forrest snapped. The two scientists hadn't shut up about their various discoveries in the data they'd mined from Hugo Base. He glanced up at the chrono which displayed their time to destination. The shortest route to Delta Pavonis was a roundabout route, which took them as far out as the Anvil system, in short three and four day jumps. Their last jump was five days, from the 987E21 system to Delta Pavonis. Forrest had wanted the navigational data uploaded for a jump to Golgotha so that they could escape, just in case this was a trap.

"We have all that," Feliks waved a hand dismissively. His excitement made his accent heavier. "That was trivial. You can't begin to imagine the wealth of information to be learned in the system. Amalgamated Worlds discovered ships and wreckage from at least *five* different species, ranging in age from a million to just over..."

"Two billion years!" Rory finished excitedly. "And lots of the equipment there was still active! Weapons systems, sensors, all kinds of technology that we could use! I've found notes that correlate to the lost Agathan Fleet... the technology that Alexander Agathan used to design and build those ships originated at Golgotha! That means there's potentially equipment there that we could build incredible ships and weapons!"

"I don't care," Forrest grated. "I need to know where to find Marius Giovanni and Reese Leone."

"I can upload that--"

"Uh, Skipper?" Petty Officer Godbey interrupted. The noncomissioned officer looked up from his sensor console. "I'm getting an odd reading from the automated sensors."

"What?" Forrest demanded. They were in shadow space, which normally meant that sensors stood down to a minimal watch. With how short-handed they were, Forrest had set the automated systems to monitor the sensors while they performed what maintenance they could with the people they had. Rory and Feliks *could* have been helpful in that regard, but they'd been too focused on their damned data.

"It picked up some kind of anomaly... and it seems to be closing," Petty Officer Godbey frowned.

That shouldn't have been possible. Ships couldn't see one another in the chaotic, high energy environment of shadow space. But Forrest remembered the last time such an anomaly had occured... when Shadow Lord Imperious had a ship match course with the UCS *Nova Rosnik*... and Forrest had been the one to notice.

"Go active sensors," Forrest snapped. "Sound battle stations and--" A siren began to wail and Forrest's eyes went wide. "Collision warning! Brace for impact!" The collision sensors picked up a ship or object when it was only a dozen meters or less from the hull.

Yet there was no impact. A light on Forrest's panel blinked and Forrest stared at it for a long moment in confusion. It was a docking confirmation. Someone had docked with them. In shadow space. It should have been impossible.

He shook his head, realizing just how dangerous this could be. "Corporal Wandry and Corporal Wicklund, report to starboard airlock, all other personnel, suit up and prepare to be boarded."

Yet even as he started to turn away from the command chair, a communications chime pinged to announce an incoming call.

Forrest looked over at Petty Officer Godbey who stared at his communications panel as if it had been replaced by a large and venomous snake. Forrest stepped over and reached out a hand, pausing a few centimeters from the control panel. He swallowed, feeling a wave of unease. He understood that not answering the call wouldn't change the circumstances or make this mystery ship go away... yet some part of his mind seemed to hope it would.

Ghost ships that boarded you in shadow space were spacer legends. The United Colonies Fleet knew that Shadow Lords could manage the feat, but there remained plenty of superstition in general about shadow space... and everyone knew that the longer the jump, the more... strange things could become.

Forrest wasn't about to allow superstition to guide him. He jabbed on the accept with a bit more force than necessary.

"Ah, Lieutenant Commander Perkins," a man's face appeared on the display, "I'm glad you took my call personally, it saves some time." He had slightly Asiatic features, with long, loose black hair, dark brown eyes, and a smug smile.

"Who are you?" Forrest demanded. "Why have you docked with our ship?"

"I'm aware that this could be taken as a hostile act," the man nodded, "and for that you have my apologies. I have no desire to harm you or your crew, Lieutenant Commander. I am Aromata Atagi, and I am an emissary of Shadow Lord Invictus, who would like to meet you in person."

"I'm a little short on time," Forrest said, glancing at the chrono. It showed only thirty minutes to their arrival at Delta Pavonis. He didn't know if he could dissuade the man or possibly delay him, but he'd take the chance to avoid whatever they wanted from him.

"Not a problem at all," Atagi smirked. "This will only take a few minutes and then you can go on your way. I promise you that you, your ship, and your crew will not be harmed."

Forrest seemed to remember the Emperor saying something about the Shadow Lords being good for their word. "Fine," Forrest grated.

"Excellent," Atagi replied. He gestured at someone off-screen. A moment later, the universe seemed to shift around Forrest. It was indescribable, as if the *Widowmaker* had turned in a direction that didn't really exist. He must have gasped or said something, because Atagi spoke up, "We have shifted your course, slightly, Lieutenant Commander. Your vessel is now in an area of shadow space where time doesn't pass as quickly as in normal space. This should allow you to meet with Shadow Lord Invictus."

Forrest managed a weak smile, "Oh, great."

***

Forrest joined Corporal Wandry and Corporal Wicklund at the hatch. Both Marines had suited up, though Forrest assumed they'd had someone else on watch while they did so. "Anything?"

"Negative, sir," Corporal Wandry replied.

Forrest went over to the hatch and opened it. A moment later, the external hatch opened, to show an opulent corridor, with wood flooring and what looked like brass lighting fixtures. Atagi stood in the hatch, "Lieutenant Commander Perkins, I'm glad you can take the time to meet with my master. He's quite anxious to make your acquaintance."

"Oh?" Forrest asked. The last thing he wanted was for a Shadow Lord to know who he was.

"Yes, he's learned quite a bit about you," Atagi replied with a slight smile. "Please, follow me." He turned, and then over his shoulder said, "if you prefer, you may bring an escort, but I'll vouch for your safety. You will experience no harm while aboard the *Baramis*."

Forrest turned to Corporal Wandry and Corporal Wicklund. "Stay here. Guard the hatch. If anyone but me tries to board before I get back..." He shot a glance at Atagi as the man walked away. "Kill them."

"Sure thing, Skipper," they both grinned.

Forrest walked through the hatch. The corridor was just as opulent as it had appeared. Persian rugs lay on the wooden floors, tapestries and artwork lined the walls. Some of that artwork was bizarre, even jarring. Forrest thought he recognized a weird impressionistic painting of a screaming man, but the one next to it was simply a blank white canvas.

"Why is Shadow Lord Invictus interested in me?" Forrest asked, coming alongside Atagi as the man led the way.

Atagi smirked a bit, like a kid who knew a secret. Forrest figured that a man working for someone like Invictus probably liked secrets. "You're at the center of quite a bit of events, Lieutenant Commander. You have accompanied *Emperor* Lucius Giovanni in battle, you served on his staff during the conquest of Nova Roma, and you're moving up the ranks quite rapidly."

"Liberation of Nova Roma," Forrest corrected automatically.

"Was it, then?" Atagi grinned. "I suppose it's all a matter of perspective. In any case, my master has a natural interest in Lucius Giovanni and those close to him."

Forrest didn't like the sound of that. It was almost as if Atagi were suggesting that Forrest had curried favor with Emperor Giovanni. The truth was that Forrest had worked hard for everything he'd done and he hadn't ever asked for favors.

Forrest had heard that the previous meeting with Shadow Lord Invictus had been in some sort of shadowy court, but Atagi led him into what was to all appearances a garden, complete with trees, plants, and a starry night sky. The garden's only light was from a pair of luminous moons above. The night sky seemed oddly familiar, but it wasn't Faraday's night sky, nor was it the night sky of Saragossa. Forrest thought he recognized a constellation, but he didn't want to spend too much time staring.

The "garden" seemed to have a fog, and the further inside they went, the deeper it grew, pooling around his feet, then up his calves, until he waded through it. The cool moisture clung to his uniform in an unpleasant, cold and clammy fashion.

There was no way that the chamber could be so big, he knew. It had to be at least partially holographic projections. On impulse, Forrest shifted over a step and ran his hand across a tree-trunk, halfway expecting it to vanish as his hand passed through the projector.

Instead, his hand met rough bark and sticky sap. As he pulled his hand away, he smelled pine sap. He didn't miss the smirk that Atagi shot at him.

They continued to walk through the garden, the path twisting here and there around dimly lit fountains and statues, until they came to a broad, green field. Dozens of men and women, many of them cloaked against the damp chill, stood in small groups. The buzz of conversation, the eerie sound of laughter, and the gleam of eyes heralded his arrival. At the far end of the field, a man stood, staring up at the stars. "Welcome, Lieutenant Commander Perkins," Shadow Lord Invictus's soft voice cut through the night air.

The conversations around them ceased and Forrest followed Atagi forward, his feet feeling damp and hearing wet grass squelch under his shoes. "Thanks, I suppose," Forrest said. "Why is it that you've gone to so much effort to meet me?"

Shadow Lord Invictus turned, and as he did so, the fog billowed around him, hiding his features. "Less effort than you might imagine... to some extent. Far more effort than you realize in other regards. Tell me, did you not find it convenient that someone at Formosa Station knew exactly where you needed to go to find Reese Leone?"

Forrest's jaw clenched, "So you're saying you put Ricky One-Eye, there?" He had suspected the pirate hadn't told him everything. Now it seemed he could add working for a Shadow Lord to the slaver's many crimes.

"Who?" Invictus asked, cocking his head. "I'll assume your contact from the station is what you mean." He chuckled a bit, "Reese had to stop at Formosa Station to conduct repairs after several of my ships ambushed him and damaged his vessel."

"Why didn't you kill him, then?" Forrest asked.

"Because that wasn't my intent," Invictus smiled and moonlight glinted off his teeth in an unsettling fashion. He went on, his voice soft but intense, "I wanted to put *you* on his trail. One, because I know you're highly motivated to find him, and two... well, I wanted to test your mettle."

Forrest scowled at the man. He wished he could banish all the darkness, look Invictus in the face, and feel like he was on even terms. *I'm not, though, I'm so far out of my league that I'm probably insignificant... but to hell with him.*

"Well, you've seen my mettle. I'm headed to get a crew and do what I wish I could have done at Kapteyn's Star," Forrest snapped. "So if you don't mind, I'll just be on my way."

"Ah, you mean to rescue Princess Alannis Giovanni, then?" Invictus sounded amused, rather than offended. He let drop that he knew Forrest's intent in such a way that Forrest didn't see any point in denial. "A worthy prize, she's valuable as a bargaining chip. You might even get you way back into the United Colonies Fleet if you return to her... assuming your goals aren't somewhat higher than that."

Forrest scowled, "She's not a game piece to be moved around the table. She's a woman, a fine officer, and she deserves a measure of respect, even from you."

The entire garden went quiet, even the chirp of crickets faded into silence.

Shadow Lord Invictus stalked forward, the pools of fog billowing around him, concealing his features. He stopped only a few feet away from Forrest. Up close, he seemed shorter than Forrest had expected, though it was hard to get a sense of scale with the fog and darkness. Forrest steeled himself for some kind of explosion, but Invictus simply smiled again, his white teeth glittering in the moonlight, "Not one to back down, are you? How should I expect less, I suppose, from a man who survived the fall of Saragossa." He nodded slightly, "Lieutenant Alannis Giovanni *is* worthy of respect, I'll give you that... but like all of us, she *is* a game piece."

Invictus turned away, and for a moment Forrest caught his profile, a hawk-like face with a goatee. "You plan to take on a crew, mount a rescue, then? Charge in like the prince from faerie tales?"

"I'll do what I must," Forrest growled.

"Why chose the Centauri?" Invictus turned back around, the light of the moons gleaming in his dark eyes.

"Not a lot of options for a wanted man," Forrest replied.

"Oh, there are always options... but I think a man like you has limits, yes? You wouldn't accept my help, if I offered it?"

Forrest considered that for a moment. He weighted the risk of betrayal by Invictus, of the Shadow Lord capturing Alannis... versus the risk of her being in her father's hands. "No," Forrest said, "No I wouldn't."

"I didn't think so," Invictus paced in a circle around Forrest, waves of fog breaking around him. "You don't trust Tanis, you can't rely upon the United Colonies, and to you, that leaves only the Centauri. Do you think they'd help you out of a sense of righteousness?"

Forrest scowled, "I don't trust them, either, but I think I can take precautions." He shrugged, "Besides, I'm out of money and options."

"No... but you *do* have something worth trading, if you had a place to trade it," Invictus grinned. "You took the data from Hugo Base. You might be surprised what that would be worth... to the right kind of people."

"I'm not giving that to you, either," Forrest said. "When and if I get Alannis back, I'll turn it over to the United Colonies."

"Nothing on it would benefit them. Quite the contrary, much of that information will bring them difficulty or even harm," Invictus scoffed. "But I didn't *ask* you for it. I merely pointed out that it has value... a great deal of value to the right person. My goals and your goals align at the moment. You want to rescue Alannis Giovanni...

and having her free will undermine Reese and his master's objectives, which will benefit me." He stopped his pacing and turned to face Forrest. "Keep that in mind." With that he turned and stalked away, passing quickly out of sight in the gloom.

Forrest blinked and then realized that he stood alone in the moonlight. The others of Shadow Lord Invictus's gathering had vanished as well, the fog seeping away and the garden becoming still and empty.

"Well, perhaps we should get you back to your ship," Atagi spoke, humor evident in his voice. "We wouldn't want to delay your arrival unnecessarily."

Forrest started a bit. Atagi had stood so silently that Forrest hadn't picked him out. "Yes," Forrest replied, "I need to get back."

He wasn't certain what Invictus's goals had been. The meeting left Forrest with more questions than answers. He did know that he needed some time to consider all this and to get his head on straight for the meeting with the Centauri.

He just hoped that the Shadow Lord hadn't done anything to sabotage Forrest's one hope of rescuing Alannis.

***

"Exiting shadow space in thirty seconds," Petty Officer Godbey reported as the *Widowmaker* went to battle stations. He'd uploaded the coordinates to Golgotha, which meant that once they arrived and gained a solid approximation for their location, then it should only take a few minutes to jump out of the system... just in case the Centauri weren't entirely forthright.

Forrest glanced at his sensor display, but it showed no sign of the *Baramis*. That fact hardly reassured Forrest, because he remembered that Shadow Lord Invictus's flagship seemed possess some kind of stealth technology on it's visit to Faraday.

Still, Shadow Lord Invictus and his emissary, Aromata Atagi hadn't harmed the ship or crew in Forrest's absence. After returning to his ship, they'd somehow *turned* again, so that they were back on track through the gray nothingness of shadow space. It seemed that all was in order, to include the resumption of the countdown from the nav-computer for their arrival at Delta Pavonis.

The meeting with the enigmatic Shadow Lord had eroded much of Forrest's conviction about seeking help from the Centauri.

Yet it wasn't as if he had any choice. He couldn't very well sell the data he'd stolen to just anyone, and it would take time and organization to turn money into people, parts, equipment, and weapons.

Alannis was running out of time and every minute that Forrest wasted was time that she remained under Reese Leone's control.

"Emergence, calculating position now.... *holy shit!*" Petty Officer Godbey looked up, his eyes wide in surprise, "Skipper, we're being hit by *major* targeting sensors, they've got our position nailed. I'm receiving a transmission..."

"Attention unidentified warship, this is restricted space, power down your systems immediately or you will be destroyed," a cold, almost robotic voice spoke over the speakers.

It seemed that they'd run out of time.

***

Chapter VI

"I say again," Forrest repeated, "we have powered down all our defensive and offensive systems, do not open fire." He had no idea what was going on. The sensors were basically blind, visual sensors showed almost nothing but some kind of dust or gas cloud.

"We detect your systems powered down," the woman replied. Her voice remained cold, "Identify your vessel and stand by to be boarded."

"This is the *Widowmaker*," Forrest replied, "I'm Lieutenant Commander Forrest Perkins. We're out of the United Colonies..."

"You stand in violation of Port Klast traffic space and security regulations," she cut him off. "If we find that you deliberately violated our zoning regulations we will seize your vessel and you will be imprisoned or executed, depending upon a ruling by our our shift administrator. Should we detect any emissions spike from your vessel that might be systems powering online, we will destroy you, do you understand?"

"Yes," Forrest replied. He looked over at Petty Officer Godbey, "Did she say Port Klast?"

The enlisted man nodded, his eyes wide. "Sir, how did we get here? That's got to be *hundreds* of light years off course!"

Forrest scowled as he considered that. There was only one way that they could be so off course... and it wasn't an accident. "Shadow Lord Invictus," Forrest snapped. "That *bastard.*"

"*Widowmaker,* this is Port Klast Security Interdictor *Violator*, we're coming alongside, prepare to be boarded. Any resistance will be met with lethal force. I want your commanding officer to meet me at the hatch, am I understood?"

"Roger," Forrest replied, even as he stood up from his command chair, "I'm headed there now." He looked at Petty Officer Godbey. "Get on our intercom, tell everyone to stand down, I have *no* idea what's going on, but at least Port Klast shouldn't care about the fact that we hijacked this ship or that I'm wanted." From what Forrest had heard, Port Klast was run by Thomas Kaid. The man ran the remote world as his own private fiefdom, and it was reputedly a haven for pirates and smugglers.

He hurried down to the airlock, where he found Corporal Wandrey and Corporal Wicklund standing by, the two Marines armed and suited up. "Stand down," Forrest said. "I don't know what is going on, but for now, we play nice." The two Marines set their weapons to the side, but he could tell they weren't happy about it.

There was a tap on the airlock hatch and Forrest rushed over to toggle it open.

A boarding team swept in. Forrest followed their instructions and got down on his knees, his hands behind his head. A stocky, bulldog-like woman followed the team in a moment later. "Who is in charge here?" She demanded in a harsh, sand-papery voice.

"I am," Forrest replied. With the weapons aimed at him, he didn't try to stand.

"No," the woman snapped, "I am Commander Zahn of the PKS *Violator* and *I* am in charge. Why did your vessel trespass inside our no emergence zone?"

Forrest chose his next words with care, "We encountered a vessel of Shadow Lord Invictus in our shadow space jump. I believe he rerouted our course. Our destination was Delta Pavonis, our arrival here was unintentional on our parts."

"Search his ship, identify and question his crew," Commander Zahn snapped. "Access their flight log and navigational computer as well." Her boarding team moved out, all but a pair of armed and armored men, their weapons leveled on Forrest and his two Marines.

"You hijacked your ship out of Sanctuary Station almost six months ago," Commander Zahn read off her datapad. "Tanis Defense Force has reported that you were in the Sol system two months ago... where apparently you slipped through their security perimeter over Mars. Were you trying to do the same thing here?"

Forrest shook his head, "No. As I said, our arrival here was unintentional..."

"Are you in league with Shadow Lord Invictus? Did he send you here to scout our perimeter?"

"No!" Forrest protested, "Look, I didn't even know where we were until your traffic control contacted us. We were headed for the Delta Pavonis system--"

"That's Centauri space, are you working for President Spiridon then?"

Forrest shook his head, "I'm not working for anyone. I did hijack this vessel, but I'm going after Reese Leone and Marius Giovanni..."

"What was your intent on breaching our security perimeter!?" Commander Zahn demanded.

"I didn't even know we were here!" Forrest snapped back.

She struck him across the face, hard enough that his head snapped around and he saw stars. "Keep a civil tone." She said the words in such a detached fashion that he realized her angry tone had to be a calculation. This was a game to her.

One of her people returned, "Ship is secure. There's one injured woman in their infirmary, two civilians, and six other crew aboard. All have been secured."

"What did you determine from their navigation logs?" Commander Zahn demanded.

"Last plotted course was the Delta Pavonis system, and their flight log confirms encountering a vessel in shadow space," the machine-like response came as a relief to Forrest. He hadn't even thought to check that the systems were running during their encounter.

"Damn," Commander Zahn muttered. "Ship like this would have been a nice prize." She gestured at one of the guards. "Get him up."

The guard jerked Forrest to his feet. Commander Zahn scowled up at him. "Seems like your story checks out. Damned Shadow Lords like their games, I guess. We're going to bring your ship in for landing at Port Klast. I'm sure that Security Control will want to confirm your logs match up to your story, but for now, I don't get to vent you or your crew."

"I suppose that's good," Forrest replied.

"However," she said, her voice cold, "you will still have to pay fines for violating our traffic zone, docking fees, and..." she paused and sniffed at the stale air, "probably resupply fees since this ship smells like a can of ass. So unless you're richer than you look,

I'd guess they'll give you thirty hours to show you have currency or trade goods, and then they'll impound your vessel for fines due."

"What?!" Forrest demanded.

"Welcome to Port Klast," Commander Zahn smirked. "Hope you enjoy your stay."

***

"Docking fees will come to five hundred PKDs, your administrative fine for violation of our traffic control procedure with the additional time for a Security Interdictor to intercept your vessel and conduct boarding operations, will come to seven thousand PKDs," The short man said. "Your total comes to seven thousand, five hundred PKDs, plus an additional five hundred PKDs per day that you remain docked."

Forrest winced, "What's a PKD?"

"Port Klast Doubloon, roughly the equivalent of six grams of gold," the man replied. He sized up Forrest's expression and smirked, "Do you have any cargo to register for sale or should I begin proceedings to impound and sell your vessel?

"Do I have some time to run an inventory to see if anything aboard is salable here as cargo?" Forrest asked.

"Commander Zahn of the *Violator* and my inspection team both conducted an appropriate inventory, and tacked it to your administrative fine," the man replied, "Short of disassembly of parts and components, total value of personal possessions and limited firearms aboard value at just under nine hundred PKDs."

Forrest's expression went gray. He couldn't afford to strip the ship, they still needed supplies, they needed to go to Golgotha and save Alannis. But the potential cost was losing the ship...

"I'll be paying their fees," a drawling voice spoke up. Forrest's head snapped around and just as a man in black strode up. The man was a bit shorter than Forrest, but whereas Forrest was gaunt and thin, he was lean and muscular, with a broad chin and slight stubble.

The administrator's expression went sour. "Ah, Captain King, of course. I'll charge the fees to your account."

"Anything else?" The stranger asked.

"No, that concludes our business," the man replied. "However, if the Lieutenant Commander decides to make any sales, he must register it with my office prior to sale."

"I'm sure he'll keep that in mind. Run along now," the man waved a dismissive hand and then walked up to Forrest, shaking his head, "Damn, boy, you managed to get on the wrong side of Port Klast's administrators. They're all practically drooling over the chance to seize your vessel and auction it." He held out a hand, "Captain Tommy King."

Forrest had taken the other man's hand and then stared at him in shock, "Wait, *the* Tommy King, the pirate?!" Forrest hadn't encountered the man, but the pirate was infamous throughout human space. He'd been a former Amalgamated Worlds officer who'd taken over a battlecruiser and then carried on his own private war against the Colonial Republic as a pirate. He'd looted entire colonies, humiliating Colonial Republic officers across human space, leading entire fleets of pirates... and then he'd disappeared. When he'd reemerged, he'd become an ally of Lucius Giovanni and he'd helped to turn the course of the war with the Chxor. *Of course,* Forrest reminded himself, *he's become extremely rich in the process... assuming he wasn't already.*

"The one and only," Tommy King smirked. He released Forrest's hand and shook his head, "And currently I'm a *privateer* for the United Colonies. Which is part of why I'm not sure whether I should detain you or be proud of you with how many people are demanding your arrest."

"My arrest?" Forrest's eyes went even wider.

"You don't know?" Tommy King's smile went broad. He pulled his datapad from inside his black jacket, "Here, we are," he tapped his display and it showed an image of a Forrest, with a large number of Centauri Dollars's offered for a reward.

"This hit the ansible network about two hours after you arrived here," Tommy King laughed. "I looked up the actual bounty, which names your ship as a key part of the deal... apparently you pissed off Annabelle Spiridon pretty bad. What'd you do, knock her up and skip town?"

"Uh, no," Forrest shook his head. "I was supposed to meet her at the Delta Pavonis system. Shadow Lord Invictus apparently had other plans for me."

Tommy King's eyebrows went up, "Invictus sent you here, huh? I'd imagine he wanted to test out Port Klast's security again. He does that from time to time. Well, you've also got a wanted notice from Chairman-Admiral Ortega of the Tanis Defence Force, for violating their enforced neutrality zone at the peace summit on Mars... that one's from six days ago. This other one is from Tau Ceti, where they didn't put a price on you, but they did put a detain on sight notice for you and your ship."

"It's all a misunderstanding," Forrest said with as genuine a smile as he could manage.

Tommy King raised an eyebrow, "I'm sure, I'm sure. Trust me, I entirely understand how these kinds of misunderstandings can occur. So, how about we go aboard your ship and discuss all this?"

***

August 27, 2410
Alpha Canis Majoris
Tau Ceti Separatist Aligned, Centauri Confederation

Captain Daniel Beeson rubbed his face tiredly as he awaited the arrival of Chairman-Admiral Ortega. Admiral Kaminsky had asked him to deliver the news personally, as he'd worked with her before... as well as to make a final plea on the behalf of Lieutenant Medica.

The hatch to the meeting room opened and Chairman-Admiral Ortega stepped through. Daniel rose to his feet and snapped to attention. To his surprise, she didn't have her normal escort with her. The tall, dark-haired woman waved for him to take his seat. She looked as tired as he felt, he realized. Her eyes were sunken, her expression was bleak.

"Well, Captain," she said, "I hope you have some good news for me."

I wish I did, he thought to himself. Maybe if he had good news or at least valuable information, he could have bargained with it for Lieutenant Medica's life. "I'm afraid I don't, ma'am," Daniel replied. "We just received a response from our Fleet Headquarters. It seems that while a copy of the location of Golgotha was within the Dreyfus Fleet's archives, we don't have it now."

She cocked her head, staring at him. Her severe, serious face didn't leak anything. Daniel envied her that self control. "Lost during the Dreyfus Coup?"

Daniel hesitated. Admiral Kaminsky had given him permission to release some information, but it went against his nature and training to share so freely. *Then again,* Daniel thought, *in this, we are allies.* "Before the Coup, there was an engineering project. An antimatter production facility based on some very theoretical quantum physics." He shrugged, "Due to the value of the facility as well as a variety of safety concerns, the decision was made to construct it in deep space at an undisclosed location. The only navigational coordinates to the facility were stored in two locations: the engineering lab on Faraday that designed it and aboard Admiral Dreyfus's flag bridge."

"Go on," she nodded.

"We think the conspirators used the facility as a remote staging area, funneling personnel and even a few ships through the site, off the books and out of sight of the rest of the Fleet. We also think that they moved considerable amounts of valuable data there," Daniel sighed. "It turned out that the director of the program was part of the overall conspiracy. She, or one of her subordinates, wiped the coordinates from the lab computer. During the coup, the main computers of many of the Dreyfus Fleet ships were wiped as well, and there was a serious firefight on the Admiral's flag bridge, destroying the main storage for Admiral Dreyfus's personal files. So we don't know what all resources and materials ended up there... although we suspect that some surviving conspirators might have contact with the facility."

"How do you know the coordinates to Golgotha would be there?" Chairman-Admiral Ortega asked.

Daniel pulled out a sheet of paper and handed it over, "This is the file that our people did recover on Golgotha. It contains the executive summary of the reports on the system, but the coordinates are a null code. It was scrubbed. The attachments were also scrubbed. So we have almost no data on the system or what could be found there. That could only be done with complete access to the system."

"I see," she sat back. For the first time, some real emotion leaked through her control: disappointment. "I had really hoped for better news."

"Me too," Daniel said. He took a deep breath, "Chairman-Admiral--"

She held up one hand, "Captain Beeson, do you have family?"

Daniel's expression went blank. "Not anymore, ma'am. All of my immediate and extended family were killed by the Chxor during the occupation of Faraday."

"Ah," She shook her head, "I am sorry. I remember that from your file, now." She looked away and to his surprise, he saw tears well up in her lavender eyes. "Captain --*Daniel*-- for the past two weeks you have come to me, asking for the freedom of your former crewman. And believe me, as a person, I have wanted nothing more to deliver him to you. He did his duty as he saw it. This... all this, is politics."

She met his gaze, "I have no love for the Centauri Confederation. Particularly for Annabelle Spiridon and her father. My brother, Paul, he fell afoul of one of their plots and they killed him. It was politics that prevented my father from making them pay for it and it is politics that has prevented me from getting my revenge."

Daniel didn't really know what to say to that.

"I've just received word that the *Widowmaker* arrived at Port Klast," she said. "It will only be a few hours until word reaches President Spiridon. I can only guess at what his response will be... but it will not bode well for either of our nations, I am certain."

Daniel winced. President Spiridon would probably put his forces on combat footing, one step short of war. "What are you going to do?"

"We are going to withdraw to Tanis," Chairman-Admiral Ortega replied. "We cannot leave our home system exposed. I will mass forces there until he makes his move. At this point, without the *Widowmaker*, he could place the blame on anyone: Tau Ceti, Tanis, United Colonies, Shogunate... *anyone*. For all I know, he will use the momentum to ferret out internal enemies."

Daniel hadn't missed that she didn't mention the one bargaining chip she had left. "What do you intend to do with Lieutenant Medica, ma'am?"

She gave him a level look, "Turning him over now would be pointless. One man can be made to disappear... and then reappear at a convenient time to tell whatever story they wish. With Medica, he could attack Tanis over the violation of the peace and then bring him out later to justify an attack on the United Colonies." Ortega shook her head, "No, it is not worth turning him over. We have his video testimony and data from Hugo Base. That is enough to sway what public opinion we could. He's of no further use to me."

She waved a hand, "I'll authorize his turnover to you. What the United Colonies Fleet decides to do with him... or with the *Widowmaker* is irrelevant to me, at this point." She sighed, "I've communicated with Tanis System Control board, and they have authorized me to issue a request for a mutual defense treaty with the United Colonies."

Daniel's eyes widened. Tanis had never before broken their neutrality. Even under Amalgamated Worlds, they had been an independent, neutral system.

"It will have severe restrictions on expectations and allowances for our force utilization, however, we wish to put it forward as quickly as possible. I ask that your Admiral Kaminsky make use of one of his cyphers to send the terms we request, ahead of our diplomatic ship which should arrive at Faraday in thirty days."

"I'll pass those along, ma'am," Daniel said.

"Thank you," she stood. "My people will have Lieutenant Medica delivered to your shuttle. Consider his return an act in good faith towards our future alliance."

She departed without another word.

***

"Well," Boris mused, "this is an interesting puzzle."

"Sir?" Captain Beeson asked.

"Without confirmation of her information, we'll need to go to Idarian Station and see what we can learn," Boris said. "I find the whole news that Forrest decided to go to Port Klast, instead of taking Annabelle Spiridon's offer, rather fishy. Then there's the timing factor. There's no short-time route to Port Klast, we've checked the navigational routes twice. His arrival, from what she told us, would have been on time for a least-time route to Delta Pavonis."

"You think she's setting us up?" Captain Beeson asked in surprise.

"Maybe not intentionally," Boris mused, "but perhaps President Spiridon is trying to throw us all off the track of his latest plot. Or maybe something else has happened. Either way, we don't know what we don't know." He sat back and pulled out a cigar and lit up, puffing at it to get it going as he thought, before he blew a big haze of smoke at the air intake.

"Alright," Boris thought out loud, "We know that Forrest didn't stay at Idarian Station long. Maybe there's something to learn there. We'll plot jumps for the system; immediate departure."

"Sir," Captain Beeson nodded. He turned to go and then paused. "Admiral, what do we do about Lieutenant Medica and also about Chairman-Admiral Ortega's offer?"

"I've already sent the details to our communications section, they'll send it out before we depart the system," Boris said. He sighed as he considered Lieutenant Medica. "Do you consider Medica a flight risk?"

"No sir," Captain Beeson replied, his voice level and confident.

"Then put him on your ship, assign him some duties, and keep him restricted to your vessel, pending charges," Boris shrugged. "If Forrest Perkins's assumptions prove right, then I doubt Medica will face any real repercussions."

"What if he is wrong?" Captain Beeson asked.

"Then most likely he's going to be dead soon," Boris said grimly. "As the sole survivor of the *Widowmaker*'s crew, and as the senior surviving officer, I'd imagine he'll take the brunt of any courts martial. I imagine he'll spend a very long time in prison."

He gave a grim smile, "So, let's all hope that Forrest isn't crazy and that Alannis Giovanni is still alive, right?"

＊＊

Chapter VII

August 26, 2410
Golgotha
Unclaimed Space

Princess Alannis Giovanni, Lieutenant, United Colonies Fleet, and prisoner for just over five months, twenty-one days, and seven hours, glared at her opponent. She moved her knight up to capture the threatening bishop.

Her opponent smirked at her, moved up her queen to capture Alannis's rook, and smiled broadly, "Checkmate." Princess Lizmadie Doko, Lieutenant, United Colonies Marine Corps, pumped a fist in the air, "I win *again.*"

Alannis frowned down at the chessboard. It was the only bit of entertainment that they'd had since their capture. Reese hadn't been stupid enough to provide either of them with any kind of electronic device. Alannis learned how to hack as way to bypass her private tutor and Lizmadie... well, the illegitimate daughter of Emperor Romulus III had a far rougher childhood.

Alannis scowled at her friend and distant cousin, "You cheated."

"What, because I *won?*" Lizmadie rolled her eyes.

"You *always* win," Alannis growled. "I think I'm not going to play you anymore." Lizmadie was worse to play at in chess than Alannis's brother... and that was saying quite a lot. Even Lucius let her win, once in a while. Lizmadie just liked to grind it in her face.

"Well, you do kind of suck at chess," Lizmadie admitted. "Maybe it's not your thing?"

Alannis rubbed her eyes, "I hate you." She said it without venom though. This had become something of a daily ritual. They woke up, they did physical training, they got cleaned up and had breakfast. After that, they played their game of chess to kill time and then, like clockwork...

The door to their shared suite opened and four guards entered. There were always four, now, after their last escape attempt. There would be four more in the corridor beyond. "The Lord Admiral asks that you join him for lunch," the senior man spoke. He wore the uniform of a Nova Roma Marine, as did the other guards, but Alannis tried not to think of them as human.

Since she'd killed at least five other guards, she tried not to think of any of them as human.

"Of course," Alannis replied. She had no idea if it was day or night, or where they were... or if the place even *had* a day/night cycle. She thought it was a planet, with slightly lighter gravity than she was used to, but it could be a station, airless moon, or even a large ship.

The four guards escorted Alannis and Lizmadie out of their quarters, down the only corridor, and directly to a gathering hall. As usual, the man who claimed to be her father sat at the head of the table. Most of the time the table had one or more guests. Often his senior officers, or more occasionally one of his guests.

"Welcome, Alannis, Lizmadie, thank you for joining us," Marius Giovanni rose. His singular guest rose with him, tall in his black Nova Roma uniform. His bright blue eyes and blonde hair stood out starkly against the network of scar tissue that criss-crossed his face and scalp.

"Reese," Alannis hissed in anger.

"Alannis," Reese nodded, his face creased in a friendly smile. His smile was somewhat less sanguine as he nodded at Lizmadie, "Princess."

"Shall we eat?" Alannis asked. Not that she wanted to share her meal with her ex-husband, but she knew it would go better if she just got it over with. Reese's last visit had been... *a disaster would be a generous label,* she thought to herself. She and Lizmadie had tried to use silverware to kill Reese and Marius. Lizmadie had at least been able to stab Reese in the leg, but Alannis had been taken down by the guards before she could get within arms reach of Marius. They'd both been hit by stunners and now...

Alannis looked down at the plastic spoons that she and Lizmadie had to eat their meal with. The meat and vegtables had all been sliced into small portions, like what someone might feed a child.

"Ah, our other guests," Marius Giovanni said with a broad smile.

Alannis looked over. Her expression hardened as she saw Spencer Penwaithe enter the room, Admiral Collae close behind. The Colonial Republic officer gave Alannis a slightly apologetic shrug, as if he felt bad about all this, but his expression remained stony.

Behind them, though, came a third man, tall, with familiar features. Alannis blinked in shock as she saw him, "Commander Bowder!?"

The man paused, taken aback by the sight of her. He looked between Reese and her for a long moment, and then he shook his head and chuckled. "I should have known... if Reese wasn't dead, then why would the princess be?"

Lord Admiral Marius Giovanni chuckled in reply, as did Reese and Spencer Penwaithe. "Ah, forgive me," Marius said. "I'd forgotten that my daughter had met you in your previous guise." He nodded at Alannis, "My dear, might I introduce you to Colonel Price, formerly of Amalgamated Worlds Security Branch."

Alannis's eyes went wide as she began to put things together. "You never were Bowder, were you?" She felt sick to her stomach. She'd respected Commander Bowder. He'd been the Executive Officer aboard the *Constellation* during her first cruise as an Ensign. She'd respected him, she never would have suspected him... and apparently he'd never been who she thought he was.

"It was a guise I had to play," Colonel Price nodded. He shot a calculating look at Marius Giovanni, then looked back at Alannis. "In truth, I served Admiral Dreyfus during his conspiracy. I survived the purge that your brother conducted after the failed coup. Lieutenant Commander Bowder was a good fit, so I took his identity."

"You mean you killed him and took his place," Lizmadie said, her voice cold.

"You could put it that way," Colonel Price said. He cocked his head as he stared at her. "And since we're laying all the cards on the table, I also plotted the murder of you and Anthony Doko. It was something of an embarrassment that you managed to survive the assassination attempt, but I must admit, you and your husband did very well to survive, that squad was one of my best."

"If that was your best, then no wonder Admiral Dreyfus lost," Lizmadie said with false sincerity.

Colonel Price's smile turned feral, "Don't mistake their... caution for incompetence. They were instructed to make a minimal presence attempt on your life. Had Admiral Dreyfus followed my advice, they would have leveled your home."

"Well," Marius said cheerfully, "let's all be grateful that they didn't, as now we're afforded the opportunity to share a meal." He gestured at the chairs, "Please, sit."

Alannis took her seat with the others. At this point, she hoped that she'd finally learn what Marius's plan was. That he'd brought in a spy from the United Colonies, clearly a man who seemed to have a sense of importance, gave her hope that she'd learn enough to figure things out.

Yet Marius seemed to enjoy drawing things out. He ate calmly, commenting now and again on this or that feature of the meal: the wine, the beef, the salad greens from Tau Ceti. If she hadn't already been through five months of it, she would have screamed in frustration.

When the meal ended, servants came to take their plates.

"I think I've been patient enough," Colonel Price said. "Now, how about you tell me what this is all about?" From the tone of his voice, he was rather less patient than Alannis.

"I see that Captain Leone has followed my orders," Marius smiled. He stood up and activated several commands on his datapad. A moment later, the wall behind him turned opaque, to show a starry night sky.

Alannis's eyes narrowed as she saw a dimly lit landscape, lights glinting here or there from structures.

"Although you can't tell, it's just after noon here on the planet," Marius said. "The star is a spectral Type K, a red dwarf, the light from it isn't visible at this distance, the planet is warmed mostly through the non-visible radiation spectrum."

Alannis shivered at that. She didn't want to imagine living on a world without daylight.

She looked around the table and saw that Spencer Penwaithe and Reese both wore smug expressions. Admiral Collae's expression was stony as always, while Colonel Price's expression was suspicious. "There's only two systems humanity colonized that were red dwarf stars with worlds outside of the visible light spectrum. One at Boon's Star, the other at Par. I don't think you'd be able to set up operations at either without someone noticing..."

He trailed off and his expression went tense. "Golgotha. We're at Golgotha, aren't we?"

Alannis blinked surprise at that. Golgotha was a myth... wasn't it?

"Indeed, Colonel, we are," Marius Giovanni smiled. "I'm happy to see that Admiral Collae's impression of your intelligence wasn't wrong. We are at Amalgamated World's dirty little secret... how familiar are you with the system?"

Colonel Price scowled, "Enough to know how dangerous this place is. The Bureau of Research lost over five thousand people here in just six months. They resorted to conscripted colonials before the Command Council shut everything down."

"I'm aware," Spencer Penwaithe said, his voice light. "My father was one of those conscripted colonials. Very few of them survived."

"Which is how I learned about the system, originally," Marius went on. "While Amalgamated Worlds sought to bury the system and pretend it never existed... well, there has been a thriving colony here of men and women whose ancestors were brought here as labor forces and who have returned to learn more."

"What did you find?" Colonel Price asked.

"More than the original report estimated, but not as much as I'd like," Marius Giovanni admitted. "The system *was* the site of a battle, several of them from what we can tell. The ancient precursor civilizations fought over this system not just once, but dozens, possibly hundreds, of times. Amalgamated Worlds thought the system had strategic importance, but they didn't know why."

"From the little I read on the research, they thought it was a combination of the system's location and the older alien structures found throughout the system," Colonel Price admitted.

"The location... well, it might have had some importance," Reese said, his voice adopting a strange tone. "But it is the artifacts found throughout the system that are of chief importance."

Alannis had to suppress a shiver at the odd note in Reese's voice. It wasn't anything she could put her finger on, it was simply strange. One part reverence and another... almost alien. When she'd encountered Reese before the Temple of Light, he'd been obsessive about her and her son. Ever since, he'd seemed almost manic, all nervous energy, with occasional rants about how important his work was... about how it would change everything.

"The race that built the ruins was of definite extra-galactic origins, their civilization consisted of an entire star cluster... what has been known as the Omega Centauri star cluster. Sometime around a billion years ago, their star cluster reached our galaxy and Golgotha, Kapteyn's Star, and a dozen other star systems were thrown free. We think that originally the Golgotha system served as their main installation and that the technology here served as the motive force when they broke free of their parent galaxy to come to the Milky Way," Reese went on.

"Wait..." Alannis interrupted, "What do you mean broke free?"

Reese looked at her, his blue eyes lit up with a strange light. "I mean this race had the power to move entire star systems and star clusters, masses millions of times the size of a single star. They harnessed the mass of a singularity and provided motive force to it to leverage a cluster of two million or more stars on an extra-galactic journey... through the void between galaxies."

Alannis couldn't help but shiver at that. "What happened to them?"

"That we don't know," Marius quickly replied, even as Reese opened his mouth to answer. Alannis didn't miss the look on her ex-husband's face. Clearly he knew more than he'd let on. "Golgotha was their ark, a star that will continue to burn long after most other stars go out. Sometime around a billion years ago the star cluster reached our galaxy. At that point, the indigenous population had vanished, no one was there to guide their machinery, and gravitational forces from our galaxy ripped their star cluster apart. Golgotha has split off from the others, it has drifted further away over that time, counter-rotation to the rest of our galaxy... until the precursor races discovered it."

"Which sparked a huge war," Colonel Price snorted. "So these races wanted super tech for themselves, and your group is picking over the remains. Find anything useful?"

"Quite a bit, though of varying applications," Marius replied, his voice sanguine. Alannis, however, had come to read his emotions, she could see the slight tensing of the skin around his eyes... he was irritated by Colonel Price's interruptions. This was a presentation that he had wanted to enjoy and it wasn't having the impact that he had hoped.

"Some of the most valuable things we've learned are not technological at all... they're historical." Marius said. He activated the table's holoprojector and the diagram of a vessel appeared. The smooth, sleek lines were predatory and ominous. "Colonel Price, you might recognize the vessel?"

The former Amalgamated Worlds officer nodded slightly, "It's a Balor dagger-class destroyer, same class as your son used to put down the Dreyfus Coup." Alannis hadn't forgotten about the captured alien ship. She'd helped her brother to reach it during the chaotic events of the coup. Her brother had captured it and a handful of other Balor ships at the Third Battle of Faraday, when he had defeated a large Balor attack on the system.

"Look more closely," Marius said with a smirk.

Alannis leaned forward, and after a moment she *did* notice slight differences in the hull and layout, but they were tiny things... like the addition of portholes and what she thought looked like larger crew quarters.

"This is the hull of a damaged vessel we found here at Golgotha," Marius smiled. "It's over a million years old, damaged and abandoned by its crew around the same time as humanity learned to use fire."

Alannis looked over at him in shock, "You're saying that the Balor..."

"Or their predecessors, yes," Marius spoke, "were one of the four races that fought here. Also, that their technology has not progressed much, if at all, in that time." He brought up another diagram, this one of a heavily damaged structure... though after a moment Alannis recognized the flowering, star-like remains. "This, is the remnants of an Illuari Enforcer Platform. There were *five* of these structures in the Golgotha system, all of them destroyed." He brought up a dozen other images, "This is the remains of a Zarakassakaraz, or Zar, dreadnought, *that* is the wreckage of a Ben-Yam-Gar mothership, and those other vessels and stations are remnants of their mobile bases."

"This was a war of massive scale, all focused on control of this one star system," Spencer Penwaithe said. "The star system that we now control."

"To what purpose?" Colonel Price asked, looking around at the group. Alannis wasn't certain, but there seemed an edge of nervousness to his voice. *He senses it,* she realized, *he senses that these men are all unhinged, that they'll do anything to accomplish their goals.*

"To the capture of the very device that allowed the original owners to move stars," Marius said. He brought up another image, this of a massive construct. It took her a moment to realize just how massive as Marius scaled them down, smaller, and smaller until they were looking at a tall spire... and then into this very room. "This: a station so large it could be confused for a planet, with millions of kilometers of corridors. A station so large that it has earth-like gravity and its own atmosphere, with livable conditions outside." He waved a hand. "This facility was the point of their war... and it is a war that I believe continues to this very day. Whoever controls this station can rule not just all of human space, but potentially the entirety of our galaxy."

***

"I think I've heard enough," Colonel Price said, pushing back from the table and leveling a glare on Spencer Penwaithe and Admiral Collae. "I came here to talk about exchanges of weapons and personnel, about building up a real force, about making humanity strong. All of this alien crap sounds like the plot of some b-list holovid."

Alannis certainly couldn't disagree. Huge alien constructs, wars fought a million years in the past, she didn't see the significance and she didn't know why Marius and Reese seemed to feel it was so essential. *I just want out of here.*

"Sit down, Colonel Price," Marius said, "I assure you that it will all make sense."

Colonel Price drew a pistol from inside his waistband. "To hell with--"

Before he could level it, Marius struck. A wave of force ripped the pistol out of Marius's grasp and then picked him up and slammed him into the wall. His pistol clattered to the floor and slid under the table. "That was hardly called for, Colonel. We are civilized people here... aren't we?"

The officer's lips pressed in a flat line, "You're a psychic?"

Marius rolled his eyes and released him. As Colonel Price dropped to the floor, he went on, "My mother was a powerful psychic who saved the life of the Nova Roma Emperor. My grandmother and grandfather were both powerful psychics... even my daughter has shown psychic abilities. Tell me, what makes you think that I wouldn't be?"

Colonel Price scowled, "You're insane."

"Please, Colonel, you are my guest. You are a potentially valuable ally. Cease insulting me or I'll be forced to change the conditions of your stay here," Marius's voice remained light, but Alannis ground her teeth at the reminder of her and Lizmadie's current predicament.

Colonel Price took a seat.

"Now, as I was saying," Marius said, "This station is is a construct of extreme significance. All written records we've located refer to it as the Star Engine... and we believe that the entirety of the precursor aliens went to war over it."

"So this thing can move a star... so what?" Lizmadie asked.

"It utilized immense forces to do so," Reese snapped in reply. "From everything we can tell, it opens conduits to shadow space and siphons energy from there simply to kick-start its main power source. Just judging by the size of the power conduits, it can harness more power in a second than its star will put out in its entire eleven trillion years of existence."

Alannis blinked at that. Thinking at a scale like that made her head hurt.

"So why is this important?" Colonel Price demanded.

"It is missing a piece," Marius said. He rose from his chair and went to stand at the window. "The core piece, the key that makes all of it work." Behind him, Reese tapped commands on the holodisplay so that it showed a huge gulf in the planet's surface, a pit that went over a hundred kilometers deep. "We think that the Illuari had control over the system and that their rivals, the Miniari and their Zar allies, launched a raid to seize part of the station's key components. They attacked with some new weapon, a suicide attack where they bored their weapon deep into the station and then," he snapped his fingers, "they jumped part of the station into shadow space."

Alannis blinked in shock at that. The size of the missing piece meant that the shadow space drive would have had to be massive, far bigger than any dreadnought or superdreadnought mounted.

"The components stolen included control equipment as well as... well, what we've taken to calling the ignition," Spencer Penwaithe said. Alannis looked over at the tall black man and she didn't miss his calculating expression as he stared at Colonel Price. "We really don't understand the *full* design of it, but think of it as a massive power source that jump starts the full power siphons... which in turn activates the device's full capabilities."

"That's why you want my station," Colonel Price growled. "To kick start your little doomsday device." He sounded dubious, as if he still found the idea dangerous and wasteful.

"Station?" Alannis asked in surprise.

"Ah, yes," Spencer Penwaithe smiled, "You didn't know. I imagine your brother kept the secret at the highest levels." He nodded at Reese.

"Doctor Sheryl Gaspodschin worked for Admiral Dreyfus. She and Doctor Randal Wade had a design for an alternate antimatter platform, which would draw upon theoretical zero point energy to create raw power. It had a projected antimatter production far exceeding any other installation's power output."

Marius spoke up, still looking out at the dark sky. "A standard solar array wouldn't work here for obvious reasons. Adapting a solar array for the high ultraviolet and infrared range of the spectrum that the star emits would be prohibitively expensive. Our outposts here operate on fusion power, but it would take us a hundred years to build a fusion reactor big enough for the task and another two hundred years to bring in enough hydrogen to accomplish the task... assuming we could *store* that much hydrogen."

He turned back to face them, his expression stark, "Humanity doesn't have that kind of time. I've mapped the attacks of the Balor along with humanity's actions tied to this system and other remnants of the Omega Centauri star cluster."

"The first Balor attack occurred within days of humanity settling the Kapteyn's Star system, which was another outcast from the Omega Centauri cluster. The main offensive began against New Paris shortly after they mounted an expedition to the Arkan system," Marius said. "I think the variety of disasters here in this system were engineered by the Balor... and I think they are aware of or soon will be aware of my efforts here."

Colonel Price scowled, "So what do you intend to do? I've already told Captain Leone that my facility isn't fully operational. Without Doctor Gaspodschin or Doctor Wade, the scientists I've been able to recruit or had on staff weren't able to make the thing work."

"Doctors Gaspodschin and Wade were both recently allowed to resume work under a monitored program," Reese said. "The program is overseen by Professor James Harbach and its being run out of the penal colony on the ice planet in the Faraday system. It should be possible for you to break them out and get them to your facility."

"How do you know that?" Colonel Price asked.

"I have agents in place within the United Colonies Fleet," Marius Giovanni said. "While my son, Lucius, may think he has rooted them all out... well, there are some that he still does not suspect and I've recruited others who are not nearly so altruistic as they pretend to be."

Colonel Price shot a glance at Alannis, who met his gaze levelly. "I'm not here of my own free will, if you're asking," Alannis bit out.

"I didn't think so, but I'm not particularly interested in the cult following that your brother --and apparently father-- possess," Colonel Price replied. He looked to Marius, "I'm here for what it can accomplish: to safeguard humanity, to make it stronger."

"And perhaps to further your own ambitions?" Spencer Penwaithe asked.

"If I come out in a position of power..." Colonel Price gave a tight smile, "well, at least I know I'm competent enough to do a good job of running things."

"Of course," Marius said. "That is something I think all of us here can agree upon... we're the right people to be in charge, aren't we?"

"Point of order," Lizmadie said dryly, "I'll have to abstain from that vote."

Alannis snorted a bit, though no one else thought it was funny. *To be the only non-meglomaniacs in the room...*

She looked around at them. Colonel Price she didn't know well enough, but that he had supported Admiral Dreyfus and then killed an innocent man simply to replace him, that told her plenty. Spencer Penwaithe had manipulated and schemed behind the scenes in the Colonial Republic for decades. He'd helped to destroy Amalgamated Worlds and had betrayed many of his compatriots for more political clout in the creation of the Colonial Republic. Admiral Collae was as paranoid and suspicious as any man could be... and while she didn't doubt his motivation to save humanity, she distrusted the methods he would take to do so.

Reese had been dangerously obsessive about "protecting" her ever since the war with the Chxor had gone badly for Nova Roma. He'd become irrationally angry when she decided to join the Fleet, then resorted to drink and gone as far as to hack her medical implant to induce a pregnancy in order to sabotage her efforts. When she'd confronted him, he'd never accepted responsibility for his actions and in the time since, he'd resorted to violence, worked in league with pirates, and instigated war, all in his efforts to somehow "protect" Alannis and their child. Alannis stared at her ex-husband, his once handsome face crisscrossed with a patchwork of scars from the Illuari Temple of Light. Whatever he'd undergone there had changed him, left him erratic and obsessive to a whole new level.

And then there's Marius, she thought, looking at the man who claimed to be her father. If he really *was* Marius Giovanni, and not a clone... then he had led a failed coup attempt against his nephew, then Emperor Romulus III. Alannis knew all too well how many military officers and enlisted men had died in the attempt. He'd officially been executed for the crime and her mother had killed herself only a few weeks later.

In the time since, he'd backed Admiral Lucretta Mannetti, a pirate who had murdered her way across dozens of star systems. Admiral Mannetti had led a failed coup attempt of her own against Emperor Romulus III, destroyed colonies, trafficked in slaves and weapons, and had tried to kill Alannis's brother at least twice.

Marius had since backed Reese in his efforts to unlock alien technology, which had left a trail of bodies, including some of Alannis's friends and people she'd served with.

She wondered if any of them would be willing to trust or share power with any of the others. Certainly Spencer Penwaithe had betrayed Lucretta Mannetti at Halcyon, and by extension, Marius Giovanni. Each of them had to have plans to remove one or more of their partners.

And here we are, she shot Lizmadie a look, *prisoners to these nut-cases.*

***

After the luncheon finished, the standard eight guards escorted them back to their quarters. As they stepped inside, Lizmadie stumbled a bit and caught herself on the arm of their couch. None of the guards stepped within reach to assist her, and they kept hawk eyes on both of them as Lizmadie straightened, "Sorry, a bit too much wine for me, I suppose."

Two of them pulled out wands and began to frisk them down, while two more kept their weapons ready.

After that was complete, the guards departed and Alannis moved over to the couch and took a seat. "Well, that was educational," she said, even as her hand dropped down into the join between the couch cushion and the arm. She'd barely noticed when Lizmadie had adjusted her boot at lunch, and only because she had did she take note of her friend's action when she'd stumbled just now.

They both operated under the assumption that they were under constant surveillance. The knowledge that they were on a planet, or massive station, completely under Marius Giovanni's control only reinforced that assumption.

"Yes, wasn't it?" Lizmadie said dryly, taking a seat across from her in the chair.

Alannis's fingers brushed the back of something angular and metallic. *Price's pistol.* Alannis remembered how it had fallen to the floor and slid under the table. Lizmadie must have stopped it with her boot and then slipped it inside when she bent over to adjust it.

Now they had a weapon. A real weapon. They knew where they were, they knew that there was breathable atmosphere outside, that meant there should be wildlife of some kind.

"We need to plan," Alannis said, thinking both about the escape and about how to stop Reese and Marius. If they could get out, they could bring back a fleet. Her brother would send an entire fleet, if necessary.

"Do you know anything about Golgotha?" Alannis asked.

"Everything I know, I learned today," Lizmadie snorted. She went to one of the windowless walls and tapped at it. "I thought this was some kind of industrial plastic or ceramic... now I'm not sure."

"Too tough to cut through," Alannis said, "even if we had a knife." This had been the topic of so many of their conversations that Alannis didn't know why they bothered. Any escape would have to go through the door... wouldn't it?

"We know it is an alien facility," Lizmadie said. Alannis followed her friend's gaze to the bathroom. *Aliens wouldn't use a human-shaped toilet...* That meant it was likely retrofitted... toilet, sink, possibly the shower, too. In theory, it would be as sturdy and hard to break as the walls, but the *join* between the existing wall and the new fittings might not be.

Alannis smiled a bit. They had a weapon. They had a plan. They were going to get out of here.

* * *

Reese stared at the image of his wife, projected from his datapad. He reached out a finger and ran it over the holographic projection. The smile that Alannis wore was so familiar... yet he knew that she didn't smile for him.

He rubbed at the scars across his forehead and his fingers trembled. She hated him. He'd tried to explain to her, tried to get her father to explain to her, but she didn't understand. *Why doesn't she understand... everything I've done I've done for her.*

His hands clenched into fists. He would *make* her understand. So far, Marius had refused to use his mental abilities to compel her, but Reese knew that sooner or later they'd have no choice. Alannis had to be made to understand.

Reese closed out the security footage and brought up a schematic of the Star Engine. He couldn't begin to understand the device's full functions, but he was on his way to understanding what he needed to know. Ever since the Temple of Light he had found himself understanding and learning more and more.

But he needed to know far more than he did. Time was not on their side. Sooner or later, the Balor would come to Golgotha and there was no way that Marius could face them. Reese smiled a bit as he considered what they'd told Colonel Price. It wasn't the full truth... the Star Engine itself wasn't a weapon... it was a key.

Reese had begun to figure out how to use the key... he just needed a little more time.

***

Chapter VIII

August 29, 2410
Gogotha System
Unclaimed Space

Colonel Price had spent the past three days touring Marius Giovanni's facilities. Overall, he was impressed. Both by the organization and their numbers. The Lord Admiral had put together a disciplined, capable force and he'd shown none of the squeamishness of his son. Those who didn't serve voluntarily were mentally conditioned to do so. It was a brutal, but effective, means to compel loyalty... and it had allowed Marius Giovanni to assemble a truly impressive force.

Admiral Collae's forces were extensive enough, with over a dozen converted Chxor dreadnoughts that served as carriers and over a hundred cruisers. Most of the Colonial Republic personnel were actual volunteers, many drawn from worlds that had already been overrun by the Balor. The level of dedication that brought was something that Colonel Price appreciated.

Marius Giovanni's people, on the other hand, had only a core of his key personnel who had none or minimal mental conditioning. The vast majority of the rest had been programmed for loyalty. Colonel Price had already met Lieutenant Patricia Hersey, who'd formerly been of the United Colonies, but he'd also recognized dozens of 'missing' officers from several nations who'd apparently been recruited and reprogrammed.

Marius seemed to have tens of thousands of people and hundreds of ships. Many of them were stolen or purchased Colonial Republic vessels of dubious quality... but many more were state of the art ships he'd recently captured from dockyards in the Centauri Confederation. In all, Colonel Price wouldn't pit their forces against the entire might of the Dreyfus Fleet... but he *would* give them even odds against any other major force in human space.

Of course, the downside of an alliance with the man was that he seemed entirely focused upon this alien technology when, in Colonel Price's opinion, he should be focused on tactical and strategic methods to fight the Balor. On top of that, Marius

Giovanni was a psychic, with Psi Kappa and probably Psi Gamma capabilities.

He walked with the Lord Admiral, even as he wondered if he could trust his own senses. *Of course, I've taken a few precautions of my own.* He glanced back at his escort, men he'd trained and worked with for decades, men who knew how to watch for psychic meddling.

"Tell me more about your mental conditioning program," Colonel Price said.

Marius raised an eyebrow, "Are you concerned that you're a target?" He didn't wait for Colonel Price to answer, but instead gestured down a side corridor. "Not a worry, Colonel. I entirely understand your interest. It's a fascinating way to build up forces. My indoctrination facility is just down here, actually."

Colonel Price went down the corridor and waited patiently as the Lord Admiral used the biometric scanner. After a moment, the doors opened and they stepped into a large, open room. Hundreds of raised pedestals held men and women, each cocooned in a network of cables and equipment.

"It's a procedure that I actually uncovered in my research of this system... though it has no direct relation to the technology found here. I've said before that they utilized conscript labor. Many of those first conscripts were criminals that they re-purposed for the task using mental conditioning." He gestured at a platform. "They had mixed results, they were able to erase and rewrite memories as well as adding skills and training, but they many of their subjects suffered mental breakdowns."

"Oh?" Colonel Price asked.

"Yes, I think they were either too invasive and erased too much, or they didn't take enough of the core personality out. From what I can find, the project was abandoned before they could iron out the issues. I found some cryptic notes about a secondary program, something called Archon, but it doesn't look like they did any more research into the project."

Colonel Price went still at the mention of Project Archon. He wondered if Marius Giovanni even suspected the importance of that project... but he decided to change the subject. "So you use it to indoctrinate captured personnel?" *Archon was a failure that is best forgotten,* he thought to himself.

"To greater and lesser levels of success," Marius replied. "It took me ten years of fine-tuning to get the systems up and working, and each subject has to undergo a series of mental scans and tweaking." He walked over to one of the platforms and rested a hand on the machinery. Inside, Colonel Price saw a young woman, her eyes wide and unseeing, the muscles of her face twitching as the equipment rewrote her mind.

"I've found that younger people, those with fewer life experiences, are far easier to fully condition. With them, you can replace one authority figure for another. Some minds are more malleable and adaptable, others... not so much."

"What happens to someone you can't program?" Colonel Price asked.

"There are some," Marius snorted. "But they're fewer than you'd think. With older people, it's much harder. It would take me at least a month to program a man like you and if I did, I'd lose a great deal of your critical thinking skills. You'd probably be severely reduced in mental capacity." He said it off-handed, as if it were of minor consideration.

Colonel Price scowled, "You think it would be that easy?"

"Not easy," Marius turned, "Simple, but not easy. This is a process I have developed and refined over two decades, Colonel. And in any case, this process is only for full conditioning. I have other methods, some designed to compel someone to accomplish a single task and others are more complicated."

"And if I refuse to give you access to my antimatter production facility?" Colonel Price asked.

"Then I will allow you to leave, Colonel," Marius said, "I promised you safe passage to and from my base of operations. I am a man of my word, Colonel. I will allow you to leave unhindered, if you decide to do so."

And I'll trust that just as far as I can throw this facility, Colonel Price told himself. If he'd had an alternative to being here himself, he would have taken it. As it was, he'd planned in multiple fail-safes, to include orders for his people to kill him rather than to allow him to be taken hostage or mentally programmed.

"In any case, most of those I program are happy to serve. They're ideal people, dedicated to the cause, eager to defend humanity, and fully trained in military doctrine." Marius Giovanni stepped away from the platform and led the way out of the room. "I'm showing you all of this so that you see the value that I bring. With my help, you could increase your forces rapidly, Colonel. I've taken pirates and riffraff and turned them into loyal Marines and spacers. Give me a year and I could give you an entire army, all of them entirely loyal to you."

"What about ships?" Colonel Price asked.

Marius hesitated. When he did speak, his voice was reluctant. "Colonel, there is only so much that I can provide. I have limited access to shipyards, most of my vessels I've acquired are filling those slots undergoing refits. I would assume you have access to at least some vessels?"

The honesty threw Colonel Price off, a bit. He had expected an offer of vessels as a matter of course. "I have a few ships," Colonel Price admitted. A single squadron of destroyers, though he wouldn't tell Marius that. Ships and crews were in short supply, throughout human space. The wars with the Balor and the Chxor had destroyed thousands of vessels. Normally there were some available for purchase on the black market, but the two recent campaigns against pirates, led by the United Colonies, had destroyed dozens of those types of ships.

"I can't expand my forces quickly enough, you understand" Marius said. "Though I'm certain if I provide you with the manpower, you'll be able to acquire further vessels of your own."

That was true enough. With more manpower he could hijack vessels, much as Marius had. He'd also be able to leverage some of his other resources. *Speaking of which,* he thought. "Did your people find the stock of Illuari artifacts I told Admiral Collae about?"

"They did," Marius smiled, "Reese heard back from the team we sent there. Regardless of what you decide, here, I've already transferred payment for that information. And should you have additional locations, we will pay quite well for those, too."

Colonel Price didn't mind selling further locations. The Illuari artifacts discovered by Amalgamated Worlds ranged from non-functional to extremely hazardous. He'd overseen the burial of several facilities, where Amalgamated Worlds had used convict labor load up abandoned mine shafts in several star systems with dangerous artifacts and then sealed the entrances with concrete.

Most of the time, the work crews were sealed inside to maintain secrecy. Price knew about several other locations and while some had been looted over the past ninety years, many more had not. *Despite any shortages, enough money will buy weapons and ships,* he thought to himself.

And selling the locations to Marius bought goodwill, so in the remote event that he was successful, then Colonel Price at least would be on good standing with the man.

They continued down the corridor and then stopped at what he assumed was their destination. The chamber overlooked a broad valley, with several large projections rising from the surface. "What are we here for?" Colonel Price asked. He saw a cluster of guards around Alannis Giovanni, the young woman so clearly a prisoner. *This coming show will be as much for her sake as mine, then.* Colonel Price wondered if her estranged father had spent time showing her his mental conditioning system... and whether she'd be cocooned inside some of the equipment someday soon.

"A slight demonstration," Marius said. He brought up a display, showing a planet and a variety of ships in orbit. Colonel Price stepped forward and he recognized the identification symbols on the ships as Centauri. He looked back at the Lord Admiral, raising an eyebrow.

"This is the Volaterra system. It is live footage, transmitted from a civilian freighter that I've rigged up as a covert observation platform," Marius said. He toggled the controls and brought up a second system, "This is the Lavinium system. Both systems requested my support, both were taken by Centauri and their..." Marius trailed off and his lips twisted in a sneer, "their *imposter.* Since that time, President Spiridon of the Centauri Confederation has utilized his secret police and the threat of orbital bombardment to keep both systems in lock down. All Nova Roma military personnel have been disarmed and their ships interned."

"I believe both systems asked your son for help," Colonel Price said, gauging the other man's reaction. Unlike Reese's intense, almost obsessive attitude, Marius didn't seem unhinged, he seemed focused, dedicated, and calculating. Despite himself, Colonel Price found himself liking the man. Still, he wanted to see if he could get under his skin.

"They have," Marius said. "But Lucius doesn't want to risk going to war with the Centauri, not that I can blame him. The Balor and Chxor are both significant threats, as are the Shadow Lords." Marius gave a cold smile, "I am not so constrained. I have no nation to defend, no systems to garrison besides this one... and no one currently knows the location of my forces."

He adjusted the controls and centered them on the two fleets of ships. "As I told you before, the core power for this station isn't online and we're missing the ignition system. But the facility retains secondary power systems, enough to power lighting, support systems, and a few weapons."

As he said that, one of the pillars in the valley lit up. A solid column of baleful blue light jabbed upwards, driving through the night sky, lighting up the entire world for the span of a few seconds. It was a harsh, blue light, one that disturbed Colonel Price, it was seemingly unnatural, almost cobalt in color, and indescribably *alien.*

The display lit up with synchronized flashes of light. It took a moment for Colonel Price to make sense of what he saw. The same blue energy appeared, leaping from ship to ship, rupturing hulls and detonating power relays, even as it seemed to *consume* the vessels. The attacks took less than a minute, but at the end of it, the ships in both systems were gone. Moments later, a returning column of blue energy drove out of the sky above them and down into the valley, where it vanished. On the screens, there were no spreading clouds of debris, no wreckage at all. The ships were simply gone... as if they had never existed. Colonel Price looked over at Marius Giovanni, whose cool smile didn't so much as waver. "What you see is in real time, Colonel. I just destroyed two forces of warships over a hundred light years away."

"How?" Colonel Price demanded. He didn't see why Marius would fake such an attack. If this were totally fabricated, then Colonel Price would be able to confirm it within a few hours or days. If he'd somehow managed to sabotage those vessels, then this *could* be some kind of bluff, but again, Colonel Price didn't see the margin in it.

"The lighter defense weapons of this facility operate on similar principles to those of the ansible network: sending pulses of energy through shadow space. But while an ansible projects wide band in all directions, this is a highly focused beam, projected and amplified to a thousand times as powerful." Marius shrugged, "This is our first official use of the weapon, outside of a few tests. As you can see... it is very effective."

Colonel Price looked over at Alannis Giovanni. The Lieutenant had as shocked expression as Colonel Price wore. This wasn't just a powerful weapon, it changed the way that war could be fought. No ship would be safe. Entire fleets could be wiped out without risking a single vessel. It was worse than the Illuari Enforcer Station at Kapteyn's Star. That, at least, had some kind of range limitations.

"Now," Marius Giovanni smiled, "I think that concludes our tour, for the day, Colonel. Captain Leone please have someone show him and his people back to their quarters."

Colonel Price could only nod in response. This was something that he'd need to factor into his plans. It changed everything. *Perhaps,* he thought to himself, *perhaps I will have no choice but to ally myself with him.*

***

"You don't look happy, my daughter," Marius Giovanni said, looking over at Alannis.

Alannis still stared at the displays. Two more had popped up, both showing news feeds from the two star systems. On the one, a Centauri military officer was trying to give a response, but reporters were shouting questions at him. On the other, people shouted and threw stones at a line of riot police in the streets.

"The Centauri will blame Lucius for this," Alannis said.

"Of course," Marius smiled. "They'll need a target and they'll blame the United Colonies... but they were going to go to war with them in any case. Don't worry too much about your brother and his experiment in ruling, I'll take claim for the attack, soon enough."

Alannis, however, was thinking about the weapon, how it had worked, and what it had done. "The Enforcer Platforms, this is the same kind of weapon, isn't it? Only, it's more powerful..." When Chuni had fired the Enforcer Platform at Kopal Pesh, it had left debris, rubble, the remains of ships. This weapon had *consumed* the vessels.

Marius nodded, "Very good. You see now, why my priority wasn't the enforcer platform."

"What other capabilities does this station have?" Alannis demanded. "I can read you well enough that you aren't telling Colonel Price everything."

"Is that your intuition or your psychic abilities talking?" Marius asked, his smile going broad. Alannis looked away. She didn't want to think about that... she especially didn't want to think that it was something she shared with him. *He's not my father,* she told herself. Odds were that he was just another clone.

Either something of her distaste showed on her face or he was reading her thoughts. Marius's face went hard. "I'm not another of those imposters, as I've told you before." He stalked over to the displays and waved a hand, "Do you think any of them could have accomplished this?!"

His brown eyes had gone dark with anger and as he gestured sharply, some of his brown hair came loose. "I have told you, I am the real deal, I am Marius Octavius Giovanni. I am your father, Alannis, and you are my daughter."

Alannis didn't look right at him. She didn't want to meet his eyes. She pushed her unease and fear out of her mind and focused on her anger. She'd been kidnapped and threatened. Reese had tried to kidnap her son, on Marius's orders. The two of them had been behind the deaths of hundreds, probably thousands, of innocent men and women. She wrapped that anger around herself and then she met his eyes. "So, what, then?" Alannis demanded. "You're going to use this doomsday device of yours to blast anyone in your way? You're going to kill people until they surrender to you?"

Marius's intense expression didn't ease, "I'm not doing this for myself, Alannis. I'm doing this for all of humanity. The Balor started this war... this is just a continuation of a fight that has gone on for over a million years. Do you think it's coincidence that they've begun attacking humanity as we started developing colonies and expanding... or as we developed psychic abilities?"

Alannis's eyes narrowed. "I'm not sure what you're talking about."

He turned back to the display and brought up imagery of Balor drones. The lean, angular, almost insectile forms disturbed Alannis in a way she couldn't quite explain. They were alien, but they were sinister in appearance, every bit of them jagged and sharp. They looked like living weapons.

"You can sense it... I think the Balor are just a cog in the machine... I think they are weapons, designed and engineered by their creators for this war... and I think their masters, the Miniari, *won* the war a million years ago against the Illuari," Marius snapped. "They won that war just before the Illuari could achieve victory."

"So they defeated this station," Alannis waved a hand, "what makes you think they can't do it again?" As insane as it seemed, she couldn't really argue with the evidence he'd presented so far, the similarities between artifacts and Balor ships made sense. She didn't have a reason for why the Balor technology hadn't advanced, but that was a job for engineers and scientists. *Feliks and Rory would have a field day with these theories,* she thought to herself.

"The Miniari won a single battle, they hit the Illuari when they were most vulnerable... but they didn't finish them off... they weren't strong enough to do that." Marius adjusted the display and a moment later, it showed Halcyon Colony's single, rugged continent. "Halcyon's Zar base at Broken Jaw Mountain. It was a Zar Gamma base, one of their *kuruk* bases. Until recently, my best scientists didn't know why the mid to late war Zar facilities and colonies were all underground or hidden in remote moons or asteroids... the answer is the Illuari's Enforcer Platforms... technology developed from the Star Engine."

"They were hiding..." Alannis's eyes narrowed and despite herself she walked forward to stare at the screen. "You can't destroy what you can't see."

Marius nodded, "Exactly. I think the Illuari's enemies all adopted similar strategies, hiding their facilities, hiding their vessels. They built up their strength in secret and they launched an all-or-nothing attack on the Illuari at the crucial moment."

"And they won," Alannis said, "obviously."

"No," Marius grimaced, "or at least not as much as you would think." He shifted the display again and it showed the Star Engine once more. "You're right, Alannis, I *didn't* tell Colonel Price everything.... and I don't intend to do so. He's a material man, he believes only in the things he can see and touch."

Marius waved at Reese, and Alannis's ex-husband came forward, his blue eyes alight. "This wasn't a war of conquest or extermination... nor was it over access to the Star Engine... not directly, anyway."

Alannis tried to pull her gaze away from Reese, but she couldn't. His blue eyes were too intense, his expression a mix of rapture and excitement. "The Illuari didn't *care* about conquest. They realized why the creators of the Star Engine went to so much effort to come to another galaxy." He pointed out nodes within the schematic, "These sections of the station would have enabled the Illuari to ascend to a higher plane of existence, to *transform*. It would have allowed them to achieve an energy state... and their enemies, in their pettiness, wanted to steal it for themselves."

Alannis tore her gaze away from her ex-husband and looked at Marius, "Wait, what?"

"They'd have god-like abilities," Marius said, "near-immortality, abilities that defy imagination. The Illuari had *every* system online, prepared for the effort, their entire race assembled in a fleet, ready to be transformed. The process would have required an open tear between real and shadow space, which is where the Illuari assembled." Marius adjusted the display and a tear between real and shadow space appeared over the surface of the Star Engine, icons of ships assembling inside it. "It's a pocket, created within shadow space... all but inaccessible, so that their process would only effect those within."

"And that is when their enemies struck... the cowards," Reese sneered. "The Balor, or their masters the Miniari, hit the Illuari with a massive fleet to distract them, while the Zar launched a raid that ripped the key component from the Star Engine."

"Which trapped the vast majority of the Illuari in their pocket of shadow space," Marius said. "The handful that escaped before the tear closed were hunted to extinction. Some created a temporary refuge in the Ghornath's Sacred Stars, protecting their client species from the wrath of the Miniari and their allies for as long as they could... but they, too, were eventually found and destroyed."

"But the rest of them, *all* of them," Reese waved a hand through the air, "they're all there, trapped just outside of our reality, their ships, their weapons, and their infinite knowledge!"

"An entire race, a species that dominated our galaxy." He smiled, "Our potential allies."

Alannis looked between the two of them. The enormity of their plan left her feeling overwhelmed. "You want to resurrect a species from a million years ago? How do you know they'll be our allies?"

"We'll have saved them from their prison," Reese blurted, "we're already at war with their enemies, how could they *not* be our allies?! Think of how much we can learn from them! They could save our entire species... not just from the Balor and Miniari, but from ourselves! They could end our petty wars, bring an end to scarcity and poverty!"

Marius put a hand on Reese's shoulder to calm him, and then looked at Alannis, "We'll be well-positioned. It's not a plan without risks... but in the time of my exile, I scouted far beyond normal space. There are thousands of lifeless worlds where the Balor wiped out the extant species, there are Balor fleets to be found a *thousand* light years away. This is a war that we cannot win on our own. The relatively small forces that we have encountered so far are merely the garrison for this region. As we fight them, there will come more and more, until their entire might, all of their forces, bear down upon us. We need a powerful ally, one that can match them on their own terms, one that *surpassed* them. We need the Illuari."

Alannis shook her head, "We don't know what this species is capable of. Multiple races worked together to defeat them--"

"The Miniari and their Balor minions killed off the Zar almost as soon as the Illuari were defeated," Reese snapped, spittle flying from his lips. "Just as they hunted down all their other puppets in the war. They were jealous of the power of the Star Engine and they could not bear to let anyone else have it! This power is only safe in the hands of the Illuari!"

"Reese," Marius interjected.

Reese shook his head, "Sorry, Lord Admiral." He nodded at Alannis, "I get a little passionate about this. It's just the more that I learn, the more that I realize that we need their help."

"I entirely understand, Reese," Marius said gently. "Now, I'll walk Alannis back to her quarters. Why don't you see to the evaluation team at work on the weapons systems?"

"Of course, Lord Admiral," Reese nodded and turned back to the controls. Marius gestured to her, and Alannis followed him out of the control room.

"He's crazy, you know," Alannis said as the doors closed behind them.

"Oh, utterly mad," Marius nodded. "Passionate about a war that was lost a million years ago... mentally obsessed about Illuari technology... and you." He shook his head, "I'd understood that the mental process at the Temple of Light would have side effects, but if I'd realized how *focused* it would make him, I would probably have insisted it be someone else."

"You can't be serious about going through with this," Alannis demanded.

"It's one of many options," Marius said. "The weapons on this station will only be so effective. As you realized, the main flaw is that we cannot fire on a target that we can't see. The Balor forces are constantly on the move, we'd need scouts positioned who could relay target coordinates through ansible or psychic transmissions.... and even then, we are vulnerable here to a sustained, massive attack. They cannot destroy the Star Engine, not with the firepower of a hundred fleets... but they could knock out our modifications, damage our human components, and kill our fragile human bodies."

"What do you want from me, then?" Alannis demanded. "Why am I here?" She couldn't help a desperate note in her voice. She hated to admit it, even to herself, but the forced inactivity was as wearing on her as captivity.

"I want you to pick a side, my dear," Marius replied. They stepped into an elevator and she couldn't help but shy back from him in the small area. They'd left the guards behind, but she knew from personal experience that Marius would meet any physical attack with his psychic defenses. The last time she'd went against him, he'd held her helpless in the air, like an adult holding a child throwing a tantrum.

"You are loyal to your brother... which is admirable. I respect what Lucius has accomplished. I respect the people he has assembled and the cause to which he fights... but he cannot win this war," Marius said. "I am patient enough to give you time to realize that."

"And if I refuse to see things your way?" Alannis asked.

The elevator door opened and Marius led the way out without responding. He paused outside the door to her quarters, the guards out front watching her, their faces hidden behind their helmets. "I am a patient man, Alannis, and you're family, just as Lucius is family," Marius spoke in a calm voice. "Just as your son and

Lucius's daughter are family. More than that, you, like me, are a psychic, with incredible potential. I need those with such abilities more than anyone else. I want you to succeed, to work with me... but my patience is not without limits." Marius's voice went hard. "If you cannot accept my methods, if you --or your brother-- get in the way of my plans, I will do what I have to do."

He gave a slight wave and one of the guards opened the door, while the other three stood ready. Alannis stepped inside her suite, noting where Lizmadie stood, just having come out of the bathroom. Marius's next words chilled her to the bone, "If you force me to, I will use mental conditioning to make you see the truth... and if that doesn't work, I'll have to settle for your son."

He shut the door and left Alannis with that to mull over.

***

"Have you experimented with your abilities at all?" Lizmadie asked, after Alannis had finished relating what she'd seen and heard.

Alannis could only shake her head. Even thinking too much about her abilities gave her a headache. She felt more and more certain that her grandmother had put some kind of mental block on her abilities, probably to protect her. Though *why* she'd thought it would protect her, Alannis didn't really know. "It hurts, a lot, if I try."

"It could give us an edge," Lizmadie said, obliquely referencing their escape.

"It could backfire," Alannis growled. She didn't know if she'd be able to control her abilities. She might incapacitate herself or injure or kill Lizmadie.

"Well, I made some progress," Lizmadie said as she pointed at the chessboard. She'd arranged the pieces in an odd fashion. Only because she knew what it was supposed to look like did Alannis realize it was a representation of their bathroom... with the area around the toilet missing.

"Ah," Alannis smiled, "our new game. Should be interesting. Do you think we could play tonight?"

Lizmadie shook her head, "I think we'll need to wait longer than that. But we can look at things and see what mechanics we need to develop." They'd spent the past few days discussing a new "game" to play with the chess pieces. She wondered what their security thought of it... if they tried to follow it or if they saw through the escape plan and watched with amusement.

Stop that, Alannis told herself, *they're not all knowing or powerful, you can defeat them.* She *would* defeat them.

Alannis reached over to where the king stood and tilted it forward. Her smile grew broader. Even if she couldn't escape, she would do what she could to make her son safe from Marius. She thought about the pistol they had concealed. She didn't know if this Marius was really her father, but whether he was or not, she'd put a bullet in Marius's head before she let him get his hands on her son.

***

Chapter IX

August 29, 2410
Port Klast
Port Klast System

"So that's what I think is going on," Forrest finished explaining his theory about Alannis and Reese's survival and the encounter with Shadow Lord Invictus. Telling the entire story in detail had taken most of three days, off and on due to Captain King having to depart to see to his business here at Port Klast. *Whatever that business may be,* Forrest thought, *it sure does seem to take a lot of his time.*

"In my opinion, Invictus did you a favor," Tommy King said after a moment of thought. "No way that you could trust Annabelle Spiridon, not if she's anything like her father, anyway." He stroked the stubble on his chin, "The timing of all this, though. I got to wonder his game..."

Forrest wasn't sure that he followed. "Who, Shadow Lord Invictus?"

"No," Tommy King waved a dismissive hand. "Well, probably him in a way. I'm talking the way that peace summit fell apart, just as you showed up. I got to wonder if they didn't have some kind of tracker or something, see you coming, and decide to torpedo the whole thing. Then they invite you to Delta Pavonis, seize your ship, and say that the United Colonies was behind the whole thing. In fact..."

His comm unit began to buzz and Tommy King frowned. "I need to take this." He pulled out his datapad and it projected a hologram of Prince Alexander of Nova Roma. "Captain King, are you monitoring the news feeds?" Forrest recognized the young prince with shock. *What is he doing with a pirate like Tommy King?* The last that Forrest had heard, the young Prince led some kind of force in exile, made up of Nova Roman military personnel who didn't accept Lucius Giovanni as their new emperor. Prince Alexander's goals seemed to be to liberate human worlds still held by remnants of the Chxor Empire.

"Uh, no," Tommy King said, "I've been looking into the *Widowmaker* situation, what did I miss?"

"Someone just hit Volaterra and Lavinium, hard," Prince Alexander said. "The Centauri forces in both systems have been virtually wiped out. I'm prepping my forces to go there now. With how the Centauri are overextended, I think this is our opportunity."

"Your opportunity?" Forrest asked, realizing only a moment later that he should have kept his mouth shut.

Tommy King looked up and grinned. "Yes, Lieutenant Commander. As a part of my duties for Emperor Giovanni, I'm assisting Prince Alexander in preparing the secret liberation of the Volaterra and Lavinium systems... which presents something of an issue as far as having a rogue United Colonies officer running around."

The pirate looked back down at Prince Alexander, "Lieutenant Commander Perkins thinks that Princess Giovanni and your sister might both still be alive."

"What?!" Prince Alexander demanded.

"He's got... well, *had* a witness that gives him a bit of weight. I think you should come over and hear this yourself," Tommy King said.

"With transit time," Prince Alexander snapped, "if I don't leave within the next hour, we may miss our window."

"I'm aware," Tommy King said. "But this involves your family, so..."

"I'll be there in a few minutes," Prince Alexander said.

* * *

"So this Ricky One-Eye is the only witness?" Prince Alexander asked a few minutes later. He looked at Tommy King, "Is he a trustworthy source?"

Tommy King snorted, "Just because I *was* a pirate, you assume I know every piece of lowlife scum in the universe?" As Prince Alexander scowled at him, he smirked, "Okay, I do know him --by reputation only, I might add-- and he's about as untrustworthy as they come. He'd sell his own mother into slavery and lie about it to her while doing it... but this seems a little too crafty for someone like him to pull off." He shook his head, "There's no margin in it for him, either. The Golgotha system? Half of those who heard of it think it's just a myth, the other half wouldn't want to go there because it's cursed."

"So Reese may be alive..." Prince Alexander mused. His expression went hard. "If he is and my sister isn't... I will not be happy."

"My Lord," Forrest spoke, "While I think that Marius and Reese would both be inclined to preserve the life of Alannis, I don't know for *certain* that--"

The younger man raised a hand to forestall him. "I know more than you might realize about the relationship between Reese and Alannis. I also know that Marius-- if this *is* the real Marius-- would see my sister as a potential bargaining piece. She'd be valuable as a hostage or for him to twist with his mental conditioning program. So there is a chance that she's alive."

"The problem is the timing. If I *knew* for certain, I'd not hesitate to launch my ships to Golgotha," Prince Alexander said.

Tommy King shook his head, "Against the lives of everyone in the Volaterra and Lavinium systems?" He managed to say it in a way that sounded respectful, which surprised Forrest. He would not have expected the pirate to be so tactful.

"That being the problem," Prince Alexander said. "And also as the source of my worry about the timing. If Marius Giovanni is behind the destruction of the Centauri vessels there, then this information would be just the kind of thing he'd leak to get both Emperor Lucius Giovanni and myself headed in the wrong direction."

"Well, sir," Forrest said, "I don't have an answer for you."

"I do," Tommy King said. "We need to conduct the attack on the Volaterra and Lavinium systems. The Lieutenant Commander here has plenty of fire, let him play prince charming and rescue the princesses from the tower."

Prince Alexander shook his head, staring at Tommy King as if he'd lost his mind, "Out of the question. If Alannis and Lizmadie are captive there and you tip our hand, then Marius may take action. Either he could evacuate and escape *again* or he could use them as hostages. You could directly endanger their lives. I can't allow you to go to Golgotha, not without sufficient forces to defeat him and seize his base."

Tommy King's eyes narrowed, but he didn't interrupt.

Forrest gritted his teeth. It seemed that even when someone believed him, they didn't want to take action. "My Lord," Forrest said, as politely as he could manage, "the longer that Reese and Marius have them, the more likely it is that they'd do something permanent to them, either mental conditioning like those poor Centauri bastards or even injuring or killing them if they attempt an escape on their own."

"In all likelihood, Lieutenant Commander," Prince Alexander said, his voice stern, "either that has already happened or it *won't* happen. If they're alive, they've been prisoner for over six months now. I cannot allow you to potentially give Marius Giovanni warning that we know his location. The man is extremely dangerous and if we give him the opportunity, he *will* escape. No, I forbid you to go."

Forrest stood and glared at the shorter man, "With all due respect, *sir*, I am not under your chain of command. And, I might remind you, I *hijacked* this vessel. What makes you think you can stop me?" He couldn't help a sneer at that... he'd come too far to let anyone stop him now, especially from someone so far outside his chain of command. *He's in league with a pirate and he's got a bunch of Nova Roma personnel who refuse to recognize Emperor Lucius Giovanni and the United Colonies as a legitimate authority.*

Tommy King snorted in laughter. "I think he's got you there. We *are* at Port Klast, and as long as his debts are paid, he's free to go." Forrest looked at King in surprise, he hadn't expected any kind of support.

"You're covering his docking fees, right?" Prince Alexander demanded. "Simply say that you won't if he doesn't cooperate!"

"That's not really how this all works, I'm afraid," Tommy King grinned. "Once I said I'd cover him, I'm in for it, under verbal contract. And even if I *could* go back on that, they'd impound and auction this ship. Do you *really* want this stealthy little vessel going to the highest bidder, especially with the data for Golgotha already programmed into their navigational computer?"

Prince Alexander scowled. He straightened his black Nova Roma Fleet uniform. "You *can't* go, Lieutenant Commander. You'll put millions at risk. We still don't know *how* the ships at Volaterra and Lavinium were destroyed. If this is some new weapon... if Marius Giovanni realizes that we know his location..."

"I'm in the stealthiest vessel I could get my hands on," Forrest said. "I'm going there and I'm going to rescue Alannis... and Princess Lizmadie, if she's there too."

"Well," Prince Alexander said, his voice and face stiff with anger, "I suppose we have nothing left to speak about." He stalked off the bridge without another word.

"You know," Tommy King drawled, "if you'd played your cards right, you might have got him to front you crew, supplies, even some munitions. Instead I think you just pissed him off." As Forrest looked over at him in surprise, the former pirate shook his head, "Seems you have a knack for that. You know, if you're dating a noblewoman, you might want to work on your diplomacy... just a smidge." He held up his finger and thumb, pinched together.

"In any case," Tommy King stood up, "I've got to prepare my own force."

"You won't offer me any help?" Forrest asked in surprise.

The amusement drained from Tommy King's face. "Boy, let me tell you this. The last time I looked into alien crap, I lost everything I cared about... *again.* No, I might have covered your tab at the bar, but it's up to you to do what you need to do." There was an echo of pain, still raw and fresh, in the pirate's voice.

"Good luck to you," Tommy King said as he headed for the hatch.

***

"What have we got?" Forrest asked a few minutes later.

"I went down the inventory and everyone's turned out their pockets, skipper, but not much," Staff Sergeant Witzke said. The Marine had taken over most of the logistics while Forrest was busy with their guests. "If we all chip in, we *might* be able to afford some of the parts we need, but no way will it cover hiring any crew, at least, not any crew we could trust. Munitions are there to be bought, some of it stuff I never heard of... but again, we can't afford any of it."

Forrest sighed. He looked over at Rory and Feliks, who had left their self-declared lab only under protest. Both of them were still poring over the stolen data. "Can you two make repairs if we get the parts?"

"What?" Rory looked up from his datapad. "Repairs? Yes, yes... did you know they have just fascinating data on here. There's coordinates for over a dozen as-yet-unexplored alien facilities! One of them may be a Zar base even bigger than the one at Halcyon!"

"Fantastic," Forrest said dryly, "Unfortunately, that doesn't matter, it's not like we could sell..." He trailed off, staring at the scientist. Without saying another word, Forrest turned to his console and pulled up a link to the customs administrator. "I'd like to post an item for sale."

"Oh?" the weasel-faced man asked. "Just one item?"

"Yes," Forrest smiled, his gaunt face lighting up, "It's the entirety of Hugo Base's data network, one package, every file that Amalgamated Worlds had in their archive. I'd like you to enter that into the market for as open for bids."

***

Well into the next morning, Petty Officer Godbey looked up from his console, his eyes bloodshot from the sleepless night. "Skipper, I'm not sure I what to do... this, this is just insane."

"You *can't* sell this information," Rory said for what had to be the hundredth time.

"This offer comes with a yacht," Feliks said. "And the crew. It makes special mention that the entire crew is female and that they are certified disease-free."

"I'm not going to..." Rory trailed off as Feliks held up his datapad. "There's no way those are real!" Rory protested. "Those women have to be surgically augmented, otherwise they're defying the laws of physics!"

"Stay focused, please," Forrest said, even as scrolled through a dozen more offers that had appeared in the time they'd spoken. Every major dealer in Port Klast had already made their offers, it seemed. Now they were receiving offers sent through the ansible network as agents forwarded the information to the wealthy and powerful throughout human space.

He would have taken the first offer, but then he'd realized that he might be able to leverage together some kind of real rescue force. With a couple of the most recent offers, he could afford to hire an entire mercenary fleet.

"This is like selling the Library of Alexandria!" Rory protested again. "You can't sell a library! This information should be researched. Feliks and I have already found dozens of plans and schematics that might be useful, the locations of alien ruins and facilities..."

"Skipper, there's a transmission from Port Klast Security," Petty Officer Godbey said.

"Put it through," Forrest said.

"Attention *Widowmaker*, prepare to receive a VIP. A PKS team will secure your vessel prior to arrival," a voice spoke.

"What..."

"Skipper, there's a platoon of armed men at the hatch," Corporal Wandry said. "They said they're here to secure the ship."

Port Klast *might* be trying some kind of double-cross and hijacking, but Forrest didn't think they'd violate their vaunted neutrality, not even for such a lucrative prize. "Let them aboard."

The team swept through the ship, four of them moving aboard the bridge within under a minute. Staff Sergeant Witzke surrendered his pistol with a scowl, and the four men moved to the sides of the bridge. A moment later, a man stepped in. He wore a tailored suit, and he had silver in his black hair and well-trimmed beard. His charcoal-colored suit was impeccible, almost like a second skin. His blood-red tie contrasted with his pale, blue eyes. Without asking, he moved to take the command chair and then waved at Forrest's people to resume their seats. The arrogance should have rubbed Forrest the wrong way, but it was as if the man simply assumed the most authoritative position as a matter of course.

"Lieutenant Commander Perkins," the man said, "I'm Thomas Kaid."

Forrest's eyes went wide, "Uh, good to meet you, sir." He hadn't expected to draw the attention of the ruler of the planet.

"You've presented my planetary administrators with a series of conundrums," Thomas Kaid said holding up one hand, as if weighing something. "On the one hand, you violated our no-fly zone and your ship possesses interesting, possibly unique, stealth systems that could pose a danger to my defenses." He held up his other hand, "On the other, you didn't do it on purpose and by all appearances, you're a catspaw to Shadow Lord Invictus, who likes to *test* me at times."

"That was an easy enough solution. Slap you with a fine that you couldn't pay, seize your vessel, and send appropriate signals to those who might otherwise take it into their heads to launch some kind of surprise attack on my pleasant world." Forrest's stomach sank at Kaid's words. "That was the plan that my former security administrator went with. He didn't expect Tommy King to bail you out, which I could excuse. His inspection team didn't think to check for something like your data archive, which I could not excuse... especially when information is far more valuable than material goods." Thomas Kaid gave a narrow smile, "He has since been relieved."

Forrest's stomach sank a bit more.

"It's good to stir things up a bit, especially as people become complacent or ambitious," Thomas Kaid settled back into the command chair. He tapped at a couple of the controls that adjusted its comfort and then frowned and stood, "Poor design. The Centauri manufacturers always go for ostentatious appearance and rarely achieve true luxury." Thomas Kaid dusted his hands. "My people could do some fantastic upgrades to this vessel."

He stroked his beard as he considered the situation. "Now, then, Forrest Perkins, I'm a pragmatic man. You have offered for sale something that I want." Thomas Kaid leaned forward and cocked an eyebrow, waiting.

"The data archive?" Forrest asked.

"More precisely, I want one file in your archive, but I want to buy all of it to keep what I took private from anyone else," Thomas Kaid replied. "This opportunity is the kind of thing I've waited for for... well, quite some time."

"What will you do with the rest of it?" Rory demanded. The portly scientist stood, "There's important files, things that would allow humanity to learn so much--"

"Humanity had a chance to do that already," Thomas Kaid interrupted. "I want my single file. The rest will remain in storage, where it can't cause any further damage."

"Any further damage?" Forrest asked.

Thomas Kaid reached over and touched a control. A moment later, a news feed appeared on the display. "...riots began on Altair IV after Technocrat Loftis's suicide note became public. In the note, he confessed to his role in the Altairian Massacre, an apparently false-flag terrorist attack conducted by Amalgamated Worlds..."

The footage changed over to a different news feed. "...General Hian mobilized the Third Mobile Infantry Brigade and seized the capital only hours ago, liberating it from the corrupt politicians who have stolen from the people of Xiang Lung for too long. He has immediately instituted a full seizure of all media and communications outlets to prevent the spread of their propaganda..."

Thomas Kaid cut off the news feeds, leaving the bridge deathly quiet. "There's a dozen more I could show you. Everyone is terrified that their dirty little secrets are going to come to light. If they go to me, they'll know that they'll be safe." He smiled, "Well, *mostly* safe. There's the one file I care about, after all." He waved at the screen, "It saves us any more of this... and I'll resupply your ship and screen personnel so that you can recruit a loyal and capable crew for your mission, as well as sufficient recompense for your efforts to recover this data."

"Recompense?" Rory sputtered. "This is irreplaceable data! There's dozens of alien facilities, weapons designs, and..." he trailed off as his datapad pinged. He looked down at it for a long moment, "Oh, my, that's a *lot* of money."

Feliks looked at his datapad, "This would fund our research for a decade, maybe more..."

"I'll match that for each of you," Thomas Kaid said. "And I'd consider it a bargain, to be honest. I like stability, gentlemen, and this auction presents instability." He held up a hand, "I've taken the liberty of marking your auction closed and as soon as I leave here, I will make a press conference confirming that I purchased the data archive and intend to keep its secrets secure."

"Hugo Base sold its data before, why is this any different..." Staff Sergeant Witzke trailed off as Thomas Kaid's cold gaze fell on her, "..sir."

"Hugo Base's personnel edited the data access and limited access to files dependent upon who paid them and who wanted to access their files," Thomas Kaid replied. "Among the files, I'm sure you'd find proof that many former Amalgamated Worlds officers paid monthly or yearly to keep their atrocities hidden. It was something of an open secret... which is one reason I couldn't access the information I needed."

"What if I don't want to sell it to you?" Forrest asked quietly.

"You're on my planet, Mister Perkins," Thomas Kaid said. "Which means quite a bit and at the same time... quite little." He held up his hands, "You could sell that data to someone else for many fortunes... but you won't find anyone here willing to sell so much as a used tissue to you if I express my displeasure. You are paid up, thanks to Tommy King, so you can depart at your leisure... but as soon as you leave our neutral zone you would be set upon by anyone seeking to curry favor with me. You would be marked for death... because the file that I want is contains information that I have sought for a *very* long time."

Forrest swallowed. "You know what we plan to do?"

Thomas Kaid waved a hand, "Some kind of suicidal rescue mission. I don't really care. So long as you give me what I want, I will guarantee that you'll have every resource that can help."

"Well," Forrest said, "I guess we've found our buyer."

***

Chapter X

September 6, 2410
Port Klast
Port Klast system

"Skipper," Staff Sergeant Witzke said. "I've cued up a list of all the munitions for the launch cells and the rest of the parts we need, rush delivery, just need your authorization."

"Yep," Forrest brought up the list on his datapad. He scrolled down it for a bit and then signed off at the bottom. With the money and blessing of Thomas Kaid, it felt like everything was moving faster than he could keep up. Petty Officer Godbey had reported that there were already over two hundred prospective crew waiting to be interviewed. Forrest didn't know how he was going to select the best people for the job in time.

"Skipper," Petty Officer Godbey said. "I've got Prince Alexander of Nova Roma on the net, he says he'd like to talk with you."

Forrest scowled. He really didn't want to have to listen to the nobleman complain. Maybe it was the Saragossan in him, but he didn't much like the prince. *Still, perhaps I shouldn't piss him off more than necessary.*

"My Lord," Forrest said as the Prince's image came up on the screen, "what can I do for you?"

Prince Alexander gave him a grim smile, "Well, Lieutenant Commander, other than waiting for the right time to launch a full attack on the Golgotha system, you can allow me to help you."

"Oh?" Forrest asked.

"Rather than hire a bunch of mercenaries or pirates who might well bungle things, let me provide you with a volunteer crew from my forces. I have a crack platoon of Marines with powered armor and just over fifty volunteers to man your vessel to retrieve my sister as well as Princess Alannis Giovanni." As the Prince spoke, he transferred a record to the *Widowmaker*'s network. Forrest gave a low whistle as he saw the records, and military decorations, on many of the personnel. "You're giving me some very skilled people, my Lord."

"They stepped forward with the offer," Prince Alexander replied. "The platoon used to be Princess Lizmadie's security platoon, before she joined the United Colonies Marine Corps. The other volunteers are among some of my forces' best people." He frowned a bit, "And before you think this is some kind of attempt to take over your ship... I give you my oath that these people will do their best to help your mission succeed."

Forrest nodded, "Very well, my Lord. I'll accept the offer of help."

"Excellent," Prince Alexander gave a relieved smile. "They're already on their way over. And just so you know, the proper form of address is *your Highness.*" He cut the connection before Forrest could respond.

"Nova Romans," Forrest shrugged.

Godbey looked over, "Sir, *I'm* from Nova Roma."

"Y'all are a little touchy on titles," Forrest said with a lax wave.

"He's the *Prince*," Petty Officer Godbey said staring at Forrest uneasily. "Skipper, you wouldn't call Emperor Lucius Giovanni the wrong thing, would you?"

Forrest thought about that for a moment. He'd been irreverent before meeting Lucius Giovanni, but after serving with him.... he pursed his lips, "No, I suppose I wouldn't."

***

Forrest stared in disbelief at the grizzled, gray-haired officer. "Sir... you're a Captain, and you want to serve as my XO? That will be a reduction in rank to Lieutenant, you know."

The older officer shrugged, "It's the slot that was open. My last command was over ten years ago, Lieutenant Commander. I've been serving as Admiral Mund's chief of staff." He gave a painful smile, "Not a lot of ships to serve aboard anymore."

Forrest didn't know much about how Prince Alexander's all-volunteer force operated. He knew that most of his forces were made up of former Nova Roma Imperial Fleet officers and senior NCO's, many of whom had lost their families during the war with the Chxor Empire.

Officially, they were a fully independent force. They were made up of Nova Roma Fleet vessels that had survived the war and their chain of command lay outside of the United Colonies Fleet. Their supplies, manpower, and munitions all came from donations and pre-war stockpiles that Prince Alexander's family had stashed. Forrest wondered about that, though. "Why not serve in the United Colonies Fleet?"

Captain Malatesta's face went hard, "I swore my oath to Emperor Romulus III and to the Nova Roma Empire. I'm a loyal servant to Nova Roma and to Emp... that is, to Prince Alexander."

Not a fan of Emperor Lucius Giovanni, then. Hopefully that animosity didn't translate to Alannis. If it did, then Forrest was going to have a problem with the man.

"Alright," Forrest said, "welcome aboard... Lieutenant Malatesta."

He'd already met with the new tactical officer and engineer officer. The thing that had surprised Forrest was the general age of all those who came aboard. Most of them were old, Forrest's age or older. All of them had received life extension therapies, so many of them didn't *look* old, but their records held decades of experience. They moved around the ship with a familiarity born of more time spent in space than anywhere else. They might not know the specific layout, but they'd been aboard so many vessels that they figured things out quickly enough.

"We'll depart in another thirty minutes, do you have any baggage to bring aboard?"

Lieutenant Malatesta shook his head, "No, Lieutenant Commander, just what I have with me." The man had a single satchel that looked to hold a few changes of uniform and his ship suit. *Apparently he likes to travel light.*

"After we depart, I'd like your input on drills and rehearsals. It seems like we've got a lot of experienced personnel, we just need to get everyone used to the ship and working together," Forrest said. "Anything else for me, XO?"

The olive-skinned officer hesitated. When he spoke, his voice was harsh, "Just so you know, Lieutenant Commander, I commanded a vessel that took part in the attack on Saragossa." He shrugged, "I can't say I'm proud of what we did there, but it was my duty and I did it."

Forrest didn't reply for a long moment. The attack had crippled his homeworld's infrastructure and left the world open to

Chxor invasion. It had come at a time when war with the Chxor Empire seemed inevitable... and the Nova Roma Empire had betrayed an ally in order to turn the focus of their invasion.

Forrest understood the strategic implications... but he'd lost his wife and newborn daughter in the fall of the planet. While the Nova Romans hadn't directly killed them, they'd died in the confusion, lost in the chaos as the planet's cities had starved and the Chxor Empire had invaded.

It was an old wound, but that didn't mean that Forrest felt good about the reminder.

"Lieutenant Malatesta," Forrest said, "I have served under and with other former Nova Roma officers. So long as you don't hold *my* loyalty to Emperor Lucius Giovanni against me, I won't hold your service against my homeworld against you."

Malatesta straightened his shoulders, "That works for me... sir."

"Excellent," Forrest replied. "Go get yourself settled."

***

"So, sir," Lieutenant Malatesta said, "I think that, given this vessel's capabilities, we should definitely alter some of our rehearsals and doctrine." The XO brought up a diagram, showing the various standard tactics for fighting a destroyer. "Most of them are focused on evasion and stealth... but I think we can completely alter combat parameters."

The *Widowmaker* had just broken orbit and Forrest had queued up the shadow space jump to Golgotha. He was impressed by what the ship's new XO had put together in only a few minutes.

"Go on," Forrest nodded.

"I served aboard one of the old Pugil-class frigates," Lieutenant Malatesta said. "We tried to use what we'd labeled a 'fire and relocate' doctrine, leading up to the surprise attack on Ghornath Prime."

Boy, Forrest thought, *the number of surprise attacks on allies this guy's been on must make him a real hit at formal functions with foreign dignitaries.*

"It didn't work very well, our frigates were small, but their stealth systems weren't up to it and they stocked so few munitions that we were forced to engage with our primary batteries, which then put off so much heat and other emissions that the Ghornath located and destroyed most of our frigates after our second volley."

Forrest nodded. He hadn't much studied the Nova Roma Empire's attack on Ghornath Prime. It wasn't exactly encouraged reading, even among the Nova Romans. The little he knew about it, the Nova Roma Empire had sent in a mix of volunteer and drafted crews to attack their allies by surprise.

"In any case, given this vessel's advanced stealth systems, I think it would work very well with an adapted effort. The launch cells allow us to keep stealth parameters and to launch several separate missile attacks. The primary weapon system has a far better cooling and emission profile, we can probably fire it multiple times before it becomes an issue."

Forrest nodded as he considered it. Standard destroyer doctrine for stealth operations was to fire once, and then adjust course slightly to clear the expected search region. Most often there was a trade-off between putting distance between the expected and actual vector change, running the risk of higher emissions to get a sharper change and to make it harder for an enemy ship or ships to box them in and localize them.

"I think we could adopt a fast course alteration," Lieutenant Malatesta said. "Crank up the acceleration, maybe even give the enemy an initial burst of emissions so think they know exactly where we are... but in actuality we're doing a seriously radical shift in course."

Forrest rubbed his chin in thought. "That's extremely risky."

"We won't be able to fool them more than once or twice," Lieutenant Malatesta nodded, "but when we do, they'll be looking for us in entirely the wrong location. If we could back that with the use of emissions from one of the decoy probes your people acquired at Port Klast..."

Forrest remembered seeing the order. He personally had doubts about a probe-sized decoy, but he hadn't had time to examine the thing's parameters.

"Okay," Forrest said. "We'll try it." He glanced at where their new tactical officer was at work, going over data on the ship's weapon systems. Forrest felt a grin grow on his face. "Lieutenant Malatesta can command the opposition. You have the con for the exercise. We'll see how it works on someone who's unsuspecting."

They had just over nine days in shadow space before they reached Golgotha. They'd have some time to drill and prepare for a fight, but Forrest wasn't under any misconceptions. This was a raid, the sole purpose to locate Alannis Giovanni and Lizmadie Doko and to rescue them. If they had to fight, then it had better be as they successfully fled the system.

Nine days, Alannis, just hold out for nine more days...

As he thought that, they jumped to shadow space.

***

Chapter XI

September 15, 2410
Idarian Station, 804E31 system
Unclaimed Space

"Evasive pattern gamma!" Captain Daniel Beeson snapped as the *Constellation* shuddered. The missile's warhead had detonated well clear of their defense screens, but still close enough to rattle the entire vessel.

The Centauri force had opened fire less than a minute after Task Force Hunter's arrival near Idarian Station. Admiral Kaminsk had ordered the task force to reverse course and extend the range. So far the long range and their defenses had prevented any direct missile hits, though both of the battlecruisers had taken damage from near-misses. Daniel hated to take fire without responding in kind.

"Orders from the flag, sir," Lieutenant Meyers reported, "we're switching vector to five five seven."

Daniels eyes went wide at that, but he queued up the maneuver change and authorized it immediately. That course change altered their plan significantly: it brought them right into the teeth of the advancing military force.

"Target priorities updating, sir," Lieutenant Commander Miller reported. "Sir, Admiral Kaminsky has authorized us to engage with our Mark V's. We are to engage in synch with the rest of the task force."

Daniel had a brief moment of indecision. They were about to fire upon the Centauri Confederation. This wasn't a mutinous force, they were ships of the Centauri Confederation. This would be an act war.

They fired first, Daniel thought. "Bring up attack pattern three," he said. They'd synchronize their missile launches with the rest of the task force. The *Constellation*'s missile tubes could fire more rapidly, but Admiral Kaminsky would want them to fire in sequence with the other ships to overwhelm the Centauri ship's defenses.

"Alter course, *mark*," Daniel snapped. The Constellation whipped around, matching the motion of the rest of the squadron and they began to decelerate. The distance between them and the Centauri force dropped rapidly.

"This is Admiral Boris Kaminsky, United Colonies Fleet, Commander of Task Force Hunter," Admiral Kaminsky said, his transmission going across on all bands. "You have engaged us unprovoked. I give you one final opportunity to stand down and then I will engage."

Daniel watched as the distance dropped. Lieutenant Commander Miller had acquired firing solutions on their targets. Their first one was a Centauri cruiser, whose stealth systems had gone online. *Those will make hits hard at this range.*

The Centauri vessels alternated their use of active sensors, Daniel noted, switching back and forth between the other ships in their force in an effort to make target lock difficult. Performance-wise, their missiles were almost identical, with similar accelerations, sensors, and warhead yields. *Assuming those intelligence estimates are right and they don't have any surprises for us...*

***

Counter Admiral Vasili Blokhin scowled as the United Colonies force turned around and began to decelerate. He really didn't want to fight them. Captain Kruchev of the *Antonov* had opened fire without orders when the other force had appeared out of shadow space.

But with the recent losses at Volaterra and Lavinium, and the terrible losses at Kapteyn's Star, Vasili knew that if he backed down, his head would roll as a result.

In another time, that might have been figurative, but Counter Admiral Vasili Blokhin had read the dispatches from his uncle. There was enough bad news that President Spiridon would want a scapegoat, someone he could throw to the wolves. If Counter Admiral Vasili Blokhin stood down it would look nearly as bad as a retreat and would bring disgrace to the Centauri Fleet, another failure after a string of defeats.

He listened to Admiral Kaminsky's request to surrender and he scowled. He recognized the name, the former Centauri officer had been discussed in Centauri media. *His force is smaller than my own,* Vasili thought to himself. *I can defeat him, it will be a costly victory, but I will win.*

The only uncertainty that he felt was that normally his squadron operated independently, the ships performing policing actions and interceptions. They had some experience fighting the Separatists, but nothing like a full-on engagement.

His lips drew back in a sneer, though. "Prepare for close range engagement. Squadron, prepare to volley remaining missiles just before we hit maximum energy engagement range." The United Colonies might have fought dirt farmers like the Colonial Republic or incompetents like the Chxor, but they hadn't faced skilled combatants. Besides, everyone knew that the United Colonies must have vastly inflated the numbers and size of Chxor vessels in their war with the Chxor Empire.

Counter Admiral Vasili Blokhin controlled a squadron of the newest Zhukov-class cruisers, with advanced stealth systems, supported by two squadrons of Khalakhin Gol-class hunter-killers. He'd pit them against any equivalent force... and he had the edge in numbers, if not mass. The two enemy battlecruisers would be tough prospects, but they were old, Amalgamated Worlds built Nagyr-class vessels. The technology hadn't improved *much*, but those differences would be important. Besides, a third-rate nation like the United Colonies couldn't possibly maintain such ships. They would be lucky to have them at fifty percent readiness.

Counter Admiral Vasili Blokhin's ships all mounted the newest pulse fusion energy weapons, a generation advanced from Amalgamated Worlds' directed fusion weapons. Those should penetrate cruisers and even battlecruisers defense screens, a pulsing attack designed to disrupt the ionized gasses of the defense screens and then penetrate the gap.

With his stealth systems and as long as his ships operated their weapons and and sensors in sequential patterns, the enemy shouldn't even have any good targeting solutions. "Disperse to formation Victor and prepare to engage targets on my command." The dispersed formation should allow each vessel to freely maneuver and gain the full use of their stealth and countermeasure systems.

With his communications, he would be able to control the entire squadron's fire, preventing any wasted shots as the two forces swept towards one another.

Counter Admiral Blokhin settled back into his command chair and he watched as they closed the distance. He already pictured his award ceremony for this victory.

***

"They're dispersing?" Daniel asked incredulously.

"Yes, sir, all indications are that they're giving their individual ships room to maneuver," Lieutenant Commander Miller reported.

"Damn," Daniel said, "I wish we had a few squadrons of fighters..." Dispersed ships were more vulnerable to large missile salvos and fighter-bomber strikes. A dozen Harrassers would be able to follow up the initial salvo and kill any crippled ships.

He watched the chrono and his sensors as the time to strike dropped. Admiral Kaminsky had already coordinated targets and priorities, all that remained was for the vessels of Task Force Hunter to launch in sequence. *Right about...* "Engage!"

The three Kriss-class destroyers didn't mount any missile ordinance, they were designed around strong, mid-range energy batteries, but the rest of the formation made up for that lack. The *Constellation* launched only four of the Mark V ship-killer missiles, as did her sister ship, the *Champion*. The two Nagyr-class battlecruisers, *Roosevelt Forest* and *Black Hills*, both launched four each, while the *Lancer* and *Gallant* each volleyed ten missiles. The two Archer-class destroyers, designed around large external missile racks, each volleyed forty Mark V shipkiller missiles in a single salvo.

The total missile count was one hundred and sixteen Mark V missiles. Daniel had to hide a slight smile as the complicated rhythm of the Centauri formation staggered for just a moment in response. *No way had they expected to see that kind of launch.*

***

"Orders, sir?" Counter Admiral Blokhin's flag officer asked.

The squadron commander's lips pinched. "Launch counter-missiles. Maintain dispersion." It was too late to close formation, and even if he'd ordered it, his ship commanders hadn't rehearsed close-quarters, overlapping fields of fire. No one fired such absurdly large volleys of missiles, not with the ridiculous expense involved.

Still apparently the enemy seemed willing to bankrupt their nation to generate a few extra casualties.

At least the enemy shouldn't have good locks on the ships of his squadron. Their accuracy would likely be terrible due to his advanced stealth systems.

He watched as the interceptor missiles fired, the individual ships picking targets among the swarm headed their way. His frown deepened as he saw the poor synchronization, with large numbers of missiles avoiding interception within the overall salvo.

Still, of the one hundred and sixteen missiles launched, almost a third of them died to the interceptor missiles. And at least it wasn't as if the enemy force could sustain such a salvo...

"Second launch, sir," his flag officer reported. Vasili Blokhin bit back a curse as he saw the second flight of missiles. This one was smaller in number, but it was still more than he'd hoped. "Launch additional interceptor missiles," the Counter Admiral said. Surely the enemy would be low on such munitions, he hoped. This would empty the Centauri force's external racks. Most of his cruisers had already fired their five missiles per tube of capital missiles, which meant they had only one volley left. His hunter-killers had already fired their missile cells. *I haven't killed any of them, yet.*

The question now was whether he should hold his fire on his remaining missiles or volley them. If he fired them now, at long range, he'd score fewer hits. Neither force had probes out, the situation had been too kinetic to launch and position them.

"Hold our return fire," Counter Admiral Vasili Blokhin said. "Maintain engagement parameters."

***

The closing force of Centauri ships went into evasive maneuvers and opened fire with their point defense weapons. Daniel's eyebrows went up as he saw the rapid-fire pulse lasers. He'd expected interceptor fire more like what he'd seen at Kapteyn's Star. Yet the enemy squadron was dispersed, each vessel defending only itself... and the entire massive flight of missiles had been focused on only eight ships.

The vast majority of missiles *couldn't* see the enemy cruisers under their stealth systems, but they were guided in by Task Force

Hunter's tactical officers. The missile salvo detonated in and around the eight cruisers of Counter Admiral Blokhin's squadron and the chain of antimatter detonations blurred together so quickly that they temporarily lost tracking on the entire enemy formation.

Eight cruisers and sixteen destroyers flew into the missile salvo. As the detonations cleared, only fourteen enemy destroyers emerged from the chain of explosions. Three destroyers broke course immediately, headed on an escape vector that would take them clear of the fight, but the other eleven continued on their course, either unable to comprehend what had happened or just too stubborn to accept it.

"Target priority updated," Lieutenant Commander Miller said, his voice calm despite the deaths of eight cruisers in less than fifteen seconds. "Coordinating second salvo."

The enemy destroyers were harder targets. They were smaller, more nimble, and their stealth systems seemed to be more effective. They also faced a smaller flight, only thirty-two missiles, fired with staged acceleration so that two volleys of sixteen missiles combined into a single strike.

Still, they were far more fragile targets and as the salvo went in, focused on the lead eight vessels, Daniel said a silent prayer for the spacers who were about to die.

When the detonations cleared, five of the enemy destroyers remained. At this point, they were too close to get clear of any follow on missile salvos and all five began to broadcast their surrender.

"Stand down from combat operations," Daniel said. "Prepare to launch search and rescue operations with our shuttles." Not that he expected to find many survivors. The enemy destroyers were too small, the hundred megaton antimatter warheads would have killed everyone aboard.

There *might* be survivors from the wreckage of the Centauri cruisers, but Daniel wasn't willing to bet any money on it. The spreading clouds of debris suggested that each of the ships had taken one or more direct hits.

"Message from Admiral Kaminsky, Captain," Lieutenant Meyers reported. "He sends his complements to the Task Force for a job well done."

Daniel just nodded in response. It hadn't been much of a fight. The Centauri *had* fired as a surprise. They'd scored at least a couple of hits on the Task Force's battlecruisers. But the straggling method that they'd fired initially had failed to capitalize on the element of surprise. The return fire had been more of a slaughter than a battle.

Of course, now the question is whether or not we just started a shooting war with the entire Centauri Confederation.

***

"Attention on deck!" someone snapped.

Admiral Boris Kaminsky looked around for a moment, then nodded, "As you were." He waited for them to take their seats, the assembled captains looking attentive and confident. None of them showed the worry that they all must feel.

"We've now confirmed that the attack on us began as a mistake," Boris growled. "Captain Third Rank Kruchev of the *Anton* opened fire in a panic. We have also confirmed that their squadron commander decided to continue the attack, without orders, for unknown reasons."

He took a deep breath, "What we just learned is that the Centauri are on edge from losing their garrison forces at the Volaterra and Lavinium systems. From what I understand, the vast majority of their forces in both systems were annihilated, without warning and with no sign of space forces. The Centauri haven't made an official statement about it, but word from contacts on Tau Ceti is that President Spiridon has called in all of his trusted allies for a strategy session at Elysia."

None of his officers looked happy at that. They might have defeated this Centauri force, but only because they'd had an edge in missile firepower from the Archers. If the Centauri had utilized their stealth systems and staged their surprise attack well, it might have gone entirely the opposite way.

"I've sent the formal report back to Fleet Headquarters," Boris said. "With the heavy expenditures of our munitions and our current distance from resupply, we're going to have to curtail our operations." He cleared his throat, "We have *also* obtained confirmation of the intel we received earlier: *Widowmaker* did indeed arrive at Port Klast, directly after departing Idarian Station.

Our agents there have confirmed that Lieutenant Commander Perkins arranged for resupply and crew and departed, his stated destination was the Golgotha system."

His statement met with mutters and confusion. Commander Ronald Shaw of the *Spathae* spoke up, "Admiral, how is that he traveled so far? There's no charted routes that could get him to Port Klast from here in under a month!"

"The information I've received suggests the involvement of Shadow Lord Invictus," Boris said. The messages sent through ansible went by a cipher code, each one a single use. That limited the information that could be sent... and it also made messages rather terse. *Even more so as we still don't understand how the ansible network is compromised... or the capabilities of the aliens who compromised it.*

"Admiral," Captain Beeson stood, "have we been able to acquire the coordinates for the Golgotha system?"

"We have not," Boris replied. He suspected that Forrest would have given those to Captain Tommy King at Port Klast, but the brevity of the message that King had sent suggested that he had little time... given other news, Boris had to wonder at what the privateer was doing at Port Klast. *It's information that doesn't apply to our current situation.*

"Fleet Intelligence is still evaluating data and searching archives for information on the system. Right now, it looks like Admiral Dreyfus or one of his conspirators erased or transferred the data," Boris said. The information about the hidden antimatter facility was still on a need-to-know basis. At least, until they learned for certain that there were no surviving conspirators in their ranks.

"In the meantime, Fleet has scrounged up several resupply vessels and escorts, who will meet us at the Garris Major system, near Halcyon Colony." He nodded at his chief of staff. "Captain Tyrell will go into detail on our resupply plan."

Boris took a seat and listened as his chief of staff began to speak. This entire operation had shifted radically as soon as Forrest decided to go to the Centauri. He didn't know *why* his old friend had made that call. *Maybe I wasn't clear enough about why he shouldn't trust the Centauri Confederation.*

Boris closed his eyes. He wished that damned ship had an ansible... and that his task force wasn't so far behind. At this point,

Boris figured there had to be enough evidence to support Forrest's decision... but the mess all this had made with their already poor relations with the Centauri Confederation was going to come down on someone.

Boris's gaze went to Senior Captain Beeson. The commander of the *Constellation* listened attentively, but Boris wondered if he knew just how political this had become. Senator Harris Penwaithe had begun to howl for military oversight and accountability. The news of this battle hadn't gone public yet, but it would soon.

When it did... and when the five captured Centauri vessels returned to United Colonies space, it was certain to start a furor. Boris personally thought that war with Centauri was inevitable. The core systems were too arrogant, their "leaders" were too corrupt. He'd risen through the ranks, seen the worst of the enlisted ranks and the nastiest side of the officer ranks. He'd left all that behind to start over on the frontier... only to be captured by the Chxor and spend ten years in their prison labor system.

Boris didn't want a war. Good men and women on both sides would die. But to remove the corrupt officials at the top of the Centauri Confederation, to protect his new home, he'd fight that war.

He just hoped that people like Senior Captain Daniel Beeson and himself weren't the ones blamed for it.

***

"I am not happy," Minder snapped at his daughter. She flinched away from his tone, not just because he had real anger in his voice, but because he spoke aloud.

It meant he didn't trust her enough to communicate mind to mind. It also meant he didn't trust her enough to discuss the things they couldn't talk about out loud. "I'm sorry, father. I expected him to come to me, he messaged me directly, I..."

"Do you have any idea how much of a mess this has become?" Minder demanded. He waved a hand at the imagery from the Volaterra and Lavinium systems. All evidence suggested the method of destruction could only be the use of Illuari weaponry. Either Marius Giovanni had acquired and activated an Enforcer Station...

Or worse, she thought to herself, *he's activated the Star Engine itself.*

"I've put all of our forces on high alert, I'm calling in all of our allies," Her father's expression shifted as he displayed his anger. It was all the more terrifying for the fact that she knew how much attention he had to put into it to project physical emotions. Up close, she could sense his rage... and she was quickly becoming a focus for it. "I've also received official notice from the United Colonies that several hours ago one of their task forces encountered the squadron you sent to Idarian Station to investigate the *Widowmaker's* departure. One of Counter Admiral Blokhin's vessels attacked them and they returned fire. The squadron was defeated and five of our ships, our *newest* ships, were captured."

Fixer didn't have to feign shock. The squadron she'd sent to Idarian Station had some of the Centauri Confederation's best equipment and Counter Admiral Blokhin was one of the better officers. He wasn't converted, but he was competent and loyal to the Centauri Confederation. "Did they say *how* they captured those vessels?" Fixer asked after a long moment.

"They did not, though they were kind enough to offload the surviving crews to Idarian Station, but they claimed the five surviving vessels as prizes for an 'unprovoked attack.' They have also told me that they want a formal apology."

Fixer winced. "What are we going to do?"

"I will instigate a formal declaration of war," Minder said, his voice cold. "I will use the *Widowmaker's* presence at the peace summit as the trigger for the violence that happened there. You will do everything in your power to follow my orders *exactly* or I will destroy you, do you understand?"

She nodded, but she couldn't help but wonder what they were really going to do. A war between the Centauri and the United Colonies meant little to her. The Centauri had the advantage in manpower and vessel count, along with shorter supply lines and a smaller strategic front. They would win, especially with her father's direction. *We probably won't even need to use Sidewinder's force to tip the balance,* she thought. Yet that brought her to the real problem. Victory over the United Colonies was one thing, but their mission was something far more vital.

What about Marius Giovanni and the Star Engine? She sent her concern directly to Minder. *Have you contacted our superiors?*

He didn't respond to her mental query. "Now, I want you to prepare for these meetings. We need all of our allies on-board with this. What I want you to do is..."

As she listened to her father's words, Fixer felt her worry turn into something altogether different: horror. Her father hadn't responded to her question... because he hadn't done anything. Their superiors, the entire rest of their race, didn't know that a human had accessed the Star Engine and had at least some of the construct's weapons and defenses online.

She had to go around her father. She had to find what actions he had taken against their true threat... and if he wouldn't address it then she would go around him.

Their species faced total eradication otherwise.

***

Chapter XII

September 18, 2410
Golgotha
Unclaimed Space

"Welcome, my dear," Marius Giovanni said, "Thank you for joining me so promptly."

"What's this about?" Alannis growled. She was afraid that this was related to her and Lizmadie's pending escape attempt, but she focused on keeping her mind off that so that Marius wouldn't be able to catch any hints.

Marius's guards had awoken her and Lizmadie in the middle of the night. They'd practically dragged Alannis out of bed, down the corridors, and into this command room.

"It seems we have something of a visitor," he gestured at the sensors, which showed the fading icon for a shadow space emergence.

"Oh?" Alannis felt a spurt of hope.

"Probably just a routine military patrol, but possibly something more," he said. He cocked his head and Alannis could feel his gaze on her. *He wants to know if I had anything to do with this.*

She met his look, "If you think I magically summoned up a ship, I'm afraid you're mistaken."

"Hmm," he replied. "No, I just wanted to make certain you weren't experimenting with your abilities by calling for help. If that's not the case, then you won't mind if we destroy this intruder?"

Alannis looked away. She didn't know who it was who'd arrived in the Golgotha system, but she felt a bit of sympathy for them. The emissions signature was faint, very faint, probably a corvette or frigate with some kind of very capable stealth systems... but Marius had the entire system rigged with the best sensor arrays he'd been able to assemble... and the ship had emerged in the inner system.

"Captain Reese," Marius said, turning to where Alannis' ex-husband stood, "Are the Star Engine's in-system weapons online?"

"Not yet, sir," Reese admitted. "And I'm not entirely certain I trust them to fire from so close, not without a psychic to direct their fire."

Marius nodded, "Very well. Order Admiral Collae's ready fighters to engage and destroy the intruder."

Alannis listened with half an ear as she watched the display. The small, stealthy ship continued to draw closer. No doubt the vessel's Captain focused on making sense of what her sensors were showing her... how this system that should be abandoned was actually heavy with traffic.

Get out of here, she thought, and not only in the hopes that the ship would carry word to her brother's forces. But if the ship didn't make preparations to jump soon...

A squadron of Admiral Collae's active combat space patrol appeared on the display. They fired at long range, the Patriot-class fighters each launched four of the fission-fusion-fission Hellcat missiles.

Alannis wondered if the ship's captain would surrender. As the ship turned and tried to go evasive, she wondered if it was even *armed.* No fire scythed out from it as those missiles closed. Then, as if it realized that it couldn't withstand the attack, it dropped it's drive.

"Picking up a transmission," Reese said. "Lord Admiral, you should see this."

"...this is UCS *Widowmaker*," Alannis recognized Forrest's voice with shock. "We have powered down our weapons and drive, please call off the attack!"

Marius leaned over the display, his eyes narrow, "Time to intercept with a ship capable of boarding?"

"Fifteen minutes, my Lord," Reese replied.

Alannis watched the missiles draw closer to Forrest's vessel. *Thirty seconds,* she thought. She looked up at Marius, who glanced at her, "Oh, I know well enough who commands that vessel, my daughter. I know about your relationship to him... and I know he'd be able to jump out and get help if we allowed it."

Marius shook his head, "Continue the attack."

"No!" Alannis shouted, "I'll do what you want, whatever you want--"

Marius held up a hand, "A promise like that, given under duress? I know better than to trust it."

"But--"

It was too late. On the display, the warheads detonated, a chain of explosions that washed over the *Widowmaker*... and then Forrest was dead. The display cleared and nothing was left but the icons of Admiral Collae's fighters.

"My complements to Admiral Collae," Marius said. "Though we should institute a policy of saving some rounds so that his fighters could keep a ship secure until we could send a boarding team out." He gestured at the guards, "That is all." He smirked at Alannis, "Sorry to interrupt your sleep, my dear."

Alannis's face hardened. "I will never work with you."

"A conclusion I had already come to," Marius replied. "It's unfortunate... but there's always your son." He said the words so nonchalantly, that it was all she could do not to try to throw herself at him, to claw at his eyes and throttle him.

Alannis forced herself to turn away, starting to follow the guards, but she paused as she stared at the display. Forrest hadn't returned fire. He hadn't powered up his ship when it was obvious that the enemy wasn't going to call of the attack.

She continued walking, the guards falling in around her... and she was glad that Marius couldn't see her face. Forrest wasn't the type to go down without a fight. The transmission had been voice only... which was exactly the kind of thing she'd expect from a rigged-up decoy.

She didn't know what kind of capabilities this *Widowmaker* possessed, but she wouldn't rule out some kind of sophisticated stealth systems.

Forrest was alive. He was here at Golgotha... and that meant he knew she was alive.

The guards stopped at the door to her quarters and Alannis gave them a single nod as she stepped into the room. She saw Lizmadie seated at the table, her expression wary.

Alannis was surprised to see her dressed. Alannis hadn't been gone that long... or at least, she didn't think she'd been gone that long. Still, with the late hour and the real possibility of rescue, Lizmadie already being dressed meant it would save them valuable time.

Alannis sat down opposite her. "It's time to play our game."

***

"Think they bought it, Captain?" Lieutenant Malatesta asked. Despite the ten days working and drilling together, the Nova Roma officer still didn't seem inclined to adopt the more informal "skipper."

"I sure hope so," Forrest said, even as he watched the display. The probe decoy had worked as advertised, though Forrest wasn't certain how it would hold up to detailed examination. If Marius Giovanni's people were so inclined, then it should at least give Forrest an hour or two.

Examining the system's layout from the data that Feliks and Rory had pulled had suggested they focus on the system's single planet in the inhabited zone, which was why they'd emerged near the planet.

Between the decoy and the ship's stealth systems, Forrest hoped they could make orbit. The *Widowmaker*'s active stealth systems should screen them entirely from the majority of active scanning. Radar and lidar would both be bent by the stealth field, which also dampened electromagnetic emissions, converting them to heat, which the ship stored. External transmissions were bent around the ship, so even if they passed through a transmission beam, the enemy shouldn't be able to detect them.

The only thing the ship couldn't entirely mask was their gravitational and mass signature. But all types of gravitational sensors were passive and locating a ship well enough to target, even with even the most advanced gravitational sensors would require a great deal of time and effort. Hopefully, Marius's people wouldn't be inclined to spend that time and effort.

The only constraint, here as it had been at the Sol system, was their heat buildup. The ship's systems could only store that heat for so long until the efficiency of the ship's cooling and heat storage systems dropped. At that point they'd have to vent the heat in a safe direction or shut the system down entirely.

He looked over at where the two civilian scientists sat, pouring over the sensor data. "Fascinating, just fascinating," Rory muttered. Forrest had restricted them to passive sensors only, but they still seemed to be getting plenty of data.

"Do you see the emissions? Indicative that they have at least some of the overall systems online." Feliks said. "I'm not sure how they--"

"Gentlemen," Forrest said with as much patience as he could muster, "Have you found where they might be keeping Princess Giovanni and Princess Lizmadie?" Elvis Medica deserved a medal for dealing with the two men as much as he had.

"What?" Rory looked up. "Well, yes... and no. It's complicated."

"We are running low on time, gentlemen," Forrest replied. "In case you haven't noticed, there's a lot of ships in the system." In fact, there were a lot more ships than Forrest had expected, complete with a number of modified Chxor dreadnoughts that looked to have been converted to carriers.

Admiral Collae, Forrest realized with shock. That must have been how Reese got out. Admiral Collae's people must have smuggled him and his prisoners out after they landed at the Temple of Light. *That bastard.*

"You have no idea," Rory ran a hand through his hair. "We thought... well because Amalgamated Worlds thought..."

"They didn't know either," Feliks giggled, "but how could they? I wouldn't believe it myself but..."

"... an entire planet," Rory said. "You see, it's not really a planet."

"Its surface structures are buried under a hundred meters or more of debris, stellar detrius that has fallen to the surface over billions of years..."

Feliks bobbed his head in a stork-like fashion, "But with our gravitic sensors, we can see that the entire structure is engineered..."

"It's not a planet, it's a space station!" Rory and Feliks finished together.

Forrest looked between them, "Wait, what?"

"We thought that the aliens must have been fighting over a facility on or around the planet... but it isn't a facility on the planet... the facility *is* the planet!" Rory said, his words tumbling over each other.

"The planet is the facility," Feliks nodded.

Forrest closed his eyes, "Fine, then, it's not a planet. Where do we need to go to find the people we're looking for?"

"Oh, uh..." Rory tapped at his controls. "Taking over your display," he said off-hand. A moment later he stood and went to the main display, which shifted to show a massive crater, almost an abyss, what had to be a hundred of kilometers or more in depth. An icon appeared around an object near the crater rim. It took Forrest a moment to make sense of the scale enough to realize that it wasn't a small marker or building, it was ten kilometer tall tower.

It was even harder to get a sense of scale because there wasn't any light, everything was artificially lit up by the sensors in a monochromatic fashion.

"We see a lot of activity around this spire," Feliks said, highlighting ships and shuttles landing and taking off. "As well as human constructions on the surface."

"They've installed fusion reactors, dozens of them," Rory said. The portly scientist tapped at his datapad, "I think that would allow them to activate some secondary systems..."

"What is this thing capable of?" Forrest demanded.

"Well, I don't know that!" Rory threw his hands in the air.

Feliks giggled, "Next you will be asking us how to disable it."

"Disable, later," Forrest snapped, "right now, I need to know about the base's sensors, weapons, everything you can give me."

"You can't be serious!" Rory and Feliks protested as one.

Rory went on, "It would take weeks--"

"Months," Feliks said dourly.

"...years!" Rory finished. "This is a facility that Amalgamated Worlds gave up on after only six months. I mean, I can draw some conclusions..."

"*We* can draw some conclusions," Feliks muttered.

"Yes, *we* can draw some conclusions," Rory nodded quickly, "but those will only be hypothesizing on our parts."

"Then give me a reasonable assumption about this thing's purpose and design," Forrest ground out. "Will it pick up this ship? Will it detect our stealth shuttle? If they do, what kind of weapons can they engage us with?"

"Uh..." Rory looked at Feliks, who shrugged, "Maybe, possibly, and a great many?"

Forrest brought up the plotted course that the new navigational officer had created while they talked. "We have... thirty minutes before we'll be in position to drop our shuttle. At that point, I need every bit of information you can give me. Priorities are: sensors, defenses, weapons, and anything about a possible location for the princesses... understand?"

"Yes, yes, of course!" Rory waved a dismissive hand.

Not for the first time, Forrest really wished that he had Elvis Medica here to deal with the two scientists. *Make do with what we have,* he told himself.

"Any signs that they didn't buy our little stunt?" Forrest asked, looking over at Petty Officer Godbey at the sensors.

"Uh, no, sir," Petty Officer Godbey replied. "All their ships are returning to their patrol positions, the ready fighters that attacked the decoy have returned to rearm... everything looks normal, I think."

There was an edge of uncertainty in his voice though. Forrest cocked an eyebrow.

"Skipper, I *am* picking up some odd gravitic pulses, coming from the planet. They're not like anything I've ever seen before. They happen in an odd sequence and it's giving our mass detector some odd distortions trying to pick out the source."

"Possibly some side effect of the alien systems?" Lieutenant Malatesta suggested.

Forrest considered that. "Alright, monitor it, let me know if there are any changes."

"Yes, skipper," Petty Officer Godbey sounded relieved, to have passed the issue along.

Forrest didn't know if it was a real problem or not. For now, though, it appeared that they'd entered the system undetected, though he hoped that his little display would warrant some kind of notice to Marius Giovanni or possibly Reese Leone. Either of them might in turn notify Alannis... and if she saw some or part of the message, hopefully she'd realize what he wanted her to know.

Forrest pulled up an image of the spire and stared at it for a long, silent time. *I know you're there,* he thought, *hold on, I'm coming for you.*

***

Alannis shut the lights out in her room and climbed into bed. But as she did so, she counted out seconds. Lizmadie would need a minute to finish her part of the task. As she counted out the last seconds, Alannis bunched up the covers and got out of bed. The humped form of the pillows and blankets would look loosely like a human form. Alannis went to the suite's bathroom and closed the door. Lizmadie had the shower running to mask the noise and Alannis's friend gave her a nod in the dim light.

She'd taken to bathing with the main light off, ostensibly because she'd been getting headaches from the constant artificial lighting. Since Marius's people had refused to give them any kinds of painkillers, it sounded like an appropriate excuse. The dim light from under the door gave them enough light to work with as Lizmadie and Alannis went to either side of the toilet and pulled.

The plastic seal around the back of the toilet, already weakened by Lizmadie and Alannis both scraping at it every time they came to use the bathroom, cracked and the toilet came away from the wall, revealing a small hole, barely big enough for them to fit their shoulders through.

Alannis stuck her head through, half afraid that it would be too-small a space to be useful.

Instead, she found it was a meter-wide, meter-tall corridor, with pipes and conduits running along the floor, walls, and ceiling. "Jackpot," she whispered. She popped her head back out and gave Lizmadie a thumbs up.

Lizmadie passed her a towel without a word. It clinked as Alannis took it, it was the tools they'd cobbled together from fixtures in their suite. Lizmadie also patted the pistol tucked in her waistband. They had a weapon, they had tools, and they had an escape route. They could do this.

Alannis crawled through into the maintenance access. It was too low to do more than crouch and it was dark, far darker than she'd expected. Alannis paused for a moment, trying to visualize the layout of the tower. She thought that the lifts lay to her right. She started that direction and heard Lizmadie enter the corridor behind her.

She shuffled along, through the dark, gradually growing more and more worried. What if there wasn't an access point? What if this led nowhere and they'd trapped themselves?

Or worse, what if it did open up... but directly into an elevator shaft or some other vertical drop?

Alannis slowed her movement and dropped to her hands and knees, feeling ahead of her. That slowed her pace even more.

She thought she saw a bit of light ahead of her, but it seemed far away and she wasn't sure if it was just her mind playing tricks on her. She kept moving, hearing Lizmadie's breathing behind her and then, finally, she could make out the shape of a grill and beyond it a dark room.

Alannis pushed on the grill, and when it didn't move, she felt around the edges. She found a fastener of some kind and fought with it.

The grill fell and she barely caught it in time. Alannis gave a sigh of relief as she lowered it, slowly, the rest of the way to the floor, then she crawled out of the access way and looked around.

It was a small maintenance room. Pipes and conduits led from the access way and connected into various bits of equipment. Alannis went to a locker and pulled it open. Inside she found some tools and a pair of dusty coveralls. She took one set out and passed them to Lizmadie and took the second set herself.

She pulled the coveralls on over her gray United Colonies uniform. She remembered seeing similarly dressed workers in the corridors.

She pulled out a large wrench and then looked at Lizmadie, "Ready?" she asked.

"What are you doing with that?" Lizmadie asked, tucking the pistol in her pocket.

"No one ever questions someone walking around with a big tool," Alannis said. She opened the door and winced against the bright light of the corridor. She and Lizmadie stepped out and moved down the hall. Their first priority was to find a datapad or some kind of network access. From there they could get maps and floor plans, find their way to a hangar...

"You, there," a sharp voice barked out.

Alannis and Lizmadie turned.

A scowling officer stalked towards them. "This is a restricted level, there's no scheduled maintenance here," the officer glared at them both.

"Uh, sorry sir," Alannis said. "We must have got turned around, we'll be on our way..."

"Hold on," the Lieutenant scowled. He pulled out his datapad and unlocked it, looking down at it, "What are your identity numbers?"

Alannis swung the heavy wrench. She hit the officer in the side of the head as hard as she could. The man dropped limply to the ground. Alannis could tell she'd killed him, simply by the way he fell.

"What the hell!?" Lizmadie hissed. She seemed shocked by the sudden violence.

"Grab his feet," Alannis said, even as she stooped and grabbed the officer's hands. "He unlocked his datapad and his uniform will be better concealment than a pair of ratty coveralls." The dead Lieutenant wasn't a good match for either of them, but an ill-fitting officer's uniform would be better than nothing.

Alannis paused to pick up the man's datapad before they moved back into the maintenance room. She wasn't sure why Lizmadie was acting so squeamish all of the sudden. That puzzled Alannis a bit, since the other princess was a Marine officer. She'd defended herself before from pirates and assassins and she'd killed cultists during their running battle at the Temple of Light. Maybe she was worried that they'd draw attention.

It took Alannis only a few minutes to get changed again, tucking the long uniform shirt into her pants and hoping she didn't look too ridiculous. Still, the datapad was the important thing. She brought up a map, even as Lizmadie passed her the officer's pistol.

"Okay," Alannis said. "So the nearest hangar is three levels up... about a hundred meters over. It's Marius's personal hangar, though, so I imagine security is going to be tight. Down thirty levels is a cargo hangar... I think that looks like our best bet."

"That works for me," Lizmadie said quickly.

"Good," Alannis said. She was a bit surprised that her friend hadn't asked for the datapad. Alannis knew how to operate a system and she knew how to bypass security protocols, but Lizmadie was a truly skilled hacker. She would have expected the woman to snatch it out of her hands.

Still, it wasn't as if they had much time. "Let's go," Alannis said, opening the door and stepping into the corridor once more. They were getting out of here. Forrest was going to be there to pick them up, and they were going home.

And after that, she was going to get her brother to send a fleet and level this place.

**

"I'm telling you," Private Lee went on, "this shift change is pretty out of the ordinary."

Sergeant Tymun rolled his eyes. Private Lee thought *everything* was out of the ordinary. Ever since he'd been assigned he'd had strange ideas and doubts. He'd even claimed to have dreams about serving in another military. He claimed their platoon must be the target of some kind of psychic experiment.

Sergeant Tymun just thought that the private needed some medication and therapy. Half of what the Marine talked about made Sergeant Tymun's head hurt.

"Look, Private, just shut up, okay?" He growled. "They changed our patrol shift, that's it. This kind of thing happens all the time." At least, he thought it did. He couldn't remember it happening before. That thought gave him even worse of a headache though, so instead he concentrated on his new duties as he waited on the lift to arrive.

The doors opened, but Sergeant Tymun stared in surprise at the odd duo in the lift. The lead woman wore an ill-fitting Fleet Officer's uniform, while the other wore an oversized set of coveralls. "Uh, ma'am..." he trailed off. He wasn't supposed to question officers.

He looked over at Private Lee, who had an odd expression on his face, almost as if he recognized the two, but couldn't remember where.

Before Sergeant Tymun could say anything, the officer drew her pistol. He stared at her, dumbfounded as the barrel lined up with his face. Then there was a flash of light and Sergeant Tymun's world ended.

**

"Really?" Lizmadie hissed at Alannis as they dragged the two bodies into the lift. "You could have given me *some* warning. I have blood all over me."

There was blood on the floor and smears from where they'd dragged the bodies. Alannis shot her friend a sour look, "It wasn't like I had much time."

"Did you have to shoot them?" Lizmadie demanded.

"You're the Marine, would you have preferred I ask them politely to lay down their weapons and surrender? Do you think that would have worked?" Alannis couldn't help her biting tone, she didn't know *why* Lizmadie was behaving so squeamishly.

The lift stopped and Alannis toggled the emergency stop. It wouldn't prevent other cars in the shaft from bypassing it, not if it was a standard grav-lift, but it should prevent other cars from stopping at this floor.

Alannis stepped out into the hangar area, adjusting how the rifle lay slung across her shoulder. She didn't see any shuttles docked, but she saw a command booth of some kind near the doors. Alannis stalked in that direction. A couple of guards looked up at her approach, but Alannis didn't give them time to challenge her. As she drew within five meters, she drew her pistol and fired. She put two shots into the nearest man, then as he dropped back, she put three more into the other one. As the first man fumbled with his radio, she put the last round from the pistol through his forehead.

She dropped the pistol and brought up her rifle as she stepped into the command booth. A navy officer had drawn his pistol, but Alannis already had her rifle up and aimed. She put three rounds through his center of mass and as he fell back, she shot the tech next to him. As the tech fell back, Alannis heard a shout from the side. She turned to see another tech, shouting something into his comm unit. Alannis shot him from point blank, blood spattering her uniform and splattering her face.

"Clear," Alannis snapped. She tried to ignore the coppery smell of blood and the hot warmth of it on her face.

Lizmadie moved past her without a word, headed straight to the communications section. She gingerly levered the dead tech out of the way and took a seat, wiping blood off the controls. "We have radio as well as a laser transceiver, what should I send?"

Odds were that the alarm was already going out. They needed to contact Forrest's rescue operation as soon as they could.

"Send a broad spectrum distress call," Alannis said, even as she checked her rifle's magazine and picked up the dead officer's pistol. "If they have a laser transceiver, they'll be able to localize us and contact us directly."

"What if they want some kind of confirmation?" Lizmadie asked.

"Give them my access code," Alannis replied. She rattled it off, her mind on the next step.

Alannis went over to pick up the dead technician's comm unit. She pulled out the ear bud, wiped it off on her pants, and jammed it in her ear. She could hear shouted demands before she switched over the channel.

She was trying not to think of the men and women she'd killed as people. They weren't, Marius had as much as admitted to brainwashing them. They didn't have families, they didn't have friends; they were just puppets who worked at Marius Giovanni's direction.

She was doing them a mercy, putting them out of their misery. Yet the terrified expressions of the people she'd killed told her differently.

They're in my way, she told herself, *they're supporting Marius, who kidnapped me and killed innocent people.* The words dsidn't salve her conscience, but they let her move on.

She just hoped she hadn't killed them for no reason. *Forrest is coming,* she told herself, *I'm getting out of here.*

***

Chapter XIII

September 18, 2410
Golgotha
Unclaimed Space

"Skipper, we got something," Petty Officer Godbey crowed.

Forrest pulled up the distress call. He didn't recognize the woman's voice, but his new XO perked up, "That's Princess Lizmadie!"

"You're sure?" Forrest asked.

"I'd bet my life on it," Lieutenant Malatesta nodded.

"Alright, then," Forrest said. He stood up from the command chair. "I'll take the shuttle down and..."

"Sir," Lieutenant Malatesta raised a hand, "you need to stay aboard the ship. As soon as they realize that someone's here, we're going to be facing an awful lot of enemy ships. You need to be at the helm to command the vessel."

Forrest scowled, but he didn't argue. It just seemed rather unfair that he didn't go. "When the time comes to rescue the princesses from the tower, someone else gets to be prince charming," Forrest scowled. "Fine. Get the shuttle launched, we'll relay coordinates en route."

"Commander," Rory and Feliks hurried over, "you have to let us go down with the shuttle..."

Forrest shook his head, "Not going to happen. You both are irreplacable." The two scientists shouldn't have been aboard the ship in the first place, and if Forrest hadn't needed them so desperately, he would have put them off a long time earlier.

"That shuttle is going to the surface of an alien construct," Rory's words were rushed. "We have no idea what they may encounter. For all we know, they'll *need* someone with our expertise. For that matter, this is a rare opportunity to take sensor readings of the structure from up close. We might learn the purpose of this device, or at least, something of what Marius Giovanni wants to use it for!"

Forrest's lips pinched as he considered that against the risk to the two scientists. Odds were that the shuttle would remain undetected on approach... but if it wasn't, it could be shot down without warning. "One of you," Forrest bit out.

"Okay, I'll go," Rory said eagerly.

"No!" Feliks shook his head, "Nyet, you are too valuable. I should be the one to go."

"Well," Rory looked at him, "I am brilliant, I might even say vital, but..."

"If something goes wrong down there, you might be able to piece together enough information from the data we already have," Feliks said. "I could not do the same."

Rory seemed shocked, he straightened a bit, standing taller, "Thank you, Feliks, I mean, *I* knew that I'm the smarter of us, but for you to admit it..."

"Hardly," Feliks shook his head as he headed for the door, "You're more likely to make wildly unfounded assumptions and get lucky than I am."

Forrest chuckled at Rory's offended expression. Yet his humor faded as he considered the situation. He really hoped that this worked out. It had gone beyond his concern for Alannis. Marius clearly had a massive amount of resources at his disposal. He was an enemy of the United Colonies. Forrest had to let the rest of humanity know about this... Marius Giovanni had to be stopped.

He watched as the shuttle departed, even as his mind went to the situation at hand. Marius had over a hundred ships in orbit. The *Widowmaker's* course had brought them extremely close to the planet, within a high orbit of the crowded world. He had picked an orbit closer to where several civilian freighters lay clustered, mostly in the hopes that they would be less attentive to their sensors than military vessels.

The *Widowmaker's* active stealth system wasn't rated for being this close to other ships. But with how well it protected them, Forrest was actually more worried about collision than he was about being detected... at least, until the system's traffic control started looking for them. Well, that and the heat buildup. The ship's passive stealth systems converted possible emissions to heat, which it then stored. Under normal operations they could vent that heat in a safe direction. Right now, though, there wasn't a safe direction, so they had to store it... and soon systems would start to overheat.

Thankfully, the multiple large vessels in close orbit should screen the destroyer's mass. Though just what Marius Giovanni and Reese Leone needed with the five large freighters, Forrest didn't know.

"Are we still seeing those odd gravitic pulses?" Forrest asked.

"Yes, Skipper," Petty Officer Godbey replied. "Though they've dropped off, significantly."

"Any ideas as to the cause?" Forrest asked of Rory.

The engineer shrugged uncomfortably, then looked around, as if he needed Feliks's input to make some kind of guess."

Lieutenant Malatesta spoke, his voice thoughtful, "It could be a product of the facility's operations, you said it's a construct of some kind, perhaps this is a result of the object's construction somehow."

"No," Rory said, "that doesn't make any sense..." He waved a hand through his thinning hair. "It's probably just a byproduct of some of their systems operations... maybe it's even an artificial effect, not a real gravitic pulse, but just an error in your ship's sensors."

Forrest nodded, yet he couldn't help a feeling of unease. It wasn't anything he could put his finger on, just an element of uncertainty that bothered him, far more than it should. Gravitic sensors might be able to pick the *Widowmaker* out... and Marius must know how capable the ship's stealth systems were... after all, his people had hijacked it from Tanis's shipyards.

What if they have some method of sensor designed to track it? Yet even if that was the case, Forrest couldn't see the point of why they'd allowed them to get so close to the planet. No, it was better to operate under the assumption that their approach had gone unnoticed, otherwise paranoia would lead to paralysis.

"All right," Forrest said, looking around at his bridge crew. "When that shuttle comes back up here, they're going to bring a lot of attention our way. What we need to do is make things busy enough up here that no one has time to take shots at them as they leave. So, gentlemen, give me some ideas."

***

Alannis yanked the pin out of the frag grenade and threw it into the open hatch at the stairwell.

The resulting explosion left her ears ringing, but not enough that she couldn't hear the screams of wounded men and women in the stairwell.

"How much longer?!" Alannis shouted into her comm.

"I don't know," Lizmadie shouted back. "I haven't been able to get anyone after that one laser transmission. I'm a little focused on preventing them from shutting the hangar doors!"

Alannis didn't respond to that. Lizmadie had been trying to disconnect the hangar controls from external access or lock the doors open somehow. She hadn't been much help in the meantime in defending against the guards that had swarmed them to stop them.

Alannis didn't know why the guards hadn't got the lift working. The stairs were on one side of the hangar and the lift the other, she and Lizmadie wouldn't be able to counter their attempts to close the hangar doors and still cover both access-ways. She'd put it in emergency stop, but she hadn't had time to disable the controls.

The guards, in the meantime, weren't using non-lethal weapons anymore. Either her father didn't care about capturing her alive or they had a bit more self-preservation than total loyalty to orders. Whichever it was, Alannis ducked back behind the support pillar as someone lobbed in a grenade of their own.

She opened her mouth to equalize pressure. It landed far enough away from her that that it only rattled her instead of rupturing her eardrums and leaving her stunned. She popped around the pillar, rifle up, just as two more guards rushed out of the stairwell. Alannis cut one down, but the other made it into the shelter of a stack of crates.

They didn't look sturdy, so she put seven rounds through the stack until she heard a scream. As the man dragged himself away from the crates, back towards the door, she waited. She could see a long trail of blood from him, he was clearly wounded.

One of his companions rushed to aide him and she shot him too.

Gunfire rattled out from the doorway in response. Alannis ducked back as bullets whipped through the hangar.

"Lizmadie," Alannis called out, "I think I've made them angry. We really need evac... now!"

"I'm *trying*." Lizmadie snapped back. "They've got at least three hackers and one of them is better than me, I'm not sure I can leave what I'm doing to call your boyfriend!"

Alannis pursed her lips and glanced over at the door mechanism. She saw some kind of hydraulic machinery and she brought up her rifle. She fired two rounds through what looked like a hydraulic tank and then four more through the motor and pump casing. Hydraulic fluid sprayed everywhere and sparks flew up from the control panel where one of her rounds had punched through. She patted the Freedom Arms PZ-7 rifle, "I like this thing, I think I'll keep it. How'd that do?"

"Uh, the door mechanism is offline. That worked, I guess... but how did you know it was a fail open and not closed?" Lizmadie asked. If the hangar had some kind of security function where its bay doors would close due to damage or system failure, then Alannis would have closed the doors for Marius.

Alannis opened her mouth to say that she *hadn't* known for certain. Then again, Lizmadie seemed rattled enough just now, so Alannis decided not to mention that.

Alannis's comm hissed with static for a moment and then she heard Marius's voice. "Alannis, my dear. This really is counterproductive."

Alannis didn't respond. She did note that she could hear the guards in the doorway of the stairwell drawing back. Either they were moving back to give her some room or they were building up for another rush. Alannis took the opportunity to reload the rifle with her last full magazine.

"You are just making this harder on yourself, you know," Marius went on. "My people are going to get into the hangar... and the more of them you kill, the less happy they'll be when they do get inside. Surrender and I can guarantee your safety."

"My safety?" Alannis demanded. "Locked up all day, every day? Go to hell."

"You are a most precocious child," Marius said.

"You are *not* my father!" Alannis snapped back. "Get this through your head, you egotistical, self-righteous, asshole! Even if you sired me... my mother killed herself over what you did. I was raised by my grandmother. I grew up as a social outcast, prohibited from ever leaving Nova Roma, a hostage to keep Lucius in line!"

Alannis racked the slide on her rifle, so angry that she wanted to shoot someone, *anyone*. "Marius Giovanni ruined my life once, I'm not going to let his cheap clone knock-off ruin it again. I'm going to get out of this place and when I do, I'm going to bring back a fleet and level this facility. We're going to tear it down around you and piss on the ashes."

"Well," Marius replied after a moment, "I suppose I deserved some of that. I haven't exactly been there for you..."

"I don't believe this!" Alannis snapped. "Lizmadie, go to the backup channel."

Alannis switched over, "How we looking on extraction?"

"Shuttle inbound," Lizmaddie replied, her voice tense. "Thirty seconds, clear the hangar, they're coming in hot."

Alannis sprinted for the control booth. She ducked inside the hatch, just as gunfire picked up from the stairwell. She supposed it was possible that they were firing nonlethal rounds, but the impact of bullets, starring the armored glass of the control room implied that they weren't.

Alannis popped her head up in time to see a squad bound out of the doorway, the six guards shooting and providing cover for one another. Alannis kicked the door shut and cranked the wheel to secure it. "Where the hell is that shuttle?"

"Alright," Marius's voice spoke from the intercom. "I think this has gone on quite long enough. Terminate this scenario."

"Wait, what?" Alannis looked around in confusion.

"Roger, My Lord," Lizmadie said from behind her. Alannis turned in surprise as her friend drew her pistol and fired from less than two meters distance.

Alannis saw the muzzle flash and felt pain blossom across her chest. "What... why..."

The world went dark.

***

"We're taking heavy inbound fire, sir," the voice of Petty Officer Cartwright was tight. The shuttle pilot clearly was under a lot of stress. "We don't think they've picked us up, but they know *someone* is here. I don't think we can get in there."

"Break off," Forrest snapped. He watched the stealth shuttle swing around, the laser transponder their only link to the small vessel. He looked over at Lieutenant Malatesta, "Any other transmissions from Princess Lizmadie?"

"Negative, sir," the Nova Roma officer looked like he wanted to spit. "There's nothing, it feels like it was a trap."

It might have been, Forrest realized. Yet he didn't see the point of it. The enemy would only have trapped the shuttle. The nearby squadron of warships wasn't even powered up. It wasn't as if they were even sweeping the orbit over the planet with active sensors...

"Skipper," Petty Officer Godbey spoke up, "I'm getting some more of those odd grav-pulses again. They're coming from the facility, and it's weird, it's almost like it's setting up some kind of resonance..."

Forrest's head snapped around. "Ping the shuttle, tell them to go to ground, *now.* Lieutenant Malatesta, power up the shadow space drive." They already had jump coordinates plotted. They'd kept the drive in standby to save on power and reduce the heat generation.

"Sir?" Malatesta stared at him in confusion.

"They're targeting us," Forrest snapped. Forrest didn't know have time to explain. Normally gravitational sensors were passive, they detected masses and densities, but they couldn't pick out objects being masked by other masses, not with precision. Normally that would mean that the *Widomaker,* so close to the planet and the five freighters, should have been hard to spot. But these gravitic pulses were different. Forrest felt a dread certainty roll over him, even as he brought up the shadow space coordinates on his console.

Someone spoke up, "That's impossible--"

"Power spike from the surface!" Petty Officer Godbey called out, "they're preparing to fire!"

Forrest activated the drive and the *Widowmaker* dropped into shadow space.

***

"Well," Lord Admiral Marius Giovanni grimaced, "that is... unfortunate."

"I'm sorry, sir," Reese said. He winced a bit as he thought of how close they'd come to recapturing the *Widowmaker.* "At least we know that the Star Engine's sensors are capable of breaching stealth fields."

"Yes, extremely effective... at least until our opponents seek to find a solution for it," Marius gave a sardonic smile. "And it seems that the perfect vessel to do so is now on its way back to my son's forces to inform them of our location and our capabilities."

Reese flinched a bit at Marius's tone. "I am sorry, my Lord, I--"

"It isn't your fault," Marius said. "You performed your role perfectly. Our forces followed my orders and there should have been no outward sign of our impending attack... perhaps young Forrest was nervous about a trap and had his ship's shadow space drive active. Perhaps when we powered up our weapons to strike the ship, they triggered the drive. Or perhaps one of Lieutenant Commander Perkins' people lost their nerve and triggered the drive prematurely. Either way, it is done."

"Yes, my Lord," Reese responded. "Should I give the order to begin preparations and bring the system to a full war-footing?" Once he gave that order, the various facilities across the Star Engine would go to full operational status. Tens of thousands of personnel would stand to, weapons emplacements and stockpiled vessels would begin to come online. Hundreds of thousands of prisoners, many kept in cryogenic sleep, would be mentally conditioned and processed, then put to work supporting Marius Giovanni's efforts.

"Begin Phase Alpha operations, only," Marius said after a moment. "We're still awaiting supply shipments and I don't think we have enough stockpiles to go fully active. Additionally--"

The doors to the command chamber opened and Admiral Collae stalked through. "Lord Admiral, I demand to know why you allowed that vessel to leave this system."

Marius's face grew hard, "You demand? You should watch your words carefully, Admiral Collae." Reese flinched at the words. The alliance with Spencer Penwaithe was fragile, but their situation was such that they needed Penwaithe's connections and resources. Marius, though, seemed to realize that and he moderated his own tone, "Admiral Collae, I did not allow the *Widowmaker* to escape... not *this* time anyway. After our gravitic sensors detected the vessel's approach, we intended to lure it in and disable it for capture. They were here to rescue my daughter. Of course, I'm certain you and your patron have already heard about how I curtailed her escape attempt."

Admiral Collae's stern expression grew pained.   "Lord Admiral..."

"I'm not doing this out of some kind of mushy-minded sentimentality," Marius snapped. "This, as in all my efforts, has a reason." He glanced at Reese, who nodded and moved to the sensor station.

"What about their shuttle?" Admiral Collae demanded.

Reese spoke up, "We did not localize the shuttle, it was too close to the facility for our gravitic sensors to get targeting data."

"Admiral, one shuttle of whatever mercenaries that they managed to scrape together is hardly a threat," Marius said. "I'm certain that Captain Leone's people will locate the shuttle after they're forced to land."

"Lord Admiral," Admiral Collae grated, "we had an intruding vessel belonging to the United Colonies. That shuttle, possessing stealth systems, was here to extract two personnel who know far too much about this base of operations and facilities. If they had managed to leave this system, the United Colonies would know about my involvement with your operations. As it is, if the *Widowmaker* returns, then the United Colonies will also know the location and disposition of our defenses and they will *still* likely know of my involvement due to the presence of my ships."

"Your point?" Marius asked calmly.

"My point," Admiral Collae snapped, "is that we cannot hold off both the Balor and your son's forces, not in enough time for this facility to come online."

"We're stepping up the time-line a bit more than you realized," Marius replied. "But you don't need to take my word for it. Captain Reese?"

"My Lord?" Reese straightened to attention. He couldn't help a slight smirk, because he knew exactly what was coming.

Marius smiled in reply, "Please activate Operation Trojan, if you would?"

Reese brought up a star map which then displayed a line of connecting systems. "What is this?" Admiral Collae asked.

"It's the route that Colonel Price has taken back towards his station," Marius replied.   "Which is located in deep space, approximately... here." He highlighted the region, "Near the Melcer system, I believe."

"You're tracking Colonel Price's movements?" Admiral Collae's eyes narrowed, "how?"

Reese didn't bother to hide his smirk as Marius didn't reply. There were secrets that didn't need to be shared... and showing that they had the means to track their friends and enemies would keep Admiral Collae and his sponsor, Spencer Penwaithe, honest. *Or at least, more circumspect in their plans to eventually betray us.*

"We'll have the coordinates for his facility soon. That will allow us to move up all of our project time-lines... including Operation Macchius. That you need to know. The escape attempt of my daughter and the attempt to recapture the *Widomaker* were both sideshows. They're unimportant in the grand scheme of things. Do you understand, *Admiral*?"

Admiral Collae gave a grim nod.

"Excellent," Marius nodded at Reese. "Now, Captain Reese, if you'd make preparations for Phase Alpha?"

Reese bowed slightly, "Yes, Lord Admiral, of course."

***

"Got to set her down!" Petty Officer Cartwright barked as the shuttle's engines whined.

Lieutenant Ambrosio scowled, "I thought you said they'll be able to spot us if we set down?"

"They *might*," Cartwright barked back, "but our heat systems are past the red line. If I don't set us down, we'll lose one or both engines within the next thirty seconds. After that, we'll fall out of the sky."

"Roger," Lieutenant Ambrosio grunted. He looked over at the scientist. Lieutenant Commander Perkins had insisted that he come along. Ambrosio hadn't thought much of the decision, but now it looked like it had worked out in his favor. "This sensor they used to spot the *Widowmaker*, can they use it to spot us?"

"No," Felik's voice was abnormally calm. "The large mass of the construct and our close proximity to it should screen us. But once we land, we'll have to vent heat rapidly, they'll be able to detect our presence with infrared sensors from orbit quite easily."

"We'll deal with that when we come to it," Ambrosio said. He wasn't a space guy. He'd fought on a dozen worlds, boarding operations, ground warfare, and insurgency and counter-insurgency. "Petty Officer, try to put us down in a ravine or canyon, someplace low where we can screen ourselves." He brought up the shuttle's inventory and scanned it. *Thermal and radar screening camo,* he noted. Most shuttles had some kind of shelter that could be strung over to hide the shuttle's profile and most spacers didn't seem to even know the stuff existed. Hardly a surprise when they focused mostly on space combat, even the shuttle pilots.

"Staff Sergeant Witzke," Ambrosio said, "have your squad ready to deploy the shuttle's camouflage, we'll have to screen it quickly, they'll be looking for us." *Good thing it's an entire planet we have to hide on.*

Ambrosio lifted his visor and rubbed at his eyes. This whole situation had gone to hell. He hadn't expected the mission to be easy: breaking out a pair of hostages on a hostile planet was bound to be difficult. But without any kind of support, with their ship missing, and with no idea where the two missing princesses were...

One thing at a time, he told himself. "Get us on the deck."

***

"Alannis," a soft voice spoke, "Alannis, you need to wake up."

She didn't want to. She was warm, safe, and comfortable. If she woke up, she'd have to face reality, have to return to... her mind shied away from those thoughts and memories. Something terrible, she told herself.

"Wake up!" the voice insisted.

Despite herself, Alannis opened her eyes.

With horror, she realized that she lay cocooned in a network of wires, many attached to her skin. She reacted with horror, trying to shake herself free, but she couldn't move, she was held, immobile, unable to even turn her head.

"Alannis, look at me," the voice insisted.

Alannis's eyes came up and she found herself face to face with Marius Giovanni.

"Good, I'm glad you're finally awake. I'm afraid the scenario we ran you through was a bit more traumatic than we intended. I decided to let you rest for a few days, but I'm afraid that I had to wake you for this." Marius's voice was gentle, even friendly, but Alannis felt mounting horror.

"What are you doing to me?!" She forced the words past lips that barely moved.

"I haven't rewritten your mind... well, not yet," Marius said. "I have no desire to damage you, and that's exactly what would happen with how stubborn you are. I hope that in time you'll see the benefits of voluntarily joining me. But that's not why I'm here." Marius gestured behind himself, and Alannis saw Lizmadie Doko similarly cocooned. "I've had both of you hooked up since just after the *Widowmaker* arrived. I figured you had an escape plan of some sort and I wanted to see what information I could get from you. I ran you both through separate escape scenarios and between you both, I've managed to finally get the information I needed."

"What..." Alannis trailed off and her eyes went wide as she realized what he'd meant. "My access codes?"

"Yes, yours and Princess Lizmadie's. They'll do as overrides to get me through security on Faraday. The codes, delivered as you gave them and with slight modifications, will be enough to override any security lock downs on our way out of the system," Mar ius smirked. "While I could have obtained them through more brute force methods, I'm glad that I didn't have to resort to such things. I will say that you were particularly brutal to my guard forces. Princess Lizmadie as well, but I assumed that you might show some mercy to unarmed technicians or guards trying to rescue their wounded. You gunned them down ruthlessly. I'm actually impressed, and I've saved the scenario for my guard forces to practice on."

"You're saying I didn't kill anyone?" Alannis felt a moment of relief.

"Well, the systemic shock that many of them suffered did trigger aneurisms in a couple, but most of the ones I used were of marginal use anyway, so they're of little consequence," Marius replied. "In any case, I'll be departing within the hour, with Reese, to take care of the business on Faraday. You and Princess Lizmadie will be transferred to my VIP holding facility in the meantime."

"What are you doing?" Alannis demanded and Marius Giovanni turned.

"I warned you," Marius said. "I told you that I only had so much patience. For reasons which I don't care to go into, I need a powerful psychic, someone who I can trust... someone who is family. I thought... I *hoped* that you would be the one. But now I need a different option. Someone who is still young enough, impressionable enough, for me to sway. Someone whose mind hasn't been poisoned against me."

"No," Alannis gasped.

"Yes," Marius replied. "My grandchildren. They'll both have the psychic genes. And while I'm fairly certain young Kaylee will be resistant, your son, Anthony William, will be more receptive, particularly since his father is already on my side."

"No!" Alannis snapped, "Please, I'll do anything--"

"I saw just how much you hate me in your escape attempt," Marius said. "I'll not be a fool and hope to compel your loyalty. We could have left your son out of this, but *you* forced my hand, Alannis. Now, I will see you upon my return, Alannis."

"He's just a child!" Alannis called after him.

"Not for long," Marius said, the hatch closing on his last words, "They grow up so fast..."

***

Chapter XIV

September 21, 2410
Golgotha
Unclaimed Space

"Welcome to Purgatory, ladies," the officer in charge of their security section said.

Alannis shot him a glare, but he just smiled. "Don't worry, I know how important you both are... and I don't give a shit who your daddy is, Princess. My job is to keep this facility secure and the Lord Admiral has given me free rein to do what I need to accomplish that task."

"I'm sure," Alannis scowled back. "Was that before or after he mentally programmed you to be his loyal slave?"

"My name, *Princess,* is Major Daniel Scaparetti, I've been a loyal officer to Marius Giovanni for decades, long before he began his mental conditioning program. I was born and bred on Nova Roma and I understand all to well how much better things would have gone there... had *Princess* Lizmadie's father been dragged out and shot a lot sooner."

"The Chxor didn't shoot him," Lizmadie replied in a tense voice. "They gassed him. They shot my brother, the Crown Prince."

"They should have shot the lot of you, in my opinion," Major Scaparetti snorted. "I wish Marius had done it first. But that's beside the point. Don't worry, I won't be using capital punishment. Your fellow prisoners here are all valuable, it wouldn't do to harm the merchandise... but there's other methods of keeping you in line."

The shuttle settled down into a landing bay and the doors closed above them. "This," Major Scaparetti said, is Purgatory. Everyone here is being given a bit of a reprieve. Either they prove their value... in which case they go to their just rewards...."

The shuttle ramp dropped and a dozen prisoners stared at them, their eyes sunken and their skin pale. Major Scaparetti and the rest of their escort marched Alannis and Lizmadie past them. "Or else they cease to be of value and we send them to hell." He gestured at the line of prisoners, "They're all going to mental conditioning. Either the worth of their connections is gone or they've exceeded the Lord Admiral's patience and understanding."

Ten men and women were marched up the ramp. Two of them refused to move and they were dragged up the ramp by their guards. "Most of them won't do well," Major Scaparetti smirked. "Too old, they'll be next best thing to vegetables when the process is done. Still, we always need more janitors, I suppose."

Alannis glared at him, "You're a monster."

"You've no idea," Major Scaparetti chuckled. He led them forward and into a separate room. "You'll be processed here." He turned away as the guards stripped the two women down. "Your uniforms will be disposed of and you'll be fitted with jump suits. They're quite comfortable and they're laden with tracking and biometric systems. We'll monitor you at all times, if your heart rate rises, if your breathing quickens, we'll know instantly. If that's because you're attempting an escape, we'll know where you are. If you remove the clothing outside of appropriate areas, we'll know that, too."

He chuckled, "Some of our guests get up to quite a bit of extracurricular activities. Not that I'd expect ladies such as yourselves to indulge, but be advised, we monitor *that* too."

Alannis scowled as they scanned her, drew a blood sample, and then took a clipping of her hair. This Major Scaparetti seemed like a sadist. She half-wondered if Marius knew how he ran the place. The rest of her figured that Marius merely saw it as the most efficient method.

"Even if you do shuck the jump suit, there's one thing that you'll carry with you no matter what," Major Scaparetti grinned. As Alannis ground her teeth, unwilling to rise to his bait, she felt a cold bit of metal clamp around her wrist.

She looked down in surprise, the bracelet fitting flush with her skin.

"The bracelet contains a tracking device. It's a titanium-steel alloy, you won't find anything inside the facility that can cut it. It also has a dose of mild tranquilizer that will inject you should you veer outside of approved areas of the facility," Major Scaparetti went on, "along with a few other goodies that I'm not going to warn you about. It's far too much fun when you learn them yourself."

Alannis scowled and pulled on the jumpsuit that one of the two technicians passed to her. As she zipped it up, Major Scaparetti turned to face them. "Now, then, let's show you to your quarters, shall we?"

***

Purgatory, if that was the facility's real name, seemed to be a purely human construction. The walls, floors, and ceilings looked like what she'd expect to see at a moderately decent hotel, with carpeted and tiled floors, painted walls, and even artwork. Yet she saw security monitors everywhere. Other than their immediate escort, Alannis didn't see armed guards anywhere. They did pass a dozen armored doors along their path, most of them unobtrusively hidden by paintings or in alcoves, yet Alannis's eyes picked them out.

"This is your suite," Major Scaparetti stopped outside of a set of doors. "Normally we'd give such... distinguished guests their own, private, quarters, but you two are a matching pair, it seems."

Something about his behavior bugged her and Alannis stepped close to him as he turned. As he realized he was within arm's reach, he flinched. It was a slight thing, barely noticed, but she didn't miss it.

The guards caught her by the arms before she could do more but she noted his reaction. He was afraid of her... and that might be useful.

The guards pushed her into the suite and a moment later, Lizmadie stepped in as well. There was a bed, a couch, and several paper books on a desk. There was a notable absence of any electronic devices... but that was to be expected, Alannis supposed.

"Dinner will be served in two hours, would you like to eat in your rooms or partake in the dining room?" Major Scaparetti asked. The false friendliness in his voice set Alannis's teeth on edge. "We'll join our fellow prisoners in the dining room," Alannis replied.

"Excellent, it's just down the corridor. Enjoy the rest of your stay, ladies," Major Scaparetti turned away, followed by their escort. Lizmadie went to the open doorway and pulled it shut. She tried the lock on it while Alannis prowled through the suite.

"We can lock the door, manually," Lizmadie said, her voice dubious. "They can probably override it easily enough..."

"Huh," Alannis replied. She didn't trust herself to say much more than that. *It wasn't her*, Alannis told herself. Yet she saw her friend shooting her down and she remembered Marius Giovanni's words. He'd used them, both of them, to get the access codes.

"We need to talk," Lizmadie said, her voice tense.

"Oh?" Alannis turned. They hadn't spoken on the flight. They hadn't had any time from when the guards had pulled them out of Marius's simulators to when they'd been brought aboard the shuttle that led them to this prison. Alannis flinched away from her friend's gaze.

"I can only assume that your escape attempt went something like mine," Lizmadie said.

"Killed lots of guards and had everything go south at the very end?" Alannis asked as lightly as she could manage. The violence and bloodshed, the total and perverse *pointlessness* of that bloodshed ate at her, no matter how simulated it had been.

Even so, the thing that caused the real pain was the expression on Lizmadie's face when she'd shot Alannis. No emotion would have been one thing... but her friend had worn an expression of satisfaction as she did it.

"When we... when *I* got to the cargo hangar," Lizmadie said. "You manned the communications console while I held off the guards coming down the elevator shaft--"

"Elevator shaft?" Alannis asked in surprise. "For me they came out the stairwell."

"I blocked the stairwell," Lizmadie replied.

"I damaged the elevator," Alannis replied with a shrug, "Either one would have worked, I suppose."

"Yes. My point is that we may have experienced slight differences... but I gave my access codes to confirm my identity and then you..." Her lips went into a hard line. "Then the person I thought was you... well, she shot me. Once in the back and then as I fell, she walked up and put a round right through my eyes."

Alannis flinched at that. "I'm sorry." She looked down. "The process lasted a bit longer for me, Marius tried to win me over, to get me to surrender. When I wouldn't, he had you... he had the person pretending to be you... shoot me."

"It wasn't me," Lizmadie said. "And I realize it wasn't *you.*"

"There's a 'but,' there, isn't there?" Alannis asked softly.

"There is," Lizmadie replied. "I realize it logically, but emotionally..."

Alannis shivered. It hurt. It felt like a betrayal. Her senses all told her it had been real. Everything had felt so real, so lifelike. "I've never seen a simulator so real, before."

"Me neither," Lizmadie replied. "And I've done some pretty advanced simulations. I *felt* it when you--" She cut herself off. "I felt it when I got shot. I felt the recoil when I gunned down the guards. I could smell their blood and the smoke and *everything*. It was more real than real."

She nodded in reply. The visceral, brutal reality of it still clung to her. She almost felt like it had been inside her head, somehow. Which was hardly a surprise, considering the fact that Marius Giovanni experimented in mental conditioning and psionics.

Alannis wondered how much of her experiences since her capture that she could trust. Had Forrest's transmission been real? Had any of her imprisonment been real?

Is this prison even real?

She saw echoes of that same worry on Lizmadie's expression. If they couldn't trust their senses, what could they trust?

"He can't control us," Alannis said, forcing confidence into her voice. "He'd destroy our value as hostages if he breaks our minds. So there's got to be some kind of limit to what he does to us."

Lizmadie didn't argue, but Alannis knew the opposite side of that coin even without her saying it. Keeping them slightly drugged and hooked into some kind of simulated reality would be a perfect prison. Marius wouldn't even need to worry about guards, he could simply allow them to play out any escape attempt they wanted... never realizing that they were stuck in some kind of ultra-realistic simulation.

There was one way to tell the difference, Alannis knew. Yet her mind shied away from it. Presumably her psychic abilities would be able to sense outside, to feel everything around her. If this was a simulation, then she'd be able to sense the differences.

She felt a blinding headache come on just from thinking about it. Despite that, Alannis pushed at the hidden part of her mind. The pain blossomed, then doubled and tripled. She felt something inside her mind snap, just for a second.

Alannis could sense the room around her, sense Lizmadie's mind, feel her friend's uncertainty and her thoughts and nervousness.

Without thinking, she touched her friend's thoughts, more a clumsy pat than any kind of mental connection.

The pain in her head amplified again and then spiked. Alannis dropped to her knees, clutching her head in pain. "Okay," she ground out, feeling blood run down her nose and dribble down her chin. "I think I just confirmed this is real."

Lizmadie rushed over, "Holy shit, are you okay?"

Alannis croaked, "I'm great." She felt light-headed and she leaned forward, barely catching herself with her hands before she flopped to the floor. "I'm just going to sleep for a minute..."

The world rushed away.

***

She awoke to a team of medical personnel, escorted by armed guards. They'd been none too gentle in making sure she was awake and not dying. None of them had spoken to her, she didn't even see their faces, they were all hidden behind their armor and helmets. They might as well have been robots.

They'd examined her and then left. They hadn't spoke, they hadn't given her anything for her massive headache. Alannis had spent thirty minutes in the bathroom after that, with the lights off and running her head under the shower, trying to ease the pain.

A few hours later, Alannis and Lizmadie stepped into the dining room. She'd taken the time to scrub the blood off her face and make herself somewhat presentable. She realized that she probably needn't have bothered. Who cared what another prisoner looked like in this place?

Two dozen men and women sat at tables, some in clusters, and some singly. None of them made eye contact with Alannis or Lizmadie. The two of them picked up food trays and then went down the buffet. There were no guards present, it seemed that they could take whatever food they wanted. All of it was already cut into small portions and served as finger food. There was no silverware. The plates were light plastic, some kind of foam-formed material that she didn't think she could break or sharpen.

Alannis filled her plate and then took a seat at an empty table. She ignored the other prisoners even as she took a seat and started eating. They needed a way out. Earlier she'd felt pressure, a need to escape, but now there was a time limit. Marius Giovanni was going to try to steal her son. He had access codes, he surely had studied her son's security. Alannis had to escape from this prison, hijack a ship, and get home in time to stop him.

For a moment, she felt utterly overwhelmed. This wasn't just an impossible task, it was utterly out of her league. Yet she pushed any bit of doubt and uncertainty aside. She would not give up. This wasn't about her life, it was the life of her son. She had proven resistant to Marius's brainwashing program, but her son might be young enough to be indoctrinated, even without the use of Marius's equipment.

I have to save my child.

Alannis ate woodenly, the food tasting like ash in her mouth. She chewed it mechanically, her mind turning over the problem, approaching it from every angle, wondering what she could do, what she had missed, where she might find a way to escape.

She almost didn't notice as a man sat down across from her and Lizmadie.

"Lieutenant Giovanni, Lieutenant Doko," the man spoke in a familiar voice.

Alannis's eyes widened and she stared at him for a moment in shock.

"Welcome, to Purgatory," Marius Giovanni smiled.

***

"You son of a--"

Alannis and Lizmadie both leapt across the table, almost at the same time.

They both bounced off each-other even as they tackled Marius to the ground. They punched and kicked at him, hitting each other as they tried to kill the man who'd imprisoned them. Alannis could barely see, barely breathe as she lashed out, a red haze across her vison.

All too soon, hands caught her and pulled her back. "I'll kill you you son of a bitch!"

To her surprise, though, the guards didn't help Marius to his feet. Nor did the medical team do any more than to confirm he wasn't seriously injured before they withdrew, along with the guards. Alannis noted the hidden doorway that they must have emerged from. Alannis watched them go and her gaze went to Lizmadie, whose eyes were narrowed in suspicion. "What's going on?" Alannis demanded. She noticed that Marius wore a gray prison jumpsuit as well. "What... why are you a prisoner here?"

Marius wiped at a trickle of blood from his split lip, "I suppose I deserved that..." He smiled, the expression somehow at once both familiar and strangely different from the confident smirk of her captor. "I'm not exactly who you think I am." There was an element of sarcasm, almost self-depreciation in his smile.

Alannis took a moment and forced herself to think. Marius was still in charge. There'd been no sign of a coup, she didn't think such a thing was even possible with how he'd programmed his people. Therefore, this wasn't Marius Giovanni. *Or at least, he's not the Marius Giovanni who imprisoned us...*

"You're a clone," Lizmadie said, her voice harsh.

Marius shrugged slightly, "Well, technically speaking, I'm far more identical than a clone would be. I'm identical from my fingerprints to my retinal scans... but for the purposes of discussion, 'clone' is as accurate as anything."

Alannis shot Lizmadie a glance, "The other clones I've encountered haven't been so..."

"Comfortable?" Marius interrupted.

"Sanguine about it," Alannis finished. In fact, Alannis still doubted that her father was truly alive. She thought that Marius-- the *other* Marius-- was also a clone. But the other ones she'd encountered had insisted they were the real ones.

"My dear, I'm a bit more self-aware and introspective than most," Marius shrugged slightly. He gestured back at their table, "Might I sit?"

Lizmadie snorted, "Why not, isn't all this yours as well?"

"In a way, I suppose," Marius replied as he took a seat. "Nice right hook, by the way," he nodded at Alannis, "I suppose your grandmother taught you that?"

Alannis's eyes narrowed, "Your mother?"

"Also... in a way," Marius replied as she sat across from him. "I think of her that way, but I know that I'm a copy of the real Marius, so I realize that I've never really encountered her." He gave that self-depreciating smile again. "Rather distressing, actually. To realize that all of your thoughts, all of your memories are someone else's... and that they were put there for a reason." There was a hollowness to his dark eyes, an ache that made Alannis's heart twist a bit. Perhaps because it was far too similar to what she'd been through as a child.

"What reason is that?" Alannis asked, despite herself.

"It's the question that keeps me alive, I suppose," Marius replied. "Certainly our captor wants to know it. He's spent weeks, even months, trying to torture it out of me." He tugged the collar of his jumpsuit open and Alannis flinched at the scars that ran up his neck from his chest. "Like my brethren, I'm a mystery and if there's one thing we don't like, it's not knowing something."

"We?" Lizmadie demanded.

"Oh, yes, there's five of us, five copies," Marius nodded. "Our captor is one. I consider myself Two. Three works with the Centauri Confederation... or worked, I think someone killed him. Four and Five work for Shadow Lord Lachesis and Shadow Lord Imperious."

Alannis's eyes narrowed, "For a prisoner, you seem to have a lot of knowledge. For that matter, how do you know that the Marius Giovanni who has us captive isn't the real one?"

"Our captor likes to discuss things with me, to see what I would do and to use me as an opponent in tactical and strategic simulations. During some of our discussions he passes along news and information. And he *is* a copy, too," Marius replied, his expression guarded. "I know it. I don't think the real Marius Giovanni still lives. And while our captor believes he's the real Marius... well, the other copies did, too."

"All but you," Lizmadie replied doubtfully.

"I've *met* all the other copies," Marius replied. "Can you say the same?"

Alannis shrugged, "I've encountered one or two of them," she hedged. She didn't want to give him any more information than he already seemed to possess. She hadn't heard about a clone working with Shadow Lord Lachesis, but she filed that away for later consideration.

"Each has a purpose, each has a goal," Marius said, his voice going distant. "Our captor was created with a desire to explore, to learn more about the threat of the Balor. He came back to human space with a driving need to create a defense, a weapon capable of defeating them. The Marius Giovanni working for the Centauri, he wanted to unify humanity under a powerful leader, President Spiridon or whoever he thought was powerful enough and strong-willed enough to rule."

"The other two were focused upon their abilities and joined up with two of the most dangerous Shadow Lords. They've planned attacks, provided strategy and tactics..." Marius trailed off.

"And you?" Alannis asked.

"I've no idea," Marius replied. He gestured around them. "Whatever my purpose *was*, now I am a captive. Like the others, I've some fragmented memories of my creation, of horrible, unending pain... but I've spent most of the past twenty years as this other Marius's prisoner."

"Twenty years?" Lizmadie demanded. "You haven't tried to escape?"

"I have *tried* with greater or lesser success," Marius replied. "I've been recaptured..." His brow furrowed in thought, "three times. I've tried to escape dozens of times. Sometimes I tasted freedom only to find out it was a simulation..."

As Lizmadie and Alannis hissed, he smirked, "Yes, it's terrible, isn't it? Our captor likes to reveal the nature of the game in painful fashion, at times." His expression went bleak. "I've been caught and tortured by several of the other copies as well. None of them... none of *us*, I should say... are very good people."

Alannis really didn't know what to say to that.

He leaned forward across the table, his voice pitched low, "Now, I know this may sound odd, as we haven't met and in reality, I'm not your father..." he glanced at Lizmadie, "nor do I know much about you, other than what I've heard second hand." He let out a tense breath, "But I would like to help you both escape this place. Let me help you, please?"

The plea was all the more powerful for the humility in the man's voice. Alannis didn't want to trust him, didn't want to think of him as her father. He admitted that he wasn't... yet it was apparent that he'd been through hell... and he seemed to want to help.

"Well, they monitor our every move," Alannis said. "We've no resources, no weapons, and we're stuck with these." She held up a bracelet. "Besides, what makes you think we haven't given up?"

Marius smiled at her in reply. "I've had to listen to some of our captor's complaints about you two. So I'm inclined to suspect that if anyone will be breaking out of here, you two will be involved." His smiled faded. "There's nothing for me out there, but you two have families, homes... real *lives*. So let me help you, please?"

"Why not," Alannis replied. Though she didn't know how they could even plan an escape, not without some means of communication. This prison would be far too secure for some kind of improvisational escape attempt.

"What should we call you?" Lizmadie asked. "We can't very well call you Marius."

"Call me Two," he replied. A moment later, Alannis heard his voice in her mind, *and they don't monitor our thoughts.*

Alannis controlled her expression, giving no sign that she'd received his message. She didn't know if Marius already knew of his copy's psychic abilities or not, but that might prove to be a game-changer.

"Pleased to meet you, Two," Lizmadie said, her change of tone apparent to Alannis. That meant that the man had communicated to her as well. They could use him to talk between them, to organize and plan an escape.

Entire scenarios flashed through her mind as she considered that. They had a method to communicate. They had an ally, one who knew the area. She didn't really trust him, not yet, but she thought she could trust his desire to escape... or at least to spite his captor.

"Yes," Alannis smiled, "I'm glad you're here, Two."

***

Ambrosio scowled at the tarps draped over the shuttle. The smart fabric blended in to match the natural environment while the layers of thermal material screened the shuttle's heat and diffused it. The problem being, the planet was dark. There *was* no color. There was no vegetation, no shelter, just barren rock with the consistency of a gravel pit... for as far as the eye could see. Of course, since the star didn't put out much on the visible light spectrum, that wasn't very far. There were some blinking lights out along the horizon and the shuttle's passive sensors had picked out heat from structures as well as emissions... but those were things to be avoided.

Lieutenant Ambrosio didn't know how long they could hide the shuttle, not in the narrow crevasse. It wouldn't be long before someone thought to do a thorough radar sweep... and without their stealth systems online, the shuttle would show up as a difference if they compared a new radar sweep to an older one.

"How long do we need to stay offline?" Lieutenant Ambrosio demanded.

"Two days--" Petty Officer Cartwright started to say.

"More like a week," Feliks interrupted. His thick Centauri accent set Lieutenant Ambrosio's teeth on edge. He hated the Centauri, the arrogant bastards had watched while the Nova Roma Empire had bled and died holding off the Chxor. "Half of systems are fried, we pushed it way too hard. We start it up now and the stealth system is going to fail in five minutes. Our enemies will pick us off thirty seconds after that."

Lieutenant Ambrosio and Petty Officer Cartwright looked at the engineer. "It's that bad?"

"This was an experimental system that someone tacked onto an existing combat shuttle. This wasn't the best platform to do it on, there's far too much excess emissions. But the systems were grafted onto that platform, so there's no help for it. Half the stealth field emitters are burned out, the other half are marginal at best. It will take me five days to repair what I can, another two to bring everything else online."

Petty Officer Cartwright pursed his lips, "I can help..."

"You know how to do maintenance on molecular circuitry?" Feliks arched an eyebrow.

"Uh, I didn't know that was possible..."

"Only with the right tools and a great deal of theoretical physics knowledge," Feliks snapped. "I happen to have both... how is your knowledge of quantum computing?"

"Pretty much non-existent," Petty Officer Cartwright admitted.

"Then you focus on preparing to fly us," Felix replied. "In meantime, I should get busy."

Lieutenant Ambrosio didn't miss how the engineer ignored him and went to work. It bothered him, technicians knew their place within the Nova Roma Imperial Fleet. But he let it slide, for now. Apparently the engineer was some kind of super-brain. Once

Ambrosio had a better grasp on the overall situation he could worry about instilling proper discipline and decorum.

He turned and moved over to where Staff Sergeant Witzke had assembled the rescue team. Lieutenant Ambrosio had to hide a scowl at the mix of uniforms. Technically this was a United Colonies expedition. Technically. Yet it was the United Colonies that had abandoned Princess Lizmadie. It was the United Colonies which laid claim to Nova Roma... and referendum or no referendum, Lieutenant Ambrosio was loyal to the Nova Roma Empire and Emperor Romulus IV... or Prince Alexander as he currently went by.

He didn't know if Nova Roma would rise again in his lifetime, but that didn't mean he had to be happy about working with the nation that had absorbed most of the star systems that had made up the Nova Roma Empire. *Sure Prince Alexander talks good about them, but that doesn't change the situation.* The day would come when eventually the United Colonies would need to be forced out.

But for now, Staff Sergeant Witzke, Corporal Wandry, and Corporal Wicklund were part of the rescue team. And while Lieutenant Ambrosio was their commanding officer, he didn't doubt that the three United Colonies Marines would do what they wanted.

"We're grounded for the next seven days," Lieutenant Ambrosio stated. "In the meantime, our priorities are intelligence and reconnaissance. First Squad," he nodded at Staff Sergeant Witzke, who had been a *First* Sergeant up until he took a voluntary demotion to serve on this rescue operation, "I want you to establish a secure perimeter, with observation posts. Minimize our movement, I don't want to give away our position through them noticing our personnel out and about, but I want this area secure and I want to know if there are any threats inbound."

He couldn't hide his grimace as he looked at Staff Sergeant Witzke. The thought of women in combat didn't sit well with him. For that matter, in his opinion, the noncomissioned officer shouldn't even be out of the sick bay, but she'd talked her way onto the shuttle and Lieutenant Ambrosio couldn't afford to coddle her. "Second Squad will assist me with recon and intelligence. We identified three structures with moderate activity nearby. I want the squad broken down into three teams, each will move to a target, identify the activity level and force presence, and identify threats."

Staff Sergeant Witzke nodded, "Yes, sir. What if we see targets of opportunity?"

Lieutenant Ambrosio scowled, "We're severely outnumbered. Our priority is to maintain a low profile."

"What if we locate the princesses?" Staff Sergeant Witzke insisted.

One of Lieutenant Ambrosio's people snickered and he snorted himself. "In that highly unlikely event, we'll have to come to a decision. But last intel was that Princess Lizmadie was at the command spire, a quarter of the way around the planet. Maintain a low profile, don't attract attention. Once we get our shuttle online and we get a feel for the local terrain, we can think about a rescue operation."

"We aren't here for just Princess Lizmadie," Lance Corporal Wandry growled.

"I know that," Lieutenant Ambrosio snapped back, "I shortened it for brevity." He scowled again at the three United Colonies personnel. He wished he didn't have them, but he couldn't afford not to use them. And truthfully, he'd rather keep his best people back to guard the shuttle. It was their lifeline on this god-forsaken planet.

"Maintain radio silence, maintain a low profile, and no matter what, all personnel will need to be back here within seven standard days. At that point we'll relocate to a better hide position and anyone who isn't back in time will be left behind... am I understood?"

"Yes, sir," came the chorus of responses.

"I've uploaded recon targets to each team leader," Lieutenant Ambrosio said. "Move out."

***

"What's a brevity?" Lance Corporal Wandry muttered.

"It's like when you frock someone, I think," Corporal Wicklund replied.

"I ain't frocking anyone..."

"Shut it, both of you," Staff Sergeant Witzke snapped. She looked over at the fourth member of her recon team. Sergeant Archeletto looked back at her with a calm expression, but she knew exactly why Lieutenant Ambrosio had assigned him to her team.

Archeletto had been a platoon sergeant before volunteering for this mission. He had the experience to lead this entire operation himself.

He was here to watch her... and if necessary to replace her.

I'd like to see him try, she thought grimly. The Nova Roma Marines had been through some shit, but she'd been through the battle of the Throne of Kopal Pesh and then the taking of Yaitsik Station. Before that, she'd been at the Battle of Halcyon where she'd fought her way through an alien base full of pirates and mercenaries. Before *that* she'd helped to put down the mutineers of the Dreyfus Coup. Staff Sergeant Witzke had been a private during the Third Battle of Faraday where she'd boarded a Balor cruiser and fought in the dark, alien corridors against the psychic aliens.

Compared to most of the Nova Roma Marines, she'd seen far more combat, been given far more initiative, and she'd been taught to be adaptable to situations that most of them couldn't imagine. She didn't miss how Lieutenant Ambrosio looked a little rough around the edges, he was freaked out about being left behind by the *Widowmaker*. He felt outnumbered and out of his depth.

Staff Sergeant Witzke was used to being out of her depth and outnumbered. At this point, she wouldn't know what to do with herself in a fair fight.

That was why she met Sergeant Archeletto's eyes without flinching. "Draw double rations and double ammunition load out, and I want a full load of demo gear."

Sergeant Archeletto frowned, "Staff Sergeant, this is a recon only..."

"If we run into something that needs taking out, we're damned well going to have what we need to do it. They're not going to need demo charges back here. If we don't need it, it's just a bit more weight we'll carry. If we *do* need it, then we're really going to need it, understand?"

Her nominal subordinate gave her a slight nod. He didn't like the subversion of their orders, but he wasn't about to go tattle on her to Lieutenant Ambrosio. "I'll see to it," he said.

"Good," Dawn Witzke said. She waited for her recon team to move to the shuttle before she turned away and adjusted her gear. Out of their sight, she could let her hands tremble in pain. Her ribs most definitely were *not* fully healed. The impact on Mars had been the equivalent of being hit by a fast moving vehicle. Her armor had blunted that to something less than lethal, but she'd still broken several ribs, cracked her pelvis, and dislocated her shoulder. She'd had time to heal some of that, but she'd had to down more painkillers than recommended just to don her gear and walk aboard the shuttle. This wasn't supposed to be a long term mission, so she'd only brought a few more doses. The combat shuttle had some more in the medical gear, but that was for serious, life-threatening injuries, and Dawn Witzke wasn't about to steal that kind of thing from her Marines.

The last dose had worn off and she was in considerable pain. Every breath hurt... but it was the cracked pelvis that made standing almost unbearable and walking sheer agony. The upcoming thirty kilometer recon mission was going to be hell. She wanted nothing more than to crawl into the shuttle and curl up and die.

But Lieutenant Alannis Giovanni was out there, somewhere. Staff Sergeant Witzke didn't trust these Nova Roma Marines to focus on rescuing her, not when they were so obviously worried about Princess Lizmadie. While Dawn Witzke wanted to rescue the Marine Lieutenant as well, the priority had to be to rescue the Emperor's sister. Someone had to keep an eye out for the United Colonies and Staff Sergeant Witzke was the senior United Colonies person on the ground.

Suck it up, Marine, she told herself.

***

Chapter XV

September 23, 2410
Golgotha
Unclaimed Space

Alannis nodded in the direction of Two even as she concentrated on thinking about the escape plan. *We need to move soon.*

If they didn't move soon, the guards would figure things out. As it was, they had to know that *something* was going on. Alannis didn't know how this copy of Marius Giovanni had kept his psychic abilities hidden, but surely the *other* Marius Giovanni would at least suspect it and warn his people to beware.

For the moment, though, it seemed that the guards weren't aware that their prisoners had a way to get around the constant surveillance.

Two had put together quite an organization, it seemed. They didn't have any real weapons or equipment, but they'd mapped out the facility and they knew what doors the guards would come from. They knew roughly how many guards there were... and they had educated guessses about the layout of the areas outside of their secure quarters.

All they needed was a proper distraction and something to give them an edge.

Alannis stepped into line behind Lizmadie and the pair of them moved towards the buffet. Alannis tensed a bit as they approached the food. She felt her heart beat faster and she took hurried breaths as she saw the mussels. It was something they'd discussed, earlier. Lizmadie had a food alergy to soy, Alannis to seafood. It seemed that Alannis had drawn the short straw.

She hadn't even reached the buffet when a door opened and a guard team stepped out. "Princess Giovanni," Major Scaparetti spoke from behind them. "I couldn't help but notice your heart rate increase. You weren't thinking of ingesting a known food allergen to create problems for me, were you?"

Alannis grimaced. She took a half step towards the food but two of the guards advanced to cut her off. "Walk with me," Major

Scaparetti said in a flat voice. He shot a glance at Lizmadie, "Both of you."

The four guards led the two of them out of the room. Any thoughts that Alannis had of using the situation to her advantage vanished as she saw the reaction team that awaited in the corridor.

She pushed aside her disappointment and took the time to observe the surroundings. This wasn't part of the VIP prisoner areas. The access corridor was strictly utilitarian, with no frills. Metal conduits and bare concrete were the highlights.

Major Scaparetti led the way down the corridor, then up a narrow ladder. To Alannis's shock, they stepped through a doorway and then outside. She stared in a daze up at the night sky, the stars glittering above the dark world. Looking around, she saw they stood on a catwalk, which seemed to run from one section of the complex to another.

"Purgatory is a holding place, Princesses. It's a calm, quiet place for men and women who are too valuable to mistreat," Major Scaparetti said. He glanced between the two of them, "It's meant to be pleasant confinement, far superior to the treatment that most of Lord Admiral Giovanni's prisoners can expect... and you two are fucking that up."

Alannis felt things click into place. "You have us outside of normal security so that Marius won't know what you say, right?"

Major Scaparetti sneered, "I don't doubt you'd whine to your father about any perceived mistreatment as soon as he gets back to the system. I'll not give you ammunition. But here are the facts. You two entitled *bitches* think you can come into my little slice of paradise and cause trouble? I may not be able to hurt you, but I can make your lives absolutely miserable. Try another stunt like eating a food allergy and I'll make sure my people take their time about getting you medical treatment... and maybe they'll forget to give you something for the pain and discomfort. Things can get much worse than that, do you understand?"

Alannis met the man's eyes. Without hesitation she stepped forward. "You just told me the most important thing, you moron. You told me that Marius is out of the star system... and I already know what he's doing out there. He's going after my son... do you think I'll give a shit about a little discomfort compared to that?"

Major Scaparetti stepped back quickly, but Alannis stuck with him, right up until two guards stepped between them, shoulder-checking her backwards.

Major Scaparetti's face had gone pale as he realized his mistake. "Get them back to their quarters. They're restricted to their suite. Don't let them talk to *anyone*."

The obvious sign that Scaparetti was panicked should have made her feel powerful, but instead it just left Alannis feeling hollow. Marius had already left to kidnap her son. He'd probably taken Reese with him. He had a head start of hours, possibly days.

She couldn't stop him. The best she could hope to do at this point was to escape and get a message back home in time to help. *Please, God, keep my son safe.* She didn't trust Marius not to brainwash him, to use his psychic abilities or mental conditioning program to turn her son into a fanatic. She couldn't let that happen.

She wouldn't let Marius have her son.

I'm going to get out of here.

***

"Ho-lee-sheet, Staff Sergeant!" Corporal Wandry hissed, "Are you seeing what I'm seeing?!"

"Princess Giovanni and Princess Lizmadie up on a catwalk?" Staff Sergeant Witzke replied. "Yeah, I see it. I don't believe my eyes, but I'm seeing it."

"It's got to be a trap," Sergeant Archeletto said.

"I don't see how," Dawn Witzke replied. If their enemies knew they were here to set up this kind of display, then they wouldn't need to do it. They had enough personnel to flood the entire area and search them out. "Alright, new plan, we recon the facility and if there's a way to spring the princesses, that's what we do."

"Staff Sergeant," Sergeant Archeletto began, "Captain --that is, *Lieutenant*-- Ambrosio's orders were to reconoiter the area, not to stage some kind of rescue..."

"His actual words, Sergeant Archeletto, were that we'd have to 'come to a decision.' He didn't specify under these circumstances and frankly, how could he?" Staff Sergeant Witzke shook her head. "No, we need to evaluate the situation, but this may be our opportunity to rescue them."

"They should still be there after we--"

"After we hike fifteen kilometers back to the shuttle?" She interrupted. "Or how about after we put together a rescue plan and then hike all the way back here? This might be the prison where they're keeping them, it might be a temporary holding facility. Hell, it might just be a brief hold-over. We may only have minutes before their transportation spools up. We have *one* opportunity for certain, and that's now, and we have to act like it. Unless you know more than I do?"

The other NCO didn't reply. She couldn't see his face under his visor, but after the nine day journey to this planet, she could picture his frown of distaste well enough. He hated taking orders from a woman, he hated being in this position.

Brittle, she thought to herself, *like most of the Nova Roma military, very strong, but inflexible.*

In her opinion, that was why they'd lost the war with the Chxor... and that was why many of the survivors had signed on with Prince Alexander. They didn't want to change, they *refused* to change or bend. It meant they fought hard, but they had lost because they couldn't adapt.

She just hoped that Sergeant Archeletto wasn't going to be a pain in her ass for the rest of the rescue. If he got in her way too much, she'd just shoot him and be done with it.

Staff Sergeant Witzke didn't think about the agony of her body and she didn't contemplate the risk of trying to rescue the two princesses from the facility. She focused on what she needed to do. There'd be time for the rest of all that later... after she'd finished her mission.

***

Breathe, Alannis thought to herself, *just... breathe.*

She focused on keeping her heartbeat level and calm, even as she waited. The time for their escape was coming soon. The earlier distraction had been meant to serve as a bit of a test. Alannis didn't trust most of the other prisoners. In fact, she wasn't certain she really trusted *any* of the other prisoners. Yet their desire to escape, their anger at Marius Giovanni, those she trusted.

And Two. She didn't know why, but she'd come to trust him.

Right now, all that Alannis had to do was keep her heartbeat steady and not set off any alarms.

She'd had a friend who'd been into meditation. Ashtar Shan had said she found it relaxing. She said that she went to her happy place, found at the core of her being. Of course, the last time Alannis had seen her friend meditating had been right after their last workout together aboard the Constellation... right before she'd been gunned down in an assassination attempt meant for Alannis.

Think about something else, she told her mind. Yet despite herself, she couldn't help but replay the scene of Ensign Ashtar Shan's death. Alannis had killed the woman who killed her, but too late to save her friend. It was the first time that she'd killed another human, or at least, the first time she'd been close enough to watch them die, anyway. As she thought back on the death of Lieutenant Krysta Busch, the woman who killed her friend, she finally felt a coldness wash through and over her.

I'm a killer, she thought. She'd killed many times sense then. The slavers who'd tried to kidnap her on Halcyon. The alien attackers at the Throne of Kopal Pesh, who'd somehow left remnants of human DNA. Her attack on the Temple of Light, where she'd gunned down cultists without flinching. Her guards, over a half a dozen that she'd killed in escape attempts.

Her heartbeat dropped to a slow, steady pace. Her breathing slowed. Alannis's eyes opened.

Alannis didn't have a happy place. She had anger. She had rage. She had a childhood that had been stripped away, destroyed by actions outside of her control. Alannis didn't go to her happy place, she went to the violent fire at the center of her heart and let that flame wash through her.

***

"Sir," the technician spoke up, "subject's heart rate has returned to normal parameters."

Major Scaparetti gnawed at his lip as he stared at the monitors. The duty officer had called him down as several of their "guests" had moved outside their normal conditions. That his two troublesome new guests were at the center of it all, hadn't surprised him.

Major Scaparetti rubbed his face in thought. "What about the others?" He demanded.

What had surprised him was to see what other guests seemed to be involved. Several Colonial Republic officers, two Centauri Confederation officers, and dozens of the political prisoners all had accelerated heart rates, faster breathing, and increased neural activity that suggested they were about to launch some kind of escape attempt. In particular, there were five who Major Scaparetti could tell were up to something. All five were in the same area. They weren't together, but they were clustered in such a way that they could work together.

"No change, sir," the technician responded.

Major Scaparetti's first instinct was to send in his riot teams, to lock them all down. Yet it was a stick he hated to use. Marius Giovanni had created this prison to keep some of his "guests" in relatively good style. Many were hostages, many more were kept because their well-being could act as leverage at a later date. They were Marius Giovanni's golden geese, and Major Scaparetti was their keeper.

Major Scaparetti didn't trust his riot team not to injure any of those golden geese.

All the same, he had to head things off... and the fact that Alannis Giovanni's heartrate had decreased actually left him feeling even more uncertain. He *knew* she was involved, somehow. Under other circumstances, he'd make an example of her to the other prisoners... but he couldn't. Marius Giovanni had made it abundantly clear that he wanted his daughter alive and unharmed. He'd gone as far as to command Major Scaparetti to make her "happy" if that was even possible.

That left Princess Lizmadie... but she too had value and Major Scaparetti didn't want to damage the valuable goods. At least the both of them had stopped hanging around with the Marius Giovanni clone. Major Scaparetti had almost been pleased when they'd had a public falling-out.

All of these "guests" are second string, Major Scaparetti thought to himself. Their value was secondary. They were on the list of those who might, one day soon, be mentally conditioned, as their value decreased over time. "Send the level one response team,"

Major Scaparetti said after a moment. The level one team was only a dozen strong, without the heavy riot control gear.

"Yes, sir," the duty officer nodded, "should I notify Command?"

"Not, yet," Major Scaparetti replied. That was technically a violation of their standing orders, but with both the Lord Admiral and Captain Reese out of the system, Major Scaparetti hoped this would slip under the radar... much like the last two incidents involving the Lord Admiral's daughter.

There's nothing that requires Command's attention, he told himself.

***

Cameron Bueller wasn't what most people would think of as an ideal prisoner. He'd been a screw-up even before his time here, unable to hold anything remotely like a normal job, able to get by with his good looks and friendly disposition, the best he'd ever accomplished was for people to think he was a handsome moron. Cameron had been a mildly successful holo-vid actor in a couple of romantic comedies. He'd been told that his charming smile, cheerful disposition, and earnestness was a big hit with the ladies in the Centauri Confederation. They'd liked handsome and dumb. Being sort of a screw-up had seemed to make them like him more.

He didn't really know, he wasn't interested in women. But he'd been willing to pretend, and to let his lover-turned-agent to sign him onto several roles that had led to a somewhat-successful acting career. That had turned out well enough that he'd accumulated something of a cult following and he'd begun to get invitations to all sorts of events.

He and his partner had accepted just one such invitation, a journey aboard a Tau Ceti senator's yacht, because, well, it was a private freaking yacht and you only lived once, right? Unfortunately for Cameron and his lover/agent, Rodrigo, the senator's yacht had been boarded by Marius Giovanni's people. Most of the crew and passengers had been interned, vanished into whatever project Marius brainwashed them for. The senator had either made some kind of deal or been brainwashed too, Cameron didn't know.

Cameron *did* know that his lover was the cousin of the military governor in the Alpha Canis Majoris system, so Rodrigo had warranted special hostage status. As a multimillionaire with some vague recognition, apparently Cameron had as well. The two of them had made the best of things, both knowing that they were lucky to be alive and to retain their minds intact.

But there had been some kind of turmoil in the Alpha Canis Majoris system. The government had collapsed and Rodrigo's value as a hostage had vanished... and then Cameron was alone. He'd tried to commit suicide after they dragged Rodrigo away. He'd managed to light his room on fire, hoping to succumb to the smoke and flames. The guards had intervened before he did himself permanent damage, but they hadn't bothered to be delicate about the scars that he'd endured, they'd simply patched him up and kept him alive. Cameron knew that, short of massive reconstruction, he'd never be in acting again.

I'm a screw-up, Cameron thought to himself, *I've never done anything right... not even killing myself.* Cameron had lost all hope and passion. Then Two had come to him. The clone of Marius Giovanni had showed Cameron his own scars, told his own story of torture and torment... and Cameron had come to realize that it wasn't just his life that Marius Giovanni had destroyed... it was the lives of tens of thousands, possibly hundreds of thousands of people.

When he'd acted, he'd been content to channel a bit of trivial emotion, the slight impulses that had come to him as he tried to empathize with the shallow characters of his roles. As Cameron realized the full depths of Marius Giovanni's evils... he realized that killing himself wasn't just an easy way out, it was cowardice. Marius Giovanni had to be stopped. Cameron didn't think he had any real chance of stopping him by himself... but he could play a role.

Cameron knew that the guards monitored his heart rate, he knew that *they* would know that he was up to something. Cameron had been inventive before, they had only barely stopped the flames that had nearly killed him. They would be wary of anything he might attempt and they'd be far more likely to intervene early.

Cameron was fine with that. *I'm going to die, but I'm going to throw a wrench in the plans of the people who took everything from me in the process.* As a perennial screw-up, Cameron could appreciate that.

He felt his heart race as he wrapped his anger around himself. It was a righteous anger, the only real thing that he felt anymore. Marius Giovanni had to be stopped. Rodrigo would be avenged.

***

Major Scaparetti scowled as he watched his level one response team moved in towards the five prisoners. Three of them had caused trouble before, one of them had come close to burning down a wing of the prison, to date, Major Scaparetti's only black mark on an otherwise spotless record.

I think Mister Bueller will have to suffer a fatal accident, he thought to himself. The former actor had only marginal value as a hostage anyway. The only reason he'd been kept around was that his tragic "death" at the hands of pirates had launched him into fame. Major Scaparetti assumed that the Lord Admiral planned to have the actor cleaned up and used as a talking head to support his regime later on.

The two other troublesome prisoners had been in minor scuffles. They and the other two would receive some special attention from his response team, and then Major Scaparetti would be certain they saw what happened to Bueller.

Then he would have to make an appropriate example to Alannis Giovanni. Something that showed the consequences of her actions. He knew she was involved, he just didn't know how... yet.

***

Cameron Bueller looked up as three guards emerged from one of the concealed doors, only a few meters from where he stood. Cameron grinned at them, "Come on, you bastards, come and get me!"

He saw them hesitate. Clearly they had expected worry or panic. Well, Cameron knew how to give them exactly what they wanted. He turned and broke into a run.

They could have used their stunners, but the short-ranged electrical pulse weapons could cause a heart attack or stroke, under certain conditions. The guards here at Purgatory never resorted to their stunners, preferring not to risk injuring or killing a valuable prisoner.

A glance over his shoulder showed the three guards in pursuit, and Cameron couldn't help a manic grin as he stretched his legs and *ran.*

The corridor flashed past as he raced towards the common area, guards in pursuit. Everything was going as Two had suggested. Of course, that meant the next part was really going to hurt.

***

Major Scaparetti scowled as his response team, split into five groups, chased their targets through the corridors. He almost called their pursuit off. It was clear that all five of the prisoners had coordinated their sprints... and it was just as clear that they'd coordinated those runs with other prisoners, because the corridors they ran through were clear.

This had to be another stunt, designed to test security or embarrass him. He knew instantly who must be responsible for that. *That little bitch,* he thought, his gaze going to the monitor that showed Alannis Giovanni. *She's trying to make me look bad.*

The runners had reached the central hub. They'd started on the northern wing and at this point, they were well ahead of his response teams... and all five of them had remained on different floors and in different corridors, forcing his men to spread out to pursue them.

"Sir, we could end this, put the whole facility in lock down..." his duty officer spoke.

"No," Major Scaparetti snapped. If the facility went into lock down, it would go into the permanent logs *and* Purgatory's computer system would notify headquarters of an incident. The last thing he wanted was for this to escalate, especially not over five idiots.

Major Scaparetti leaned forward and toggled a control, "Mobilize team two," he snapped. "Intercept the runners, lock them down. Authorized force up to class two non-lethal." That included rubber bullets and stun batons. It was likely that his guards would kill two or more of the five that way, but Major Scaparetti had no choice, he needed to shut them down, hard.

"Sir," the duty officer stepped close, his voice pitched low, "Team two is our initial riot response team. If we send them in..."

"Our overall response will be delayed, yes, I know," Major Scaparetti waved a hand. "But these runners are headed away from our other troublemakers. We'll have time to get other people into position before any of the other troublemakers can become a real issue." They could pound on armored doors all they wanted, they wouldn't break through.

"What if this is a distraction, sir?" his duty officer asked.

"From what?" Major Scaparetti snorted. "They can't accomplish much, if anything, other than to hurt one another." He shook his head, "The situation is in hand."

Still, the man had a point. "Get our second shift personnel ready and in position to intercept the runners, send our second team to control the situation with the other potential troublemakers. Have them near section three of the north wing." That was the location with the largest group of prisoners with accelerated heart rates. If there was some kind of riot planned, that would be where they'd start. It was at the far end of the building, furthest away from the central hub. If the prisoners hoped to escape, it made some sense, though he didn't know how they planned to get out of the facility.

Not possible, but it doesn't hurt to take precautions.

***

Cameron ducked low as he heard the hiss of a stunner behind him. The guard must have missed, because Cameron's muscles didn't lock up with electrical current. *This is working,* he thought with shock, *I haven't screwed this up for the good guys.*

He dodged left and then rushed into one of the commons areas, a large, open room. Men and women in prison jumpers looked up in surprise and shock as he rushed into the room. Dozens of his fellow prisoners watched as he ran through, followed by a half-dozen guards. Cameron had plenty of ground to cover and he broke into a sprint, taking great, panting breaths as he pumped his arms and legs, racing for the far end of the room.

Cameron gave a whoop as more armed guards emerged from a hidden door just ahead of him. These guards moved to cut off his escape, but they didn't realize that Cameron had no intention of escaping.

As the guards rushed forward, they roughly shoved prisoners down and out of their way. More prisoners scattered to the sides and out of their paths. Some of them even ran behind the guards, towards the open doors from which they'd come. Cameron focused on the nearest guard, tucked his shoulder, and drove into the man with every bit of force he could muster.

The guard wore armor, but that could only lessen the impact, it couldn't stop basic Newtonian physics. Cameron weighed eighty kilograms, and he drove into the other man at a full sprint. Both of them went down, Cameron seeing stars and barely able to draw breath, landing on the guard.

He vaguely heard shouts as other guards rushed up, their attention on him. Rolling over, he looked up just as one of the guards brought up his rifle, aimed at Cameron's face. As the guard's fingers tightened on the trigger, Cameron could do nothing but watch.

Strange, he thought to himself, *I don't want to die, now... at least, not before I see the end of this...*

***

Alannis had watched as Cameron Bueller raced into the commons area. Like the other four chosen runners, he knew what was about to happen. The other prisoners, selected carefully by Two and positioned for the past few days for this occasion *also* knew what was about to happen. But the other prisoners in the room hadn't known *when* it would happen. They'd been under stress, but no more than that of any other prisoners in Purgatory, so their bodies hadn't given it away.

Alannis had known, too... she and Lizmadie and Two had planned the entire thing. As the guards rushed forward to subdue Bueller, prisoners rushed to the doors from which the guards had come, wedging them open with chairs and tables or whatever was on hand.

The guards, too focused on Bueller, didn't see other prisoners converging on them, didn't notice what happened behind them. Half of them had been sprinting after Bueller, they were winded, angry, and their attention entirely focused. The other half had just been awoken after the end of their twelve hour shift. They were groggy, irritated, and their movements were disjointed and slow. Alannis allowed herself a cold smile as she stepped in behind one of the guards, pulled his pistol out of his friction holster, and planted the barrel just at the junction between his armor and helmet.

She pulled the trigger.

At that moment, dozens of prisoners swarmed over the guards. Here and there, one got off a shot or shout of warning, but they didn't have time to react. Prisoners struck them with chairs, with prison shanks, and with their fists, even as other prisoners ripped away weapons and turned them against their former owners. In a matter of seconds, all the guards were down.

"To the control room!" Alannis shouted, waving her pistol as emphasis. They rushed to the open doors, even as alarms began to go off. Alannis stopped to pick up a datapad off one of the downed guards, and then raced after the other rioting prisoners.

***

"Move!" Lieutenant Lizmadie Doko barked, even as she shoved prisoners ahead of her through the closing door. She'd been in charge of the ambush in the dining hall, and while it had gone better than expected, it had also become a bloodbath. A couple of the guards had managed to get some space and they'd gunned down a least a dozen prisoners. Fortunately, they hadn't been able to differentiate between those in on the attack and those unfortunate enough to be in the area, so most of her strike team was still up, but there were a lot of dead and wounded men and women.

They hadn't been able to block off the doors, either, there weren't enough heavy items to do the job, so Lizmadie just barely cleared the doorway as the hatch slid shut. "Go, go!" Lizmadie shouted. They didn't know the layout of the central hub, they didn't know where the armory was or where the command center was. Each team operated off their own initiative, their goals oriented on taking down communications, power, and command of the facility.

Lizmadie continued to shove people ahead of her. She heard bursts of gunfire and here and there she stumbled over a body, sometimes in prison jumpsuits, other times in coveralls or uniform. The shouting and confusion continued, but Lizmadie skidded to a halt as she saw a code on a hatch.

It was something she recognized. Not from the base, or her previous escape attempts, but from her escape from the Chxor occupation of Nova Roma. This was a power relay station, she was certain of it. She pulled a stolen datapad up and quickly spliced it into the hatch controls. She paused to wipe a smear of the previous owner's blood off the screen, then went to work.

Lizmadie tripped the hatch's lock and then gestured at a prisoner near her to help her. They strained at the hatch for a moment, finally getting it open.

On the other side, Lizmadie gave a grin, seeing the large forms of breaker boxes and power relays. She didn't hesitate, but rushed inside and started flipping switches.

***

"What the hell?" Staff Sergeant Witzke asked as lights all across the facility went dark.

"Someone's hit the power," Sergeant Archelctto said, his voice nervous. "Ambush?"

Staff Sergeant Witzke shook her head, "Negative." She cranked up the audio on her helmet and then felt a smile grow on her face, "I hear gunfire."

"Alright," Staff Sergeant Witzke snapped, "Wandry and Wicklund, take point. I want their communications offline. If there's some kind of riot or attack, I want to make damned sure that Marius's people won't have any help coming. Sergeant Archeletto, you're with me, we're going to breach the perimeter and then run interception."

"Staff Sergeant, our orders--"

"Went out the airlock when we saw the Princesses," Staff Sergeant Witzke snapped. "Move out!"

They broke into a run and Staff Sergeant Witzke took a brief pause to inject the last of the pain-killers and a dose of stimulant. She needed to be able to move. Princess Alannis Giovanni needed her help.

She'd worry about what damage she did herself later

***

As the lights went out, Major Scaparetti felt his heart begin to race.

Red emergency lighting came on a moment later, but the baleful glow just gave everything a claustrophobic feeling. The growing sounds of gunfire and the muffled sounds of screams made Major Scaparetti's stomach twist.

This had spiraled out of control. This went beyond containment, now he realized it was a matter of survival. Prisoners that he had tormented for decades were running through the corridors of his prison, armed with weapons.

He felt an odd bit of satisfaction. Major Scaparetti had never seen combat. He'd never had the opportunity to prove himself in the theater of war. In his service of Marius Giovanni, he'd always been relegated to administrative roles. Somehow, Alannis Giovanni had sensed that. Now he'd finally test his mettle. It didn't matter anymore what Marius would think, about how Major Scaparetti had failed his task of keeping the prisoners alive and happy.

No, now it was time to fight and kill. If Scaparetti was going to fail his job, he'd at least take as many of the bastards as he could with him in the process. *Especially that little spoiled bitch.*

"Sir," his duty officer snapped, "we have reports of prisoners in the barracks, in the kitchens, we stopped them short of the armory for now, but our second response team is stuck in the north wing--"

"Arm our support staff," Major Scaparetti snapped. "All personnel. Launch an attack down the central corridor, drive them back out of the secure areas."

"Sir, we must get a message out--"

"Arm your personnel and move out!" Major Scaparetti shouted.

The technicians looked at the two of them, their eyes wide. Most of them were well-paid volunteers, men and women with technical expertise, who never expected to have to use a weapon.

"Sir, you can't expect me to--"

The duty officer didn't have a chance to finish. Major Scaparetti drew his pistol and shoved it in the man's face, grabbing him by the back of his head with his other hand. He didn't shoot him, but only because he'd forgotten to thumb off the weapon's safety. "Get. Your. Men. Moving." Major Scaparetti bit out. "Now!"

The duty officer stumbled back as he released him. Major Scaparetti waved his pistol around the control room. "All of you, move out!"

Men and women scrambled to the weapons racks. Major Scaparetti stalked over and pulled down the drum-fed TRA Hammer. The big, twenty-five millimeter rifle felt good in his hands. He glowered at his people, the red emergency lighting giving his expression a demonic appearance. He jerked out the non-lethal rubber bullet drum magazine and threw it to the side. Major Scaparetti used the keys from his necklace to open the locker next to the rack, and he drew out an armor piercing drum. It was meant to be for use against some kind of armored assault on the facility. Against an unarmored prisoner, the weapon went far beyond overkill.

Alannis Giovanni wanted to test me, he grinned as he slammed the drum in place. *She will get more than she bargained for.*

* * *

Chapter XVI

September 23, 2410
Golgotha
Unclaimed Space

Cameron Bueller wasn't really certain how he was still alive. The other prisoners had taken down the guards, sure, but he would have expected at least one of them to put a bullet in him in the process. Instead, he'd come through alive and unharmed.

After that, there'd been storming the rest of the facility. Cameron and the other prisoners had rushed through the corridors, firing at just about anything that moved, but it seemed like the guards were too confused to put up a decent fight.

They were supposed to search for an armory or command center, but many of the prisoners were simply hunting down any of their captors they could find. Cameron flinched away from the red ruin that they'd made of one of the technicians. All his anger, all his hate had evaporated with the realization that he really didn't want to die.

That didn't mean he didn't want his captor's punished, but...

He looked over as a pair of whooping prisoners dragged a screaming woman out of the corridor, her face battered and bloodied and her uniform torn open. Cameron looked around, hoping someone would intervene, but most of the other escapees either didn't seem to notice or care.

Cameron looked down at the pistol in his hands. The woman had been one of his captors. While she might not have sent Rodrigo to be programmed, she'd helped to run the prison facility. Cameron tried to tell himself he shouldn't get involved. Even so, he found himself outside the room a moment later, pistol readied.

"Stop," Cameron snapped. He saw the two prisoners had the woman down, her uniform mostly ripped off. Cameron thought she looked like one of the medical technicians.

He recognized one of the prisoners, then. *Martin,* Cameron thought, *of course.* The former Colonial Republic officer had made no bones about the fact that he'd had multiple wives and concubines or that he took what he'd wanted. He'd been little more than a well-connected pirate.

"Get out of here, pretty-boy," Martin sneered. "She's not your type."

Martin's friend snickered at that, but Cameron brought up his pistol. "Stop. Leave... now."

Martin's face went hard. "Like I'm afraid of you! Not man enough to put it where it belongs. Get out of here and go find your boyfriend you--"

Cameron lowered the pistol slightly and fired a round into the deck. Martin's eyes went wide in surprise. "I said, leave."

Martin let go of the woman. He and the other man stood, but they didn't make for the door. Instead, Martin gave the other man a nod.

Cameron realized what they meant to do just as they rushed him. He brought his pistol in line with Martin and fired twice, flinching from the bark of the pistol. As Martin fell back, Cameron brought his pistol around and fired again. The second man fell with a scream, hands going to his leg.

Martin had fallen face down, and Cameron gingerly rolled the man over with his foot. The dead man's eyes stared up at him and Cameron shivered and stepped back.

He looked at the whimpering woman and the shouting man. As a couple more prisoners appeared in the doorway, he turned to them. "Patch him up," Cameron pointed at the wounded man. "Keep him away from her."

The two prisoners looked nervous, "Shouldn't we... you know, kill her?"

"She's a medical tech," Cameron snapped out. "I'm sure there'll be a trial or something. In fact..." He dragged Martin's corpse to the side. "Any other guards or techs you guys see, tell the others to bring them here, we'll keep them under guard. Okay?"

Both prisoners nodded. The woman looked angry. That was good, maybe she'd help to prevent another rape. "I'm going to go find whoever's in charge," Cameron said.

"We don't have weapons," the woman said as he stepped past them.

Cameron hesitated, then passed over his pistol. "I'll find another, keep this place secure."

He jogged away, somehow feeling better. He'd done something. He'd done something *right*.

***

They'd breached the perimeter as soon as the power went down. Staff Sergeant Witzke had detached Wandry and Wicklund to take out the base's comms tower while she and Sergeant Archeletto moved towards the central hub on a direct route as fast as they could.

Staff Sergeant Witzke bit back a curse as Sergeant Archeletto grabbed her by the shoulder. Her barely-healed ribs and pelvis both protesting at being jerked to a halt. Sergeant Archeletto spoke in a low voice, "Staff Sergeant, we should withdraw--"

"You hear that?" She snapped back as she waved at the compound. "This is a full-scale battle, now. Our two VIP's, the whole reason we are here, are in the middle of it. We owe it to them to intervene."

"But we risk capture!" Sergeant Archeletto hissed. "If we get caught or killed, we give away the position of the shuttle and any opportunity--"

"This is Reject Three," Wandry's voice came over the radio. "Their communications relay is powering up off their emergency generator. We're too far away to disable, how should we proceed?"

"Take it out," Staff Sergeant Witzke ordered.

A moment later, she saw Wandry fire his plasma rifle at full strength. The bolt almost seemed to travel slowly, but it still covered over six hundred meters in just under a second. The plasma bolt struck the base of the comms tower and for a second, the entire facility lit up like day.

Dawn Witzke ducked her head as bits of the comm tower rained down across the facility. She turned to Sergeant Archeletto, "Either you follow my orders or you get the hell out of my way." She shoved past him, her body still aching. The painkillers were enough to take the edge off, but she worried that she'd already injured herself.

She ran forward, not caring whether Sergeant Archeletto followed her or not. She didn't know if the princesses knew where the command center was, but she assumed they'd head for the central hub, so that's where she went. "Reject Three and Four, move in on our position. Engage hostiles at will."

Staff Sergeant Witzke rushed up the external stairs, taking them three at a time. She hit the top landing and ripped a breaching charge off her belt and slammed it against the armored hatch, "Clear!"

She ducked back behind a column and saw Sergeant Archeletto flatten against the wall below her. *Apparently he decided to be helpful,* she thought as she triggered the explosives.

The breach charge was a stabilized composite explosive, wrapped in a sandwich of water and sealed to be ready. The water was incompressible, which meant on the one side it acted as a tamper, containing the blast, while on the other it smashed against the armored door like a hammer. The metal door blasted inwards, as if struck by the hand of an angry giant, ripping the doorframe apart and smashing the guards beyond into a bloody mess before they even knew they were dead.

Staff Sergeant Witzke slapped Sergeant Archeletto on the shoulder and waved for him to move forward. Below them, she saw Wandry and Wicklund racing up the stairs. *Here I am, rescuing princesses from towers,* Staff Sergeant Witzke thought to herself, then she ran through the doorway.

***

"That's got to be the command center!" Alannis snapped. "We have to move forward!"

Most of the other prisoners around her just seemed to want to take shelter. Three of the prisoners to the front had already died, their bodies riddled with bullets. There might be another way than this corridor, but there wasn't time. Power was out, but there could be back-ups and if they didn't take out the prison's communications, then someone would get the word out.

Gunfire roared in the corridor. They couldn't afford to stall out. Alannis leaned around the corner and fired her captured rifle. She didn't hit anyone, but she saw forms flinch back from the return fire. "Suppress them!" she shouted. "We need to attack!"

A couple of the other prisoners pointed their weapons out and fired, but it wasn't enough. "We need to attack!" She shouted.

"You do it!" a prisoner near her snapped back. "I'm not risking my neck for anyone else!"

There was no organization. If she led the way in, she'd just be gunned down and none of the others would follow her. Alannis took a few steps back, getting behind the group, then lowered her weapon. "We're going to clear this blockade. Now."

Most of the men and women stared at her with dull or shocked expressions. The one who'd snapped at her earlier, though, sneered. "The hell we are, I'm--"

Alannis shot him between the eyes. As the man's corpse tumbled into the open, more bullets struck his corpse. "I said move!" Alannis shouted.

The half-dozen men and women scrambled into the corridor, firing at the enemy that might kill them as opposed to the one that would shoot them if they didn't attack.

Gunfire met them and Alannis rushed out behind, pausing only to fire on an exposed guard, before she followed the panicked charge.

We are going to take this base and I'm getting off this damned planet.

***

Major Scaparetti ducked into a side room and toggled the hatch closed as the duty officer fell. For a moment, he heard his surviving technicians pounding on the hatch, but after a rattle of gunfire, that stopped. *Weak,* he told himself, *they were weak and useless.*

He heard running footsteps in the corridor. He felt the acid bite of failure, but he clutched the TRA Hammer in his hands, his knuckles going white. There was no way that he could save the facility. The Lord Admiral would kill him, if he was lucky. If he wasn't lucky, the prisoners would find him.

Then, through the hatch, he heard a voice he recognized. He couldn't hear what she shouted, but he recognized Alannis Giovanni's tone, the sense of command that she carried... the spark that he lacked.

A spark I will extinguish, he told himself. He waited a moment, and then toggled open the hatch, stepping out into the corridor and raising his weapon. Less than ten meters away, he saw her. Princess Alannis Giovanni, Lieutenant, United Colonies Fleet.

Even in the midst of the chaos, her appearance struck him. Her black hair hung loose, the curls dropping in their face, her skin pale and spotted with blood. She turned, somehow sensing him, and her dark eyes went wide as she saw him bringing up his weapon.

I've got you, he thought to himself as he squeezed the trigger.

***

Staff Sergeant Witzke saw four or five men and women in prison jumpsuits, just as they opened fire on her. She ducked around the corner and shouted, "Friendlies, cease fire!"

As she popped her head back around the corner, the prisoners stared at her in shock. *Good enough.* She moved out, followed by Sergeant Archeletto. Most of them looked shellshocked, but past them and through the open hatch, she saw what looked like a control room. "Reject Three and Four, we've breached what looks like a control room. There's some escaped prisoners here, take charge and secure the area, we're continuing to find the princesses," she snapped as she jogged down the corridor.

She found herself stepping over bodies, technicians and prisoners, then rounded another corner and found Lieutenant Giovanni. Yet before Staff Sergeant Witzke could say anything, she saw an officer step out of a side room just beyond the princess.

There wasn't time to shout a warning and Staff Sergeant Witzke didn't have a shot. She didn't hesitate, this was what she'd come seventy light-years to do: save the princess. She dove forward, shoving Lieutenant Giovanni down and out of the way, just as she heard a roar of gunfire.

She felt an impact and then she felt nothing at all.

***

Major Scaparetti hadn't expected the massive roar from a single shot of the Hammer. The muzzle flash blinded him and the rocket-assisted projectile singed his hair and eyebrows in the tight confines of the corridor. Yet he didn't hesitate to fire a second and third time.

His ears ringing and his eyes dazed, it took him longer than it should have to make sense of what he saw. The remains of someone, someone who'd worn body armor, for all the good it did, had fallen over Alannis Giovanni. That someone had pushed her down and out of his field of fire. His rounds hadn't hit her, they hadn't even come close.

Major Scaparetti realized that as he stared down the barrel of her carbine, and he felt despair as he realized that she'd waited just long enough for him to understand that he had failed. She wanted him to know that.

Major Scaparetti tried to pull his weapon back up, but it was too late. Three bullets struck him before he could so much as bring his weapon up. The heavy Hammer fell out of his hands and he screamed in a mix of pain and frustration as he fell to his knees. "No... no!"

Alannis Giovanni stood and stepped over to him. He weakly pawed for the pistol at his hip, but his fingers didn't seem to have any strength. The last thing he saw was her putting the carbine between his eyes and then a single, bright flash of light.

***

"Ma'am," Corporal Wandry saluted her as Alannis arrived at the command center, "we've secured the control room. It looks like most of the fighting has drawn down, but there's still some of the guards down in the North Wing putting up a fight, with your permission..."

"Hold up," Alannis said. "How the hell did you lot get here?" She half-worried that this was either some kind of dream or another of Marius's simulations.

"Lieutenant Commander Perkins detached a shuttle when we made orbit, ma'am," the sergeant who'd greeted her earlier spoke. *Sergeant Archeletto, he said his name was... he's got a Nova Roma accent, an upper class one.*

Alannis tried not to think about what had happened in the corridor. Major Scaparetti had her dead to rights. She'd known it, she hadn't had time to move. Then Staff Sergeant Witzke had come out of nowhere and shoved her out of the way... and she'd taken three hits from the twenty-five millimeter Hammer.

One of them would have been fatal. The three armor piercing rounds had shattered the Marine's body. Alannis had taken down Major Scaparetti, but she'd been left feeling hollow and empty. No one had ever taken a bullet for her. The importance of her own life had been a purely intellectual exercise... until now.

"Alright," Alannis said with a nod to Sergeant Archeletto. "Take Corporal Wandry and Corporal Wicklund, help secure the rest of the facility..." She looked up as Lizmadie came down the corridor, followed by several armed prisoners. "We'll secure the facility command center."

Sergeant Archeletto looked between her and Lizmadie. Alannis couldn't see his face behind his visor, but she could tell from his body language that he didn't want to leave. "Go," Alannis snapped.

They jogged off down the corridor. A moment later, Lizmadie came up. "United Colonies Marines?" she asked.

"Yes," Alannis said. "Staff Sergeant Witzke led this team. I gather there's more of them somewhere, but we can resolve that later." Some measure of her experience must have come through her voice, Lizmadie didn't ask any further questions.

"Secure the area," Lizmadie said to the cluster of prisoners who'd followed her. "Take any captives down to the holding area that Bueller set up."

"Roger!" one of the prisoners gave a sloppy wave.

We need to do something about some kind of military discipline, Alannis noted. Most of the prisoners here at Purgatory were senior officers or government officials. Those who'd joined into the fighting hadn't had much incentive to work together beyond the initial escape. Now, though, they needed to stay in control or this was going to fall apart before they could escape the system.

She stepped through the hatch and began trying to make sense of the chaos. She moved past the biometrics displays. That information didn't matter to her. The security monitors showed prisoners fighting guards and one another throughout the facility. Most of it was disorganized. The guard force as a whole had ceased to be a threat. Alannis brought up a camera that showed a group of guards huddled behind a barricade in front of what looked like a barracks. "We'll need to either talk them down or assault them, before they decide to keep fighting."

Lizmadie nodded and Alannis saw her note the location on her datapad.

Alannis pulled up another monitor, this one showing a group of prisoners in front of the armory doors. Red lights flashing on those doors suggested it had gone into lock down. "We can override the lock down," Alannis said, looking at the controls, "But I don't want to, not until we get people we can trust down there."

"I can take some people," Lizmadie said, "but we should probably wait until our Marines get back. That way we can control access."

Alannis nodded. She flipped through more screens. Most of them showed empty rooms and corridors. Then she stopped and flipped back through several of the security monitors. "What the hell?" The display showed a large room, racked along the walls and in rows, filling the room with little space to spare, were eight-foot tall metal coffins. All of them were connected into wiring and the rooms seemed to have a heavy fog.

"Those are cold storage," Two said from behind her. Alannis had to suppress a start of surprise. She turned to face him and he gave her a narrow smile. "Marius Giovanni likes to keep many of his prisoners in cryogenic stasis until he has them run through mental conditioning." Even though she knew he was another copy, some reflexive part of her distrusted him because he was the same person as the Marius who had done all this.

Alannis shivered a bit at that. The more she learned about the Marius Giovanni clone that ran this world, the more inhuman he seemed. "There seems to be a lot of these storage chambers. It looks like they're underneath the rest of this facility."

"What do you mean by a lot?" Lizmadie asked.

Alannis stopped flipping through and consulted the directory. "There's got to be a hundred, maybe a hundred and fifty people in each of these chambers," she estimated. "The directory lists ten rooms per floor and twenty floors of these chambers."

"That's..." Lizmadie shook her head, "That's twenty to thirty thousand people. That's a small city." She shook her head, "That's insane, someone would have noticed that many people going missing!"

"Not if they weren't all taken at once," Two said, his voice dull. "A ship here, a station there. Marius Giovanni has kidnapped tens of thousands to serve as cannon fodder for his war. I'd be surprised if there aren't more such facilities throughout the planet."

Alannis swallowed down her gorge. "Alright, we can figure that all out later. First we need to secure this facility. Lizmadie, Two, I want you to take charge of the prisoners. Get the fighting under control, try to find some of Major Scaparetti's officers, we need to learn everything we can about this place."

The work they had to do felt staggering, yet Alannis didn't let it weigh her down. She'd already done the impossible. From here, she just needed a ship. She would get a warning home, Marius would not take her son.

"Move out," Alannis ordered.

***

Epilogue

October 13, 2410
Elysia, Centauri System
Centauri Confederation

Fixer had spent weeks trying to set up the meeting. It would have been hard enough to slip away from her father had he only been human. President Spiridon of the Centauri Confederation had vast resources and surveillance techniques and personnel available to him. Since he was an alien hybrid capable of reading minds and telepathically controlling his minions, she had taken multiple layers of precautions.

Hello, brother, Fixer greeted her guest.

Sidewinder didn't respond for a long moment. She half expected him to attack her or to send a message of warning to Minder. But he didn't. He sat quietly for a long while, and when he finally answered, he used his voice. "Clearly I received your message. I'm here."

His human voice was so similar to that of his biological sister that Fixer had to suppress a surge of instant hostility. For all the fact that he was as much a product of Minder as she was, his exterior and his appearance were that of his original body and host.

I wonder how Chairman-Admiral Ortega would react to see her long-lost brother working with me? She quashed the thought and focused on what she needed to say. "The humans know about Golgotha. They may know the significance of the system. Minder has not warned our superiors of this knowledge."

Sidewinder's eyes went wide. "You can't be serious."

"I swear to you, I'm not lying. Nor am I misinformed. We have multiple confirmations at this point," Fixer replied.

Sidewinder's mind reached out and Fixer allowed his mind to merge with hers. She'd carefully prepared for this moment, and it was more than a shock to realize that he intrinsically reacted with hostility to her appearance just as she did to his. The humans they had once been had hated one another enough that the emotions carried over through their transformations. Yet he pushed past that and dove into her psyche, she showed him what she'd learned, how she'd confronted their creator directly and how he had ignored or deflected her questions.

We must pass along a warning, he sent to her.

We cannot, Fixer replied. *If we bypass him, the first thing they will do is confirm with him. He will kill us if he learns that we went around him.*

Sidewinder considered that. *If they then have confirmation, they can act, they can stop the humans from destroying us all.*

But it will be too late for us, Fixer sent back. *For that matter, they'll remove Minder and Minder will have removed us. There will be no one with the experience and skill to manage the humans.* Fixer paused to let him consider that.

"The others will annihilate humanity," Sidewinder spoke aloud. Fixer wondered if he did it because he wanted to distance himself from the thought... or because he wanted to hide from her any emotional overtones he might feel.

"They will try," Fixer replied. "But we've seen how tenacious they can be. Marius Giovanni has built up an entire fleet in secret, on the suspicion that we exist. Lucius Giovanni has defeated a significant force, one that should have destroyed his entire fleet. They are resourceful."

Sidewinder took a step back from her. "You can't think that they'd hold off the full weight of the Balor." As he said it, she saw him flinch, though. *He slipped,* she thought to herself, *he referred to our parent species as an outsider would.*

Fixer didn't feel shock at that. She'd spent many hours examining her own feelings about the subject, after all. For now, though, she let it slide. "Maybe they won't... but they may survive in isolated pockets or on hidden moons. And those that do survive will know the importance of Golgotha. Sooner or later some of those survivors might seek it out and do the very thing that we fear they might now."

Slowly, as if against his will, Sidewinder nodded. Like her, he understood humans as the rest of their kind did not. After all, they had been human, before their transformation. Minder had left them both with elements of their former humanity intact. In Fixer's case, those had been memories intended to help her play her role better. In Sidewinder's case, it had been his tactical and strategic knowledge. *In doing that,* Fixer thought to herself, *Minder erred.*

There has been an emotional bleed over... we are by no means human... but we are neither of us fully of the Balor. We are hybrids.

"What do you want to do?" Sidewinder asked.

"We will have to act without Minder," Fixer replied. "We may have to act *against* him. We must stop Marius Giovanni's efforts at Golgotha. Minder's human scouts haven't reported back, but it is only a matter of time before he will move. I don't think he will be successful... but the effort will require him to report to his superiors about his failure."

He will blame us, Sidewinder sent. *It is the only path open to him.*

Yes. We will be killed, the Balor will attack humanity in force, and our kind will be of no further use to them... all of us will be killed as well. She sent the thought on the tightest mental control she could manage. It was a thought that she wanted no one to intercept. The rest of their conversation would have earned them death... but the realization that she and Sidewinder had about themselves, about their nature as hybrids... that would earn their entire species extinction. If the Balor realized that their infiltrators had come to think of themselves as a separate species...

The combination of our knowledge and abilities to hide anywhere, our psionic strength, and everything we know... they would hunt us. They will eradicate any species that we might seek to hide within. No place would be safe and the Balor would eradicate any perceived threat. Unity was the only thing that the Balor accepted.

"I will take precautions," Sidewinder said after a moment.

"I will make preparations," Fixer responded. "We will stop the humans at Golgotha... we will protect *our* kind." The only way to do that was to keep the Balor in the dark about so many things. Fixer wished she had Minder on her side in this... but it was clear to her now that he was too self-interested to care about what would happen to their species.

Now they would take action.

***

He awoke and for a moment, he didn't know what was happening. There were lights, sounds, thoughts, emotions, all of them out of control, overwhelming. His instinct was to lash-out, but he was restrained, mentally and physcially.

"It's alright," a woman's voice spoke in his ear. *You are among friends,* her thoughts spoke into his mind. They were comforting, familiar... she was his creator.

What am I? Yet even as he thought that, he knew. He was a Balor Infiltrator. His mind, his very insides had been consumed by a parasite, which had converted him into an outwardly-human alien. She had made him, converted him... healed him. He reached up a hand and touched his two, whole eyes, feeling some sense of wonder. Human medicine could have done the same, but at expense that his former consciousness could not have afforded.

"Your host had connections, knowledge, contacts," Fixer spoke. "You have access to all of that. You will be my eyes and ears into the human underworld."

With what goal? Even as he asked the question, he knew the answers. Fixer had created him to find and destroy her enemies. She wanted him to destroy Marius Giovanni. She wanted access to the resources that he could provide to remove her creator.

"We will do this, together," She said, even as she removed his physical and mental restraints.

He sat up and flexed his hands, feeling stronger than he ever had as a human, feeling mentally sharper, more focused, more *alive* than he ever had before. *I spent so many years chasing money, never really understanding what true power was...*

"Together," He nodded. Yet in his deepest part of his mind, his innermost nature wondered what use she would have for him after he achieved his goals. He was her hidden dagger... but once she used him to remove her father, what value would he have to her then?

"What should I call you?" Fixer asked.

He had been Ricky One-Eye, yet the name seemed petty, simple. Before that he had possessed many names. Yet none of them had any meaning, any symbolence. Now, in his rebirth, he had meaning and purpose. *Dagger,* he sent to her, *my name is Dagger.*

***

October 15, 2410
Port Klast

Port Klast System

The bar was empty and dark, which suited Forrest's mood just perfectly.

He stared at the drink that he'd ordered over an hour earlier. Forrest had never had a drink in his life. He still hadn't taken even a sip of the one he ordered. It taunted him, a reminder. His father, his actual, biological father, Manuel Vasquez, had been a drunk. An abusive, belligerent drunk. A failure.

Forrest, too, was a failure. *I was so close,* he thought to himself. He'd been in orbit. They'd launched the shuttle. Everything had come together... and then he'd run. It ate at him, even while it felt like the right decision, but he couldn't justify it to himself. *I could have stayed a little longer...*

He still had no proof that Marius Giovanni's people had been able to detect his ship. All he had was his gut feeling. Forrest couldn't go back to Lucius with that. He couldn't face the inevitable board of inquiry over it, couldn't ruin the careers of the men and women who had trusted in him, in his hunch.

Forrest had his opportunity to save Princess Alannis Giovanni, and he had failed. On his return to Port Klast, the Nova Roma volunteers had disembarked, the officers and crew insinuating that they couldn't leave soon enough. Lieutenant Malatesta had all but called Forrest a coward. Forrest didn't have a crew and he couldn't go back to Golgotha, not when they could detect his approach.

He reached out and picked up the glass. He stared at it, the golden brown liquid representing his failure. *I could down it in a single gulp.*

"I wouldn't drink that if I were you," a light voice spoke.

Forrest turned in surprise as someone settled onto the bar stool next to him. Captain Tommy King gave him a cheshire cat grin. "Why not?" Forrest asked. "What do you care?"

"That's from a plastic bottle and has more dye in it than alcohol, I'm certain," Captain King smirked. "It'll taste terrible." He waved to the bartender, "Glennfiddich. Aged. One bottle, two glasses."

"I don't drink," Forrest said out of habit.

"That's obvious," Captain King snorted. "Besides, they're both for me."

The bartender set the bottle down in front of Captain King, who poured some into a glass. He sniffed at it, then sipped appreciatively. "So," Tommy King asked, "why are you here?"

"I screwed up," Forrest replied, "I nearly rescued her and--"

"No, why are you *here*," Captain King snorted. "I've already heard Lieutenant Malatesta's report to Prince Alexander. Who isn't exactly your biggest fan, by the way, but even he admits you probably escaped a trap by the skin of your teeth. Honestly, rescuing princesses is all well and good, but if you ask me, ones as capable as the pair you were after are probably able to rescue themselves."

Forrest scowled at that. "I was just trying to--"

"Yes, yes, young love and all that," Captain King took another sip. "God, this is good stuff. Trust me, kid, always take the time to savor the good stuff while you can."

"I'm not a kid," Forrest snapped, "I'm forty-eight years old and--"

"Then start acting like it," Captain King snapped back. He set his glass down on the bar and turned to look at Forrest. "You stole a ship, broke the law, attacked a diplomatic summit, possibly started an interstellar war... all over this girl. I can understand that... hell, I can even respect that. But sitting in a bar moping? For God's sake, buying cheap booze when you've got the money for the good stuff? Stop being a cry-baby and do something about it!"

"It's too late," Forrest snarled. "There's no way I could slip into the star system. They have an entire fleet..."

"Then get a fleet of your own," Captain King said with a wave. "If you'd like, I'll introduce you to any number of reputable pirates and mercenaries. You have a very large fortune to your name and young Prince Alexander's just finished liberating Volaterra and Lavinium, then turned them over to the United Colonies. He's ready to go save his sister. If you were out there you'd be doing a hell of a lot more than moping here in this crap bar."

Forrest straightened. Tommy King was right. He did have options. "Thanks," Forrest said as he pushed away from the bar and stood. "Thanks a lot."

He walked out, leaving Tommy King alone with the bartender. "Sorry I called this place a dive," Captain King said.

The bartender shrugged, "It's fine, kid needed a good kick in the ass."

"That he did..." Captain King poured more whiskey in his glass. "Lauren come by?"

"No, Captain," The bartender replied.

"Damn," Captain King said. He sipped at the whiskey, feeling the slow, cool burn. *Nothing to do but take the same advice I gave to the boy.* He had options too. "Thanks, Mac." Tommy tossed him payment and stepped back from the bar and headed for the door.

He backtracked a moment later, "What am I thinking, this is good whiskey," He finished off the glass, grabbed the bottle, and nodded farewell to Mac.

***

October 20, 2410
Golgotha
Unclaimed Space

"So," Alannis asked as she followed Lieutenant Ambrosio and Lizmadie Doko into the briefing room, "what's so important? I was still interviewing prisoners who seemed interested in signing on with our uprising."

That was important. There wasn't an ansible station here at the base, so they had no way to call for help. Lieutenant Ambrosio and the shuttle gave them some ability to move, but they needed a ship or a way to get a transmission off-world.

Presumably Forrest Perkins would bring help, but Alannis had no way to know who would believe him or how soon that help would be available.

Lieutenant Ambrosio looked uncomfortable, "Ma'am," he said, clearly hating to defer to her. Whether that was because she was female or because she was the daughter of Marius Giovanni, Alannis didn't know. She did know that he was the third son of a minor nobleman back on Nova Roma. So it was probably a combination of the two. *He came here to rescue Princess Lizmadie. Needing our help to stash his shuttle and learning that we'd already orchestrated our own escape hasn't made him like me. Finding himself outranked by me is bitter fruit indeed.* "Ma'am," he repeated, almost as if he had to force himself to say it again, "*Princess* Lizmadie found something that she thinks you need to see."

"Lieutenant Lizmadie?" Alannis asked with a pleasant tone. She hadn't missed how *she* earned a military rank, while Lizmadie's was discounted. There would be issues, and soon. She'd rather resolve that in private.

"We found more information on Marius Giovanni's cryogenic storage facilities," Lizmadie said. She activated the command center's holodisplay and an image of the planet appeared. Across the planet, multiple sites glowed. "As you can see, there are over a dozen of them."

Alannis leaned over the display, "So you're saying there's over a dozen of these processing facilities? They have *how* many people?"

"Twenty or thirty thousand people in each, if this place is anything to go off of," Lizmadie replied. "About a thousand caretaker staff and guards. Each of the other facilities contain uniforms, weapons and equipment to arm them after they've been processed. We think several of them are in close proximity to ship hangars so they can embark vessels as crew quickly."

Alannis shook her head. She was awed and more than a little horrified. It was one thing to think of her father as brainwashing a few thousand people. But these facilities were far, far worse than that. *There's a quarter million or more prisoners on this planet.*

"We can't leave," Alannis said, her voice wooden. She wanted nothing more than to blast her way out of the star system, to get home and warn her brother about the threat, to see her son and to be safe. Safe from this madman who broke people to his will. Safe from her insane ex-husband.

"Ma'am?" one of the Marines asked.

"We can't leave these people here," Alannis straightened and pointed at the map on the display.

Lieutenant Ambrosio frowned, "We can get help..."

"By the time we get help and get back here, these facilities will have gone fully online," Alannis shook her head, "They could process thousands, tens of thousands of people in a few months." Her lips firmed into a hard line. "No, we have to seize these facilities, quickly and quietly. We have to rescue every man and woman that we can... and *then*," Alannis jabbed a finger at the sky, "then we blast our way out of here and smash everything we can on the way out."

* * *

October 23, 2410
Faraday, Faraday System
United Colonies

One of his bodyguards gave him a friendly grin as he opened the door to the car, but Prince Anthony William Giovanni ignored the smile and the bodyguard as he climbed into the car.

Poor orphan boy, Anthony William thought to himself, *that's what they're thinking.*

That's what all of them thought, even his uncle. Oh, sure, his cousins, Kaylee and Patricia at least genuinely cared about him, but all the rest? He was the spare heir. He was valuable in the event that something horrible happened to his uncle and cousin... and other than that, no one cared about him in the slightest.

He felt tears well up in his eyes as the car pulled away from the Imperial House. *Stupid Mother had to go and get herself killed...* Loyalty, duty, honor, what did those matter when it got you killed? He wanted to hate her for it, but hate would require some real emotion, to require himself to feel... and that just opened him up to the pain again.

Anthony was only seven years old, but he knew better than to open himself to that pain. His mother was dead. His father had apparently done something horrible enough to get himself exiled and now he was dead too. He didn't know the details, but he'd listened to the guards and servants, what they said and more importantly, what they didn't say.

He remembered the odd looks his mother had given him, how she'd always been so distant. *She hated me too,* he thought, *everyone hates me.*

Even as he thought that, there was a loud crash and the protective features of the armored car locked down. Anthony couldn't move as expansive foam surged around him. For a second, he couldn't breathe, couldn't see... and then the foam retracted just enough for him to gasp for air.

He heard what sounded like gunfire and the thud of an explosion. Anthony's heart raced and he swallowed down a spike of fear. There'd been kidnapping attempts before. He remembered only two years ago his father had tried, had even convinced him that it would be best to help. *He said we'd be a family, him and mom and I... only now I know that mom hated him, even more than she hated me.*

Anthony couldn't help a trill of excitement... and a little bit of hope that this was his father, back from the dead to rescue him.

The gunfire dropped off and then someone was peeling back the protective foam. Strong arms pulled Anthony free of the car... and Anthony's eyes went wide as the men in civilian clothes pulled him away from his car. Anthony's eyes went wider as he saw his guards were down, bleeding.

They're dead, he realized, *I should feel something about that.* Yet he just felt distant. He pushed any feelings aside, even as the kidnappers dragged him away. They thrust him into a dark van and Anthony kept quiet as they drove. The kidnapping wouldn't work, Anthony knew. He carried a silent alarm, a beacon that General Proscia's security people would track.

Adults think they're so smart... Anthony thought to himself. He remained calm, he didn't ask questions. He hadn't felt anything when his bodyguards died and he would feel even less when the Guard killed these kidnappers.

Yet he hated to go back. Some part of him wished that these kidnappers would succeed. That they'd escape. Anthony almost reached over to switch off his beacon, but then he thought better of it. These men were probably criminals, they'd kill him or hurt him to get their way.

The van pulled to a halt and the men carried him out. They were in a warehouse or large building of some kind and they rushed him across it, towards a set of industrial doors. A couple of them spoke in low tones as they moved him.

The doors opened and Anthony realized that it wasn't a warehouse, it was a hangar. A ramp dropped down from the doors and his kidnappers moved him up the ramp and onto the ship. *They won't get off the planet,* he told himself.

The two kidnappers led him into what looked like a luxury suite, dropped him on a comfortable leather couch in front of an entertainment center, and then turned around and left without saying a word. Anthony looked around in confusion. Maybe this wasn't a kidnapping. Maybe it was a drill of some kind...

The doors opened and a man stepped into the room. For a second, Anthony thought it was his uncle. He was short, almost Anthony's height, with dark hair, olive skin, and brown eyes. Yet this man wore a black uniform that looked like something Anthony had seen in history lessons. He also had a thin mustache. The smile he wore, too, was arrogant and patronizing. Uncle Lucius wouldn't smile that way.

"Who are you?" Anthony demanded.

"A bossy little fellow, aren't you?" The man replied, his smile growing broader. "Good to see you've the tone of command, even at such a young age, Anthony William." He held up a hand as Anthony started to open his mouth, "Now, boy, don't worry. I'll answer you. I'm Lord Admiral Marius Giovanni, rightful Emperor of Nova Roma, and your grandfather. That is, I'm your mother's father."

Anthony's eyes went wide, "But..."

"I'm sure you have many questions, Anthony," Marius's voice was gentle. "And I'm sorry that we have to meet under these... circumstances. Unfortunately, events as they are, have forced my hand. You'll be coming with me on a trip... a very special trip."

"A trip?" Anthony couldn't help but look down at his wrist, at the tracking beacon that even now would be leading his rescuers to him.

"Yes, Anthony, a trip. And don't worry about any interruptions. My people have been jamming the distress signal. Your guardians don't even know you're gone." Marius took a seat in the chair across from him. "Anthony, we'll have plenty of time, more than you'll realize, to get to know one another. More importantly, I've got a great deal to teach you."

"Teach me?" Anthony couldn't help but scowl. He'd had plenty of tutors. Music, art, history. The last thing he wanted was to be stuck in more boring classes. The whole kidnapping, this mention of great things, it excited him.

"Important lessons," his grandfather said with another smile. "Lessons about commanding, about leading. Lessons about war and conquest. Lessons about your family and where you come from. And one day, lessons about your psychic abilities."

"My what?!" Anthony stared at the man.

"You're psychic, or you will be once I help you awaken your abilities," Marius Giovanni said. "And I can teach you how to use those."

"Why are you doing this?" Anthony couldn't help but ask. He didn't trust the man, not yet.

"Because you're family," Marius replied. "And because I need an heir. Someone to follow in my footsteps. Your uncle... well, we don't see eye-to-eye. Your mother... she didn't understand me either. But you, Anthony William? I think you and I will come to understand each other."

###

The End
The story will continue with The Star Engine

Printed in Great Britain
by Amazon

52236420R00145